"Subversion of the Given":
On the Postmodern Historical Writing in Julian Barnes's Fiction

"对已知的颠覆"：
朱利安·巴恩斯小说中的后现代历史书写研究

何朝辉 著

·广州·

图书在版编目（CIP）数据

"对已知的颠覆"：朱利安·巴恩斯小说中的后现代历史书写研究 ＝ "Subversion of the Given"：On the Postmodern Historical Writing in Julian Barnes's Fiction：英文／何朝辉著. －－广州：中山大学出版社，2024.11. －－ ISBN 978-7-306-08222-0

Ⅰ．I561.074

中国国家版本馆 CIP 数据核字第 202419AD08 号

出 版 人：	王天琪
策划编辑：	金继伟
责任编辑：	麦颖晖　蓝若琪
封面设计：	曾　婷
责任校对：	卢思敏
责任技编：	靳晓虹

出版发行：中山大学出版社
电　　话：编辑部 020 - 84111901，84111997
　　　　　发行部 020 - 84111998，84111981，84111160
地　　址：广州市新港西路 135 号
邮　　编：510275　　　传　真：020-84036565
网　　址：http://www.zsup.com.cn　　E-mail：zdcbs@mail.sysu.edu.cn
印 刷 者：佛山市浩文彩色印刷有限公司
规　　格：787mm×1092mm　1/16　14.25 印张　289 千字
版次印次：2024 年 11 月第 1 版　2024 年 11 月第 1 次印刷
定　　价：108.00 元

如发现本书因印装质量影响阅读，请与出版社发行部联系调换

Acknowledgements

This research is a brief revision of my doctoral dissertation accomplished in December 2013. The revision refers mainly to the deletion of the Chinese abstract and to the addition of a brief introduction to Julian Barnes's latest works published in and after the year of 2011 and some development of Barnes studies at home and abroad (appended in the footnotes) in the Introduction part as well as some grammatical modification about the whole writing. There is no revision about the key points of my dissertation, for they still hold water, as far as Julian Barnes's postmodern historical view or historical writing is concerned, although it was completed ten years ago.

This research would not have been accomplished without the advice and help of not a few people. My greatest gratitude would be given to my dissertation advisor Professor Zhan Shukui, in School of Foreign Languages and Cultures, Xiamen University, who unfortunately passed away on July 2, 2023. When I broached the idea of writing Julian Barnes's historical writing as my study focus, Professor Zhan encouraged me to make a thorough research on Barnes to dig out all of those issues related to history in Barnes's works and suggested that I narrow my attention on Barnes's historical views; and during the process of writing he answered all of my questions with great patience and valuable suggestions. Without his consistent help and illuminating instruction, the completion of this research would not be possible. Still, Professor Zhan's lectures have also inspired me a lot, which extends my vision and deepens my understanding of literature learning; he is both a strict mentor and a kind professor, for he not only cares for my study but also shows concern for my life. Professor Zhan is not merely an academic advisor but a fatherly figure as well, to whom I owe a great amount for his expert guidance, perceptive ideas and caring words.

My sincere thanks also go to a good many professors in School of Foreign Languages and Cultures, Xiamen University, who have, in one way or another, made great contributions to this study and to my advance in the study of literature. Professor Yang Renjing not only inspires me much with his profound knowledge of literature but also influences me with his scrupulous attitude towards academic research; Professor Cai Chunlu, my M. A. advisor, has always showed concern for my study and encouraged me to study further; Professor Zhou Yubei, whose lectures stimulated my interest in literary study, also shows her concern for me and displays her encouragement for my study. Still, the teaching of Professor Zhang Longhai, Professor Li Meihua, Professor Liu Wensong, Dr. James Martin, Dr. Brian Low broadens my mind in the study of literature, to whom my earnest thanks are also given. Moreover, I would express my genuine gratitude toward Professor Zhao Yifan from Chinese Academy of Social Sciences and Professor Chen Shidan from Renmin University of China, whose lectures at Xiamen University enlighten me a lot, especially for my study of theoretical discourses of literature. Without these professors' concern and help, without their teaching and lectures, I would not turn out to be who I am now.

I am also fortunate enough to meet several study fellows such as Professor Zhang Xiaoping, Ms. Ma Qunying, Ms. Wang Yanping, Ms. Liao Bailin, Mr. Yan Jianming in College of Foreign Languages and Cultures, Xiamen University. During these years we have studied together and discussed a lot about literature. The exchange of ideas accordingly brings about our cordial friendships. Their help for me during the difficult time of my study is unforgettable.

Still, my deep gratitude is expressed to my family members. All of these years, my parents have supported me with their love wholeheartedly. Their industry, their honesty and integrity always spur me on to study hard and behave well. My deepest thanks would be paid to them; and this research, with no doubt, would be dedicated to them. My heartfelt thanks would also go to my grandmother, who has been another "mother" for me all the time; to my wife Zhou Xiaowei, who has been standing by my side as a staunchest supporter; and to other family members, who have encouraged and assisted me during the writing process of this research and along the road of my growth. Their love and support is the greatest motivation for me to go on.

Finally, I would like to show my heartfelt thanks to Shaoguan University where I work now, which sponsors part of the fund to publish this research and provides a friendly and delightful atmosphere for my work and my life, and to the Deans, Directors, and Colleagues in School of Foreign Studies, Shaoguan University, who have encouraged and helped me a lot during these years' work and life.

Preface

Julian Barnes, one of the most outstanding, interesting and challenging novelists now writing in the English language, is often considered as one of the three giants in contemporary British literary circle, the other two being Martin Amis and Ian McEwan. As a prosperous and prominent writer, Barnes has received not a few literary awards and honors at home and abroad including the prestigious award the Man Booker Prize in 2011. Due to the originality and experimentalness of form and the richness and profundity of his works, Barnes during his more than thirty years' writing has won a variety of names, such as "a highly original writer," "a master of craftsman," "a metafictionist who challenges literary orthodoxies," "a natural satirist," "a novelist of ideas," and "a novelist-philosopher." However, because of the flexibility and versatility of his writing style, Barnes is esteemed as "the chameleon of British letters" and as such the specificity of his works taken as a whole is a strong "sense of heterogeneity." As to formal experimentation, his works often defy categorization, blurring the boundaries of genres by means of using such writing techniques as parody, irony, collage or textual hybridization; as to thematic exploration, his novels explore different areas of human experience, ranging from personal growth, love, and marriage to gender, identity, war, religion, race, history, philosophy and politics. Due to the heterogeneous feature of his writing, there are up to now few comprehensive and systematic studies on Barnes, although many an article, review and essay about his certain work could be searched out or retrieved. In China, Barnes study is in a budding state, which cannot be matched with the glaring reputation of Barnes in Britain. This provides a great opportunity for this research to study Barnes, especially the postmodern historical writing in his fiction.

Although critics observe that every book by Barnes is "a new departure" and his whole writing is typical of heterogeneity, a close reading of Barnes's works shows that an acute historical consciousness permeates in his writing, behind which there is his sharp deconstructive thought. As one of "the golden generation of British novelists," Barnes, like Martin Amis, Kazuo Ishiguro, Ian McEwan, Salman Rushdie and Graham Swift, lives under the shadow of contemporary historical reality such as the decline of the British Empire and the political conflict of the Cold War, and in the meantime is affected by various isms of postmodern culture and thoughts. This no doubt makes a great imprint on Barnes's writing, rendering his fiction an acute historical consciousness and the typical features of postmodernism. As to Barnes's concern for history, it is evident that in his works there is often such a character who is either a history professor (*Before She Met Me*; *A History of the World in 10½ Chapters* ; *England, England*; *The Sense of an Ending*) , or a historian (*England, England*), or a person extremely interested in historical figures (*Flaubert's Parrot*) , or the novel itself is a re-writing or parody of history (*A History of the World in 10½ Chapters*; *The Porcupine*; *England, England*; *Arthur & George*). Not coincidentally, a good many comments about history or the views of history turn up in Barnes's writing. More specifically, Barnes often expresses his view about the nature of history. For instance, he writes: "Nothing was set in concrete: that was the nature of history." He also calls into question history or historical truth epistemologically, stating, "History is merely another literary genre." Barnes further suggests that "The story of a louse may be as fine as the history of Alexander the Great—everything depends upon the execution." Additionally, Barnes interrogates history ontologically by stating, "History doesn't relate;" "The history of the world? Just voices echoing in the dark; images that burn for a few centuries and then fade; stories, old stories that sometimes seem to overlap; strange links, impertinent connections;" and his writing also foregrounds the ideological attribute of history: "History isn't what happened. History is just what historians tell us;" "One of the central problems of history ... the fact that we need to know the history of the historian in order to understand the version that is being put in front of us." Because of this, Barnes is often referred to as a "near-historian" by critics, and his fiction is considered a "footnote to history" and a "subversion of the given."

 Critics have noticed the views of history and historiography embodied in Barnes's works, but few global, systematic, penetrating and in-depth studies of Barnes's historical writing have come into being yet. This research focuses on Barnes's postmodern historical writing, from epistemological, ontological, and political points of view related to history, by way of a close reading of Barnes's texts such as *Flaubert's Parrot*, *A History of the World in 10½ Chapters*, *The Porcupine*, *England, England*, *Arthur & George*, and "The Revival," combining the reading strategies of Deconstructionism and New Historicism, drawing mainly upon hypotheses of postmodern discourse of history put forward by postmodern theorists (of history) such as Jacques Derrida, Michel Foucault, Linda Hutcheon, Fredric Jameson, Jean-François Lyotard, and those of New Historicism by such theorists as Frank Ankersmit, Keith Jenkins, Louis Montrose, and Hayden White, to explore how Barnes explicitly or implicitly demonstrates his postmodern view or philosophy of history through his intertextual, deconstructive, satiric, or parodic strategy of writing, to substantiate that Barnes is such a postmodern novelist whose work presents a postmodern "philosophy of history in fictional ... form." Epistemologically, Barnes, through his questioning and questing for historical truth in a way of intertextual writing, foregrounds that historical writing or historiography bears the feature of textuality and fictionality. Ontologically, Barnes, through his subversion and revision of historical (meta)narratives in deconstructive writing, stresses that history is discontinuous, fragmented, and pluralistic. Politically, Barnes, through his fabrication and representation of contemporary and future politics-history in satiric or parodic writing, highlights that history and historiography are subtly affected by political ideology and/or power relations.

This research consists of an introduction, four chapters, and a conclusion. The Introduction surveys Barnes's writing experience, major works and the literary awards he has won, and briefly reviews Barnes studies at home and abroad. The rest of the Introduction addresses Barnes's concern for history, the preview of some of his postmodern views of history and the genesis of the study angle in this research, followed by an explanation of the research's framework.

Chapter One "Historical Discourse, Historical Writing and Julian Barnes" examines the transformation of historical discourse, historical writing in British fiction and Barnes's historical consciousness, providing a theoretical and historical framework for understanding Barnes's postmodern historical writing. This chapter first of all sorts out the transformation of historical discourse (from the speculative philosophy of history to that of analytical) in a brief way, pointing out that some grand narratives or (meta)narratives of history belong to the category of the speculative. Then it summarizes the main ideas of postmodern discourse of history and New Historicism from the ontological and epistemological perspectives, arguing that these ideas challenge the traditional (speculative) view or philosophy of history and modes of historical writing. The second section mentions the origin and development of the historical novel in British literature from the late eighteenth century to the mid-twentieth century. It also explores the social, historical reasons behind the rise of "new historical fiction" since the 1960s, along with its key features. Barnes's postmodern historical writing belongs to the category of "new historical fiction." The last section deals with Barnes's historical consciousness (from its budding in his early novels to its maturity in his later ones), with an introduction to his postmodern view of history and historiography as its conclusion.

Chapter Two "Questioning and Questing for Historical Truth" explores

Barnes's postmodern historical writing epistemologically. Barnes, through his intertextual strategy of writing and his constant questioning and questing for historical truth, foregrounds the relation of history to text(uality) and the fictive character of historical writing, contending that history could be approached merely through texts, and that historical writing, just like literary writing, relies on literary execution such as fabulation. This chapter mainly examines Barnes's novels such as *Flaubert's Parrot* and *A History of the World in 10½ Chapters*. First of all, it points out that in *Flaubert's Parrot*, Barnes interprets Flaubert through various kinds of texts pertinent to Flaubert so as to construct a true image of Flaubert and in the mean time constantly queries "How do we seize the Past?" and questions the texts as historical evidence for the construction of Flaubert's image, thus investigating the possibility of questing for historical truth, highlighting the relation of history to text(uality) and the (inter)textuality of history or historiography. Then, by way of analyzing three heterogeneous texts about a historical disaster in "Shipwreck," one "chapter" of *A History of the World in 10½ Chapters*, and discussing the historical phenomenon in connection with this historical disaster in "The Mountain," another "chapter" of this "novel," the writing in this part intimates that Barnes's intertextual writing discloses the subtle mediation relation of (historical) texts to social processes, or the notion of "the textuality of history" in Montrose's sense. In its second section, the text explicates Barnes's knowledge and practical writing of the issue of the fictionality of history. In *Metahistory: The Historical Imagination in Nineteenth-Century Europe* and other works, Hayden White argues that historical writing, like literary writing, bears the fictive character and is a "poetic process." Barnes also puts forward similar views about history or historiography through his characters, such as "history is merely another literary genre" and "the technical term is fabulation." This section firstly expounds Barnes's own understanding of the view that "history is merely another literary genre," suggesting that history is imagined and fictionalized, especially when there is insufficient evidence for historical writing. This is supported by his practical writing in such texts as *Flaubert's Parrot* and *Arthur & George*. The text discusses the idea of history as fiction embodied in Barnes's *Love, Etc.* and *A History of the World in 10½ Chapters* and elaborates on how Barnes, through formal construction and content exploration, writes a "chapter" of the history of the world in the latter "novel" via the literary execution of fabulation intertextually and self-reflexively, suggesting that Barnes's writing mirrors the fictive character of history from the angle of literary writing or in the form of fictional writing.

Chapter Three "Subverting and Revising Historical (Meta)Narratives" explicates Barnes's postmodern historical writing ontologically. In an ontological sense, conventional discourse or philosophy of history maintains that history is a whole, with such characteristics as continuity, causality and totality; on the contrary, postmodern discourse or philosophy of history contends that history is discontinuous, fragmented and pluralistic. Not a few views exposed in Barnes's postmodern historical writing have some similarities to those of postmodern discourse of history ontologically. This chapter mainly studies Barnes's novels like *Flaubert's Parrot*, *A History of the World in 10½ Chapters* and *Arthur & George*. Firstly, its first section briefly explains the view of history as discontinuity put forward by Michel Foucault and Claude Lévi-Strauss, then it interprets the writing of the history of the world in *A History of the World in 10½ Chapters* from such aspects as form, genre and narrative voice as its main content, pointing out that Barnes's deconstructive writing of history breaks up the linear causality, continuity and totality in conventional history (and historiography), stressing such features of history as discontinuity and fragmentation. Secondly, this section refers to Barnes's direct expression of interrogation about (the narrative of) progress through the voices of his characters in such texts as "Junction" and *Flaubert's Parrot*, and then illuminates how Barnes in *A History of the World in 10½ Chapters* in a way of deconstructive writing displays his interrogation and subversion of the view of progress embedded in such historical (meta)narratives as those of Darwin's theory of evolution and Hegel's rational history. The second section explores the feature of historical plurality in Barnes's postmodern historical writing. The conventional Western History often underscores Anthropocentrism and Eurocentrism, excluding the Others such as the female, the racial minority and the animal out of the vision of historical writing, displaying the feature of monism. Postmodern view of history underlines the diversity and plurality of human history and civilization, proffering some prominent positions for the Others in historical writing, which is in some sense represented in Barnes's postmodern historical writing. This section first of all explores Barnes's interrogation and revision, from the angle of an animal, of the (hi)story of Noah's Ark and the Deluge recorded in the Bible in "The Stowaway," the first "chapter" of *A History of the World in 10½ Chapters*, laying bare Anthropocentrism implicated in the narrative of the Bible, providing a new perspective for the understanding of grand narratives such as Christian History; then a close reading of racial prejudice which brings about miscarriage of justice on a racial Other, and of Barnes's digging out and rewriting of this forgotten history in *Arthur & George*, indicates that Barnes's writing unearths his deep rethinking and penetrating critique of national character and racial unconscious of the English people, as well as the racial bias in the official writing of British history. Rewriting history from an animal's perspective and digging out a forgotten history of a racial Other give expression to the suppressed voices in the master narratives of history, revealing Barnes's subversion and revision of orthodox history and his potential defense for historical and racial plurality.

Chapter Four "Fabricating and Representing Politics-History" examines Barnes's thinking of the relation of politics to history and his postmodern delineation of hetero-topia worlds in the future. Leopold von Ranke's objective history highlights the writing of history as "what actually happened," which is called a "noble dream" by later scholars. Postmodern theorists (of history) like Michel Foucault and Keith Jenkins realize that history (and historiography) is deeply affected by such factors as political ideology and/or power relations, which could be also corroborated in Barnes's postmodern historical writing. This chapter discusses Barnes's two political novels *The Porcupine* and *England, England.* To start with, it analyzes from the angle of the relation of history to political ideology and/or power relations how Barnes in *The Porcupine* suggests the influence of (political) power on history and historiography and then illustrates Barnes's depiction of the ideological conflict in this novel through reviewing Jacques Derrida's critique of the hypothesis of "The End of History" proposed by Francis Fukuyama, so as to point out Barnes's acute perception of the contemporary political, historical reality and his potential critique of Fukuyama's proposal of "The End of History." Next, this chapter turns to investigate Barnes's writing of the political future (history) of England in *England, England* in its second section. Utopia is an ideal or perfect depiction of the future world, with dystopia being its reversal; Barnes delineates two worlds of hetero-topia in this novel. First of all, it recounts the process of how a world of simulacra and hetero-topia named "England, England," based on the English historical heritage, is established in the Isle of Wight, a small island to the south of England, and becomes politically independent, indicating Barnes's satirizing and critiquing of the phenomenon of commodification of history (or historical heritage) and preferring the original and authentic to the replica and fake in a postmodern society through a parody of Jean Baudrillard's hypothesis of "the hyperreal" culture. The last part of this section makes a survey of Old England's political fall and seclusion, its economic recession and ruin and its regression into a pre-industrial rural society, "neither idyllic nor dystopic," another world of hetero-topia, after the independence of the Isle of Wight, and intimates the paradox that Old England encounters in the construction of its (historical) tradition, that is, like the hyperreal world in the Isle of Wight, Old England is also "entrapped" in the situation of blurring the boundary between reality and simulacra. Through the fabrication and representation of the world of hetero-topia, Barnes's writing explores such issues as national identity consciousness, construction of history, and their relations to national political future, implying his concern for and thinking of the political future and historical orientation of England.

The conclusion reviews the main contents of Barnes's postmodern historical writing in light of his concern for the issue of truth, the paradox or shortcomings implied in his writing, and then makes a brief comparison of his historical writing with those of other contemporary British writers to highlight his peculiarity in formal experimentation. It addresses in the end some possible perspectives for the study of Barnes to arouse more interest in this writer.

All in all, Julian Barnes is a postmodern writer with a profound awareness of rethinking and strong spirit of critique, and his postmodern historical writing, bearing a distinctive feature of deconstruction, subverts "the given" notions about history and historiography, making a postmodern "footnote to [conventional] history" and historiography, presenting a postmodern philosophy of history in the form of fictional writing, thus proffering very good texts for the study of literature (and even history) from the angle of postmodern discourse or philosophy of history.

CONTENTS

List of Abbreviations ·· I

Introduction ·· 1
    I. Barnes's Literary Career and Achievements ················ 4
    II. Barnes Studies at Home and Abroad ························ 11
    III. Framework of This Research ·································· 16

Chapter One   Historical Discourse, Historical Writing and Julian Barnes
    ·· 23
    I. Transformation of Historical Discourse ····················· 26
        i. Traditional Historical Discourse ························ 27
        ii. Postmodern Historical Discourse and New Historicism ······ 31
    II. Historical Writing in British Fiction ······················ 38
        i. Traditional Historical Novel ····························· 39
        ii. New Historical Fiction or Historiographic Metafiction ······ 41
    III. Historical Writing in Julian Barnes's Fiction ··········· 45
        i. History as Background: Traditional (Historical) Novel ······ 45
        ii. History Foregrounded: Postmodern Historical Writing ······ 50

Chapter Two   Questioning and Questing for Historical Truth ············ 55
    I. Textuality of History ·· 58
        i. "How Do We Seize the Past?" ························ 59
        ii. "Turn Catastrophe into Art" ···························· 72

Ⅱ. Fictionality of History ·· 81
　　　　ⅰ. "Merely Another Literary Genre" ························· 83
　　　　ⅱ. "The Technical Term Is Fabulation" ····················· 90

Chapter Three　Subverting and Revising Historical (Meta) Narratives
　　·· 99
　　Ⅰ. Discontinuity and Fragmentation of History ················ 102
　　　　ⅰ. "History Doesn't Relate" ····································· 104
　　　　ⅱ. "Is This Progress?" ··· 114
　　Ⅱ. Plurality of History ·· 121
　　　　ⅰ. History in an Animal Version ······························ 123
　　　　ⅱ. History of a Racial Victim ··································· 130

Chapter Four　Fabricating and Representing Politics-History ········ 141
　　Ⅰ. History and Ideology ·· 144
　　　　ⅰ. History and Power Relation ································ 146
　　　　ⅱ. Not "The End of History" ··································· 155
　　Ⅱ. History and Hetero-topia ··· 164
　　　　ⅰ. "We Must Demand the Replica" ························· 165
　　　　ⅱ. "Neither Idyllic nor Dystopic" ····························· 176

Conclusion ·· 185

References ·· 197

List of Abbreviations

Throughout this research, parenthetical references to Julian Barnes's novels and other writings use the following abbreviations:

AG	*Arthur & George* (2005)
EE	*England, England* (1998)
FP	*Flaubert's Parrot* (1984)
HWC	*A History of the World in 10½ Chapters* (1989)
JBC	"Julian Barnes in Conversation" (2002)
LE	*Love, Etc.* (2001)
LT	*The Lemon Table* (2004)
P	*The Porcupine* (1992)
SE	*The Sense of an Ending* (2011)
SS	*Staring at the Sun* (1986)
WFTW	"When Flaubert Took Wing" (2005)

Introduction

> Julian Barnes is one of the most interesting, challenging figures now writing in English. ... His daring, his challenge to himself to make every book a new departure not only for Julian Barnes but for the whole history of the novel, makes each of his books an event. And his unique mixture of literary experimentation, intelligence, and dedication to the truths of the human heart ... makes every book an adventure.
> —Merritt Moseley, *Understanding Julian Barnes*

On October 18, 2011, at the age of 65, Julian Barnes (1946-) eventually won the Man Booker Prize for his latest novel *The Sense of an Ending* (2011), after being shortlisted for this prize on three previous occasions for his *Flaubert's Parrot* (1984), *England, England* (1998) and *Arthur & George* (2005). Up to now, Barnes's literary achievements have reached a pinnacle in the literary landscapes since his debut novel *Metroland* published in 1980. In fact, due to the richness and profundity in his works, Barnes, during his more than thirty years' writing career, has won a variety of names such as "the brilliant Barnes" (Allen 34), "the English wit" (Balée 664), "a novelist-philosopher" (Buxton 58), "a natural satirist" (Craig 55), "a highly original writer" (Heptonstall 117), "a master craftsman" (Kennedy 110), "a marvelous essayist" (Mallon 7), "a metafictionist who challenges literary orthodoxies" (Wilhelmus 348), and "a novelist of ideas" (Wood 40), to name only a few; still, Barnes has been acclaimed as "one of the most truly interesting writers of his generation" (Allen 32), and even as "Britain's wittiest and most cosmopolitan living writer" (Eder 2). With no doubt, it is safe to say that Barnes has become one of the most celebrated contemporary writers in the English language.

Since starting his career as a novelist in 1980, Barnes has been constantly called "the chameleon of British letters" (Stout), for, as Merritt Moseley perceptively observes, Barnes "never writes the same book twice" (5) and every book for him is "a new departure" and "an event" (17), and he "has refused to repeat himself, pressing on to innovate, straining to find new ideas for novels" (Levenson 43). As a result, Barnes is also esteemed as "the inscrutable Mr. Barnes" and "is much the hardest to pin down" among "the golden generation of British novelists" (Rees), consisting of Martin Amis (1949-), Kazuo Ishiguro (1954-), Ian McEwan (1948-), Salman Rushdie (1947-) and Graham Swift (1949-), among others; and no one knows what his next book would look like. In his writing, Barnes is always trying to find new mountains and discover new territories, his work thus revealing vivid variety and magic miscellaneousness, technically and thematically. His insightful examination and enlightening exploration of such issues as history and historical truth, the relation of fiction to reality, love and marriage, and race and politics have earned him a considerable fame. Therefore, a critic acutely argues that Barnes's "unique mixture of literary experimentation, intelligence, and dedication to the truths of the human heart," "makes every book an adventure," and that Barnes's "daring, his challenge to himself" not only makes a great significance to Barnes himself, but also marks some milestone in the "whole history of the novel" (Moseley 17), which, to my mind, constitutes the highest critical acclaim for Barnes.

Richard Locke makes a very high commendation about Barnes in a similar vein, thinking of Barnes as equally important as Vladimir Nabokov (1899–1977), Italo Calvino (1923–1985), and Milan Kundera (1929–2023): "Barnes's literary energy and daring are nearly unparalleled among contemporary English novelists. With such a passion for history, art, and formal innovation, with such fulgent wit and bright discursive skill, he will most likely push on along the high Parnassian path he's beaten beside Nabokov, Calvino, and Kundera" (43).[①] Thus, we can say that Barnes has become one of the most prominent and outstanding novelists in contemporary English literature. Thirty-odd years' writing has proven the popularity and canonicity of Barnes, to which fifteen novels, four collections of essays, three anthologies of short stories, four detective stories, a few pieces of translation, and multitudes of nonfiction that Barnes has spawned and accordingly not a few literary awards that he has received at home and abroad would testify.

Barnes is not so widely accepted and enthusiastically acclaimed in China as in Britain, America and some non-English speaking countries such as France, Italy and Germany, however. Even after he got the most significant literary award the Booker Prize in Britain, his name has not caused much sensation in the literary circle of China, which, so to speak, offers a great opportunity to make him and his works as the study focus in this research, perhaps the first one about him in China. It is, therefore and to start with, very necessary to write of the literary career and achievements of this prominent contemporary British writer in a few more pages to introduce him, although such an act might be against Barnes's own will, due to the belief held by him that a "writer's life usually isn't ... an especially interesting or instructive one. It is full of frailty and defeat like any other life. What counts is the work," and that "[o]nly the work can really explain the work" (Barnes, "The Follies of Writer Worship" 5, 7).

I. Barnes's Literary Career and Achievements

Born in Leicester, England on January 19, 1946, Julian (Patrick) Barnes was the second son of Albert Leonard and Kaye Barnes, both of them

---

① Sebastian Groes and Peter Childs have made a comprehensive comment on Barnes, which is worth reading here: "Julian Barnes is perhaps the most versatile and idiosyncratic author of an astoundingly talented generation of writers, and he is also intensely prolific and at home in many genres. ... Barnes is additionally a sharp and refined critic and reviewer, perhaps one of the finest thinkers of his generation, whose interests include politics, sports, nature, food, the arts and literature, and 'difficult' or taboo subjects such as death, religion and adultery" (1). The main ideas of this comment would be more or less referred to in the later sections.

being French teachers, which perhaps influenced Barnes's later obsession with French culture and literature (Moseley 2). One month and a half later, the whole family moved to Acton, a western suburb of London, and lived there for almost ten years. Then in 1956, the two French teachers took their two sons to settle down in Northwood, from which Barnes commuted by way of the Metropolitan Line for seven years to attend the City of London School. This experience on the metro or subway turns out to be the main concern in Barnes's *Bildungsroman* and debut novel *Metroland*. From 1959, the family took summer vacations by driving through different places in France. Though "[t]hose early holidays were filled with anxiety" (**xii**), due to a poor grasp of the French language, as recalled in the preface to *Something to Declare* (2002), Barnes in later years developed a great passion or enthusiasm for France, which he shared with Jonathan Barnes his older brother, who has settled down in France, now a Professor of Philosophy at the University of La Sorbonne in Paris. From 1964 to 1968, Barnes studied first modern languages (French and Russian), then changed to PPP (philosophy, politics, psychology), and then changed back to read French at Magdalen College, Oxford (Guppy); during this period he taught English at a Catholic school in Rennes, France for a year from 1966 to 1967 (Barnes, *Letters from London* 255). After graduation, Barnes worked as a lexicographer for *Oxford English Dictionary Supplement*, and was, as a male among a female majority, in charge of the "rude words and sports words" from 1969 to 1972 (Smith 73). Without doubt, this experience has sharpened his "connoisseurship in language" (Moseley 3). Barnes then read for the bar and qualified as a barrister in 1974, but never practiced because at the same time he started working as a freelance journalist, which appealed much more to him. Certainly, the experience of studying law helped Barnes greatly in the writing of his important novels such as *Flaubert's Parrot* (1984), *A History of the World in 10 ½ Chapters* (1989), *The Porcupine* (1992), and *Arthur & George* (2005).

Since then, Barnes started to write reviews, articles and columns under his own name and by means of pseudonyms. From 1976 to 1978, he published satirical pieces as Edward Pygge in the "Greek Street" column of the *New Review*, and in 1977 became a contributing editor under the direction of the poet, critic and literary editor Ian Hamilton (1938-2001), to whom he later devoted an essay "Bitter Lemon Days" (1999). In the same year, Barnes joined the *New Statesman* as assistant literary editor under Martin Amis. There he met and made friends with the columnist Christopher Hitchens (1949-2011) as well as the poets Craig Raine (1944-) and James Fenton (1949-), and wrote reviews about novels and television programmes till 1981. In 1979, Barnes married a well-known literary agent Pat Kavanagh (1940-2008), to whom most of his fiction was dedicated and whose surname he utilized as a pseudonym for his detective novels. From 1979 to 1982, Barnes worked as the deputy literary editor of the *Sunday Times*, and from 1982 to 1986, the television critic for the *Observer*, and in 1981, another of his pen-names, Basil Seal, restaurant critic for *Tatler*, was nominated Gourmet Writer of the Year (Guignery, *The Fiction of Julian Barnes* 2). All of these experiences as literary reviewer, critic, editor, and his friendships with literary figures pave the way to some extent for his rise as a professional writer.

On the way to becoming a journalist, Barnes commenced to write fiction. "A Self-Possessed Woman" was his first short story, printed in 1975. In 1980, he published *Metroland*, "a long-gestated coming-of-age novel about a young man growing up in the same suburbs as Barnes, with the same interest in French matters, the same loathing for bourgeois conformity" (Moseley 4), winning the Somerset Maugham Award for an outstanding first novel in 1981, adapted into a film in 1998. The outcome of this literary debut was beyond Barnes's expectation, for he lacked confidence in the process of writing. The unexpected success of *Metroland* spurred Barnes on to continue his writing. Two years later, his second novel *Before She Met Me* (1982), "a short but intense, funny but terrifying study of love and overmastering jealousy" (Moseley 6), surprised his readers with the combination of horror and humor, getting mixed reviews. These two novels were not well sold, as Barnes recalled years later: "[m]y first two novels had sold 1,000 or so copies in hardback and had just about staggered into paperback—on separate lists, each of which had collapsed shortly afterwards" (WFTW 30). Therefore, when his third novel *Flaubert's Parrot* came out in 1984, Barnes did not expect much better from his readers. This "upside-down sort of novel," as called by Barnes himself, "might interest a few Flaubertians, and perhaps a smaller number of psittacophiles [parrot lovers]" (WFTW 30). Nevertheless, it met with great success and was Barnes's first great success; it has established itself as "a minor classic, and one of the best criticism novels" (Rafferty 22), so that it is up to now still the most acclaimed and celebrated novel of Barnes. It is also the first of Barnes's works to raise the question of whether it merits to be classified as a novel. The "novel" received several literary prizes in Britain and abroad, and was shortlisted for the Booker Prize. In 1983, Barnes was selected by the Book Marketing Council as one of the twenty "Best of Young British Novelists" in a list that included Martin Amis, Pat Barker (1943-), William Boyd (1952-), Kazuo Ishiguro, Ian McEwan, Salman Rushdie and Graham Swift. Three years later, because of the success of *Flaubert's Parrot*, Barnes did not work as a journalist any more, although he still wrote some reviews, essays and pieces on painting for (literary) journals and magazines. In the same year, his fairly conventional novel *Staring at the Sun* (1986) was put out and "met critical reservations" or "subdued acclaim," though Barnes himself viewed it differently (Guignery, *The Fiction of Julian Barnes* 3).

From 1980 to 1987, Barnes published four detective novels via a pseudonym Dan Kavanagh: *Duffy* (1980), *Fiddle City* (1981), *Putting the Boot In* (1985) and *Going to the Dogs* (1987). They constitute a peculiar feature of Barnes's literary output, which is quite different from Barnes's "mainstream" novels, that resist categorization and defy expectations to a remarkable degree. As mentioned at the beginning, Barnes "never writes the same book twice;" there is no exception to these four detective novels, in which the characters and the plots are unusual. But these detective novels are not experimental in form, which is in sharp contrast with Barnes's other better-known and openly acknowledged "siblings" such as *Flaubert's Parrot* and *A History of the World in 10½ Chapters*. Merritt Moseley proffered an insightful interpretation about the relation of Barnes's detective fiction to his serious novels:

> The traditionalist side of Julian Barnes, the part of him that appreciates straightforward narration, the management of suspense, and a fairly clear moral taxonomy among the characters, has gone into the making of the Duffy [the name of Barnes's detective] books, leaving him free in his other novels to experiment, to rearrange or dispense with narrative chronology, to be playful about the relationship between art and life. (5–6)

In light of this, the four detective novels, though now in a state of oblivion, contributed much to the transformation of Barnes's writing from traditional modes of writing to experimentation and innovation in form, which is typical of Barnes's postmodern writing. After the writing of his final detective novel, Barnes in 1988 translated into English a book by German cartoonist Volker Kriegel, *The Truth About Dogs*. Barnes also wrote an unpublished non-fiction work entitled *A Literary Guide to Oxford* in the 1970s as well as the drafts for two screenplays *Growing Up in the Gorbals* (1987) and *The Private Wound* (1989), based on the novels by Nicholas Blake (Guignery, *The Fiction of Julian Barnes* 3).

Barnes's second major literary success came with the publication of *A History of the World in 10½ Chapters* in 1989. Like *Flaubert's Parrot*, this work takes liberties with the form of novel, and as such invites suspicion over whether it qualifies as a novel at all (Candel 27–28; Oates 13; Taylor 40).

The "novel" consists of ten chapters, in which Barnes tries to explore serious themes in a serious way but often remains witty and charming. The half "chapter" is a meta-fictively straightforward "disquisition on love" (Rushdie 243). Nevertheless, it is not unsafe to say that it is a typical novel of postmodernism, due to such features embodied in it as engagement with the issues of historiography, problematizing of conventional notions about truth, polyphonic voicing, achronological plotting, mixed genres, and awareness of cultural (racial) diversity.

From 1990 to 1994, Barnes became the London correspondent of *The New Yorker* and wrote long essays on his own country that were later collected in a book titled *Letters from London 1990-1995*, reflecting principally Britain's politics and scandals from 1990 to 1994, which is Barnes's first published book of non-fiction and in which Barnes's talent as "a brilliant essayist" is artistically demonstrated. In 1991, Barnes published a very delightful novel *Talking It Over*, telling a love triangle story with dialogical narrative techniques, which received the Prix Femina Étranger in France and was adapted into a French film titled *Love, Etc.* in 1996. Coincidentally, ten years later, the sequel of *Talking It Over* was also named *Love, Etc.* (2001). His seventh novel *The Porcupine* (1992) is a political fiction, depicting the downfall of a former Communist country and its chaos under the regime of the democratic and market capitalism, evoking "the moral complexities of freedom, truth, and political power" (Moseley 7), and is called "the first serious Western novelistic attempt in some time to come to grips with the Communist experience" (Puddington 62). In 1995, Barnes came to Johns Hopkins University in Baltimore, U. S. A., to teach creative writing. One year later, his first collection of short stories titled *Cross Channel* came out; it is "a remarkable book" (Kennedy 110), which exhibits "the finely nuanced knowledge of French culture" and explores "the British experience of France over the past three hundred years" (Hutchings 149). In the year of 1998, Barnes issued another (political) novel *England, England*, a satirical and/or farcical novel about the invention of English (historical) tradition and the construction of English historical heritage, which rendered Barnes the second time being shortlisted for the Man Booker Prize.

In 2002, Barnes's attention was again turned to France by publishing a collection of essays *Something to Declare*, which are "mostly about men and women in French arts and letters ... or about Anglophone writers in France" (Messud 25), and his translation into English of the remarkable *In the Land of Pain* by French author Alphonse Daudet (1840-1897), the translation of which "certainly confirms Barnes's interest in and intimate relationship with French literature and language" (Guignery, "A Preference for Things Gallic" 43). *The Pedant in the Kitchen*, printed in 2003, is Barnes's third collection of essays, which seems to play a minor part in Barnes's works and has not aroused much critical evaluation. Issued one year later, *The Lemon Table* (2004) is a volume of short stories about the theme of ageing and approaching death, "territory upon which Barnes imposes a fine variety of plots and moods," with "genuine artfulness and imaginative necessity," which "in ways both modest and grand, helps sustain a reader's faith in literature as the truest form of assisted living" (Mallon 7). Published in the year of 2005, *Arthur & George* tells of a true historical case concerned with Sir Arthur Conan Doyle (1859–1931), the world famous detective writer, and George Edalji, a historical but obscure young English solicitor. Barnes's unconventional narrative techniques, unique language style and the historical, racial motifs laid bare in it brought him a third nomination as a candidate for the Booker Prize. *Nothing to Be Frightened of* (2008) is a very Barnesian book, which cannot be easily classified; it is, among many things, a family memoir, an exchange with his older brother a philosopher, a meditation on mortality and the fear of death, a celebration of art, an argument with and about God, which again confirms Barnes's great artistry as "a brilliant essayist."

Coming out in 2011, *Pulse* is Barnes's long-awaited third collection of short stories, which are attuned to rhythms and currents: of the body, of love and sex, illness and death, connections and conversations; and in which Barnes's *tour de force* as a short story writer is well exemplified: "All the stories in *Pulse* have the absolute completeness and density of the very best short fiction" (Saunders, "What Death Has Taught Him" 51). In the same year, *The Sense of an Ending* was published, which won the Booker Prize that year. Although the novel is about 160 pages in length, its content bears rich connotations, probing into such important themes as love, memory, history, truth and self-identity cognition, and its narrative technique is also unique and breathtaking; accordingly it is esteemed by a critic as "little treasure of a book" with "subtlety and grace of Barnes's prose" (Martino 57). Since its publication, the novel has been warmly acclaimed by the academic circles.

Levels of Life, a mixture of essay, fiction and memoir, was published in 2013, in which Barnes dedicates the last section "The Loss of Depth" to his bereavement process after the loss of his wife, Pat Kavanagh, which, as Zekiye Antakyalioğlu observes, foregrounds the theme of "mourning and melancholy" in the writing (158). The hybridization of genres, a remarkable characteristic of Barnes's writing, turns up in this work. *The Noise of Time*, came out in 2016, is a fictional biographical novel written by Barnes as a tribute to the Russian musician Dmitri Shostakovich. The interest in and concern for historical figures and history, the living quandary of the artist or the writer under the control of totalitarianism, and the relations of knowledge to power—the issues told and retold across Barnes's career, are retold in this novel. As a recurring motif in Barnes's writing, history in this novel, "which is associated with the metaphor of *the noise of the time*, becomes a story and a postmodernist parody of the Russian communist world at the beginning of the 20th century" (Catană 25, italics original). *The Only Story* (2018) is Barnes's another "essayistic novel about love" (Martin), which, written in a retrospective narration or in the form of recollection and with shifting perspectives, explores the love entanglement under the patriarchal culture, the moral subversion and sexual freedom under the influence of sexual revolution, and the survival tragedy of the characters. Published in 2019, *The Man in the Red Coat* is at once a fresh and original portrait of the French Belle Epoque and a "biography" of a man, the pioneering surgeon Samuel Pozzi, ahead of his time. Witty, surprising and deeply researched, Barnes in the novel demonstrates the fruitful and longstanding exchange of ideas between England and France, which is also a constant motif and a unique feature in Barnes's writing. And Barnes's latest work is *Elizabeth Finch* (2022), in which Barnes explores love, grief, and the collective myths of history; but it is more than a novel, as the blurb on the book jacket shows, it is "a loving tribute to philosophy, a careful evaluation of history, an invitation to think for ourselves."

    Herein we would contend that a brief survey about Barnes's major works attests to the fact that every book for Barnes is indeed "a new departure," and accordingly his work as a whole (re)presents a strong "sense of heterogeneity" (Guignery, "History" 59). This for one thing represents Barnes's endless exploration in his writing, rendering his work with colorfulness and richness,[①] but for another brings about not a small difficulty for readers to do research on his works systematically and consistently, few of

---

[①] The literary awards and honors that Barnes has up to now garnered during his thirty-odd years' writing to a great extent corroborate his literary quality and achievement. They include: the Somerset Maugham Award in 1981; the Booker Prize nominations in 1984, 1998, 2005; Geoffrey Faber Memorial Prize in 1985; Prix Médicis in France in 1986; the E. M. Forster Award in 1986; an American Academy and Institute of Arts and Letters Award for work of distinction in 1986; the Gutenberg Prize in France in 1987; the Premio Grinzane Cavour in Italy in 1988; the Prix Femina Étranger in France in 1992; the Shakespeare Prize of the FVS Foundation of Hamburg in 1993; and the Australian State Prize for European Literature in 2004; what's more, Barnes was named Chevalier of the Order of Arts and Letters in France in 1988, promoted to Officer in 1995, and finally to Commander in 2004; still, in 2011 he was awarded the David Cohen Prize for Literature, which is awarded biennially, honouring a lifetime's achievement in literature for a writer in the English language who is a citizen of the United Kingdom or the Republic of Ireland. And, certainly, Barnes was the winner of the Man Booker Prize in 2011 for his novel *The Sense of an Ending*.

the theses and dissertations about him being the evidence, which could be validated in the next section about Barnes's studies at home and abroad.

II. Barnes Studies at Home and Abroad

Since 1980, there have been multitudes of essays, reviews, and academic papers about Julian Barnes and his works, some of these are critically negative, but most are warmly positive, praising Barnes's experimentation and innovation and his contribution to contemporary British literature and even to "the history of the novel." The majority of these writings are in English, with a few in French, Italian, German or even Czechoslovak and in Chinese. In this section, I shall narrow the emphasis on the critical study of Barnes in Britain and America, and in China as well. When surveying the critical study of Barnes in Britain and America, I shall focus on those monographs written and printed in English. As to the critical study of Barnes in China, I will mainly examine the introduction of Barnes in the history of British Literature by Chinese scholars and refer briefly to some academic articles published in some important Chinese journals. Hence the survey of the critical study of Barnes at home and abroad.

Understanding Julian Barnes (1997) by Merritt Moseley is perhaps the first important book-length study in English about Barnes and his works. Moseley's explication is on the whole insightful and instructive and, I would maintain, his remarks and comments, as mentioned at the beginning of this Introduction, are still helpful up to now. His observation is firstly groundbreaking in that he detects the intricate relationship between Barnes's divided career as a writer of serious novels, published under his own name, and of detective thrillers, published under the pseudonym Dan Kavanagh. Moseley then provides close readings of Barnes's major works, defending him against some charges that Barnes's works receive, and examining Barnes's commitment to writing books rich in the exploration of serious ideas. Moreover, Moseley sorts out the important motifs in Barnes and highlights his formal experimentation, perceptively points out his admiration for Gustave Flaubert, and intimates that Barnes's greatest achievement is his ability to resist summary and categorization by creating each book in a dramatically original way, or in his own words, "the keynote to his [Barnes's] career as a writer has always been versatility and change" (Moseley 172). In a word, it is indispensable for the study of Barnes, and its significance cannot be negated by anyone who wants to do research on Barnes.

Bruce Sesto in *Language, History, and Metanarrative in the Fiction of Julian Barnes* (2001) contends that Barnes's novels, marked by an urbanity, wit and gracefulness of style, represent and examine many theoretical issues that preoccupy contemporary writers—issues such as the nature of artistic representation and the relation of history to fiction, and explores the ways in which Barnes develops such themes in his early works from *Metroland* to *The Porcupine*.

Matthew Pateman's *Julian Barnes* (2002) provides a brief introductory overview of Barnes's career and a discussion of each of the novels written before 2002 in Barnes's own name. By focusing on the novels themselves, Pateman offers close readings that seek to foreground the dominant ideas in each novel, including such issues as narrative inventiveness, questions of love, notions of truth of justice, friendship and betrayal, cynicism, faith, politics and art. While each novel is discussed in its own right, the book aims to demonstrate that Barnes's writings constantly attempt to push the limits of the novel form, however subtly, and prove that Barnes is one of the most important writers in Britain today.

Vanessa Guignery is a distinguished expert on the study of Barnes, and her book *The Fiction of Julian Barnes* (2006), insightful and scholarly, provides a comprehensive and accessible overview of the essential criticism on Barnes's work, drawing from a selection of reviews, interviews, essays, and books; through the presentation and assessment of key critical interpretations, Guignery proffers a most wide-ranging examination of Barnes's fiction and non-fiction, considering key issues such as Barnes's use of language, treatment of history, obsession, love, and the relation of fact to fiction.

Julian Barnes (2009) by Frederick M. Holmes provides another comprehensive and accessible introduction to the works of Barnes, which includes a timeline of important dates to help place new British fiction in context, offers extensive readings of ten novels from *Metroland* to *Arthur & George*, explores Barnes's distinctive techniques in these novels, and finally makes an overview of the varied critical reception Barnes's work has provoked.

Peter Childs's *Julian Barnes* (2011), then, the latest comprehensive and lucidly written introductory overview of Barnes, situates Barnes's work in terms of fabulation and memory, irony and comedy, pursuing a broadly chronological line through Barnes's literary career, but also showing how certain key thematic preoccupations and obsessions such as love, death, art, history, truth, and memory tie Barnes's work together; it provides detailed readings of each major publication from *Metroland* to *Arthur & George* respectively in each chapter while treating the major concerns of Barnes's fiction, including art, authorship, history, love, and religion.

Julian Barnes: *Contemporary Critical Perspectives* (2011) proffers a wide range of current critical perspectives on Barnes's works from his early *Metroland* to his recent memoir *Nothing to Be Frightened of*, offering insights into the genesis of some of Barnes's novels and new perspectives on Barnes's complex uses of historical and biographical facts and fictional invention, reflecting the richness and diversity of Barnes, and taking scholarly analyses of Barnes's work to a new level.

In short, these works about Barnes are in the main introductory and explanatory, comprehensive in content, but lack depth from a certain perspective.

Barnes has been introduced into China by some scholars specializing in contemporary British Literature in the late 1990s. However, the study of Barnes in China is still in a low tide, compared with that in Britain and America. There are only a few theses and dissertations about Barnes, and some introductory articles appearing in the study monograph or textbooks of contemporary British Literature and some academic papers published in Chinese journals. Zhai Shijing is one of the first Chinese scholars who introduce Barnes to Chinese readers. In "The Young- and Middle-Aged Novelists in Contemporary Britain" (1997), he briefly mentions Barnes's personal attitude toward art and explicates the contents and themes of Barnes's early works, thinking highly of Barnes's exploration in motif, experimentation in form and innovation in writing style, with no negative comment (407-411).[①] Then, Ruan Wei in *Texts Against Social Contexts: The Study of British Fiction After the Second World War* (1998) introduces Barnes in one section, pointing out the French influence on Barnes, recounting the contents of *Flaubert's Parrot* and *A History of the World in 10 ½ Chapters*, celebrating their language styles but not endorsing Barnes's peculiar narrative strategies, dismissing them as "tricks" with no enduring power (211-218),[②] which is nevertheless unsound and unfair. Hou Weirui and Li Weiping also make a brief introduction to Barnes in *A History of English Fiction* (851-853), which is less insightful and less inclusive than

---

[①] The introduction to Barnes in Zhai's article is, without much change but adding more specific details by way of close reading, later included in *A History of Contemporary British Fiction* (Zhai and Ren 317-323).

[②] His introduction to Barnes is later, without changing a word, included in *A History of the 20th Century British Literature* (Ruan et al. 339-346). One error that remains is that the publication date of *The Porcupine* is still 1993 (Ruan 218; Ruan et al. 346) but not 1992, the latter the original publication date.

Zhai's and Ruan's comments on Barnes.① Compared with these introductions, the introduction to Barnes in *A History of British Literature in the 20th Century* (2006) is much more comprehensive and more enlightening. Eight novels from the earlier *Metroland* to the later *England, England* are examined, themes and language style explicated, the significance of these novels emphasized, and the unique features of Barnes summarized; more importantly, Barnes's interest in (the writing of) history and the significance of pursuit of historical truth in some of his novels are for the first time pointed out (Wang and He 220-226).

The latest research on Barnes appears in *A Historical Survey of Contemporary British Fiction* (2010) by Liu Wenrong, one section of which, "Julian Barnes: Fiction Deconstructing Fiction," is devoted to Barnes. Evidently, the content of it is richer than those by the scholars above. Ostensibly more academic and transcending than scholars before him, Liu's writing bears some resemblance to theirs literally, especially in reviewing and analyzing *Flaubert's Parrot*. However, we would argue, more errors turn up in his writing. In "Life and Works," for instance, while discussing Barnes's political novel *The Porcupine*, Liu remarks, "obviously, the novel is based on the trial of Slobodan Milosevic (1941-2006) the former president of Serbia by International Court of Justice in Hague, Netherland;" and he continues, "Barnes is not trying to defend Milosevic but to convey such a view: politics is ugly, and there is no justice for either the adjudicator or the adjudicated; and the so-called political trial is merely a farce" (Liu 388-389). In this comment, Liu makes at least two mistakes. First of all, the trial in the novel is not based on the historical trial of Milosevic, the former president of Serbia, who was arrested in 2002 and was on trial from 2002 to 2006, passing away in prison before it was over. *The Porcupine* was published in 1992, how could Barnes know of Milosevic at that time?② Secondly, that the politics is a farce is not exactly what Barnes tries to convey; instead, what Barnes thinks of is to represent the historical reality happening after the fall of old Communism in Eastern European countries and to reflect the relationship between two systems, therefore making some

---

① One mistake that should be pointed out is that Hou and Li assert that after publication *Staring at the Sun* gets the unanimous commendation from the critics, which is certainly not the fact, for it disappointed at that time many British critics due to its banal plot and conventional structure.

② In fact, the trial is based on what happened in Bulgaria in 1990 and 1991, when Barnes tried to promote *Flaubert's Parrot* there and witnessed the fall of old Communism and the trial on Todor Zhivkov (1911-1998) the former President of Bulgaria (Guignery, *The Fiction of Julian Barnes* 86).

response to the hypothesis of "The End of History." Without realizing this, the reading of this political novel would be meaningless and misleading. Another error occurs to *Nothing to Be Frightened of* (2008), which is regarded by Liu as a novel (389), but is actually a collection of essays, or a memoir. One more blunder in Liu's writing is his misreading of the title of *A History of the World in 10 ½ Chapters*. He mis-writes the title "A History of the World in 10 ½ Chapters," regarding it as "10 divided by 2" and "1 divided by 2," thus calling it as "five and a half chapters" (Liu 391). Quite obviously, such a reading registers that the author did not look at or browse the "table of contents" of the novel, not to mention read it. Anyone who has read it would tell that it is composed of ten "Chapters" and a "Parenthesis," which is a half "Chapter." All of these mistakes only evince that the author did not make a thorough reading of Barnes, which should be avoided in academic research, anyhow.

In short, the introduction to or reading of Barnes by these scholars is not comprehensive, important issues like the historical writing not thoroughly examined, some works just briefly addressed without a close reading or deep analysis, needless to say the errors and mistakes and the non-reading of Barnes's latest works.

Up to now, about 20 articles related to Barnes have been published in Chinese journals, one of which is a translation of an English article, one a translation of an English interview, four of which introductory articles, fourteen research papers. Barnes's name was first mentioned in a Chinese version of an English article in 1990, in which less than 250 words are devoted to Barnes. The four introductory articles and six papers, not important enough, would not be mentioned here. The remaining eight papers are mainly concerned with Barnes's *Flaubert's Parrot* and *A History of the World in 10 ½ Chapters*. As to the former, one of the articles expounds its narrative strategies (Zhang 3–10), one its social concern, cultural and political position (Ruan, "Barnes and his *Flaubert's Parrot*" 51–58), one its query into the narrative of "progress" (Yin 12–19) and one Barnes's pursuit of historical truth (Luo, "Searching for the Truth" 115–121); as to the latter, one article explores the issue of history from the perspective of postmodernism (Yang and Wang 91–96) and one from that of New Historicism (Luo, "Aftereffects of Shock" 98–102). Still, there is one paper about *England, England*, which exposits the complicated relationships among identity, memory and history (Luo, "A Thematic Study" 105–114), and one paper about *Nothing to Be Frightened of*, dealing with Barnes's view of death from the angle of existentialism (Zhang and Guo 81–88). This is then a brief survey of Barnes study in Chinese, which nevertheless cannot be compared with its counterpart abroad. ①

III. Framework of This Research

The critical studies about Julian Barnes, as noted before, suggest that there are few comprehensive studies about this writer yet, needless to say a research on him from the perspective of (postmodern) historical writing. In fact, a great number of elements pertinent to history or historiography in Barnes's fiction have been examined and studied in not a few papers, but not

---

① This section "Barnes Studies at Home and Abroad" was conducted before the year of 2013. As to Barnes studies abroad, it only surveyed the monographs about Barnes published at that time, and did not refer to the related academic papers, theses or dissertations, the quantity of which is certainly not a few. And now a brief survey or retrieval (in May 2023) by the key words "Julian Barnes" on the internet or through some database would evince that there are about 15 monographs, more than 1,900 academic papers and more than 90 theses and dissertations written in English about this writer. It is clear that Barnes studies abroad has gone through a rapid development during these years, especially after he won the Man Booker Prize in 2011. This phenomenon has also occurred in China. As mentioned in this section, Barnes studies in China at that time was in a low tide. But the situation has changed since he published the novel *The Sense of an Ending*. As to the Barnes studies at home, I retrieved the related literatures in 2021 and wrote a paper about the introduction, the studies and translations of Barnes's works in China. The relevant data can be detected in the following description: "According to statistics, as of September 9, 2021, in China, there are 13 introductory articles (these articles are mainly published in the foreign literature journals, with no English abstract, keywords and references, etc., listed here separately, not included in the following statistics), 24 comprehensive papers (involving Barnes's several works), 183 academic papers (about Barnes's certain work), 1 interview, 3 doctoral dissertations, 80 theses, and 2 monographs. According to the statistics, we can see that before 2013, the number of papers published per year is less than 5, which shows that the research on Barnes has been in a very slow development state. In the year of 2011, Barnes won the Booker Prize, which attracted the attention of China's academic circles. However, many researches appeared one or two years later, and there was a large increase in 2014, which displays that the acceptance, digestion and absorption of Barnes' works are not an easy task, which is in line with the development law of academic research. The increase in the number of papers since 2014 shows that Chinese scholars are making efforts quietly and painstakingly. After a period of accumulation, they have published their own research results. This increasing trend also fits in with the speed of translation and publication of Barnes's works. The translation and publication of many works by Barnes have a great influence on Barnes's research, but it also reflects the characteristics of Chinese scholars' dependence on translated works in the study of foreign writers" (He and Gan 125). As to the translation of Barnes's works in China, the retrieval conducted in 2021 shows that there were 16 works of Barnes translated into Chinese and some of these works even had more than one version of translation (He and Gan 125). And in fact in May 2023, two more works of Barnes, that is, *Through the Window: Seventeen Essays and a Short Story* (2012) and *The Only Story* (2018) have been translated into Chinese and can be bought through internet bookstore. That means 18 works of Barnes have been translated into Chinese, which would to a great exent promote the advancement of Barnes studies in China.

in a comprehensive and systematic fashion and especially not in a way of putting history in the first place, which accordingly proffers a great opportunity for this research to write of Barnes from the viewpoint of postmodern historical writing.

Any reader who has read Barnes would not deny the fact that Barnes's fiction is thick with historical views and literary theoretical suggestions, which are in accordance with those hypotheses proposed by such postmodern theorists as Frank Ankersmit (1945–), Jacques Derrida (1930–2004), Michel Foucault (1926–1984), Jean-François Lyotard (1924–1998) and Hayden White (1928–). Barnes's concern for history or historiography has given rise to a great interest of study not only for literary scholarship but for historical scholarship as well; and as Rudolf Freiburg, a German scholar in literature, told Barnes:

> [There is] almost no class in our contemporary university where the postmodern idea of history is introduced without going back to at least one of your books, *Flaubert's Parrot*, *A History of the World* [*in 10½ Chapters*], *The Porcupine*. You are exhaustively quoted in the *Oxford Dictionary of Quotations*, for instance, with the phrase, "History just burps, and we taste again that raw-onion sandwich it swallowed centuries ago." There are critical articles that quote your definition of history as "merely another literary genre," and the general critical view would be that you treat history as a "narration" and this of course is an idea closely associated with the name of Hayden White. (42)

However, interestingly enough, when asked whether he read any literary theory, Barnes offered an ostensibly negative but paradoxical answer as such: "I have never read any literary theory. I've read a few pages of Derrida, I've occasionally been sent theses on my work where there would be ... two pages of a sort of Derridaish prose" (Freiburg 37), and when the name of Hayden White was referred to, he defended that "I've never heard of Hayden White, I'm afraid" (Freiburg 42). Most readers who are not unfamiliar with Barnes's writing would not believe what Barnes said. How could a novelist like Barnes whose works are replete with postmodern views of history not read any of these postmodern theorists as aforementioned? The following statements articulated by Barnes would clarify the mystery. As he explained, "I'm deliberately unaware of literary theory. *Novels come out of life*, not out of theories about either life or literature, it seems to me; ... *I think* I know more than most critics, ... *I'm* also aware that you can be *influenced at second hand*, and you can be *influenced by things that are in the air*" (Freiburg 37, italics added). Similarly, when White was mentioned, Barnes spoke out his view like this, "all my ideas come as I write. ... Appetite comes with eating and ideas come with writing. I never start my novels wanting to prove something; I never start my novels with any sort of thesis" (Freiburg 42), and as the interviewer interpreted it as "in the sense that 'it is in the air,'" Barnes definitely agreed with it with a "Yes" (Freiburg 43). We can decode the mystery in this fashion: although Barnes did not read a great deal of literary and history theories but "a few pages of Derrida," he has been greatly influenced by the society in which he lives and by postmodern culture and thinking, especially the French language and culture which is quite familiar to him. Still, when Barnes was a university student, he studied philosophy for one year, which has naturally affected his fictional writing. Moreover, we can infer that Barnes has also read not a few books about history, since many historical figures, historical events and different historical views turn up in his novels. This could be confirmed by what he wrote in his novel *The Sense of an Ending*:

> *I still read a lot of history, and of course I've followed all the official history that's happened in my own lifetime*—*the fall of Communism, Mrs. Thatcher, 9/11,* global warming—with the normal mixture of fear, anxiety and cautious optimism. But I've never felt the same about it— I've never quite trusted it—as I do *events in Greece and Rome,* or *the British Empire,* or *the Russian Revolution.* (66, italics added)

Considering these factors, then, when we read Barnes's writing we will not feel surprised why he is so obsessed with history and why his writing is shining with the aura of postmodern views or thinking of philosophy.

In the reading of Barnes's fiction, we would come across a good many (postmodern) views of history explicitly written or implicitly suggested between his lines. Some of the important could be enumerated here as an introduction and preview. Barnes often expresses his view about the nature of (conventional) history, therefore he writes as such: "Nothing was set in concrete: that was the nature of history" (*EE* 130); "History, to put it bluntly, is a hunk" (*EE* 152); and he also calls into question history or historical truth epistemologically: "history is merely another literary genre" (*FP* 90); "We make up a story to cover the facts we don't know or can't accept; we keep a few true facts and spin a new story round them. Our panic and our pain are only eased by soothing fabulation; we call it history" (*HWC* 240); "'The story of a louse may be as fine as the history of Alexander the Great—everything depends upon the execution.' [...] What is needed is a sense of form, control, discrimination, selection, omission, arrangement, emphasis ...that[...] three-letter word, art" (*LE* 14); still Barnes interrogates history ontologically: "History doesn't relate" (*EE* 70);

"The history of the world? Just voices echoing in the dark; images that burn for a few centuries and then fade; stories, old stories that sometimes seem to overlap; strange links, impertinent connections" (*HWC* 240) ; and his writing also foregrounds the ideological attribute of history: "History isn't what happened. History is just what historians tell us" (*HWC* 240) ; "HISTORY ... often comes in incompatible versions" (*Letters from London* 160) ; "one of the central problems of history ... the fact that we need to know the history of the historian in order to understand the version that is being put in front of us" (*SE* 13). Of course, there are more such views of history implied in Barnes's lines or even embedded in his writing mode, which would not be specifically mentioned here. But then how could we as layman of history explore or explicate Barnes's literary writing from the angle of combining literature and history? Such an overall and detailed study not turning up, there are nevertheless a few insights given to the understanding of this issue, among which the comments of Vanessa Guignery, a distinguished specialist of Barnes in France, are worth reading here.

Guignery acutely argues that in most of his fiction, "Julian Barnes overtly questions the foundations of traditional historiography, a process that could be analysed from three main viewpoints: ontological, epistemological and political" ("History" 60). Then Guignery continues to interpret her argument further: from an ontological viewpoint, Barnes's novels "direct the reader's attention towards the similarities between fiction and history, stories and History, underlining their discursive and narrative dimension, their fictive and constructed character" (60); the second perspective "from which to consider the destabilisation of historical discourse in Julian Barnes's fiction is thus epistemological," which is mainly connected with the epistemological question, as Barnes puts it in *Flaubert's Parrot*: "How do we seize the past?" (61) ; a third angle "leads the author [Barnes] to foreground the intimate links that connect historical accounts and political power" (62). With no doubt, Guignery's brief interpretation of the problematizing of historical discourse in Barnes's fiction is enlightening and illuminating, but there is something not accurate or confusing in her remarks; that is, her reading of Barnes's historical writing from the perspective of ontology seems to be overlapping with or crossing the boundary of epistemology. Anyhow, Guignery's remarks make me study Barnes's historical writing more thoroughly and comprehensively; and I will use her classification as the framework of this research but in a different way and with different focalizations. Still, the reading of Barnes's works makes us believe that Barnes is a typical postmodern writer, not only in his formal experimentation but also in his expression of postmodern views or philosophy of history, bearing the distinctive features of deconstructive thought, which are against the conventional historical or historiographical views established and permeated in official history. Salman Rushdie makes an incisive comment on Barnes's *A History of the World in 10 ½ Chapters* as such: "what he [Julian Barnes] offers us is the novel as *footnote to history*, as *subversion of the given*, as brilliant, elaborate doodle around the margins of what we know we think about what we think we know. This is *fiction as critique*" (241, italics added). This comment, for my part, could be used as a footnote to most of Barnes's postmodern texts. Therefore I will use the phrase "subversion of the given" as part of the title of this research. Undoubtedly, not all of Barnes's novels are concerned with the issue of history or historiography; that is, not all of his novels are characterized by an acute historical consciousness, such as his early novels like *Metroland*, *Before She Met Me* and *Staring at the Sun*. As a result, these novels would not become the main concern of this research, and I will focus on those novels or short stories of Barnes which display an acute historical consciousness and the typical features of postmodernism, so as to underscore the postmodern features of Barnes's historical writing or the postmodern rendering of history or historiography in Barnes's fiction. Hence the genesis of the title of this research — "Subversion of the Given": On the Postmodern Historical Writing in Julian Barnes's Fiction.

To realize this, I would elaborate on Barnes's several prominent novels such as *Flaubert's Parrot*, *A History of the World in 10 ½ Chapters*, *The Porcupine*, *England, England* and *Arthur & George* and a couple of short stories, not in a chronological but thematic order, by way of a close reading of these texts, combining the reading strategies of Deconstructionism and New Historicism, and through drawing upon hypotheses put forward by postmodern theorists (of history) and New Historicists such as Frank Ankersmit, Jacques Derrida, Michel Foucault, Linda Hutcheon, Fredric Jameson, Keith Jenkins, Jean-François Lyotard and Hayden White, to explore how Barnes demonstrates his postmodern view or philosophy of history explicitly or implicitly through his intertextual, deconstructive, satiric or parodic strategy of writing, to substantiate that Barnes is such a postmodern novelist whose work presents or suggests a postmodern "philosophy of history in fictional ... form" (Buxton 58). Epistemologically, Barnes, through questioning and questing for historical truth in intertextual writing, foregrounds that historical writing or historiography bears the feature of textuality and fictionality; ontologically, Barnes, by subverting and revising historical (meta)narratives in deconstructive writing, stresses that history is discontinuous, fragmented and pluralistic; politically, Barnes, via fabricating and representing contemporary and future politics-history in satiric or parodic writing, highlights that history and historiography are subtly affected by political ideology and/or power relations.

This research consists of an introduction, four chapters and a conclusion. The Introduction makes a survey about Barnes's writing experience and literary achievements, refers to Barnes studies at home and abroad, to the preview of his postmodern view of history and the genesis of my study angle, followed by the explanation of the framework of this research. Chapter One "Historical Discourse, Historical Writing and Julian Barnes" examines in a brief way the transformation of historical discourse, the main ideas of postmodern discourse of history and New Historicism, the origin and development of historical fiction in British literature from the later 18th century to the end of the 20th century and its main features, and finally addresses Barnes's historical consciousness, with an introduction to his postmodern view of history (and historiography) as its conclusion.

Chapter Two "Questioning and Questing for Historical Truth" explores Barnes's postmodern historical writing epistemologically. Its first section "Textuality of History" investigates the possibility of questing for historical truth and highlights the relation of history to text(uality) and the (inter)textuality of history or historiography through the analysis of Barnes's intertextual writing in *Flaubert's Parrot* and *A History of the World in 10½ Chapters*; its second section "Fictionality of History" expounds Barnes's knowledge and practical writing of the view of fictionality of history by way of the elaboration and substantiation of history as "merely another literary genre" and of history as fiction or fabulation, particularly implicated in Barnes's two most postmodern(ist) novels *Flaubert's Parrot* and *A History of the World in 10½ Chapters*.

Chapter Three "Subverting and Revising Historical (Meta)Narratives" explicates Barnes's postmodern historical writing ontologically. Barnes's deconstructive writing, particularly in *A History of the World in 10½ Chapters*, breaks up the linear causality, continuity and totality in conventional history (or historiography), and also interrogates and subverts the view or narrative of progress embedded in such historical (meta)narratives as those of Darwin's theory of evolution and Hegel's rational History, accordingly suggesting and stressing such features of history as discontinuity and fragmentation and the view of incredulity toward the historical narrative of progress, which represents the main ideas of the first section of this chapter. Barnes's writing, as discussed in the second section of this chapter, explores the feature of historical plurality, embodied in his revision of Christian History from the perspective of an animal (in a "chapter" of *A History of the World in 10½ Chapters*) and in his digging out and rewriting of a forgotten history of a racial Other (in *Arthur & George*), mirroring his subversion and revision of orthodox history or historical monism and his potential defense for historical (and racial) plurality.

Chapter Four "Fabricating and Representing Politics-History" examines Barnes's thinking of the relation of politics to history and his postmodern delineation of hetero-topia worlds in the future. Barnes's postmodern historical writing in *The Porcupine* intimates the influence of (political) power on history and historiography, and makes an implicit agreement with Jacques Derrida's refutation of Francis Fukuyama's hypothesis of "The End of History." Barnes's writing of the political future (history) of England in *England, England* as the world of hetero-topia indicates his concern for and rethinking of such significant issues as postmodern hyperreal culture, construction of history and commodification of history (or historical heritage) and their relations to political future and historical orientation of a country (like Britain). The interpretation and investigation of the relation of politics to history in Barnes's two political novels *The Porcupine* and *England, England* respectively constitutes the main ideas of each section in this chapter.

The Conclusion makes a review about the main contents of Barnes's postmodern historical writing in light of his concern for the issue of truth, mentions the paradox or "shortcomings" implied in his writing, then makes a brief comparison of his historical writing with those of other contemporary British writers to highlight his peculiarity in formal experimentation, and deals with in the end some possible perspectives for the study of Barnes to arouse more interest in this writer.

All in all, this research contends that Julian Barnes is a postmodern writer with a profound awareness of rethinking and a strong spirit of critique. His postmodern historical writing, bearing the distinctive feature of deconstruction, subverts "the given" notions about history and historiography, making a postmodern "footnote to [conventional] history" and historiography, presenting a postmodern philosophy of history in the form of fictional writing, thus proffering very good texts for the study of literature (and even history) from the angle of postmodern discourse or philosophy of history.

Chapter One
Historical Discourse, Historical Writing and Julian Barnes

To history has been assigned the office of judging the past, of instructing the present for the benefit of future ages. To such high offices this work does not aspire: It wants only to show what actually happened (*wie es eigentlich gewesen*).
    —Leopold von Ranke, "Preface: *Histories of the Latin and Germanic Nations from 1494–1514*"

We can study files for decades, but every so often we are tempted to throw up our hands and declare that history is merely another literary genre... .
    —Julian Barnes, *Flaubert's Parrot*

[W]hat would be meant by the real is always something that is imagined.
    —Hayden White, "Interview"

History isn't what happened. History is just what historians tell us.
—Julian Barnes, *A History of the World in 10½ Chapters*

History is therefore never history, but history-for.
    —Claude Lévi-Strauss, *The Savage Mind*

To discuss postmodern historical writing in the works of Julian Barnes, this chapter shall, first of all, make some explanations on the concept of "history." The word "history," as explained by Raymond Williams, comes into English from *histoire* (French), *historia* (Latin), from *istoria* (Greek), having the early sense of *inquiry* and a developed sense of the results of inquiry and then an account of knowledge (146, italics original). More specifically, at its root *istoria*, it means an intellectual process, not its subject matter or its final result; but it can also mean the knowledge obtained by investigation or research, an account of the inquiry or a narrative of events, past or present. In Latin, *historia* refers more narrowly to narratives of events or to fictional tales and stories; it is true of *histoire* in French. The definition of history as such is quoted by Graham Swift in the head page of his outstanding novel *Waterland* (1983): "*Historia, -ae*, f. 1. inquiry, investigation, learning. 2. a) a narrative of past events, history. b) any kind of narrative: account, tale, story." These are beyond doubt the original meanings of "history," which is inclusive and paradoxical in that it not only includes the authentic "narrative of past events" but also means "any kind of narrative" such as fictional "tale" and "story," the latter having been forgotten when "history" is mentioned. Seeing this paradox in its origin, Swift uses it to deconstruct the conventional but orthodox historical writing in his brilliant novel, showcasing a new or postmodern line of thinking about history and historical writing.[①] In general, we can summarize that there are two related but distinct concepts about "history:" it can be the past events which actually happened, or in a more terse term, that is, "the past," or on the other hand it can also be the study of past events. The first meaning of "history," or the past, which includes all prior occurrences, is gone forever and irretrievable, therefore it is inarticulate and inaccessible in the practical world. It can only be retrieved and (re)constructed in the narrative or in the text of the past. "History" in the second sense has evolved as a discipline with the past as its exclusive subject matter, which is also called "historiography," that is, "the writing of history" and/or "the study of writing about history" (*Oxford Advanced Learner's Dictionary*; Atkinson 9-10). In common sense, the historiographical writing is simply named "history" as well. In this research, I shall use "history" to convey these two meanings, as commonly used, but will underline the latter occasionally and necessarily.

Bearing the definition of history in mind, we should be aware that those

---

[①] As Graham Swift's contemporary, Julian Barnes seems to have addressed, consciously or unconsciously, both of these original meanings of "history" in his historical writing and quite similarly challenged and undermined the conventional view of history and historiography.

related to history such as historical discourse, philosophy of history and historical writing could not be easily defined, the reading and writing of which could not be an easy task. Therefore, this chapter would first of all make an introduction to historical discourse, specifically sorting out its evolution from the speculative philosophy of history to the analytical one and then summarizing the important views of postmodern discourse or philosophy of history, to proffer a theoretical backdrop for this research; its second section would briefly explicate the origin and development of historical novels in British literature and accordingly the social and historical reasons for the rise of "new historical fiction" and its main features, thus eliciting a literary background for the understanding of the (postmodern) historical writing in Barnes's fiction; its last section addresses Barnes's historical consciousness briefly, with an introduction to his postmodern view of history and historiography as a conclusion.

I. Transformation of Historical Discourse

With the rise of historical consciousness, many critical debates or controversies about history and historiography have turned up, various schools of "historicism" or lines of historical thinking turning up during the process. I shall divide them, in a very broad sense and in light of the terminology generally used by historians proper, into two categories of historical thinking or historical discourse, that is, the traditional or conventional, which includes the ancient and the modern views of history, and the new, which represents the postmodern discourse or philosophy of history; they are coexistent and struggling with each other at present in the study of history or literary theory. Before moving on to the detailed discussion of these historical discourses, we can first of all look at two different views about the flow of events described in *Slaughterhouse-Five* (1969) by Kurt Vonnegut (1922–2007). The novel indicates that, for Billy Pilgrim the protagonist, cause-and-effect relationships govern the course of events: things happen because others things make them happen, but the Tralfamadorans have a different notion. For them, there is "no one after the other;" and "[t]here is no beginning, no middle, no end, ... no causes, no effects" (Vonnegut 88). That is, things happen merely because they happen—randomly, haphazardly, inexplicably and chaotically. Here we can see two different and contrastive views about the flow of events; in actuality, they are two distinctive worldviews about history as well. The view held by Billy Pilgrim is deeply engrained in the tradition of Western civilization, which can be roughly termed as the traditional or conventional (historical) view, whereas the latter, supported by the Tralfamadorans who live in the fourth dimension, has some affinity with the view (of history) contended by postmodern theorists (of history). These two kinds of views of world or history, not so simply and briefly as displayed by Vonnegut, need explicating in more detail, which will be examined in the discussion to follow. Therefore, the first part of this section will deal mainly with the traditional or conventional view of history (or historiography), whereas its second part will discuss the main ideas of postmodern discourse or philosophy of history and/or New Historicism.

i. Traditional Historical Discourse

In fact, history is an altogether stranger and far more difficult discipline than it is often taken to be. The difficulty lies in its varieties. Just as a critic holds, "History, ... varies as the life and spirit of different ages vary, and that is why at different times and in different countries diverse types of history have prevailed. ... Indeed at any one time different, often antithetical, histories are written" (Stern 13). It is true of the historical discourse: "The conceptions of history have been almost as numerous as the men who have written history" (Turner 198). Therefore, I will mainly and briefly mention some important views of conventional history and historiography in this part.

From the perspective of history and historical discourse, we can say that there in general exist three basic schemata of traditional historical view, that is, the cyclical, the providential, and the progressive. Without doubt, variations on each exist, and the three views overlap and intermingle to some extent. In spite of such confusion, each view maintains a measure of distinctiveness. In the first view of history, history moves in circles, repeating endlessly over and over again; in contrast, in the second and third views, history is a linear process moving through time from a beginning to a middle to an end. As to the providential and the progressive versions, each assumes some kind of advancement, or progress, through time but defines the impetus in different ways. In the providential schemata, divine guidance or God's will constitutes the first (and ultimate) cause, and in the progressive one, natural or metaphysical forces provide the momentum or motivation. The cyclical idea of history first appears in many ancient peoples and some Eastern cultures. History for them, as it were, does not exist. Although cyclical interpretations of history persist even into the twentieth century, such as in a dazzling and perplexing work called *The Decline of the West* by Oswald Spengler (1880-1936), the more characteristic form of historical discourse or the grand narrative of history in Western civilization emphasizes the linear conception of the past. A belief in providential design, or the grand narrative of Christian History, established affirmatively and exhaustively by St. Augustine (354–430) in the fifth century, appears incessantly in the historical writing of the Middle Ages. Augustine, more specifically, establishes in *The City of God* a dualism that makes a fundamental distinction between the profane and the sacred, the former being the earthly "city of man" and the latter the heavenly "city of God." Augustine's main concern in the book is sacred history and, as Mark T. Gilderhus puts it, it is an "attempt to elucidate the ways of God and correlate human events with biblical accounts" (23). Augustine's another significant contribution is that he, rejecting the Greek notion of cyclical movements, which would render history meaningless and nullify divine influence and purpose, thinks of history as moving along a time with a clear beginning marked by the Creation, a middle, and an end. In this fashion, the birth and death of Christ becomes the central events, and the salvation of all believers in the end would signify the completion of the process. Augustine's influence lasts for more than ten centuries, and his convictions attribute a great significance to the doctrines of teleology and eschatology, making a profound imprint on Western civilization. In consequence, the History of Christianity as one kind of grand narrative is established during the Middle Ages. The providential power is later manifested in Giambattista Vico's *The New Science* and Hegel's philosophical system.

The shift toward secular characterizations of the past or history in progressive, linear terms achieves particular prominence during the Age of the Enlightenment in the eighteenth century and thereafter. For instance, besides the historical views embedded in Charles Darwin's theory of evolution and Hegel's rational History, the view of history held by Marx and Engels in a later century is also linear and progressive. Their analysis and prediction of history is built on "a true comprehension of reality and a scientific understanding of historical development" (Gilderhus 58), thus endorsing the grand narrative of history espoused by them with a new name—historical materialism.

In general, the historical discourses aforementioned are mainly the speculation on the course and aims of history. The views of history as such are the main concern of the so-called speculative philosophy of history,[1] which seeks to "obtain profound levels of truth by discerning patterns in the past and connecting them with expectations for the future" (Gilderhus 52). Or as William H. Walsh asserts, its aim is "to attain an understanding of the course of history as *a whole*" and "to show that ... history could be regarded

---

[1] Ronald F. Atkinson prefers "substantive" to "speculative" in his writing (9), but it is obvious that William H. Walsh's terminology receives more attention and is accepted by more historians or critics.

as forming *a unity* embodying *an overall plan*, a plan which, if once we grasped it, would both illuminate the detailed course of events and enable us to view the historical process as, in a special sense, satisfactory to reason" (11, italics added). In the twentieth century, the traditional, speculative philosophy of history has lost much of its appeal, partly because of its traditional grandiose aims, but never dies out. Indeed, they live on, often in somewhat different and modified forms, and continue to influence the historical writing proper and even the history of the world.

Contrary to this discourse of history is the analytical or critical philosophy of history, in an epistemological sense (Walsh 119). The focus on problems in methodology, particularly in the area of epistemology, constitutes the main concern of the analytical or critical philosophy of history. Simply speaking, the analytical discourse of history addresses one crucial question: on what grounds can historians reasonably demonstrate that they know what they claim? In other words, the verifiability of historical knowledge comes under review. The turning-up of this historical discourse results from the emergence of natural sciences, specifically when Francis Bacon (1561–1626) and René Descartes (1596–1650) and other scientists try to establish more reliable means for studying the natural world. In general, they favor mathematical formulations and high levels of generality. Thereafter, many historians assert that all forms of knowledge must conform to the methods and techniques of natural science or else forfeit any rightful claim to the status of knowledge. Positivism represents this trend of historical discourse. Instead of focusing on unique or individual events, Positivists concentrate their attention on uniformities and similarities in the course of history and then lay bare the invariable relationships that connect the same kinds of experiences. In this way, Positivists presume the existence of general laws governing the outcomes of activities in the human world, just as in the natural world, and their task is to find them. Leopold von Ranke's view of history and historiography is in effect similar to that of the positivist thought. Ranke's objective view of history represents a forerunner of today's university-based, professional history which aspires to find out "what actually happened" in the past through careful investigation based on archival research. Four prominent features can be detected in Ranke's practice of historical writing or historiography: the objectivity of historical truth; the priority of facts; the particularity of historical events; and the kernel position of politics in historical writing.[①] In the preface to one of his greatest historical works, Ranke states, "To history has been assigned the office of

---

[①] See Huang Jinxing, *Postmodernism and Historiography: A Critical Study* (Beijing: SDX Joint Publishing Company, 2008) 130, footnote 1.

judging the past, of instructing the present for the benefit of future ages. To such high offices this work does not aspire: It wants only to show what actually happened (*wie es eigentlich gewesen*) " ① (57). Although expressed in simple terms and within only a couple of sentences, Ranke's method of writing history as "what actually happened" or his view to describe a historical event as "it had really been," has become a niche for the later historians. As a result, we can see that the similarity of Ranke's view of historiography to Positivism lies in that they both endeavor to accumulate historical data and examine historical records, so as to write history objectively and scientifically.

In stark contrast and as an opposite school of thought to Positivism, a different sort of historical discourse of idealism appears in the end of the nineteenth century and continues to develop in the twentieth century, typically represented in the writings of Wilhelm Dilthey (1833-1911), Benedetto Croce (1866-1952) and Robin G. Collingwood (1889-1943). Croce's view of history that "all true history is contemporary history" (12), along with Collingwood's notorious declaration that "[a]ll history is the history of the thought" (215), has made a sensation among the historians and in the writing of history. However, whether the view of history as "contemporary history" or as "the history of the thought," they are both idealistic, violating the principles of Positivism and eventually going awry in the historical writing that is in pursuit of historical truth.

All in all, the positivist view of history and the idealistic view of history constitute the main components of the analytical philosophy of history. Their controversies and debates promote the development of history and/or historiography to a great extent. Later in the twentieth century, the advancement of natural sciences, the process of industrialization, the emergence of mass culture, and a shift in perceptions of a global world, all together shatter the uniform picture of history and result in great divergences in historical writing or historiography. Be it in economic history, social history, new colonial history or in institutional history, be it for the school of "New History," the Progressive school of historiography in America, or the school of *Annales* in France, or for other schools of history in other countries all over the world, the criterion of objectivity in historiography still holds water; or in other words, "that noble dream" (Beard 315-328) of

---

① There are different versions about Ranke's works. Cf: "History has been assigned the office of judging the past, of instructing our times for the benefit of future years. This essay does not aspire to such high offices; it only wants to show how *it had really been—wie es eigentlich gewesen*" (qtd. in Gilderhus 47, italics added). William H. Walsh translates the German phrase as "precisely what happened" (32).

Ranke—writing history "as it actually happened" or "as it really was" and the search for the historical truth is, as it were, still the aim of historical writing. This is a most distinctive element in the traditional discourse of history or historiography. It does not mean, however, that there are no divergent voices against the traditional philosophy of history, especially after the 1960s.

ii. Postmodern Historical Discourse and New Historicism

Since the 1960s, postmodern discourse or postmodernism as a cultural thought has aroused great attention for its fierce position against tradition. The representatives of this thought embrace, among others, Jacques Derrida (1930–2004), Michel Foucault (1926–1984) and Jean-François Lyotard (1924–1998). Postmodernism originates from the areas of art and architecture and gradually permeates through the fields of linguistics, literature, philosophy and eventually history; and it has up to now become one of the most influential discourses of theory among all of the aspects of western society. Postmodern theory, just as the authors of *The Postmodern Turn* (1997) observe:

> has penetrated almost all academic fields, producing critiques of modern theory and of alternative theoretical practices in philosophy, politics, economics, anthropology, geography, environmental theory, education, and just about every domain from the humanities to the sciences. Consequently, nearly every academic discipline and profession have been challenged and confronted with alternative approaches that often fly the banner of the postmodern, and every domain of society is undergoing transformation to which the term "postmodern" is applied. (Best and Kellner 19)

As a philosophical, cultural and social thought, postmodernism or postmodern theory does not arouse so much sensation in history as in other fields such as art and literature. Its influence on history is mainly upon the view of history or the philosophy of history rather than on the practical operation of historical writing. Nevertheless, the postmodern discourse of history is gradually taking shape and influencing the historical writing proper and even the historical writing in literature. Next, I shall briefly refer to the new or postmodern challenge towards the traditional discourse of history.

The traditional discourse or philosophy of history, as mentioned before, views history as a whole or totality, and accordingly constructs the so-called universal History.① Its significant features lie in the emphasis on continuity, causality and totality, on the unification of time and space. For the postmodernists, the views of history as such and the narrative of history which tries to disclose the plan or program of the world and the entire meaning of history, are the so-called grand narratives or metanarratives of history, upon which they launch their attack, Lyotard being such a postmodern theorist, for instance. Postmodernists challenge the traditional discourse of history from the aspects of both ontology and epistemology. Simply speaking, postmodernism regards history as discontinuous, fragmented and pluralistic ontologically, whereas epistemologically postmodernism endeavors to undermine the objectivity of historical writing, highlighting its textual, fictional and ideological attributes. The following discussion would expound these views in detail.

a. Postmodern View of History

In the first place, the postmodern view of history puts forward its challenge toward the continuity in the traditional, progressive view of history. The progressive view of history is firstly established in the History of Christianity and later extends to the Age of the Enlightenment and thereafter, but the subject of progress is shifted from the divine to the rational and from God to man. To the historians of this sort of view, history is evolutional progress with direction and causality, and can be divided into such periods as ancient, middle and modern in general. In this linear process, progress is continuous, universal and dominant. Continuity and progressiveness thus turn out to be the key concern of conventional history or historiography. Postmodernists or postmodern theorists like Derrida, Foucault and Claude Lévi-Strauss (1908-2009), on the contrary, are suspicious of such progress and deny the continuity of history. To their mind, history is discontinuous, with no continuity and causality.

Postmodernism rejects a total History; it not only denies the continuity of history, but also highlights the fragmentation of history. The rupture of historical continuity and the fragmentation of history are two aspects interconnecting with each other, for when historical continuity is dismantled

---

① Universal History is "based upon the assumption that history displays one single plot" (Kotte 112). The idea can be traced back at least to Augustine's *The City of God* and received wide popularity and currency only in the last decades of the eighteenth century, when thinkers such as Kant and Schiller reflected on the notion of it. Universal History bears such features: first of all, it claims that all human events unfold in a single story with a single central subject or theme; based on the principle of uniform human nature, it further implies that individual events can only become intelligible when integrated within the single movement of History at large (Kotte 112-113).

and demolished, the so-called total History would turn out to be fragmented. Therefore, for postmodernists, history has no internal structure and unity, and everything can be altered, dismantled and ruptured, thence fragmented. In this vein, fragmentation, to postmodernists, constitutes the constant of history. In short, for postmodern(ist) historians, history has become fragmented, the total History no longer existing. In consequence, the study of history would become localized and fragmented, micro-history taking the place of marco-history, which in some sense undercuts the grand narrative or (meta)narrative of total History.

When historical continuity is broken and history consists of but "historical scraps," historical writing as such would take on a picture of differences and varieties. Tolerating difference and recognizing otherness is an essential position of postmodern theory, which is also the basic element of postmodern pluralism or plurality. This position embodied in the postmodern view of history lies in its negation of Eurocentrism or Westerncentrism, which holds that the history of Europe bears the feature of universality and that its development trajectory represents the normal, typical and standard development mode for human society, whereas histories of other countries and areas are mere exceptions and variations. In other words, the historical view of Eurocentrism only recognizes one kind of History, that is, the History of Europe, which is, so to speak, a sort of monism (embodied in racism and Eurocentrism, for instance), and as a consequence other countries and areas all over the world are included and internalized in the same time framework, hence the spatial differentia of world histories reduced to the sole temporal differentia. In this way, history is often considered as "the Western myth" (Descombes 110, qtd. in Rosenau 62) and "a creature of the modern Western nations" and "as such it is said to 'oppress' Third World peoples and those from other cultures" (Rosenau 63). In fact, before the 1960s, Oswald Spengler and Arnold Toynbee (1889-1975) have made some challenge against this historical view in their writings. The strongest counterattack appears to be in *Orientalism* (1978), which is no doubt a corollary of postmodern theories, and in which Edward Said (1935-2003) theorizes and systemizes Orientalism, thinking of it as a sort of power discourse utilized by Europeans or the Occidental to describe, colonize and control the Oriental, thus proffering a forceful punch against Eurocentrism. [1] In a word, history, for postmodern theorists (of history), is pluralistic, bearing more than one center, or no center at all. Highlighting

---

[1] Jacques Derrida's writing also indicates that history or civilization of the world is pluralistic and thus often uses the strategy of deconstruction to subvert the given meaning, thinking, idea and structure, etc., which constitute the basis of Logocentrism and Eurocentrism.

the pluralistic characteristics of history can liberate historians from the limitation of the traditionally Eurocentric writing mode, thus representing different trends and possibilities in history or the evolution of civilization, and reconstructing the historical landscape with diversity and variety.

The aforementioned three aspects in general represent the postmodern, ontological challenge against the traditional discourse of history; and these views subvert and revise the grand narrative or (meta)narrative of history from the perspective of ontology. Postmodernism or postmodern discourse of history thus subverts the continuous, total and monistic History, and recognizes the discontinuous, local and pluralistic histories, giving up the search for and the investigation of grand history or macro-history. For postmodern(ist) historians, the grand narrative or (meta)narrative of history as the dominant in the writing of history, is but a kind of (ideological) bias; it is not the representation and revelation but the covering and masking of historical truth and verity. In a nutshell, postmodern discourse or philosophy of history provides different and new ways of viewing and rethinking history, which merits our attention and cannot be dismissed.

As a postmodern "novelist-philosopher," Julian Barnes in his fiction such as *A History of the World in 10½ Chapters* and *Arthur & George* also exposits some postmodern views of history, suggesting that history is discontinuous and fragmented, that the views of progress embedded in some historical (meta)narratives are vulnerable to be challenged and that the Others have their own histories. Therefore, the third chapter of this research will explore Barnes's postmodern views of history from the perspective of ontology and with a close reading of his fiction, to demonstrate how he subverts and revises the conventional (meta)narratives of history.

b. Postmodern Discourse of Historiography

Objectivity is, epistemologically speaking, one of the most essential notions for historicism and/or modern scientific historiography, which is one of the very reasons for its difference from literature and philosophy. For the Western world, the nineteenth century is the century for history to become a scientific discipline and also the century which is most obsessed with the search for objectivity in the aspect of epistemology. Ranke, for instance, upheld the view of writing history "as it actually happened" or "as it really had been" —*wie es eigentlich gewesen*. Like Ranke, most of the historians at that time contended that historical writing could be objective only if the historians kept an impartial and detached attitude, seriously abided by research processes and thoroughly evaluated historical materials. However, from the later period of the nineteenth century, some philosophers (of history) and historians started to challenge the objective view of historiography of Ranke, by dint of highlighting the experience of historians, foregrounding the difference between history and natural sciences, and throwing out such idealistic views as "all true history is contemporary history" (Croce) and "[a]ll history is the history of the thought" (Collingwood). The objectivity as the basis of modern scientific historiography was thus being shaken. Postmodern thoughts and New Historicism since the 1960s have endeavored to interrogate and subvert this historiographical objectivity with no hesitation. Keith Jenkins, for instance, affirmatively claims that "[t]he idea of writing an objective, neutral, disinterested text [history or historical narrative], where explaining, describing, and 'introducing' something is done for a position that isn't ostensibly a position at all, is a naïve one" (*Why History ? Ethics and Postmodernity* 1). The postmodern challenges alike can be roughly illustrated in three aspects, which would be briefly mentioned in the following discussion: (1) highlighting the textuality of history, embodied in the theoretical assumptions by Postmodernism and New Historicism; (2) the equalization of history with literature (and art)—due to its fictive characteristic; that is, historical writing, like that of literature, is a poetic process, typically manifested in Hayden White's work; (3) the emphasis on the (political) power domination behind the production of historical knowledge—history is no more a scientific and objective discipline, but a sort of ideological (re)construction and subtly affected by (political) power relations.

  First of all, unlike traditional historians or philosophers of history, postmodern theorists (of history) or New Historicists all stress the textuality of history. What is past is past, and cannot be retrieved in the practical world. It can only be retrieved and reconstructed in the narrative or text of the past or history. Fredric Jameson thus asserts, history "is inaccessible to us except in textual or narrative form, or in other words, that we approach it only by way of some prior textualization or narrative (re)construction" ("Marxism and Historicism" 42). This is the "formula" for Jameson to further examine historicism, without which his analysis would be groundless. Linda Hutcheon also argues for the textuality of history. For her part, the "accessibility [of history] to us now is entirely conditioned by textuality" (16), and "[w]e cannot know the *past* except through its texts: its documents, its evidence, even its eye-witnesses are *texts*" (*A Poetics of Postmodernism* 16, italics original). New Historicists place the textuality of history in a very important position in their writing; and just as Louis Montrose claims:

> By *the textuality of history*, I mean to suggest, firstly, that we can have no access to a full and authentic past, a lived material existence, unmediated by the surviving textual traces of the society in question—

traces whose survival we cannot assume to be merely contingent but must rather presume to be at least partially consequent upon complex and subtle social processes of preservation and effacement; and secondly, that those textual traces are themselves subject to subsequent textual mediations when they are construed as the "documents" upon which historians ground their own texts, called "histories." (20, italics original)

Montrose's view of "the textuality of history" foregrounds the textual traces' functions of mediation, negotiation and exchange in the "social processes" of history. The mediation, negotiation and exchange among different "textual traces" and/or documents would to a great extent reshape historical writing, if I can say so. Hayden White, another prominent figure who has made significant contributions to the study of history, holds a similar view about the textuality of history, but further emphasizes the linguistic attributes of history-texts. "Historical events," as he reasons, "are no longer directly accessible to perception. As such, in order to be constituted as objects of reflection, they must be described, and described in some kind of natural or technical language" ("New Historicism: A Comment" 297). Then White continues to point out that "[t]he description is a product of processes of linguistic condensation, displacement, symbolization, and secondary revision of the kind that inform the production of texts" and that "[o]n this basis alone, one is justified in speaking of history as a text" (297). Therefore from the perspective of linguistic construction, White challenges the traditional view of historical writing or historiography and suggests at the same time another attribute of history, that is, the narrative construction or fictionality of history and historiography.

  The linguistic attribute of history or historiography can also be detected in Roland Barthes' elaboration on the discourse of history. As he notes, historical discourse is "in its essence a form of ideological elaboration, or to put it more precisely, an *imaginary* elaboration, if we can take the imaginary to be the language through which the utterer of a discourse (a purely linguistic entity) 'fill out' the place of subject of the utterance" (Barthes 16, italics original). Here, Barthes stresses the imaginary or linguistic characteristic of historical discourse, which is in fact similar to White's view of historiography, as just noted. Or to put it precisely, White's view echoes and reflects Barthes's discourse of history, since White admires the latter much (Domańska 32). The stress on the linguistic attribute of historiography also intimates the fictitious character of historical writing proper; that is, historiography necessarily "employs" or "involves" literary conventions (Rubinson 161, 162). Or as White puts it, like literary works, historical works or histories "contain a deep structural content which is generically poetic, and specifically linguistic, in nature" (*Metahistory* ix). Therefore, White underscores the similarity between novelists and historians like this: "Novelists might be dealing with imaginary events whereas historians are dealing with real ones, but the process of fusing events, whether imaginary or real, into a comprehensive totality capable of serving as the object of representation is a poetic process" and "the historian must utilize precisely the same tropological strategies, the same modalities of representing relationships in words, that the poet or novelist uses" ("The Fictions of Factual Representation" 125). In simpler terms, the writings of postmodern theorists like White equalize history with literature as a poetic construction, thinking of history as fiction. Hence the feature of fictionality of history or historiography.

If the views such as the textuality of history and the fictionality of history undercut the objectivity of historical writing in a dramatic way, then the ideological attribute of history would undermine this objectivity more subtly. By means of introducing the concept of power (relation) into the study of history, postmodernism or postmodern discourse of history breaks down the myth of objective knowledge, pointing out that the search for an absolutely scientific objectivity is merely wishful thinking made by historians. Under the postmodern circumstances, "knowledge is related to power and that, within social formations, those with the most power distribute and legitimate 'knowledge' *vis-à-vis* interests as best they can" (Jenkins, *Re-thinking History* 31). That is, for proponents of postmodernism and New Historicism, it is power that determines or distorts the objectivity or the truthfulness of knowledge. Again, as Keith Jenkins maintains, "ultimately what has stopped anything being said, and has allowed only specific things to run, is power: truth is dependent on somebody having the power to make it true" (*Re-thinking History* 38), especially those who have the political power.

Postmodern theorists like Foucault and Lyotard have also made great contributions to the investigation of the relation of knowledge to power. Foucault has made a deep analysis about the power relations behind knowledge production. He puts forward a different notion of knowledge, that is, the production of knowledge is not merely a cognitive activity, not merely for the objective truth, but more significantly for the service of power control of the dominant. The demarcation between knowledge and power is not set up definitely and once and for all, for in Foucault's mind "the development of all these branches of knowledge [of the human sciences] can in no way be dissociated from the exercise of power" ("On Power" 106). In short, knowledge and power cannot be separated, so is true of history and power. In this way, history or historical writing would by no means become objective; that is to say, the scientific, objective history would be a wishing dream and to write history "as it actually happened" would never be realized.

As to Julian Barnes, I would contend, his postmodern historical writing explores the relations of history to text, history to literature and history to (political) power, and rethinks the nature of history, the objectivity and truthfulness of history or historiography from the perspectives of epistemology and ontology. Or in other words, Barnes's fictional writing to a great extent substantiates the postmodern view or discourse of history aforementioned, which constitutes the main concern of this research.

II. Historical Writing in British Fiction

After an introduction to discourses of history, traditional and postmodern, this section makes a brief introduction to historical writing, more exactly the historical novel in British literature, its tradition and new development or ramification from the end of the 1960s to the present, and the reasons for this new development, thus illuminating the historical and social contexts in which the (postmodern) historical writing in Julian Barnes's fiction is embedded.

To start with, we can say that the traditionally called "historical novel" is different from historical writing in fiction. The historical novel "makes use of historical personages or events in a fictitious narrative," in which "historical events, processes, and issues are central to the story line rather than providing peripheral or decorative touches" (Murfin and Ray 201). Or as Avrom Fleishman observes, the "historical novel is distinguished among novels by the presence of a specific link to history: not merely a real building or a real event but a real person among the fictitious ones," and "when the novel's characters live in the same world with historical persons, we have a historical novel" (4). Historical novels "are often vehicles for their authors' insights into historical figures and their influences or into the causes and consequences of historical events, changes, or movements" (Murfin and Ray 201). Historical writing has a bit broader meaning than the historical novel as such, however. For my part, historical writing in fiction refers not only to the historical novel aforementioned but also to those writings that involve and investigate the matters concerning history, historical view or philosophy of history. According to this line of thinking, a great number of novels are associated with historical writing. This research would discuss historical writing in Barnes's fiction in this sense; accordingly Barnes's "postmodern historical writing" would signify his postmodern rendering of history or historiography and of related issues in his fiction, behind which his postmodern view or thinking of history is expressed or implied. Hereinafter it is rewarding to examine the historical novel in British literature before the further discussion of the historical writing in Barnes's fiction.

i. Traditional Historical Novel

The historical novel as a literary genre in general started from the novels written by Walter Scott (1771-1832), the father of English historical novel. The rise of the historical novel, as Avrom Fleishman notes, was "the outcome of the age of nationalism, industrialization, and revolution" (17). It turned up in "the age when the European peoples came to consciousness of and vigorously asserted their historical continuity and identity," in "the century when widening commerce, population shifts, and factory organization created a new pattern of day-to-day life and consequent nostalgia for the old," in "the time when the French Revolution and its successors precipitated out what we have come to call the modern world" (Fleishman 17). The political-economical influence on the historical novel, nevertheless, was effected through a cultural intermediary, that is, the speculative view of history and the corresponding historiography, since the time in question was the very period for the rise of the speculative philosophy of history.

As for Scott, the specific context was that, as a man of letters in early nineteenth century Edinburgh, Scott was "caught between antiquarian affection for Scottish national and folk traditions and pragmatic satisfaction in the commercial progress that was making Scotland one of the first modern countries in the world—a leader in the industrial revolution and in the development of a dominant middle class" (Fleishman 38). Scott's problem was typical of the "ambivalence of Scottish writers toward the transition between agrarian tradition and capitalist modernity;" therefore, Fleishman rightly remarks that the reason "the historical novel begins with Scott is that the tension between tradition and modernity first achieved its definitive form in Scotland" (38). More directly, Scott's historical novel was shaped by and around his speculative view of history, which was affected by the "governing theories of the Scottish school of speculative historians," and especially those of a forerunner of modern sociology and a friend and mentor of Scott, Adam Ferguson (1723-1816), who aimed to "bring Enlightenment theory of history to bear on the problems of Scotland in the latter half of the eighteenth century" (Fleishman 40-42). Fleishman is correct in pointing out that Scott resembles Ferguson and other speculative historians not only in moral sentiments and political temper but also in his attitude toward the pattern of history. Thus Scott's vision of history is a dynamic picture of constant change, stressing growth, the development of the present from the past and even the broad principle of progress, which is in accordance to the progressive view of the Enlightenment narrative of history, evinced in most of his historical novels such as *Waverley* (1814), *Rob Roy* (1817), *The Heart of Midlothian* (1818) and *Ivanhoe: A Romance* (1819).

The year of 1837, five years after the death of Scott, was the commencement of the Victoria Era (1837-1901) in British history. This was also "the period in which almost every major Victorian novelist felt called upon to attempt the historical novel" (Fleishman 36). These attempts were for the most part not satisfactory but nevertheless saved the genre from falling into "utter bathos," before a number of major modern writers brought it a renewed life. These writers in the main included William Makepeace Thackeray (1811-1863), Charles Dickens (1812-1870), George Eliot (1819-1880), among others. Narrative techniques and views of history revealed in their historical writings are no doubt in the line of Scott's tradition. In the Victoria Era, beside and after Dickens, not a few major writers such as Thackeray and George Eliot and some minor writers like Elizabeth Gaskell (1810-1865), Charles Reade (1814-1884), Anthony Trollope (1815-1882), Joseph Henry Shorthouse (1834-1903), Walter Pater (1839-1894) and even Arthur Conan Doyle, all wrote historical novels, usually with such great events as the French Revolution and the age of "world-historical individual" like Napoleon as the main subjects, representing the traditional view of history sponsored by the speculative historians such as Thomas Carlyle (1795-1881), Thomas Macaulay (1800-1859) and those embedded in the Biblical writings.

The historical novel did not take some changes until Thomas Hardy (1840-1928) touched (peripherally) on this genre. Although Hardy is never labeled as a historical novelist or accused of writing a historical novel, his interest in history "is demonstrably greater than that of any English novelist after Scott," which leads him "to create what is probably the greatest historical poem" in English, i. e., *The Dynasts* (1904, 1906, 1908), and therefore his Wessex novels collectively could be considered as "a history of an English rural county in the nineteenth-century" (Fleishman 179). However, as the critic insightfully indicates, Hardy's determinism or deterministic view of history, "emphasizing the impotence of any historical explanation" and "ascribing historical causality to a stream of tendency in the order of the universe and its components," is a little different from his progenitors (Fleishman 180).

Some minor changes occurred to the historical novel at the turn of the twentieth century. A number of writers influenced by French naturalism and impressionism such as George Moore (1852-1933), Maurice Hewlett (1861-1923) and Ford Madox Ford (1873-1939) brought "a new subjectivity to the portrayal of the past and pave[d] the way for the distinctively modern historical novels of Conrad and Woolf—the one moving from impressionism toward perspectival narration, the other in the direction of archetypal symbolism" (Fleishman 208). Joseph Conrad's sense of the past or view of history is representative among the intellectuals of his time. His historical novels display that "history is the shaping power in modern experience," but "recent developments" "have made so sharp a break with the political values of the past that history may be said to have ended and an era of anarchy to have been ushered in" (Fleishman 212). As to Virginia Woolf, her contribution to the writing of historical novel lies mainly in her innovative, modernist writing techniques and her thematization of consciousness-of-history, represented prominently in her *Orlando* (1928) and *Between the Acts* (1941). To Fleishman's mind, Woolf's historical novels "bring the tradition of the English historical novel to a close" (233). Certainly, this is a precocious conclusion about the English historical novel, for it has not ended yet, and would not end either, to which the different and refreshing historical writings in contemporary British literature could attest.

In a word, whether the liberal view of progress embodied in the Enlightenment narrative of history, or the cyclical view of eternal return, the views of history disclosed by the (historical) novelists from Scott to Woolf are all in the line of traditional speculative view or philosophy of history. Therefore we would suggest that the "historical novel" from Scott to Woolf did not alter its trajectory, although there were some minor alterations in their writing modes; it marched along a fixed line and never walked out of it to a ramificate road to make radical changes. This lasted to the end of the 1960s until the rise of "new historical fiction."

ii. New Historical Fiction or Historiographic Metafiction

Dismissed as "escapism," as Antonia S. Byatt observes, to write the "historical novel" in the 1950s "has been frowned on, and disapproved of, both by academic critics and by reviewers" (*On Histories and Stories* 9). The circumstances took on a radical change about ten-odd years later. The historical novel since the 1960s has taken "a quite different sense of direction," for "a sense of endless change," "the rapid turnover of novelties" and "the commodification of artistic experiment" are dominant and the "attitudes to the past have been influenced by marketing, by a consumer demand for the *retro*, by an investment in history reproducible as style" (Mengham 1). The more significant reasons lie in the transformation of history and society. A critic acutely argues that the major historical experience of Britain in the twentieth century, other than the two world wars, is "the final flourishing, later decline and eventual loss of the Empire" (Stevenson 126). But the importance of these two wars cannot be dismissed and they no doubt have directly influenced the change of society and the mind of its subjects. World War II, for instance, helped to accelerate the breakup of the British Empire. After that, India and Pakistan gained independence from Britain in 1947 (Sri Lanka one year later), with the African nations of Kenya, Nigeria, South Africa, and Uganda following in the years 1960–1963, and the vast majority of British-held Caribbean countries such as the Bahamas, Barbados, Dominica and Jamaica gaining independence between 1962 and 1983. Still, closer to England, the Irish Free State was internationally recognized in 1921; Scotland, although remaining a part of the United Kingdom, moved in the direction of devolution, re-inaugurating its Parliament in 1999; and Wales inaugurated a Welsh Assembly in the same year. All these together have altered the definition of Englishness or Britishness, in which the English people have taken great pride for centuries. And during the process, Britain's abortive intervention in the Suez Crisis of 1956 and the war of Falkland Islands in 1982 with Argentina bring about different psychological shocks for British subjects. If the former event, as Brian W. Shaffer suggests, "marks the demise of British imperial heritage" (15), then the latter seems to bring back some proper pride for English people, among whom the nostalgia for the past glory of the Empire starts to extend and enlarge. Thus, not a few British writers including Julian Barnes endeavor to seek out from the past and history some answers for the present issues.

What's more, as David Leon Higdon argues, a new historical "sensibility" may have been inspired by the Festival of Britain in 1951, the accession of Queen Elizabeth II in 1952, or her coronation in the following year (*Shadows of the Past in Contemporary British Fiction* 6–7). However, that the interest in history turns to be prime in the 1980s, is related to the Mrs. Thatcher government's neoconservative emphasis on "Victorian" values, which, "coinciding with a contradictory de-emphasizing of national identity in the face of a redefined relationship with continental Europe, could have fueled an impulse toward fictional re-examination of the English past" (Janik 187). In addition, as Antonia S. Byatt notices, the new interest in historical writing in literature is connected with "the vanishing of the past from the curriculum of much modern education in schools and increasingly in colleges and universities" (*On Histories and Stories* 93). In other words, the "de-emphasis on school history" (Keen 169) does not mean that students are indifferent to it, but on the other hand stimulates the students' appetite for narratives based on the past, which in some sense affects the historical writing in literature and accelerates the appearance of "new historical fiction. "

Besides the social and historical reasons aforementioned for the rise of the historical turn in contemporary British literature around the 1970s and for its prominence since the late 1980s, the rise of "new historical fiction" is closely correlated to the narrative turn in historical writing proper and to the impact of poststructuralism and postmodernism on fiction. The linguistic turn in postmodern literary criticism, along with the narrative turn in the postmodern philosophy of history,① reshapes the direction of the writing of historical fiction to some extent. Still, the influence of World Literature on British Literature turns out to be enormously great. The (historical) works of great writers of other countries such as Jorge Luis Borges (1899-1986), Italo Calvino (1923-1985), García Márquez (1927-), Carlos Fuentes (1928-2012) and Umberto Eco (1932-) have tremendously inspired a number of British writers in their historical writing. A notable example is Salman Rushdie, whose *Midnight's Children* (1981) is deeply influenced by Márquez's *One Hundred Years' of Solitude* (1967) and becomes one of its intertexts. All in all, it is generally under such circumstances that a number of contemporary British writers try to find inspiration from the river of history for writing, to uncover historical truth, to erase historical unfairness and prejudice, to explore the relation of the past to the present and history to narrative, so as to represent "the past to approach contemporary issues" (Keen 180), or to "use the past to cast light on the present" (Furbank 112).

Due to these circumstances, "the history of Britain and of the peoples inhabiting it, the temporal and spatial relationships that determine the margins of Britishness, have all been questioned and amended by the more ambitious fictional projects of a time in which the scale of history itself has been revised" (Mengham 1). The contemporary historical fiction consequently presents some different features from the traditional historical novel. First of all, one of the prominent features of the contemporary historical novel since the 1960s could be its "ambitious varieties," with "an array of different constituencies," and voicing "fragments of the history of various communities" (Mengham 7). Moreover, different from the old historical novel, contemporary historical fiction is not confined by its generic

---

① As a novelist, Antonia S. Byatt is consciously aware of this, as she refers to it: "The renaissance of the historical novel has coincided with a complex self-consciousness about the writing of history itself" (*On Histories and Stories* 9). Her own writings, especially *Possession: A Romance* and *The Biographer's Tale*, are also written according to or by the postmodern philosophy of history. If Byatt could detect the influence of postmodern philosophy of history especially that of Hayden White, other contemporary British writers such as Julian Barnes, Salman Rushdie and Graham Swift may also take note of it and thus write their fiction by way of this philosophy.

boundaries. Suzanne Keen makes a not so clear but more inclusive definition about "historical fiction." For her part, historical fiction "includes a wide range of works with a basis in biographical details and historical events, set in periods other than the writer's and contemporary readers' times, and representing characters in interaction with settings, cultures, events and people of the past" (167) ; and generic boundaries "are by no means tightly policed" (168). Another feature is that contemporary historical fiction has become "objects of study in and of" itself (Keen 168) and has "become respectable, even intellectual" (Duguid 284). Certainly, the most important event in contemporary historical fiction is the rise of "new historical fiction" or historiographic metafiction as defined by Linda Hutcheon—the fiction on the one hand "works to situate itself in history and in discourse" and on the other "to insist on its autonomous fictional and linguistic nature" (*Narcissistic Narrative* xiv). It is safe to say that, due to its postmodern style and philosophy (of history), this "new historical fiction" or historiographic metafiction, as "a quintessential postmodern genre and an important subset of historical fiction in the contemporary period" (Keen 171), has not only altered the development trajectory of the historical novel but also reshaped to a great extent the territory of contemporary literary landscape.

John Fowles's *The French Lieutenant's Woman* (1969) is often acknowledged as the first influential fiction of this new trend, due to its self-reflexive style, its postmodern formal experimentation and its thematic and metaphysical interrogation on (historical) truth, engendering the ensuing writing of "new historical fiction." After Fowles in British literature, in consequence, many writers such as Peter Ackroyd, Martin Amis, Julian Barnes, Antonia S. Byatt, Ian McEwan, Salman Rushdie and Graham Swift all engage in the writing of this "new historical fiction."[①] However diverse and different their styles and approaches to history, these writers address similar subjects and share much in common. Just as Suzanne Keen acutely claims, "new historical fiction" "emphasizes postmodern uncertainties in experimental styles, tells stories about the past that point to multiple truths

---

① Some striking examples of contemporary British fiction in this category include Peter Ackroyd's *Hawksmoor* (1985) and *Chatterton* (1987), Martin Amis's *Time's Arrow* (1991), Julian Barnes's *Flaubert's Parrot*, *A History of the World in 10 ½ Chapters*, *The Porcupine*, *England, England* and *Arthur & George*, John Banville's *Dr. Copernicus* (1976), *Kepler* (1981), Anthony Burgess's *Earthly Power* (1980), Antonia S. Byatt's *Possession: A Romance* (1989) and *The Biographer's Tale* (2000), John Fowles's *The French Lieutenant's Woman* (1969) and *A Maggot* (1986), Ian McEwan's *Atonement* (2001), Salman Rushdie's *Midnight's Children*, *Shame* (1983) and *The Satanic Verses* (1988), Graham Swift's *Waterland* (1983), D. M. Thomas's *The White Hotel* (1981), Adam Thorpe's *Ulverton* (1992), and Jeanette Winterson's *The Passion* (1987).

or the overturning of an old received Truth, mixes genres, and adopts a parodic or irreverently playful attitude to history over an ostensibly normative mimesis" (171). In addition, the most significant differentia between "new historical fiction" and the traditional historical novel lies in the fact that they display different views of history. While the latter showcases the speculative view or philosophy of history and emphasizes the objectivity of historiography, the former reveals a postmodern thinking or philosophy of history. Julian Barnes is such a typical writer whose postmodern historical writing explicitly presents or implicitly suggests the postmodern views or philosophy of history, which will be briefly dealt with in the next section, along with a brief introduction to his conventional (re)presentation of history in his early novels such as *Metroland* and *Before She Met Me*.

III. Historical Writing in Julian Barnes's Fiction

A careful reading of the works of Julian Barnes would tell us that history and related issues occupy a very important place and permeate in almost all of his works, be it in his short stories or novels. History is thematized in some of Barnes's works, but only peripherally dealt with in others, and the views of history revealed in his writing vary accordingly. In general, when history is written as background in Barnes's fiction, the view of history is in line with the traditional discourse or philosophy of history, his writing strategies being realistic and traditional; when history becomes a topic or leitmotif or foregrounded in his writing, the views of history turn out to be postmodern or unconventional, his writing strategies being experimental. Therefore we would contend that history written and rendered in Barnes's works could be broadly classified into two types: "history as background" and "history foregrounded." This section will refer briefly to them, so as to demonstrate a general picture of Barnes's rendering of history or historiography.

i. History as Background: Traditional (Historical) Novel

In some short stories and early novels, Julian Barnes does not show a strong sense of historical consciousness or an intense interest in history; therefore, when addressing some issues pertinent to history or views of history, he does not attach much importance to history, but only mentions or refers to it briefly. History is then presented as background or foil in his writing (at most). For instance, in some short stories, Barnes depicts some interesting and intriguing events happening in the past, with no reflection on history itself, as in "Harmony" (*Pulse* 158–184) and "The Story of Mats Israelson" (*The Lemon Table* 23–48), and aiming to reflect on the relation of art to life, as in "Hamlet in the Wild West" (100-103), or unearths some historical events through and historical trauma on fictional characters, as in "East Wind" (*Pulse* 3-18), or discloses some historical figures' love affairs with a view of meditating on love, marriage and their relationship, as in "Carcassonne" (*Pulse* 185-195), history itself not mattering much in these stories. Still, Barnes examines in some short stories like "Melon" (*Cross Channel* 63-87) the relation of important historical events such as the French Revolution to (historical) characters, his focus is on the character's personality, his rendering of history being conventional. The issue of historical forgettery or forgetting history is one of the main themes in Barnes's writing, and he explores in one short story— "Evermore" (*Cross Channel* 89-111) —the effort of a fictional character to fight against this forgettery, his strategy of narrating being psychologically realistic. I would suggest, all in all, that not only the style but the historical views embodied in Barnes's short and essay-like stories are conventional, with no traces of experimentation or innovation. So is true of some of his early novels, such as *Metroland* and *Before She Met Me*. Next this part shall exposit the writing relevant to history, among other things, in these two early novels to investigate the issues such as the rise of historical consciousness in Barnes's writing and how it is related to his later postmodern historical writing.

Metroland is Barnes's first novel, "a rare and unusual first novel" (Boyd 96). When he authored it, Barnes "had absolutely no confidence in it," so that the process of writing "was a long and greatly interrupted process, full of doubt," and Barnes "shelved the book for long periods of time" (Guppy). But it was a success as a debut novel, and well acclaimed by critics. More importantly, it presages several vital motifs and narrative strategies in Barnes's later novels. To be specific, Barnes's passion for French language, literature and culture, including the first signs of his great admiration for Gustave Flaubert, has been firstly manifested in this novel. Intertextual references and allusions, a typical characteristic of Barnes's writing, can be also detected. Such motifs as the relation of art to life, love triangle and adultery and narrative strategies like the first person narration and the triptych structure, firstly turning up here, would reappear again and again in Barnes's later novels.

On the other hand, the novel also arouses some criticism, as to its theme of coming of age, the sexual itch and its lack of other characters, and its *sui generis* (unique) way of addressing the historical event. The way of dealing with the important historical moment, that is, *lesévénements* of 1968 in Paris, disappoints some reviewers, but other critics insightfully grasp Barnes's strategem. The title of the second part, "Paris (1968)," would arouse the readers's interest immediately, but frustrate them after reading, for Barnes does not depict the event in detail and not engage Christopher Lloyd the protagonist with this event. Nevertheless, Barnes's exact intention is to show that, as David Higdon perceives, Christopher "may be one of those unfortunate enough never to experience the exciting moments in life" ("Unconfessed Confessions" 176). Christopher's embarrassment or regret lies in that he has inadequate engagement with the historical event of 1968, just as he narrates in the novel:

> The point is—well I was there, all through May, through the burning of the Bourse, the occupation of the Odéon, the Billancourt lock-in, the rumours of tanks roaring back through the night from Germany. But I didn't actually see anything. I can't, to be honest, remember even a smudge of smoke in the sky. Where did they put up all their posters? Not where I was living. (*Metroland* 76)

Therefore, as Matthew Pateman perceptively points out, "Barnes refuses the expected history, ... giving us instead the personal history of Christopher's falling in love, losing his virginity, meeting his future wife, visiting art galleries and completely avoiding (hardly even noticing) the students' rebellion" ("Julian Barnes and the Popularity of Ethics" 183). History herein is displaced to the margin and background, while Christopher's personal history is given a central place. The novel thus follows the form of *Bildungsroman*, focusing on the personal development of the protagonist, especially his sentimental and sexual education, so that it is regarded as a novel "about a modern sentimental education" (Bradbury 487). Hence the understatement of historical event in *Metroland* undercuts the relationship between individual development and social change. In this sense, we would maintain that Barnes's consciousness of historical writing has not come to the fore yet in this novel, but we cannot deny the fact that his historical consciousness is budding. Just as Barnes ridicules Christopher's emphasis on historical dates for the writing of a thesis on art: "You always need to shove at least one *big date* (1789, 1848, 1914) into your title, because it looks more efficient, and flatters the *general belief* that everything changes with the eruption of war" (*Metroland* 83, italics added). Behind the satiric tone of Barnes, there is the suspicion about the "big date" and "general belief" in the "totalising discourse of received history which bases itself on cause and effect in an inevitable linear progression" (Pateman, "Julian Barnes and the Popularity of Ethics" 183). That is to say, Barnes implies through his fictional character his incredulity towards traditional grand narratives, which are replete with "big date" and "general belief." It is in the similar vein in his later novels such as *A History of the World in 10 ½ Chapters* that Barnes displays his reflection on the nature of traditional historical discourse and his postmodern view of history.

John Lukacs, an American historian, argues that "[e]very novel is a historical novel, in one way or another" (120). If we embrace this broad definition about the historical novel, we can say that Barnes's *Metroland* is a historical novel in that an important historical event looms as a backdrop, that Barnes indeed touches a little on something correlated with history and that it "is [the] product of its historical moment" (Taunton 22). But according to the definition about the historical novel as noted before, it is not a historical novel but a *Bildungsroman*. For in *Metroland*, Barnes's thematic concern is mainly about the protagonist's growth as a man and/or his experiences in love affair and marriage. Similarly, Barnes's second novel *Before She Met Me* is not a historical novel either, but worth our attention. It is first of all a novel about love, infidelity and jealousy, yet more significantly a novel about reflection on the relation of art to life and fiction to reality. It, written at times in crude language and terrific horror, satiric humor and melodrama, focuses on Graham Hendrick, a history teacher who divorces his first wife Barbara, remarries Ann Mears a former actress, whom his friend Jack Lupton the novelist introduced to him. After watching all the films Ann has made in the past, Graham finds himself consumed with jealousy as he investigates his new wife's former love affairs she had "before she met him," both on and off the screen. His obsession with Ann's past love affairs and his ensuing jealousy gradually deepen until he becomes convinced that Ann had an affair with his friend Jack. Deeply hurt and in a state of disorder, Graham kills Jack in the end and commits suicide in front of Ann. The portrayal of the slow deterioration of Graham is quite spunky, shocking and moving, which is quite peculiar in Barnes's works, so to speak.

Compared with *Metroland*, *Before She Met Me* is quite different in theme, plot and tone: it is "more thematically ambitious, more psychologically concentrated, and certainly darker" (Higdon, "Unconfessed Confessions" 176). Again, the cleverness and wit displayed by Barnes are highlighted and its limited characterization is criticized by critics, thus mixed views accompanying this novel as well as the first one. Three prominent features of this novel have drawn much attention from the critics: the mixture of horror and comedy and the possible origins that influenced Barnes; the jealousy theme; the (postmodern) reflection on the relation of art to life. The relation of art to life is Barnes's critical objective in this novel, which will be briefly discussed here due to its close relevance to the issue of "history." Graham's obsessive investigation of Ann's past affairs also results from his confusion of art with life, and fiction with reality. More specifically, he considers that some of the affairs Ann had in the movies are really-happened affairs, thus falling into a sort of uncontrollable jealousy and mental disorder, his "constant" love for Ann causing him to find out a real past of Ann. As a historian who should be adept at selecting and interpreting source of information, however, Graham's "version of history [of Ann's past] is deeply subjective" (Guignery, *The Fiction of Julian Barnes* 25). Graham wants to be accurate in searching for the truth of Ann's past, just as he confesses, "[t]here was no point in getting jealous unless you were accurate about it" (*Before She Met Me* 60). However, his obsessed jealousy blinds his mind: he makes no selection among the archives which construct Ann's biography or history; he eventually confuses art with life, fiction with reality, Ann as constructed by his imagination with her real self. And Graham confuses art with life to such an extent that he reckons that the affairs his friend Jack described in his novels are "disguised versions of his friends and altered retelling of his own life" (Moseley 64), on which Jack must rely, for he believes Jack lacks the imagination to make up his novels, thus supposing that during their marriage Ann has an affair with Jack. Obsessed with uncovering the past (or historical) truth, just like a historian or detective, but finally aware that the past is irretrievable, Graham kills Jack and commits suicide in front of Ann, when he "discovers" the affair between them. In so doing, Barnes is addressing a typical postmodernist topic in this novel, that is, the confusion of reality with fiction, or as Brian McHale calls, "some violation of ontological boundaries" (16). Since then, Barnes as a postmodern novelist is looming and emerging, and the "violation of ontological boundaries," firstly demonstrated here, comes to the fore dramatically and daringly in his later fiction, especially in *Flaubert's Parrot*, *A History of the World in 10½ Chapters*, *The Porcupine* and *England, England*. Still, the "paradox implicit in having, as central character, a [fictional] historian who predicates his theoretical conclusions on cinematic 'fiction' rather than on empirical 'fact' embodies the contemporary novel's concern with the problematic relationship between fiction and historiography" (Sesto 26), which also prefigures Barnes's exploration of the fictionality of history in his later postmodern (historical) writing.

Like *Metroland*, *Before She Met Me* is not an authentic historical novel due to its want of actual historical elements, although there is a fictional historian in it and his pursuit of the past truth. In a word, history and related issues have not become the centre or foregrounded in these two early novels. However, what should be emphasized is that these early novels of Barnes, although not historical novels in a strict sense, display the growing historical consciousness in Barnes's writing anyhow. In other words, from the historical event of Paris in 1968 as mere background in *Metroland* to the searching for the past (historical) truth of a fictional character by a fictional historian and the insinuation of sexual liberation in the 1960s in *Before She Met Me*, Barnes's historical consciousness is on the rise, which becomes manifest in *Flaubert's Parrot*, continues in his such later novels as *A History of the World in 10½ Chapters*, *England, England*, *Arthur & George* and *The Sense of an Ending*, and would be briefly illuminated in the next part.

ii. History Foregrounded: Postmodern Historical Writing

In *Metroland* and *Before She Met Me*, Julian Barnes does not emphatically reflect on the issues concerning history and/or historical truth in a postmodern way, then after them and starting with *Flaubert's Parrot*, Barnes through his writing sets out to question and quest for history and/or historical truth, to subvert and revise historical (meta)narratives, and to fabricate and represent contemporary political-cum-historical reality from the perspective of postmodernism, which is built on and corresponding with his postmodern thinking or philosophy of history. The discussion below will refer to Barnes's exploration of the issue of history in *The Sense of an Ending* and then to the main postmodern historical views upheld by Barnes or intimated in his works.

Like Salman Rushdie and Graham Swift, Barnes often expresses his postmodern view or philosophy of history through his characters or narrators. In his postmodern historical fiction, there is always a historian, a history teacher, or a fictional character or narrator who is obsessed with or interested in historical figures or historical events. For instance, similar to Swift's *Waterland*, there is a history teacher in Barnes's latest prize-winning fiction *The Sense of an Ending*, in which Barnes depicts a significant scene in relation to history, in which Old Joe Hunt the history teacher at the end of the semester asks his students to discuss history, to "look back over all those centuries and attempt to draw conclusions" (*SE* 18). The following excerpt is the discussion initiated by the history teacher but fabricated by Barnes the novelist:

> "We could start, perhaps, with the seemingly simple question, *What is history?* Any thoughts, Webster?"
> "*History is the lies of the victors*," I replied, a little too quickly.
> "Yes, I was rather afraid you'd say that. Well, as long as you remember that *it is also the self-delusions of the defeated*. Simpson?"
> Colin was more prepared than me. "*History is a raw onion sandwich*, sir."
> "For what reason?"
> "*It just repeats*, sir. *It burps*. We've seen it again and again this year. *Same old story, same old oscillation between tyranny and*

rebellion, war and peace, prosperity and impoverishment."①

"Rather a lot for a sandwich to contain, wouldn't you say?"

We laughed far more than was required, with an end-of-term hysteria.

"Finn?"

"*History is that certainty produced at the point where the imperfections of memory meet the inadequacies of documentation.*" (*SE* 18, italics added)

In this excerpt, Barnes indeed touches on several views of history through his characters, such as the issues of perspective, repetitiousness and documentation of and in history. Behind the voices of the innocent students lies Barnes's profound and postmodern reflection on (the nature of) history. For instance, behind the lines of this discussion, such views of history are implied: history is not "what actually happened;" historical progress does not exist; historical documentation is inadequate and history cannot be objective. In light of this line of thinking, we can say that, although *The Sense of an Ending* is not a traditional or authentic historical novel, it can be considered as part of Barnes's postmodern historical writing, for in it the issue of history is foregrounded and through it Barnes explores such important issues as the nature of history. This is one of the vital features of Barnes's postmodern historical writing and also evinces that, like Peter Ackroyd's, Barnes's "interest isn't so much in writing historical fiction as it is in writing about the nature of history as such" (qtd. in Finney, "Peter Ackroyd, Postmodernist Play and *Chatterton*" 258). Moreover, as to this excerpt, what should be pointed out is that the definition of "history" articulated by Finn the fictional character is *de facto* (in fact) an exegesis of the whole novel, i. e., what Barnes writes of in the novel confirms Finn's thinking of "history," hence the feature of self-reflexiveness of this novel, a typical feature of Barnes's writing as well.

Besides this sort of presentation of historical thoughts through fictional characters as in *The Sense of an Ending*, more importantly, Barnes presents his postmodern view or philosophy of history through his postmodern historical writing itself, which will be exemplified in the following chapters and therefore not examined here in detail but briefly. For instance, Barnes in his fictional writing questions the objectivity of history or historical truth

---

① This view of repetitiousness of history is but a repetition of what Barnes has articulated years ago in his *A History of the World in 10 ½ Chapters*, just as he wrote in this book: "History just burps, and we taste again that raw-onion sandwich it swallowed centuries ago" (*HWC* 239). It also indicates that Barnes has consistently reflected on the issue of history in his works.

from the perspective of epistemology. Therefore he often expresses through his characters (especially in *Flaubert's Parrot*) that how we could seize the past. When questioning the objectivity of historical truth, Barnes indicates that we can grasp the past or history merely through traces or texts such as papers, letters, diary, works, etc., which have become historical texts and been often used by historians to reconstruct histories as such. In so doing, Barnes's writing suggests such a view of history—the textuality of history. Still, Barnes further questions the writing of history from the epistemological angle, arguing that the objective historiography is but an illusion or a wishful thinking of historians. For him, historians write history in such a way: "We [historians] make up a story to cover the facts we don't know or can't accept; we keep a few true facts and spin a new story round them. Our panic and our pain are only eased by soothing fabulation; we call it history" (*HWC* 240). Therefore he demonstrates another postmodern view of history—the fictionality of history, viewing history as fiction, being "a poetic process."

When questioning history from the viewpoint of epistemology, Barnes also endeavors to launch his attack upon the traditional historical (meta)narratives or grand narratives of history from the angle of ontology. His postmodern historical writing interrogates the traditional linear view of history, the progressive view of history, and the continuity or cause-effect relationships in the total, unifying or universal History, implicating that "[h]istory doesn't relate" (*EE* 70) and that history is discontinuous and fragmented. Because of this, to Barnes's mind, not total History but the fragmented histories do hold water and history is not monistic but pluralistic. Thus, Barnes ontologically backs up such postmodern views of history, that is, the discontinuity and fragmentation of history and the plurality of history, by subverting and undercutting the traditional view of total and universal History, to which his revision of the historical (meta)narratives and his presentation of pluralistic pictures of histories in *A History of the World in 10 ½ Chapters* and *Arthur & George* could testify.

Finally, Barnes showcases his postmodern view or thinking of history from the perspective of politics or political ideology. Like some postmodern theorists, Barnes also detects the (political) power relation behind history or historiography. As a result, the same historical figure like Francis Drake would be portrayed quite differently in British and Spanish history and thus viewed quite differently by British subjects and Spanish people (*EE* 7). The power relation, especially the political power struggle, is made manifest in Barnes's political novel *The Porcupine*, in which the victor could re-write or fabricate history for the defeated, and which becomes remarkably unique in Barnes's works due to its writing of the issue of "The End of History" at the very moment when it was a heated topic. Therefore, the exploration on the relation of history to (political) power, and accordingly the (political) ideology-ness of history, is looming large in Barnes's postmodern historical writing. Still, the traditional speculative view or philosophy of history always presents a utopia at the end of so-called History. Barnes in his writing does not present a picture of utopia, but a picture of hetero-topia, which is neither pastoral nor dystopia, but heterogeneous. This hetero-topia is depicted in *England, England*, Barnes's another political fiction. Through these two novels, Barnes explores such important issues as the relation of history to politics and the history of human future from the perspective of postmodern discourse of history, proffering a new vision about "the end of history" and the hetero-topia of history politically.

These views briefly mentioned above from the perspectives of epistemology, ontology and the political are the main ideas demonstrated or suggested in Barnes's postmodern historical writing, which constitute the main contents of Chapter Two, Chapter Three and Chapter Four of this research respectively. Undoubtedly, Barnes also touches on other views of history, which will not be explicated but referred to, if necessary, in the discussion of his historical writing. What should be pointed out in this end is that the division of Barnes's postmodern historical writing into three sections from the epistemological, ontological and political perspectives does not mean that these three aspects are clearly cut and separated from each other. In fact, they are closely interconnected and intertwined with each other, and such a division is but an expedient strategy for analysis, so that we can explore and exposit Barnes's postmodern historical writing more conveniently and efficiently.

Chapter Two
Questioning and Questing for Historical Truth

The [historical] Truth is rarely pure and never simple.
—Oscar Wilde, *The Importance of Being Earnest*

There is not one true story about the past, but a multiplicity of complementary, competing, or clashing stories. ... Such stories do not come only in written texts purporting to tell us about the past, but in a variety of other ways too.
—Peter Lee, "Understanding History"

His book celebrates the textuality of history, [and] the narrativity of historical narration.
—Brian Finney, "A Worm's Eye View of History: Julian Barnes's *A History of the World in 10½ Chapters*"

In the nineteenth century and especially at the urge of Leopold von Ranke's objective history since the 1830s and under the influence of the Positivist science, the historians had a strong belief in the objectivity of history, historical truth and "ultimate history" as such. For instance, Lord Acton an English historian asserted in 1896 that "[b]y the judicious division of labour we should be able ... to bring home to every man the last document, and the ripest conclusions," for "all information is within reach, and every problem has become capable of solution" (qtd. in Carr 3). However, about sixty years later, such optimistic prospect has been abandoned and the objective historical truth has been suspected or interrogated.① It is commonly acknowledged that postmodern theory questions established or orthodox knowledge, norms, principles, value judgement, order and system. There is no exception to historical knowledge. Just as Sir George Clark a history professor claimed in 1957 that some historians tended to "take refuge in skepticism, or at least in the doctrine that, since all historical judgments involve persons and points of view, one is as good as another and there is no 'objective' historical truth" (qtd. in Carr 4). Since the view or philosophy of history all along affects the writing of the historical novel, historical skepticism also turns up in the (historical) writing of postmodern novelists. As of the end of the 1960s, postmodern novelists started to write a new kind of historical fiction, different from the traditional historical novel inherited from Walter Scott, in which on the one hand these postmodern novelists "use Realist conventions," but on the other hand "they simultaneously seek to subvert them," as Alison Lee puts it (36). This sort of historical fiction is labeled as "new historical fiction" by some critics but also termed "historiographic metafiction" by Linda Hutcheon, as noted before.

Julian Barnes is no doubt such a novelist who writes "new historical fiction" or "historiographic metafiction," which could be corroborated in his masterpieces such as *Flaubert's Parrot* and *A History of the World in 10 ½ Chapters*.② However, as discussed before, Barnes's postmodern historical writing consists of not only these "new historical fiction" but also those

---

① In fact, before the 1960s, some historians or philosophers of history have started to question the nature and objectivity of history. For instance, in 1910 the American philosopher, Carl Becker, argued that "the facts of history do not exist for any historian till he creates them" (qtd. in Carr 22-23). Later, Benedetto Croce, Robin George Collingwood and Michael Oakeshott, among others, also challenged the objectivity of history but more or less fell victim to historical idealism, as mentioned in the first section of Chapter One.

② The title of *A History of the World in 10 ½ Chapters* would be later abridged in this research as *A History* for the convenience of writing, with no further explanation.

novels which involve and investigate the issues concerned with the nature of history and thinking or philosophy of history, for Barnes's writing demonstrates that he not only writes unconventional, postmodern historical fiction but also authors some novels reflecting on history and historiography, which could not be termed "historical fiction" but are postmodern(ist) fiction in a certain way, such as his *Talking It Over*, *England, England* and *The Sense of an Ending*. This chapter elucidates from the perspective of epistemology two salient postmodern views of history or historiography—the textuality of history and the fictionality of history exemplified or implied in Barnes's writing, particularly in *Flaubert's Parrot*, and some pieces of writings like "Shipwreck" (*HWC* 113-139), "The Revival" (*LT* 85-101) and "The Survivor" (*HWC* 81-111), in light of postmodern theoretical hypotheses about historical textuality and fictionality or narrativity put forward (especially) by Fredric Jameson, Linda Hutcheon, Jacques Derrida and Hayden White, with a view of foregrounding Barnes's postmodern questioning and rethinking about historical objectivity and historical truth.

I. Textuality of History

Postmodern theorists and/or New Historicists underline the view of the textuality of history, arguing that we can know history only through texts such as "documents," "evidence," "eyewitnesses" and any other traces and relics of the past or history. Fredric Jameson, Linda Hutcheon and Louis Montrose are such prominent figures, although their theoretical emphases bear some differences. Jameson, for instance, refers to the relation of history to text(uality), and ostensibly denies history as a text in his *The Political Unconscious: Narrative as a Socially Symbolic Act* and in such an article as "Marxism and Historicism," but history in his view can be approached in and only in the form of text. As he writes of it in this vein: "History is *not* a text, ... it is inaccessible to us except in textual form, and that our approach to it and to the Real itself necessarily passes through its prior textualization" (*The Political Unconscious* 35, italics original). In the same book, Jameson later restates the view emphatically: "History ... is *not* a text ...; what can be added, however, is the proviso that history is inaccessible to us except in textual form, or in other words, that it can be approached only by prior (re)textualization" (82, italics original). In short, Jameson's view of history "in textual form," like those of Hutcheon and Montrose, from the perspective of epistemology, implies that due to its prior (re)textualization, the writing of history proper is a sort of construction, suggesting that history as such is inevitably involved with the subjectivity of the writing subject, which is a social construct or even a linguistic construct for some postmodern theorists, thus undermining and undercutting the objectivity of historiography supported by Ranke the historian and his proponents.

Jacques Derrida also illustrates his concept of text in *Of Grammatology* (1967), especially in the part about Jean-Jacques Rousseau (1712–1778). For Derrida, if we want to know the life of Rousseau, we can only consult the texts that Rousseau left for us; that is, if we want to (re)construct a true Rousseau or adumbrate a picture of Rousseau's life, we must search for the traces of Rousseau in the texts that he wrote and left; and there is no other framework or external reference to consult. This is, as it were, the kernel of Derrida's notorious pronouncement that "there is nothing outside the text" —*Il n'y a pas de hors-texte* (*Of Grammatology* 158). In so doing, the (history-)text would turn out to be an endless play of signs, without substantive referentiality, which is mind-bogging for and cannot be accepted by historians of the traditional sort, although it is innovative as a theoretical hypothesis and reading strategy. For my part, Derrida's textual strategy, along with those of other postmodern theorists, could be used to explain Barnes's (re)construction of the image of Gustave Flaubert in *Flaubert's Parrot*, which will be discussed in the first part of this section. Its second part mainly analyzes "Shipwreck" in *A History*, through the view put forward by some New Historicists, to elucidate how Barnes's writing highlights the view of the textuality of history.

i. "How Do We Seize the Past?"

Ronald F. Atkinson, a history professor, argues that "[t]he evidence we have does not guarantee the truth, even though our only access to the truth is via that evidence" (11). It seems very apposite for the understanding of Julian Barnes's *Flaubert's Parrot*, in which Barnes through the character-bound narrator Geoffrey Braithwaite, a doctor and an amateur for Flaubert, in his all-consuming pursuit of Flaubert, seeks to (re)construct a true or real Flaubert by way of "evidence," firstly the stuffed parrot which Flaubert used as a model for the writing of the parrot Loulou in his short story *Un Coeur Simple* ("A Simple Heart"), and subsequently various, heterogeneous "texts" such as novels, letters, travel notes, records, memoirs, etc., which are pertinent to Flaubert. From the very beginning, Barnes assures us that we can know the real Flaubert only through texts, although he uses the word "paper" instead of "text," just as he writes: "Nothing much else to do with Flaubert has ever lasted. He died little more than a hundred years ago, and all that remains of him is paper" (*FP* 12). Therefore, from the start, Barnes conveys the message that, in Jameson's words, history (or historical figure) is inaccessible to us except in textual form, or in other words, it can be approached only by prior (re)textualization. It is in this sense that Alison Lee the critic points out that "Gustave Flaubert is an historically verifiable entity, but we can only know him through the written evidence of novels, letters, and reminiscences" (39). In addition and more importantly, Barnes tells us that history is textualized and that the (objectivity of) historical truth as such is vulnerable to be questioned or challenged. In spite of this, Barnes endeavors in *Flaubert's Parrot* to seek for the historical truth, firstly the authentic parrot, then the real Flaubert, and lastly the past in general. All of these start from two stuffed parrots encountered by Barnes in his personal experience.

Barnes has been a Flaubertiste since his adolescent years. He admired Flaubert's books greatly (McGrath 15), and "had first read *Madame Bovary* at about 15; had done a special paper on Flaubert at university; and felt that at some point ... would want to write about him" (WFTW 30). What he wanted to write about Flaubert is not the conventional biography, "any kind of biography, for instance, or something in that charmingly illustrated Thames & Hudson series about writers and their worlds" (WFTW 30), but something different, which is to a great extent fulfilled in *Flaubert's Parrot*.① The chance of writing this novel is unique and personal, as Barnes recalled after its completion and on various occasions (Birnbaum 93; JBC 257-258; WFTW 30). His article "The Follies of Writer Worship" seems to provide the answer for those who want to know the genesis of this novel. Barnes's recountal briefly goes like this: in September 1981 Barnes visited the hometown of Flaubert but didn't expect there would be very much to see, for "the writer's house had been demolished a century ago, and most of his possessions were scattered or lost. But a few scraps of memorabilia had survived, and their aura would be enhanced by their scarcity;" still, he went firstly to a small museum in the Hôtel-Dieu hospital where Flaubert's father was chief surgeon and came across "a stuffed green parrot," which was explained on a label as "the very parrot that Flaubert borrowed from the local natural history museum when he was writing the story 'A Simple Heart';" two days later Barnes visited the second Flaubert shrine, a pavilion at Croisset, on the outskirts of the city where he came across another stuffed parrot, "also entirely authentic" and was assured that "this was definitely the parrot borrowed by Flaubert when he was writing 'A Simple Heart'" ("The

---

① See also "Julian Barnes in Conversation," p. 256. In the "Conversation," Barnes retold his interest in Flaubert and the genesis of writing this novel.

Follies of Writer Worship" 2-3).① It is the second parrot that disturbs Barnes, engenders his questioning of the past truth and inspires him to write this novel, to explore the issue of historical truth and of how to "seize the past" (*FP* 14, 90, 100). From Barnes's recountal, we can perceive that he is just like a historian who is searching for the (historical) truth in historical sites, i. e., the museum at Hôtel-Dieu hospital and the pavilion at Croisset, through investigating the historical "possessions" and "scraps of memorabilia" of and about Flaubert.

By artistic execution, Barnes the writer turns out to be Geoffrey Braithwaite the doctor and the "amateur Flaubert scholar" (*FP* 95), and what Barnes has done in a real world turns out to be what Braithwaite does in a fictional world. Barnes even endows Braithwaite the fictional character and narrator with the ontological status as a "real" writer of the novel, for in the "Note" at the beginning of the novel he confirms that "[t]he translations in this book are by Geoffrey Braithwaite; though he would have been lost without the impeccable example of Francis Steegmuller [a distinguished Flaubert scholar]" (*FP* 8), "so that ontological tension is created between the author and the narrator, and therefore between reality and fiction" (Joseph-Vilain 184, qtd. in Roberts 32). This blurring of the boundary between reality and fiction, Barnes's typical writing strategem, represents one of the prominent characteristics of the novel. Anyhow, critics tend to believe that Braithwaite is but the incarnation of Barnes. Just as Keith Wilson perceptively points out:

> Parodies of literature examination papers and of Flaubert's *Dictionary of Accepted Ideas*, sophisticated excurses on novelistic theory and practice, the three alternative versions of a Flaubert chronology and Louise Colet's revisionist account of her relationship with Flaubert—*all bespeaks the actual Barnes rather than the nominal Braithwaite*, even without

---

① Barnes later recalled this "incident" in his writing "When Flaubert Took Wing" and in an interview "Julian Barnes in Conversation," which is recorded in his travel notebook. One paragraph can be identified in these two texts as follows: "Then, crouched on top of one of the display cabinets, what did we see but Another Parrot. Also bright green, also, according to the *gardienne* & also a label hung on its perch, the authentic parrot borrowed by GF when he wrote *UCS*!! I ask the *gardienne* if I can take it down & photograph it. She concurs, even suggests I take off the glass case. I do, & it strikes me as slightly less authentic than the other one: mainly because it seems benign, & F wrote of how irritating the other one was to have on his desk. As I am looking for somewhere to photograph it, the sun comes out—this on a cloudy, grouchy, rainy morning— & slants across a display cabinet. I put it there & take 2 sunlit photos; then, as I pick the parrot up to replace it, the sun goes in. It felt like a benign intervention by GF—signaling thanks for my presence, or indicating that this was indeed the true parrot" (WFTW 30; JBC 257-258).

confirmatory evidence drawn from the recurrent preoccupations and cadences of his other work. (362, italics added)

This critic continues to indicate that "a distinctive, readily recognizable authorial voice supplies the dominant narrative tenor in much of his [Barnes's] fiction" (363). Geoffrey Heptonstall also maintains that the "voice [in *Flaubert's Parrot*] is singularly and brilliantly his [Barnes's] own" (117). As a result, it is safe to contend that Braithwaite is Barnes's fictional *alter ego*, through whom Barnes the writer expresses his own views in the form of fictional writing. In this way, *Flaubert's Parrot* is not merely a novel about Flaubert's parrot.

It is first of all a story about Flaubert's parrot. Braithwaite's (or Barnes's) questioning the authenticity of these two parrots in the novel, especially in the first section "Flaubert's Parrot" and the last section "And the Parrot …," registers that Braithwaite (or Barnes) is really a keen truth-seeker. Just as the narrator tells us:

> After I got home the duplicate parrots continued to flutter in my mind: one of them amiable and straightforward, the other cocky and interrogatory. I wrote letters to various academics who might know if either of the parrots had been properly authenticated. I wrote to the French Embassy and to the editor of the Michelin guide-books. I also wrote to Mr. Hockney.① I told him about my trip and asked if he'd ever been to Rouen; I wonder if he'd had one or other of the parrots in mind when etching his portrait of the sleeping Félicité. If not, then perhaps he in his turn had borrowed a parrot from a museum and used it as a model. (*FP* 22)

After writing these letters, Braithwaite hopes to get his replies quite soon, but they "produced nothing useful; some of them weren't even answered" (*FP* 180). Two years passed, the problem unsolved yet, Braithwaite decides to re-visit the two sites to re-examine the two stuffed parrots and to visit M. Lucien Andrieu, a Flaubertian scholar, "the secretary and oldest surviving member of the Sociétédes Amis de Flaubert" (*FP* 186). What happened two years ago is resumed: the *gardien* in the Hôtel-Dieu museum and the

---

① David Hockney (1937–) is an English painter, draughtsman, printmaker, stage designer and photographer. As Barnes told us, Mr. Hockney in 1974 "produced a pair of etchings: a burlesque version of Félicité's view of Abroad (a monkey stealing away with a woman over its shoulder), and a tranquil scene of Félicité asleep with Loulou" (*FP* 19–20). Reality and fiction are here united. Hockney's etching of the parrot corresponds to Flaubert's description of Loulou in *Un Coeur Simple*: "He was called Loulou. His body was green, the ends of his wings pink, his forehead blue, and his throat golden" (qtd. in Barnes, *FP* 185).

gardienne at the Croisset pavilion both assure Braithwaite that their stuffed parrot is the real one. Braithwaite photographs the two stuffed parrots and compares them with the one described in *Un Coeur Simple*, leaning to believe that the Hôtel-Dieu parrot is the authentic one.

Still, Braithwaite visits M. Lucien Andrieu and talks with him about his questioning of the authenticity of the two parrots. The latter, as an expert on Flaubert, assures the former that there were fifty parrots in the Museum of Natural History at Rouen from which Flaubert borrowed one as a model for Félicité's Loulou. After his writing, as the expert tells, Flaubert returned it to the Museum; thereafter, the Croisset pavilion in 1905 and the Hôtel-Dieu museum in 1945 asked the Museum of Natural History for the return of "Flaubert's parrot," and they got one parrot respectively from the parrots in the Museum according to Flaubert's description of Loulou. When hearing this, Braithwaite changes his mind and tends to believe that the parrot at Croisset pavilion might be the true parrot, for it was the first choice from the fifty parrots. At this moment, Andrieu the expert explains that two things should be kept in mind. The first one is that Flaubert was an artist, "a writer of the imagination" and "he would alter a fact for the sake of a cadence" (*FP* 188). "Just because he borrowed a parrot, why should he describe it as it was? Why shouldn't he change the colours round if it sounded better?" as the expert refutes (*FP* 188). The second thing is that Flaubert returned the parrot to the Museum after he'd finished his writing, which was in 1876 and the pavilion at Croisset was set up in 1905, about thirty years later. The expert assumes that stuffed animals would get the moth and fell apart and the color would change with the passing of time (*FP* 188). Therefore, from Andrieu, Braithwaite does not get the answer he wanted and the authentic parrot is still a mystery. Finally he goes to the Museum to examine the remaining three parrots of all the fifty parrots. "Perhaps it was one of them" (*FP* 190) is the conclusion that he reaches in the end. In consequence, the parrots, as "evidence" and "the only access to the truth" of Flaubert's parrot, "does not guarantee the truth" (Atkinson 11). However, the ostensible conclusion is *de facto* not a conclusion: "It was an answer and not an answer; it was an ending and not an ending" (*FP* 189). The indeterminacy or "postmodern uncertainties" behind it does not mean that it is impossible to "seize the past" truth but suggests that the door is open to possibilities, the very idea Barnes upholds and reveals in the novel.

This is the overview of the exact search for (the authenticity of) Flaubert's parrot in the novel, mainly turning up in its first and last sections, the middle thirteen sections unknown to us yet. If Barnes stopped at this, this novel would become another conventional story of quest for (historical) truth, and he would not get international fame overnight due to it and could not be named as one of the eminent postmodern(ist) novelists in contemporary British literature. "But Mr. Barnes hasn't written this novel directly or simply. Rather, he has appropriately given us the story of an obsession with Flaubert. The result is a splendid hybrid of a novel, part biography, part fiction, part literary criticism, the whole carried off with great brio" (Brooks, "Obsessed With the Hermit of Croisset" 7). Peter Brooks here insightfully indicates the very feature of this novel, that is, "part biography, part fiction, part literary criticism," which stylistically results in the quandary for critics of whether or not it should be classified as a novel and undoubtedly "opens the door to the spirit of fictional postmodernism" (Bradbury 487), which will be manifested in the discussion below. The novel's "great brio" starts from the search for Flaubert's parrot, a historical truth, but lies in more than that.

Barnes's questioning of the historical truth, through his *alter ego* Braithwaite, consists of the interrogation not only about the authenticity of the parrots but also about the true Flaubert, so is true of his questing for the historical truth. In actuality, Barnes's questioning and searching for truth occur at the same time, or to put it another way, the questioning means the searching as well; that is, when Braithwaite questions the authenticity of the two stuffed parrots, he is searching for the (historical) truth about Flaubert's parrot. However, the parrot is not merely the parrot; it is "a fluttering, elusive emblem of the writer's voice" (*FP* 182-183), and represents the "Pure Word" or "*un symbole de Logos*" (*FP* 18), or "language ... and finally the pursuit of truth itself (for just as there are many parrots by the end of the novel, so are there many ways of apprehending the truth or, better still, many truths to be apprehended)" (Sesto 37). Moreover, as a critic correctly claims, Barnes's relationship with Flaubert "is the real relationship that spawns the book," and "the twelve or so chapters (out of fifteen) devoted exclusively to Flaubert indicate quite obviously that the real concern of the book is Flaubert" (Berlatsky 187). Thus, for my part, what Barnes endeavors to question and quest for in the novel is not just the authenticity of the parrot but also the voice of Flaubert, the historical Flaubert and the past in general. It is in light of this that at the very beginning Barnes voices his bemusement about the nature of the past (or history) and about how to "seize the past:"

> *How do we seize the past? Can we ever do so?* When I was a medical student some pranksters at an end-of-term dance released into the hall a piglet which had been smeared with grease. It squirmed between legs, evaded capture, squealed a lot. People fell over trying to grasp it, and

were made to look ridiculous in the process. The past often seems to behave like that piglet. (*FP* 14, italics added)

How does Barnes question and quest for a historical Flaubert, a true Flaubert? Or in what way? Since all that remains of him is "paper," we can only reach him through "paper" or text. After reading we can discern that the whole novel is composed of the (inter)textual traces related to Flaubert: just as a reader remarks, the "intertextual investment" is announced "right in the title" (Versteegh 16). The discursive quotations from Flaubert's works including novels, travel notes, letters and notebook or diary are multitudinous and omnipresent in the novel. For instance, the third part in "Chronology," the second section of the novel, consists of thirty-two entries of quotations (long or short, and covering almost six pages) by Flaubert from 1842 to 1880. The discursively quoting of a great number of quotations by and about Flaubert foregrounds the textuality of the novel, through which Barnes aims to underline the textuality of history. A close reading would evince that it does "put itself very self-consciously within the field of postmodern explorations about textuality and history" (Brooks, "Interred Textuality" 46). Next I will discuss how Barnes realizes this through his (inter)textual references which go off in various directions.

The search for the authenticity of Flaubert's parrot lasts "a good two years," that is, "two years elapsed between the question arising and dissolving" (*FP* 182). The spatial or textual distance "between the question arising and dissolving," however, includes thirteen sections or about 175 pages in the novel, in which the parrot exits but Flaubert looms large, be it true or false. It is therefore a novel about Gustave Flaubert. Section Two "Chronology" presents three versions of Flaubert's biography. The first one is a positive picture of Flaubert the writer, offering an altogether optimistic view of his life, starting with " [a] stable, enlightened, encouraging, and normally ambitious background," and concluding with his death: "Full of honor, widely loved, and still working hard to the end, Gustave Flaubert dies at Croisset" (*FP* 23–27). Opposed to the first one, the second depicts Flaubert "the family idiot" and the loser, whose life is fraught with deaths (of relatives and friends), diseases, hopelessness, rowdyism, disobedience and financial ruin, and who dies impoverished, lonely and exhausted (*FP* 27–31). The third one is composed of quotations from Flaubert's own writing, from which we can vision a different Flaubert—his high literary sensibility and rich inner life, through many of his literary metaphors and similes (*FP* 32–37). Flaubert once wrote to a friend that "[w]hen you write the biography of a friend, you must do it as if you were taking *revenge* for him" (qtd. in *FP* 6, italics original). In this novel, Barnes as a Flaubertiste does not take revenge for Flaubert, although he indeed displays his disagreement with Jean Paul Sartre (1905-1980) and with the depiction of Flaubert in the latter's *L'Idiot de la Famille.* Is the juxtaposition of three chronologies contradictory and confusing, as some readers might assume? On the contrary, Barnes thinks it is illuminating: "I don't think that, if you read the three chronologies, all the facts, all the statements there are incompatible with one another in terms of human life and human psychology. I think it's like giving an extra dimension or extra depth of focus" (JBC 261). As such, we can say that the point is not that there is no truth to be found in these chronologies, but that there are many truths here as well as many paradoxes, confusions and omissions, which indicates the difficulties involved in the writing of history (or biography), chronology being an ancient genre of historical writing. These three chronologies are very simple overviews of Flaubert's biography or "some sort of account of Flaubert's life" (JBC 260), which is only part of the historical Flaubert. Too much about Flaubert has not been uncovered yet.

Section Three "Finders Keepers" is about Braithwaite's encounter with a fictional academic Ed Winterton who occasionally obtains 75 (love) letters between Flaubert and his mysterious mistress Juliet Herbert but burns these letters according to Flaubert's own will in them, which enrages Braithwaite, for he eagerly wants to get these letters to decode the mystery or "the fascinating relationship" between Flaubert and Herbert. Without these letters the mystery remains; without these letters, "more exactly what Flaubert was like" and "how the writer behaved in London" (*FP* 41) cannot be solved; without these letters, "[w]e know little about his four trips to England" (*FP* 42). Behind Braithwaite's (Barnes's) search for these historical letters and his subsequent interrogations, what is clear is that these letters as historical texts are the only means to approach Flaubert in a particular period or to decode the mystery between Flaubert and Herbert; without these history-texts, the historical truth cannot be laid bare in any way, which confirms that history does exist only in the textual forms, as some postmodern theorists and New Historicists strongly suggest. Then Braithwaite tells us that there is "one overt reference to Juliet Herbert" "in a letter [by Flaubert] to Bouilhet [Flaubert's *alter ego* in reality], written after the latter had visited Croisset" (*FP* 40). Does this mean that Flaubert and Herbert had affairs or anything special? "Should we jump to conclusions?" (*FP* 41). At this very moment, the narrator warns us that "this is the kind of boastful, nudging stuff that Flaubert was always writing to his male friends" (*FP* 41). Is Braithwaite's or Barnes's description objective? It is evident that Barnes (through Braithwaite) realizes this so that he assures us that "you must make your judgement on me as well on Flaubert" (*FP* 41). It is here that Barnes directly addresses a significant issue concerning the objectivity in history (or biography). That is, in his search for the letters (or the historical truth), Barnes interrogates their truthfulness at the same time. This "contradictory phenomenon" (Linda Hutcheon's term), or these "contradictory impulses," "may be the only means to truth" (Elias 27), which figures prominently in Barnes's writing and would be referred to in the discussion to follow.

The next eleven sections in *Flaubert's Parrot* represent Barnes's alternative, creative, (inter)textual and referential reading and interpretation of Flaubert and his works. Several important sections will be mentioned to exemplify Barnes's pursuit of historical truth and his exploration of the relation of history to text(uality). In Section Four "The Flaubert's Bestiary," Barnes explicates the image of Flaubert via the writing of bestiary in relation to the writer. Various kinds of animals turn up in Flaubert's writing, and Barnes chooses some of them which are best concerned with Flaubert, that is, the bear, the camel, the sheep, the parrot and dogs, so as to decode Flaubert. Take the parrot and the dog for example. Parrot is perhaps the most important animal turning up in Flaubert's works; it can be found in his short story *Un Coeur Simple*, in a long clipping from *L'Opinion Nationale* of June 20th 1863 in the dossiers of *Bouvard et Pécuchet*, in *Salammbé*, *La Tentation de Saint Antoine*, and his letters to Louise Colet. Does Barnes merely lead us to search for a parrot in the "paper" or "dossiers" of Flaubert here? On the one hand, following Barnes, we are searching for various parrots in Flaubert's texts; on the other, we are searching for Flaubert, for the past and for historical truth. Barnes's own comment seems to have conveyed the very idea:

> It isn't so different, the way *we wander through the past. Lost, disordered, fearful, we follow what signs there remain*; *we read the street names, but cannot be confident where we are. All around is wreckage. These people never stopped fighting.* Then we see a house; a writer's house, perhaps. There is a plaque on the front wall. "Gustave Flaubert, French writer, 1821–1880, lived here while—" but then the letters shrink impossibly, as if on some optician's chart. We walk closer. We look in at a window. Yes, it is true; *despite the carnage some delicate things have survived.* A clock still ticks. Prints on the wall remind us that art was once appreciated here. *A parrot's perch catches the eye. We look for the parrot. Where is the parrot ? We still hear its voice*; *but all we can see is a bare wooden perch. The bird has flown.* (*FP* 60, italics added)

This excerpt tells us that a historian is wandering through the historical relics, finding that all around is wreckage, due to the never-stoppable "fighting" and "carnage." Who are "these people" in Barnes's mind when he writes these sentences, and what are the "fighting" and "carnage"? A close reading reveals that Barnes reflects on the war in history in a general sense, although he has mentioned the relics of the Second World War and a war about nine centuries ago in the first section of the novel. In a word, what Barnes does in the search for the parrot is just like what a historian does in the search for historical truth. Parrot is thus becoming a symbol, a signifier of Flaubert, of the past, and of history. Dogs also play a vital role in Flaubert's life and works. Barnes summarizes four types of dogs closely connected to Flaubert, i. e., *The Dog Romantic*; *The Dog Practical*; *The Dog Figurative*; and *The Dog Drowned and the Dog Fantastical* (*FP* 60 – 65). For my part, what is important here is not merely Barnes's detailed investigation of dogs' importance or role in Flaubert's life and works but Barnes's comments in the end as well. The last sentences of each subsection under "Dogs" go as follows: "What happened to the dog is not recorded" (*FP* 61) ; "What happened to the dog is not recorded" (*FP* 63) ; "What happened to the dog is also not recorded" (*FP* 64) ; "What happened to the dragoman is not recorded" (*FP* 65). Here what Barnes really means to say is that what happened to the dog and the dragoman as (part of) history are not recorded. Therefore in his conclusive note, Barnes stresses that " [w]hat happened to the truth is not recorded" (*FP* 65). Even if they are recorded, as the last story about dog and dragoman was both recorded in the writing of Maxime Du Camp a friend of Flaubert and in Flaubert's "journal," whose narrative is authentic and reliable, when they are, as Barnes assures us in the novel, different versions of the (hi)story? What is suggested in Barnes's writing, naturally, is his interrogation of (historical) truth or his interrogatory attitude toward the objectivity of history and truth.

Section Six "Emma Bovary's Eyes" transfers our attention to Barnes's critique of critics' criticism on Flaubert's "inaccuracy" in the description of the colors of Madame Bovary's eyes (embodied by Dr. Enid Starkie) , defending Flaubert's different depictions of the colors of Emma's eyes in light of textual evidence from *Madame Bovary* and from Du Camp's *Souvenirs Littéraires*, the "earliest substantial source of knowledge about Flaubert" (*FP* 80), and eliciting in general Barnes's critique of academic critics, such as Cambridge professor Christopher Ricks,① who are obsessed with finding faults in literary works. When Barnes (through Braithwaite) tries to confirm the reliability of Flaubert's writing of the colors of Emma's eyes, he warns us that Du Camp's narrative is "historically essential" but "gossipy, vain, self-justifying and unreliable" (*FP* 80). That is to say, for one thing Barnes tries to establish the historical truth pertaining to Flaubert, but for another he interrogates the reliability of historical documentation, thus challenging and undermining the authenticity of historical truth. It is in this sense that *Flaubert's Parrot* is often considered as "historiographic metafiction" by critics such as Linda Hutcheon and Alison Lee.

Section Seven "Cross Channel" is the longest and perhaps the most complicated and complex one in all of the sections in *Flaubert's Parrot*, which is a good instance in point to show that this novel is a "trans-generic prose text" (Scott 58), and in which Barnes addresses a number of topics (be it related to Flaubert or not), such as Flaubert's attitude toward progress, the relation of book to life, authorial absence in Flaubert's works, the relation of style to subject matter and language to reality, unreliable narrator and multiple endings in contemporary fiction, the importance of casual details in seizing the past, the writing of unconventional memoir, the bans on the themes in novel writing, the controversy about Flaubert's sex-life, Flaubert's regret about his unmarried life, Flaubert's relationship with his niece Caroline (by reference to Willa Cather's narrative), the coincidence between Flaubert and Sartre, among others (*FP* 82–106).② Among the issues mentioned above, the crucial one is about "how to seize the past." Barnes directly discusses it on at least two occasions and with specific illustrations. For the first time in this section, Barnes questions, "How do we seize the past? How do we seize the foreign past? We read, we learn, we ask, we remember ... and then a casual detail shifts everything" (*FP* 90). The casual details in Barnes's argumentation refer to the concepts of "the tall, the fat, the mad" and "the colors." For Barnes, the concepts of these terms would alter with the passage of time, or be different in the past and the

---

① Enid Starkie (1897–1970) was an Irish literary critic, known for her biographical works on French poets and writers. *Flaubert: The Making of the Master* (1967) and *Flaubert: The Master* (1971) were her two biographies about Flaubert. Christopher Bruce Ricks (1933–) is a British literary critic and scholar. In the novel, Barnes displays his critique on four real critics: Edmund Ledoux, Jean-Paul Sartre, Starkie and Ricks. He thinks that these four critics distorted and vilified the image of Flaubert in their writing. See Barnes, *Flaubert's Parrot*, *Passim*.

② Discursive quotations and (inter)textual references in this section are involved at least with Roland Barthes's text, Flaubert's *Bouvard et Pécuchet*, *Madame Bovary* and *Dictionaire des Idées Reçues*, Turgenev's, Sartre's, Arthur Frederick Payne's painting, G. M. Musgrave's, Mauriac's, Edmund Ledoux's, Emile Faguet's, Caroline's, and Willa Cather's memoir.

present. In light of the examples about the height of Flaubert the giant (only six feet tall), the largest Fat Boy in France in the 1850s, the mad man in the Rouen asylum and the color of redcurrant jam in Flaubert's writing, Barnes tends to argue that the referents about height, weight, saneness and color in Flaubert's time are not the same as those at present, therefore the understanding of them would be different, and as such the image of or the truth about the past would be altered. ① Then, Barnes continues to question, "how do we seize the past? As it [the past] recedes, does it come into focus? Some think so. We know more, we discover extra documents, we use infrared light to pierce erasures in the correspondence, and we are free of contemporary prejudice; so we understand better. Is that it? I wonder" (*FP* 100). Next Barnes obviously turns out to be a historian proper again. He takes the controversies about Flaubert's sex-life as an instance to demonstrate his "wonder." To Barnes's mind, the "shape" of Flaubert's sex-life as "ambi-sexual, omni-experienced" (*FP* 100), surrounding Louise Colet, Juliet Herbert, Elisa Schlesinger, actresses, Cairo bath-house boys, and Bouilhet, etc., is gradually and incrementally dug out and (re)constructed but still in controversy and no conclusion is conclusive. In short, in this section, through examining historical truth in connection with Flaubert, Barnes explores the issue of "how do we seize the past" in a general sense. Just as he questions and searches for the authenticity of the parrots, with no certain answers offered, Barnes in his exploration of the issue of "how to seize the past" does not proffer a definite solution either. His questioning and questing is illuminating, however.

After reading Flaubert through Barnes or Barnes's interpretation of Flaubert so far, what is our impression of Flaubert the man and the writer? Subsequently, Barnes decides to test our reading ability so that in Section Fourteen "Examination Paper" he puts forward some questions concerning Flaubert for us to answer in three hours. All of the questions are about Flaubert, among which various kinds of quotations from and about the writer are brought together and different perspectives of reading Flaubert are offered as well. For instance, in "Section A" of the "paper," the relation of Flaubert to literary criticism is explored to the extent that two questions about Flaubert should be answered, that is, "to discuss the relation of art to life" and "to analyse Flaubert's attitude toward critics and criticism" through

---

① This is in effect a very thorny problem in the study of history. James B. Scott has discussed in his article the "infinite deferral of meaning" relevant to Barnes's writing, so that I will not repeat what he has argued. See James B. Scott, "Parrot as Paradigms: Infinite Deferral of Meaning in *Flaubert's Parrot*," ARIEL: A Review of International English Literature 21.3 (July 1990): 57-68.

reading quotations by and about Flaubert listed in the "paper." Is this just a test on our reading of Flaubert, or a parody on literary examination, or an experiment in fiction writing? What is possible is that we can, in light of many a quotation by and about Flaubert, know more about Flaubert.

All in all, after a brief reading of these important sections pertinent to Flaubert in this novel, it is safe to maintain that one of the crucial and recurrent motifs in it is about "how do we seize the past," which is put forward by Barnes in the novel three times. The use of multitudes of and various kinds of (inter)textual and discursive references including novels, letters, memoirs, notes, records, diaries, stuffed parrots, etc., intimates that we can only know Flaubert through the texts by and about him, which is, for Barnes's part, the very means to know the historical (or biographical) truth, and also indicates one of the typical features of the novel—intertextuality,① the others being parody (or pastiche), fragmentation, decentredness, and self-referentiality, which to a great extent result(s) in John Updike's view of this novel as "the most strangely shaped specimen of its genre ... since Vladimir Nabokov's *Pale Fire*" (86). Again we can restate that Barnes's idea of knowing historical truth is very similar to the view upheld by some postmodern theorists. That is, history turns up in the form of texts, and before we can know anything about it, it has already been (re)textualized. In so doing, is history the history itself? Barnes suggests something occasionally in his writing. As mentioned before, when Barnes deals with the search for the love letters between Flaubert and Juliet Herbert, he reminds us that "you must make your judgment on me as well as on Flaubert" (*FP* 41) ; and when he corroborates the reliability of Flaubert's writing of the colors of Emma Bovary's eyes in light of Du Camp's narrative, Barnes warns us that Du Camp's writing is "gossipy, vain, self-justifying and unreliable" (*FP* 80). It is clear that on the one hand Barnes, through a good many quotations or (inter)texts, tries to construct a real Flaubert, to establish the historical truth, or in his own words, to "seize the past," but on the other hand he calls into question the objectivity and authenticity of these texts on which the truth about Flaubert and the past could be built. In this way, he undermines what he has established. Later, in his twelfth section "Braithwaite's Dictionary of Accepted Ideas," the parodic writing of Flaubert's *Dictionaire des Idées Reçues*, Barnes refers to the "unreliability" of the "texts" again in the entry about Goncourts:

---

① *Flaubert's Parrot* has similarities with Flaubert's *Bouvard et Pécuchet* and Ford Madox Ford's *The Good Soldier* in theme and structure. In general, *Bouvard et Pécuchet* and *The Good Soldier* are both intertexts of *Flaubert's Parrot*. See more discussion about this issue in Bruce Sesto's and Neil Brooks's writings.

GONCOURTS

Remember the Goncourts on Flaubert: "Though perfectly frank by nature, he is never wholly sincere in what he says he feels or suffers or loves." Then remember everyone else on the Goncourts: the envious, unreliable brothers. Remember further the unreliability of Du Camp, of Louise Colet, of Flaubert's niece, of Flaubert himself. Demand violently: how can we know anybody? (*FP* 155)

Barnes's reading and understanding of Flaubert or the past is by the square based on the texts by Du Camp, Louise Colet, Flaubert's niece Caroline and Flaubert, as noted before. If these texts are of "unreliability," then, could the reading and understanding of Flaubert be reliable? Is the past as such reliable? Is the historical truth truthful? Bearing these questions in mind, we can sense that Barnes's questioning and questing for historical truth in this novel bears the very feature of "new historical fiction" or "historiographic metafiction:" when the writer tries to search for the historical truth and confirm what he has established, he also suggests occasionally his skepticism about the reliability and the objectivity of the texts he utilized, thus undermining or deconstructing the "historical truth." This is then the postmodern questioning and questing for historical truth in *Flaubert's Parrot* by Barnes, a postmodern writer with a strong interrogating spirit.

ii. "Turn Catastrophe into Art"

In *Flaubert's Parrot*, Julian Barnes refers to "a small watercolour of Rouen" painted on May 4th, 1856, by Arthur Frederick Payne (born Newarke, Leicester, 1831, working 1849-1884), displaying "the city from Bonsecours churchyard: the bridges, the spires, the river bending away past Croisset" (91). Then the narrator asks, "[i]s this history, then—a swift, confident amateur's watercolour?" (*FP* 91). Is this history? Broadly speaking, and for a historian proper, it is the document of history; it is the evidence or relic of history of a particular period, and thus part of history; it is pictorial or visual history, and history of an instant moment. But its value for the study of history is under consideration. If it is just a painting of natural landscape like the small watercolor of Rouen by Payne, its value perhaps could not be compared with a painting in which a significant event of history is depicted. There is a piece of well-known oil painting—*The Raft of the Medusa* by Théodore Géricault (1791-1824), an influential French artist, painter and lithographer—commented on and affiliated in Barnes's *A History*. This painting is about an important event or catastrophe happening in the history of France in the early nineteenth century; it is thus part of history, a text in history and for historiography. In this part, I shall discuss how Barnes, in light of his comments on the oil painting *The Raft of the Medusa*, writes of a historical event in "Shipwreck," one "chapter" of *A History*, so as to illustrate how he connects history to text(uality), and/or how the view of "the textuality of history" is suggested in his writing.

Before probing into how the view of "the textuality of history" is implied in "Shipwreck," I shall first of all examine its general demonstration in *A History*. Glancing at its title, we can discern that it is about "a history of the world" in more than ten "chapters," although "10 ½" in the title seems a little odd at first sight. A close reading of the novel evinces that it relates more than ten (hi)stories, be it factual or fictional, secular or sacred, about the world. For instance, Chapter One "The Stowaway" is a revision of the story of the Noah's Ark from the eyes of a very tiny animal. Evidently, Barnes's rewriting is intertexually built on a sacred, historical text, i. e., the Bible. As a text of history, the Bible has survived after some "complex and subtle social processes of preservation and effacement" and "textual mediations" (Montrose 20) in the river of history and turned out to be the most authoritative historical text about God and Christian History. Similarly, Barnes's writing in other several "chapters" of this "novel" also verifies that we can have access to history only through texts or "the surviving textual traces" of the historical events. Barnes, for instance, confirms in his "Author's Note" at the end of the "novel" that, "Chapter 3 is based on legal procedures and actual cases described in *The Criminal Prosecution and Capital Punishment of Animals* by E. P. Evans (1906)," which shows that Barnes's knowledge and rewriting of this "chapter" of the "history of the world" is based on another (historical) text, so is true of Chapter Five "Shipwreck" and Chapter Seven "Three Simple Stories." In a word, *A History* explores, among other things, the relation of history to text(uality), implicating that we can know the past or history only by the "surviving textual traces" such as documents, evidence, and even eyewitnesses, which in consequence and through mediation, negotiation and exchange of social processes become historical documents for the writing of history. Next I will explore how Barnes's writing in "Shipwreck" manifests the relation of history to text(uality) or what Louis Montrose has claimed about "the textuality of history."

"Shipwreck" is the fifth "chapter" in *A History*, which can be extracted as a short piece of writing and as an essay of artistic criticism; and like any one of the "chapters" in this "novel," it can be read as an independent article and would not lose its significance. It consists of two parts: the first one is a retelling or overview of a historical text, *Narrative of a Voyage to*

Senegal in 1816 written by Jean Baptiste Henry Savigny and Alexander Corréard, two of the fifteen survivors of the catastrophe of "the raft of the *Medusa*" in 1816. The second part, as Barnes tells in "Author's Note," "rel[ying] heavily on Lorenz Eitner's exemplary *Géricault: His Life and Works* (Orbis, 1982)," is an artistic review about Géricault's painting *The Raft of the Medusa*. After reading the "chapter" and the note at the end of the "novel," we can perceive that Barnes's historical writing is dependent heavily upon these two texts: one is about the shipwreck, the other about the painter. Certainly, the readers who are familiar with the specific historical event and the political scandal behind it and Géricault's most famous painting would tell that the feature of (inter)textuality of history is evidently embodied in this "chapter." Moreover, affiliated after the first part and before the second part of this "chapter" is a color replica of the very oil painting *The Raft of the Medusa* composed by Géricault in 1819. Simply speaking, the historical text, the artistic text and the literary text are linked together here by Barnes's postmodern textual practice.

Barnes's retelling of the *Medusa* shipwreck in the first part of "Shipwreck," as he tells in "Author's Note," "draws its facts and language from the 1818 London translation of Savigny and Corréard's *Narrative of a Voyage to Senegal*."[1] Savigny and Corréard's narrative as a (historical) text seems to have been almost forgotten by later readers, and Barnes's retelling of the historical event and/or his (inter)textual reference to it in some sense renders us in pursuit of the prior text, for his description of the "shipwreck" is too brief to know more details about the event and about the (hi)story behind it. The view of the textuality of history is implicitly intimated in Barnes's writing, so to speak. Without the prior textualization (by Savigny and Corréard in this case) of the history of this catastrophe, we could never approach the shipwreck. History has been gone forever, and cannot be

---

[1] The specific event briefly goes like this: on June 17th of 1816, a French government frigate named *Medusa* set sail with three other ships to Senegal; wanting to make good time, the ship *Medusa* stuck close to the African shoreline and quickly outpaced other ships but unfortunately it was too close to shore and inevitably hit a sandbar, the ship was thus abandoned; due to an insufficient provision of lifeboats for all, a makeshift raft was quickly built to load the remaining one hundred and fifty persons, including officers, soldiers, sailors and passengers, among whom there was one woman; at first, the raft was tied to the lifeboats in front of it, but at some point, it was either intentionally or accidentally cut loose, and what followed for those on the raft was about fifteen days' nightmare of stormy seas, hunger, disease, brutal murders, insanity and cannibalism, and only fifteen men survived the ordeal on the sea, five of them died shortly after their rescue (*HWC* 115-124). This is a brief overview of the *Medusa* shipwreck in light of Barnes's description, which covers less than ten pages. Savigny and Corréard narrative in the 1818 edition covers about 360 pages.

retrieved but can only be (re)cognized through the texts that relate it. Savigny and Corréard's narrative is the first and perhaps the most authentic history-text about this "shipwreck" that one can rely on, for they experienced the ordeal and therefore could write it first-hand. It is assumed that, as two of the fifteen survivors of this harsh catastrophe, they could depict it "as it actually happened," to tell the truth to the public, so as to fight against the injustice imposed upon them as well as other low crews, due to the political "corruption, incompetence, and arrogance of not only the French naval officer-class but also the government which had appointed them" (Sesto 78). Naturally, in his retelling of the catastrophe, Barnes does not show suspicion about the truthfulness of the two survivors' narrative. Barnes's brief rewriting of this event makes a page of almost forgotten history of France in the early nineteenth century come to the fore. Why does he retell this shipwreck?

Barnes does not merely retell the *Medusa* shipwreck. He occasionally comments on the event and links it with what he has written before in *A History*. For instance, when recounting that there are twenty-seven persons on the raft, fifteen healthy, the rest wounded and "with smallest chance of survival" (*HWC* 121), "the most terrible decision [comes] to be taken" (*HWC* 120) —the fifteen healthy universally agree to cast the rest unhealthy into the sea due to the limited supply of provisions, Barnes remarks that "[t]he healthy were separated from the unhealthy like the clean from the unclean" (*HWC* 121). Thus, another picture of a journey on water emerges from our mind and becomes clear, that is, Noah's Ark and the Flood episode in the Bible (and in the first "chapter" of this "novel"). It is commanded by God that Noah should bring the clean animals and the unclean ones together onto the Ark (Genesis: 7). The only difference is, for Barnes's part, that on Noah's Ark some of the clean would be killed by Noah as food, the unclean surviving, while on the raft of the *Medusa* only the healthy would survive in the end. The Flood is no doubt a catastrophe, especially for those species that cannot embark on the Ark and survive the Flood, which is manipulated by God in light of Christian History. In Salman Rushdie's view, the raft of the *Medusa* is "also a sort of ark" and "just as Noah ate his animals, so the *Medusa*'s survivors turned to cannibalism" (241-242). In this sense, Barnes associates the history of the *Medusa* shipwreck with that of Noah's Ark, so as to suggest that human history or the "history of the world" starts from a catastrophe and a journey on the flood of water, of which the catastrophic journey on the raft of the *Medusa* is but a reproduction and/or a repetition. In other words, behind the intertextual references to the similar event happening in the river of history, be it secular or sacred, Barnes's writing tends to substantiate that history repeats itself and are fraught with catastrophes, an important motif in this "novel." Therefore, Barnes's retelling of the historical event surrounding the *Medusa* shipwreck does not merely mean recounting a forgotten chapter of "history of the world;" its (inter)textuality endows the "novel" with a linked motif related to history. On the other hand, it is evident that Barnes's brief account of the *Medusa* shipwreck prepares a historical background for his reading of Géricault's oil painting *The Raft of the Medusa* in his second part.

The second part of "Shipwreck" is a critical reading of the painting *The Raft of the Medusa* [1] and also a reading of another two texts, that is, *Narrative of a Voyage to Senegal in 1816* and *Géricault: His Life and Works*. By reading the three (historical) texts including the oil painting, Barnes tells us the "history" of how Géricault composed his most celebrated artistic work, what Géricault did not paint and what he did paint, and examines how Géricault's composition of a historical catastrophe was turned into a sempiternal artistic work. "How do you turn catastrophe into art?" Barnes at the inception of this part puts forward the question for the reader and himself as well. Then he refers to the "chronology" of the catastrophe being turned into art very briefly:

> The expedition set off on 17th June 1816.
> The Medusa struck the reef in the afternoon of 2nd July 1816.
> The survivors were rescued from the raft on 17th July 1816.
> Savigny and Corréard published their account of the voyage in November 1817.
> The canvas was bought on 24th February 1818.
> The canvas was transferred to a larger studio and restretched on 28th June 1818.
> The painting was finished in July 1819.
> On 28th August 1819, three days before the opening of the [Paris] Salon, Louis XVIII examined the painting and addressed to the artist what the *Moniteur Universal* called "one of those felicitous remarks which at the same time judge the work and encourage the artist." The king said, "Monsieur Géricault, your shipwreck is certainly no disaster."
> (*HWC* 125-126)

---

[1] As noted in the Introduction, in his early writing career, Barnes wrote various kinds of essays such as television review, cooking review and artistic review. Therefore Barnes is often called an essayist, apart from a novelist. His essay writing to a great extent affects his novel writing so that critics often consider some of his novels not as novels but essay-like prose. "Shipwreck" is such a case in point. See also Vanessa Guignery and Ryan Roberts, "Julian Barnes: The Final Interview," in *Conversations with Julian Barnes* (Mississippi: The University Press of Mississippi, 2009, 177-178).

Although this timeline of turning catastrophe into art leaves out a lot of things occurring during the process, it nevertheless includes two very important issues, which are closely connected with Géricault's composition, that is, Savigny and Corréard's account, and Louis XVIII and his comment, the former affecting its composition and the latter its reception and dissemination. Without the former, Géricault's painting could not be initiated; without the latter, this painting might not be successfully exhibited and preserved.

From Barnes's retelling of what is recorded in Lorenz Eitner's text, we know that Géricault's turning the *Medusa* shipwreck into a different kind of text, an artistic text, is based on another historical text, Savigny and Corréard's narrative. The significance of this "historical" text cannot be understated, just as Bruce Sesto comments, "[i]ncited by the writings of Savigny and Corréard, disaffected intellectuals and political malcontents all over France elevated the *Medusa* scandal to a *cause célèbre*" (78), which was witnessed by Géricault the artist, anyhow. Therefore and first of all, "[i]t begins with truth to life" (*HWC* 126). As Barnes retells, the artist "read Savigny and Corréard's account; he met them, interrogated them" and eventually "compiled a dossier of the case" (*HWC* 126). Besides this, Géricault did do a lot of other work. For instance, he "sought out the carpenter from the *Medusa*, who had survived, and got him to build a scale model of his original machine," on which "he positioned wax models to represent the survivors" (*HWC* 126); and he even "placed his own paintings of severed heads and dissected limbs, to infiltrate the air with mortality" (*HWC* 126). Among all of these, the most important for Géricault's composition would be Savigny and Corréard's narrative, without which Géricault's oil painting would be groundless. With no doubt, the event of the *Medusa* shipwreck or, to be exact, Savigny and Corréard's narrative about it, moved Géricault, stimulating him to paint or represent an instant moment of the shipwreck with his art. Then Barnes summarizes what Géricault did not paint in his work and the reasons for it and what the artist did paint by comparing it with Savigny and Corréard's description in their narrative, from which we know more about the social, political, historical and cultural background about the shipwreck, Géricault and his painting. ①

It is certain that Barnes's careful eyes do not leave out the discrepancy

---

① Certainly, Barnes refers to in a few pages the artistic transcendence and eternalness of this painting, which will not be discussed here due to its irrelevance in the analysis of the relation of history to textuality.

between Géricault's painting and the description in Savigny and Corréard's text. "Comparing paint with print, we notice at once that Géricault has not represented the survivor up the mast holding straightened-out barrel-hoops with handkerchiefs attached to them. He has opted instead for a man being held up on top of a barrel and waving a large cloth" (*HWC* 131). Still, Barnes informs us of another detail that there are twenty persons on Géricault's raft but in the writing there are only fifteen survivors. Does Barnes interrogate the truth represented in Géricault's painting? Yes and no. Barnes's quest for the historical truth here indicates that on the one hand he did do a lot of careful and even precise research for his (historical) writing to the extent that he is very familiar with the texts in question, be it in print or in paint, and on the other hand he does not mean to override its untruthfulness but foregrounds its transcendence and universalization: what Géricault painted is not just a specific shipwreck, but also "our human condition, fixed, final, always there" (*HWC* 139). Hence the discordance between Géricault's painting and the narrative by Savigny and Corréard. And for Barnes's part:

> The painting [text] which survives is the one that outlives its own [hi]story. Religion decays, the icon remains; a narrative is forgotten, yet its representation still magnetizes … . Time dissolves the [hi]story into form, colour, emotion. Modern and ignorant, we reimagine the [hi]story: do we vote for the optimistic yellowing sky, or for the grieving greybeard? Or do we end up believing both versions [texts]? The eye can flick from one mood, and one interpretation, to the other: is this what was intended? (*HWC* 133)

Here Barnes suggests that when the story and the narrative of the *Medusa* shipwreck by Savigny and Corréard are forgotten, "its representation" (text) *The Raft of the Medusa* "still magnetizes," and the "form, colour" and "emotion" embodied in the painting (text) can help us quest for the story, the narrative "forgotten" but still existing and the history behind it, in spite of the fact that its truthfulness is questionable. In short, Barnes's writing exemplifies that Géricault's oil painting (text) is basically built on Savigny and Corréard's narrative, a prior historical text, and, as it were, represents a page or picture of history, through which we can know a specific historical event happening to France in the early nineteenth century, not merely an oil painting of French Romanticism, from which a constant picture of human history is emerging.

Barnes also briefly mentions Louis XVIII's comment on Géricault's painting, which reveals the painting's particularity ("no disaster" about and for a catastrophic shipwreck) and is in effect a sort of endorsement from the dominant class as well. When the painting was offered for sale, it is the very Louis XVIII who stepped in and rescued it from being shipped overseas to a wealthy English chap or hacked to pieces if it was obtained by a consortium of French nobility, who planned to chop the canvas (about 5 m×7 m) into smaller, more easily sold pieces, and then the King denoted it to the *Louvre* and now it still remains there. Still, the innovation registered in Géricault's artistic work (or text) is not snuffed out by the conventional vision or the traditional dominant thought (the then Neo-Classicism in painting in particular), which ushered in the commencement of the Romantic age for the oil painting in France and ensured its dissemination thereafter.

Its dissemination is attested to in Barnes's next chapter "The Mountain" in the "novel" (*HWC* 144-146). As Barnes writes, the female character in "The Mountain" was "excited by reports of the exhibition at Bullock's Egyptian Hall in Piccadilly, London, of Monsieur Jerricault's [sic] Great Picture, 24 feet long by 18 feet high, representing the Surviving Crew of the Medusa French Frigate on the Raft" and went without her father's knowledge to view it in Dublin, "where it was put on view at the Rotunda: Admission 1s 8d, Description 5d" (*HWC* 144). Although Géricault made some (Romantic) innovation in his painting, as is implied in Barnes's writing (*HWC* 134-139), the people at that time tended to acknowledge that it was a representation of the *Medusa* shipwreck, and desired to view the catastrophe through the painting. Just as Barnes tells, those "who saw Géricault's painting on the walls of the 1819 Salon knew, almost without exception, that they were looking at the survivors of the *Medusa*'s raft, knew that the ship on the horizon did pick them up ... and knew that what had happened on the expedition to Senegal was a major political scandal" (*HWC* 132-133). Géricault's painting was not the only visual representation of this catastrophe at that time, however. Barnes mentions another "mobile canvas" turning up as a rival for *The Raft of the Medusa* in another exhibition at the same time. The female character was brought by her father to view this "mobile canvas," that is, " Messrs Marshall's Marine Peristrephic Panorama of the Wreck of the Medusa French Frigate and the Fatal Raft," in which "an immense picture, or a series of pictures, gradually unwound: not just one scene, but the entire history of the shipwreck passed before them," and "[e]pisode succeeded episode, while coloured lights played upon the unreeling fabric, and an orchestra emphasized the drama of events" (*HWC* 145). It is reported that this "mobile canvas" was directed by one of the fifteen survivors of the *Medusa* shipwreck. Moreover, this showing picture seems to be more representative than Géricault's painting, for it displayed a series of scenes about the *Medusa* shipwreck instead of an instant moment, thus appealing to a great deal of more viewers and being showcased for more days (*HWC* 146). Accordingly, we can sense that the relation of history to text(uality) is implicated between Barnes's lines. These two different kinds of pictures are both a sort of (historical) texts, "the surviving textual traces" of the *Medusa* shipwreck; and the rivaling exhibition of these paintings in fact involves themselves in, in Montrose's words again, the "complex and subtle social processes of preservation and effacement" and in consequence they become some sorts of "documents" or evidence for the later us (Julian Barnes and his readers, for instance), be it historians or not, to consult or even to ground our own texts about the (hi)story of the *Medusa* shipwreck. Therefore, Barnes's exploration of the relation of history to text(uality) is implicitly evinced in these two "chapters" of the "history of the world"—"Shipwreck" and "The Mountain."

Why does Barnes write such a "chapter" ("Shipwreck") of the "history of the world?" It is no doubt that the *Medusa* shipwreck has made its imprint in the history of France and could become one of the "chapters" in the "history of the world," for it reflects or represents "our human condition" in a historically typical or typically historical way: a journey on the sea, with "the oscillation between hope and despair" (*HWC* 139). Is this not the very condition of human history? It is because of this that Barnes considers it as one of the chapters in his "history of the world in 10 ½ chapters." Many narratives and various other types of "texts" about the shipwreck have come out since Savigny and Corréard's narrative. ① How can Barnes make some breakthrough? "Shipwreck" is composed of two parts, with no titles but the Roman numbers "I" and "II," between which there is a color replica of the very oil painting by Géricault. As noted before, the first one is an overview of the (hi)story written by Savigny and Corréard, and the second part is a critical reading of Géricault's painting. There are in fact three different (types of) texts co-existing here, through which we can know a specific "chapter" of the "history of the world," and through which Barnes explores, among other things, the relation of history to text(uality) and suggests what Montrose has defined as "the textuality of history." In a word, this textual hybridization or the juxtaposition of heterogeneous "texts," the very typical feature of this "chapter" as well as the "novel," foregrounds Barnes's postmodern(ist) formal experimentation, which also comprises his contribution to the writing of fiction.

---

① A survey through Google evinces that there are about 22 versions of Savigny and Corréard's narrative, and at least 31 other books about the *Medusa* shipwreck.

II. Fictionality of History

    As mentioned in the first chapter, postmodern theorists and/or New Historicists foreground the fictional character of history or historiography while highlighting the relation of history to text. This foregrounding in fact refers to a very ancient issue, i. e., the relation of history to literature, an interesting but thorny topic for centuries. At its very inception, history is but a branch of literature and has no distinct difference from it; or in other words, they are not independent from each other. It is Aristotle that firstly and influentially made a distinction between them in *Poetics*: "[T]he historian and the poet differ ... in this, that the one speaks of things that have happened, but the other of the sort of things that might happen" and "[f]or this reason too, poetry is a more philosophical and more serious thing than history, since poetry speaks more of things that are universal, and history of things that are particular" (32). Due to the tremendous influence of *Poetics*, the distinction between history and poetry (literature) or the relation made as such has been recognized and dominated the Western world for thousands of years. In the nineteenth century, when history established itself as an independent, scientific discipline, the distinction between history and literature was finally fixed. Thereafter, the "distance" between them turned out to be further and further, especially in a highly specialized society. In general, the difference between them lies in the fact that history seeks for objective truth and factual authenticity while literature is in quest of artificial felicity and fictional conception. Certainly, there are other distinctions between history and literature. For instance, "[h]istory demands, among other things, blinding clarity, while literature can be impressionistic, frenzied, symbolic, [and] romantic" (Karl 149). However, the circumstances lasted not for a long time and evoked interrogations and critical reactions. As Hayden White argues, "[c]ontinental European thinkers—from Valéry and Heidegger to Sartre, Lévi-Strauss, and Michel Foucault—have ... stressed the fictive character of historical reconstruction, and challenged history's claims to a place among the sciences" (*Metahistory* 1–2). White himself also reconsiders "the nature and function of historical knowledge" from a postmodern perspective, and "consider[s] the historical work as what it most manifestly is—that is to say, a verbal structure in the form of a narrative prose discourse that purports to be a model, or icon, of past structures and processes in the interest of *explaining what they were* by *representing* them" (*Metahistory* 2, italics original).

    Simply speaking, for postmodern theorists or New Historicists, history and literature do not have much significant difference, for they are both a sort of fictive construction, relying heavily on language. Or again, as Hayden White puts it, like literary works, the historical work or histories "contain a deep structural content which is generically poetic, and specifically linguistic, in nature" (*Metahistory* **ix**). Therefore, by way of stressing the importance of language in historical writing, postmodern theorists or New Historicists underline the fictive character of historiography. For them, any kind of history is above all a sort of verbal artifact and the product of language exertion. White highlights the similarity between novelists and historians like this: "Novelists might be dealing with imaginary events whereas historians are dealing with real ones, but the process of fusing events, whether imaginary or real, into a comprehensive totality capable of serving as the object of representation is a poetic process" and accordingly "the historian must utilize precisely the same tropological strategies, the same modalities of representing relationships in words, that the poet or novelist uses" ("The Fictions of Factual Representation" 125). Like White, Frank Ankersmit is also one of the postmodern theorists of history who uphold such a view. He compares history to art to the extent that in his view (postmodern) historiography "is similar to art" and "should therefore take to heart the lessons of aesthetics" ("Historical Representation" 228). In simple terms, for these postmodern theorists of history, what historians really do is to transform or translate the historical facts into a historical narrative. The process of transformation or translation is dominated by at least one of the four tropes, that is, metaphor, metonymy, synecdoche and irony, as demonstrated in White's *Metahistory: The Historical Imagination in Nineteenth-Century Europe* (1973). These "techniques of *figurative languages*," as White asserts, are "the only instruments" for historians to emplot their narratives ("The Historical Text as Literary Artifact" 295, italics original). Thus, historical writing as such is often considered as an art of language tropes and a poetic act. Still, in historical writing one of the important parts is the process of emplotment. ① Corresponding to the four tropes aforementioned, there are four types of emplotment techniques: romance, comedy, tragedy and irony. Via these techniques of figurative speech and of emplotment, the literary qualities of historiography are foregrounded; thence for postmodern theorists like White and Ankersmit, historical writing displays no significant difference from literary narratives. As a consequence, the fictionality and narrativity of historical writing is

---

① White in "The Historical Text as Literary Artifact" makes an introduction about "emplotment" like this: "By emplotment I mean simply the encodation of the facts contained in the chronicles as components of specific *kinds* of plot-structures, in precisely the way that Frye has suggested is the case with 'fiction' in general." (280, italics original)

suggested, the differentiation between history and literature erased.

Julian Barnes, his fiction being considered "as footnote to history, as subversion of the given" (Rushdie 241), also addresses the fictive character of history or historiography in his postmodern historical writing. This section will expatiate on how the feature of the fictionality of history is implied in Barnes's writing, especially in his *Flaubert's Parrot*, "The Revival" and *A History*, so as to exhibit Barnes's peculiarly insightful understanding and postmodern practice of the writing of the fictive character of history or historiography.

i. "Merely Another Literary Genre"

In his insistent and intense pursuit of the authentic Flaubert's parrot, the real Flaubert and the true past in *Flaubert's Parrot*, Julian Barnes the novelist turns out to be Julian Barnes the historian, who often comments on what the past is and how to seize the past and has an insightful vision about the elasticity of history or the past. Due to this nature of the past or history, historical truth is thus not easy to approach and get at. Moreover, the difficulty in seizing the past truth or taking cognizance of the objective truth of history lies in its fictionality as well, on which Barnes the near-historian also has his own understanding, just as he remarks in his search for the true past in *Flaubert's Parrot*: "We can study files for decades, but every so often we are tempted to throw up our hands and declare that *history is merely another literary genre*: the past is autobiographical fiction pretending to be a parliamentary report" (*FP* 90, italics added). This remark is often quoted to confirm Barnes's agreement with the suggestion that history is a fictive narration or fiction, just like literature, as indicated in Hayden White's writing. Such a reading does not distort the literal meaning of this remark. But how does Barnes interpret his own remarks? In an interview with Vanessa Guignery, a distinguished scholar on Barnes scholarship, Barnes comments on his view of history as "merely another literary genre" in this way:

> I suppose one of the things I meant there was that most of the evidence of history, most of the evidence of lives of people who have lived and what they did and what happened to them, has disappeared, that what we think of as historical evidence is a very very tiny fragment of all the total evidence that was there during the lifetime of most of humanity. And therefore, inevitably there is bias; there are one or two sorts of bias. *Either you only write the history for which there is evidence, or, if you try to write more than that, if you try to write a more complete history, then you have to fictionalize or imagine. And so, to that*

extent, history, if it attempts to be more than a description of documents, a description of artefacts, has to be a sort of literary genre. But often the greatest historians write narrative as well as the best novelists. (Guignery, "History" 63, italics added)

Here Barnes mentions one of the constant situations encountered by historians, that is, the lack of evidence. Under the circumstances, historians would use their imagination or fictionalize like novelists to (re)construct a more complete picture of the historical figure or historical event. How many histories that we have read are not "written" as such!? In fact, even if there is evidence, historical writing proper could not hold water without literary executions, as suggested by White. Certainly, if we consider another original meaning of history, i.e., "any kind of narrative" or "story," as noted in Chapter One of this research, we would contend that Barnes in fact deconstructs the fixed meaning of history as truth unconsciously; that is, Barnes's view of history as "merely another literary genre" is quite similar to the notion of "history as itself a fiction" (Brooke-Rose 125), a notion having been predominantly discussed in postmodern discourse or philosophy of history. Anyhow, the following passages will discuss what Barnes the near-historian does when there lacks evidence for his historical or biographical writing about historical figures.

As noted before, *Flaubert's Parrot* is a novel with the mixture of fact and fiction. In his endeavor to (re)present a more complete or overall image of Flaubert, Barnes indeed makes good use of a lot of historical texts by and about Flaubert on one hand and has to fictionalize or use his imagination on the other, due to the lack of historical evidence. Section Eleven "Louise Colet's Version" in the novel is a fictional (re)construction about Flaubert from the perspective of his paramour Louise Colet. As mentioned by Barnes, Flaubert stressed the impersonality or absence of a writer in his works and in public life as well [1] so that this French writer destroyed or burned a good many personal letters and required the opposite parties to burn them too. Therefore, up to now, only a small number of letters by or related to Flaubert are identified. Because of this, the fascinating relationship between Flaubert and Juliet Herbert remains to be decoded, as discussed in the first section of this chapter; and even the notorious (steamy) affair between

---

[1] Barnes mentions many times Flaubert's view of impersonality of the writer in *Flaubert's Parrot* and other essays. For instance, in "The Follies of Writer Worship," Barnes refers to the fact that Flaubert considered it " a principle of fiction that the personality of the writer, and the expression of subjective opinion, were irrelevant: ' Man is nothing, the work of art everything'" (6). One of the favorite maxims quoted by Flaubert is "Abstain, and Hide your Life," which is mentioned by Barnes more than once in the novel.

Flaubert and Colet needs more evidence to clarify. However, not all of the evidence has survived yet. In light of this, as Barnes argues, "if you try to write a more complete history, then you have to fictionalise or image." Then, what does Barnes fictionalize about Flaubert in Colet's version?

"Louise Colet's Version" is a first person narrative about Colet's relationship with Flaubert, narrated or "confessed" by Colet but fictionalized by Barnes. Through Colet's version, we know of some facts about these two historical figures: how they met with each other at the studio of a French sculptor in 1845; what were their social status at that time; why did Colet the then Paris poetess fall in love with Flaubert "the big, gangling provincial;" how did Flaubert act as a lover; the twisted love affair between them; Flaubert's capricious personality; and his attitude toward life and love (*FP* 138–148). After the "confession" about the complicated relationship with Flaubert, Colet eventually refers to Flaubert's work and his lecturing of her on art and their ultimate conflict as writers, which deserves our attention hereinafter due to its relevance to the knowledge and understanding of Flaubert the historical figure.

As Colet "narrates," Flaubert sent her his work but rebuked her comments and cautious suggestions of alterations. In spite of this, Colet, unlike "the odious Du Camp," did not deny Flaubert's genius, although Flaubert undervalued her talents. And how did the "unknown, unpublished provincial" educate the poetess on Art? Colet used to sent her work to Flaubert as well, but the latter complained of her style and her titles, told her to write with the head instead of the heart, not to put herself into her work and not to poeticise things, and told her to have the religion of Art instead of the love of Art, to write objectively, scientifically, without "personal presence" and "opinions" (*FP* 149–150). This is for Colet the vanity of Flaubert as a writer and of writers in general. Moreover, this vanity of Flaubert is not merely literary: Flaubert "believed not merely that others should write as he did, but that others should live as he did" and "wanted all writers to live obscurely in the provinces, ignore the natural affections of the heart, disdain reputation, and spend solitary, backbreaking hours reading obscure texts by the light of a tiring candle" (*FP* 150). Could Colet, a woman, a poet, and "a poet of love" take what Flaubert lectured? Certainly not, for her talent "depended on the swift moment, the sudden feeling, the unexpected meeting" and "on life" (*FP* 151). In the very end of her "confession" Colet defends herself against others' accusation of her vanity to get married to Flaubert, to visit his home at Croisset, to share with him the authorship of some literary work, and even against posterity's taking side with Flaubert and prejudice against her. Her final defence seems to proffer a different perspective to rethink their true images in history and the injustice imposed upon her by history:

> People will take Gustave's side. They will understand me too quickly; they will turn my own generosity against me and despise me for the lovers I took; and they will cast me as the woman who briefly threatened to interfere with the writing of the books which they have enjoyed reading. Someone—perhaps even Gustave himself—will burn my letters; his own (which I have carefully preserved, so much against my own best interests) will survive to confirm the prejudices of those too lazy to understand. I am a woman, and also a writer who has used up her allotment of renown during her own lifetime; and on those two grounds I do not expect much pity, or much understanding, from posterity. (*FP* 152)

Be it justifiable or not, it is certain that Colet's "confession" or defence against historical prejudice merits our attention and rethinking: it represents one of the "different angles" from which Barnes did "pay homage to Flaubert" (McGrath 14).

In short, this is then Flaubert the writer and the lover in Colet's eyes. Should we believe her "confession" or Barnes's narrative? Is it the mere fictionalization by Barnes? It is narrated from the perspective of a historical female who *de facto* did not write such an account about Flaubert; it is executed by Barnes anyhow. On the other hand we can discern that Barnes's writing is based on some historical texts, such as Flaubert's travel journals and letters to Colet and Du Camp's memoir; therefore it is not groundless, although "Louise Colet's Version" is no doubt a mere fictionalization. Is Barnes's description objective or reliable? Still, we can consult entry "G" in his "Dictionary" in *Flaubert's Parrot*. Simply speaking, it is a mixture of fact and fiction, as confirmed before, but Barnes blurs their demarcation, leaving the quandary for the reader, especially the academic reader, as he mentioned in an interview (JBC 261). This is, however, one of the very features of Barnes's postmodern (historical) writing: in his representing the historical facts, he undermines its very authenticity; in other words, in his pursuit of the historical truth, he never ceases to question its reliability.

Barnes's short story "The Revival" in *The Lemon Table* also deals in some sense with the issue of fictionality in the writing of the historical figure's personal (hi)story. After reading it, we can discern that it is a narrative about the love affair between aged Turgenev and a young celebrated actress S—. ① It consists of four parts. The first part "Petersburg" is concerned with Turgenev's first meeting with the actress because of her abridging of a "juvenile" play of Turgenev and his watching of her performance: "She was twenty five, [and] he was sixty" when they fell in love with each other (*LT* 87–88); the second one "The Real Journey" recounts the only but cryptic "real journey" happening to and between them on a train, lasting for thirty miles, due to the fact that he was "an institution, the representative of an era" whereas she was married (*LT* 89–94); the third one "The Dream Journey" is Barnes's assumption of a dream journey that would occur to them, a pure imagination of what will happen to them if only they could have traveled together to Italy (*LT* 95–98); the fourth one "At Yasnaya Polyana" narrates what happened to Turgenev when he stayed with Tolstoy: their shooting, party dancing, and the former's psychological changes after his falling in love with S— (*LT* 99–101). It is ostensibly a simple short story or essay, but replete with meanings if viewed from the perspective of the relation of history to fiction(ality).

What merits attention here is the second part, in which Barnes briefly writes of what happened to Turgenev and S— after their love affair and "depicts" an actual journey on the train where they travelled together, relying basically on their letters and memoirs. More specifically, the old playwright clandestinely arranged the train timetable for the actress and successfully embarked on it where she was already on:

> He sat in her compartment for those thirty miles. He gazed at her, he kissed her hands, he inhaled the air she exhaled. He did not dare to kiss her lips: renunciation. *Or,* he tried to kiss her lips and she turned her face away: embarrassment, humiliation. The banality too, at his age. *Or,* he kissed her and she kissed him back as ardently: surprise, and leaping fear. *We cannot tell: his diary was later burned, her letters have not survived. All we have are his subsequent letters, whose gauge of reliability is that they date this May journey to the month of June.* We know that she had a travelling companion, Raisa Alexeyevna. What did she do? Feigh sleep, pretend to have sudden night vision for the darkened landscape, retreat behind a volume of Tolstoy? *Thirty miles passed. He got off the train at Oryol. She sat at her window, waving her handkerchief to him as the express took her on towards Odessa.*

---

① It is not difficult to note that Barnes's study of Russian literature in his university days, as mentioned in the Introduction, makes some influence on his writing of this story. See also Michael March, "Into the Lion's Mouth: A Conversation with Julian Barnes," rpt. in *Conversations with Julian Barnes* (Mississippi: University of Mississippi, 2009) 23–26.

> *No, even that handkerchief is invented.* But *the point is, they had had their journey. Now it could be remembered, improved, turned into the embodiment, the actuality of the if-only.* He continued to invoke it until his death. It was, in a sense, his last journey, the last journey of the heart. "My life is behind me," he wrote, "and that hour spent in the railway compartment, when I almost felt like a twenty-year-old youth, was the last burst of flame." (*LT* 90–91, italics added)

In these two paragraphs Barnes has actually touched on the issue of fact and fiction in biographical writing about a historical figure's (hi)story. The "journey" was a historical fact, but what happened on the train journey was an enigma, for the evidence was absent forever so that Barnes "invented" several versions or possibilities here of what they could do on the train. Barnes even suggests in his later passages that they could probably have sex in the train compartment, in spite of the fact that Turgenev the prominent playwright upheld "renunciation" after the age of forty in his life (*LT* 89, 91; Koval 120). There is no reason to deny such a possibility, however, since Turgenev passionately mentioned this incident in his subsequent letters. Here again Barnes refers to the "reliability" of the historical texts, the letters of the playwright: "May" is altered to "June." Later in his writing, via examining Turgenev's letters, Barnes finds that there is discrepancy as to who is "the suitor" and who is "the recipient" in their love affair, and the indeterminate meanings of the "bolt" ("the lock on the compartment, on her lips, on her heart? Or the lock on her flesh?"). However, her letters have not survived. Barnes questions the authenticity of the historical truth as such: "Is this the truth, or is that the truth? We, now, would like it to be neat then, but it is rarely neat; whether the heart drags in sex, or sex drags in the heart" (*LT* 94). As Virginia Woolf contends, "[t]he biographer is inventing when the evidence runs out" (qtd. in Barnes, JBC 263); it is perhaps all the more true of historical writing proper. In this short (hi)story (or discursive essay) Barnes carries it out in his construction of the affair between the aged Turgenev and a young actress, and self-consciously manifests its artifice of writing; in the meantime, he also interrogates the historical texts utilized in his writing so as to question the historical truth implied in it, thus displaying his constant, postmodern skepticism about the objectivity and authenticity of the (historical) truth.

Similarly, in his (re)writing of the life (hi)stories of historical figures such as Arthur Conan Doyle and George Edalji in *Arthur & George*, one of his finest and most compelling novels, Barnes again combines the historical facts and fiction, due to the absence of the evidence and documents. The novel in question is a "gorgeous, epic retelling of a true story, that of the famous Arthur Conan Doyle and the largely forgotten George Edalji" (Lewis). The former was an imperialist, a Knight of the Realm, and the creator of Sherlock Holmes, whereas the latter was the son of a Parsee country vicar, a solicitor, and author of the 1901 pamphlet, *Railway Law for the "Man in the Train;"* the one is still world-famous today but the other has fallen into a state of oblivion for more than a hundred years. There is little evidence about the latter, although the Court of Criminal Appeal in Britain was established in 1907 due to the injustice done to him. Nevertheless, to write the forgotten history of and between Arthur and George, Barnes does do a lot of research and read a large number of documental papers, just as he explains at the end of the novel: "*Apart from Jean's letter to Arthur, all letters quoted, whether signed or anonymous, are authentic; as are quotations from newspapers, government reports, proceedings in Parliament, and the writings of Sir Arthur Conan Doyle*" (*AG* 445, italics original). Due to this authentic aura it is often considered "a true story," "a careful and predictably astute retelling of the story, a double biography that describes the strange convergence of these very dissimilar figures" (Winder 50). Anyhow it is a mix of fact and fiction, "a marvelously readable account, written as fiction but entirely based on fact, of how Conan Doyle becomes involved in a great judicial injustice, and how he tries to solve a great mystery, Holmes-style" (Bernard 2–3). With no doubt, the "sensational miscarriage of injustice" imposed upon George Edalji and Doyle's great efforts to win George a full pardon and compensation are "historically verifiable" (Bernstein 146), but the vital and intriguing portraits of its title characters are a sort of fictionalization. For instance, Barnes, for lack of documental evidence, fictionalizes the ten years of Arthur's life story in which the famous detective writer was involved with another woman while his wife was suffering from tuberculosis (Schiff).①

In a nutshell, Barnes's (historical) writing in these texts substantiates what he has articulated, that is, "if you try to write a more complete history,

---

① There have been some documents preserved and existing about Conan Doyle, but it seems that Barnes has no access to some of the historical evidence, especially the private documents such as Conan Doyle's letters. Barnes in an interview spoke of his predicament in getting at the source materials about Arthur: "There are some letters, but the Conan Doyle estate is a very curious estate. It has been very keen on milking money, as much as possible, and also very secretive, refusing to answer any approaches from any writers. I got a contact for the chief fellow—chief beneficiary or something—through a Conan Doyle biographer who was greatly approved of, and he said 'this is the person to email' and 'I will email the fellow in advance, follow up after that.' And so I did, and got absolutely no response" (Lewis). Under such circumstances, in his (re)writing of Conan Doyle's (hi)story, Barnes comes across the problem of lack of documents and has to "invent" or "fictionalize." So is true of Barnes's writing of George's life (hi)story.

then you have to fictionalize or imagine," especially when the evidence runs out or the documents are not available or accessible. Many of histories we have read are *de facto* written in this way; therefore Barnes's interpretation of history as "merely another literary genre" unconsciously undermines the authenticity of historical truth and refers back to "story," one of the almost forgotten original meaning of "history." It is also in this sense that Barnes's understanding of history as "merely another literary genre" fits in well with Hayden White's argument that "what would be meant by the real is always something that is imagined" (Domańska 35).

ii. "The Technical Term Is Fabulation"

What is discussed in the preceding part only refers to one of the aspects in relation to the fictionality of history or historiography represented in Julian Barnes's postmodern historical writing; that is, history as "merely another literary genre" lies in the fact that we cannot get at all of the historical evidence so that it is unavoidable to invent or fictionalize in order to represent a more complete (hi)story of the past. In this part, other aspects about the fictionality of history will be dealt with, such as Barnes's use of "story" as "history" or vice versa, consciously or unconsciously, and Barnes's comments on the "fabulation" of history and its self-reflexive writing in his fiction.

In the reading of Barnes's postmodernist novels, we can perceive without much difficulty that on many occasions Barnes views "story" and "tales" as "history," or vice versa (*FP* 136; *HWC* 133; *EE* 12-13, 25-26, 91, 97, 123-124, 133; *LE* 14). Under such circumstances, Barnes's writing suggests one of the original meanings of "history," as noted in Chapter One of this research, that is, "history" involves any kind of narrative, be it an account, a tale or a story. Accordingly, the fictive feature of history or historiography is brought to the fore. For instance, in one of his postmodern (but not historical) fiction *Love, Etc.*, a narrative of a peculiar love triangle, Barnes proffers a *très* (very) postmodern(ist) view of history through one of his character-bound narrators:

> "The *story* of a louse may be as fine as the *history* of Alexander the Great— *everything depends upon the execution.*" An adamantine formula, don't you agree? *What is needed is a sense of form, control, discrimination, selection, omission, arrangement, emphasis ... that* [...] *three-letter word, art. The story of our life is never an autobiography, always a novel*—that's the first mistake people make. *Our memories are just another artifice*: go on, admit it. And the second mistake is to assume

that a plodding commemoration of previously feted detail, enlivening though it might be in a taproom, constitutes a *narrative* likely to entice the at times necessarily hard-hearted reader. (*LE* 14, italics added)

This excerpt reveals what Barnes the novelist has written in the novel and to his characters; therefore it becomes an exegesis to the novel itself, which constitutes its self-reflexive feature. More significantly, we would suggest that herein Barnes broaches the view of the fictionality of history or historiography, similar to those put forward by postmodern theorists of history like Hayden White and Frank Ankersmit. Specifically but briefly, in the first sentence Barnes equalizes "story" with "history," which blurs the demarcation between them, and between "fiction" and "reality." This, as observed before, not only turns up in this novel but in Barnes's other fiction as well, which evinces that the conflation of "story" with "history," or vice versa, is engrained in Barnes's mind. Then, Barnes further endorses the view that history, like art or literature, "depends upon the execution" and needs "form, control, discrimination, selection, omission, arrangement, emphasis," which reminds us of what White has claimed in his works, and intimates that life, memory or commemoration are all "novel," "artifice" and "narrative," thus foregrounding the artificial constructedness of life and reality as well. In short, in this excerpt by way of the equalization of "story" with "history" and of "life" with "artifice," Barnes proposes implicitly that historical writing or historiography " necessarily employs literary conventions" (Rubinson 161), and that history, as story, bears the feature of fictionality, just like that of art.

In *A History*, Barnes also addresses the issue of the fictionality of history. In one "chapter" of "the history of the world" titled "The Survivor," through his female character Kathleen Ferris, abused by her drunkard boyfriend Greg and terrified by the outside world's crises such as nuclear disaster and war, Barnes implicates what happened to and in the "history of the world" and expresses such a view of history: "the technical term is fabulation. You make up a story to cover the facts you don't know or can't accept. You keep a few true facts and spin a new story round them" (*HWC* 109). Here Barnes in fact refers to the fictive feature of historiography; and perhaps it is more appropriate for the official history or historiography. Still, later in his self-reflexive half chapter "Parenthesis" between Chapter Eight "Upstream!" and Chapter Nine "Project Ararat," the narrator camouflaged as a "Julian Barnes" directly makes comments on history, love, truth and the entwined relationships among them. The narrator "Julian Barnes" deals with history in it, for instance, in a very postmodern fashion:

> History isn't what happened. History is just what historians tell us. There was a pattern, a plan, a movement, expansion ... ; it is a tapestry, a flow of events, a complex narrative, connected, explicable. One good story leads to another. ... [A]ll the time it's more like a multimedia collage, with paint applied by decorator's roller rather than camel-hair brush. ... —*we fabulate. We make up a story to cover the facts we don't know or can't accept; we keep a few true facts and spin a new story round them. Our panic and our pain are only eased by soothing fabulation; we call it history.* (*HWC* 240, italics added)

Over again, in this "½ chapter," the most authoritative "chapter" of the novel, Barnes mentions "fabulation" in history or historiography, which, as it were, exposits his underscoring of the fictional feature of history. The following discussion will explore what Barnes "fabulates" specifically in "The Survivor," and generally in the "novel" under discussion, so as to evince that Barnes's postmodern view of history is not only a self-conscious exegesis to his own writing but also a "subversion of the given" and a "footnote to [conventional] history" (Rushdie 241).

"Fabulation" in "The Survivor" is first of all a sort of psychological syndrome detected in a special type of patients called "persistent victims." The victims of such sort as the heroine Kathleen Ferris fabulate their life (hi)stories, as mentioned in this "chapter" by a male doctor, so as to evade the physical hurt and emotional trauma imposed upon them from "severe stress in private life" and some (political) crises in the outside world (*HWC* 110). To understand this term, it is rewarding to know of history (of the world) from Ferris's perspective. Then what is the "history of the world" in Ferris's eyes like? In the first place, history is chronologized by "[n]ames, dates and achievements" (*HWC* 99). When about ten years old, Ferris is taught in history class to recite historical events by "dates" and "achievements" of famous men, such as "[i]n fourteen hundred and ninety-two/Columbus sailed the ocean blue" (*HWC* 83). Although indoctrinated as such by conventional education of history, Ferris does not believe in history written in this vein. On the contrary, she hates "dates," for "[d]ates are bullies, dates are know-alls" (*HWC* 99).[1]

Moreover, Ferris's dislike of history (identified by "dates") also extends to the view of history as a chronicle of events dominated by men, especially

---

[1] Barnes's incredulity toward "big dates" could be also detected in his writing in *Metroland*, as discussed in the first chapter of this research, and in his depiction of the teaching of history in *England, England*. All these indicate Barnes's attitude toward the total History or historical (meta)narrative, another issue discussed in the next chapter.

"famous men." Even in her childhood, when she was told by her father that all the reindeers appearing and pulling the sleigh in Christmas cards were stags, Ferris "felt disappointed" at first and grew resentful later. "Father Christmas ran an all-male team. Typical. Absolutely bloody typical, she thought" (*HWC* 83). Her life as a young woman is accompanied by this resentment against male domination as well. Ferris intensely senses that the world is dominated and controlled by men, the "men in dark-grey suits and striped ties" (*HWC* 89). And the "big accident" happening in Russia and the "Big Thing" about politics are "men's business" instead of women's, as told by Greg, Ferris's boyfriend (*HWC* 84–89). Still, her concern about the big accident in Chernobyl, about its nuclear leakage and radioactivity, are but despised by Greg as pre-menstrual tension. When rebuked by men including Greg that the "men in dark-grey suits and striped ties" would "sort something out," Ferris turns angry and refutes agitatedly but reasonably:

> Listen to them, listen to them and their connections. This happened, they say, and as a consequence that happened. There was a battle here, a war there, a king was deposed, famous men—always famous men, I'm sick of famous men—made events happen. ... [B]ut I can't see their connections. I look at the history of the world, which they don't seem to realize is coming to an end, and I don't see what they see. All I see is the old connections, the ones we don't take any notice of any more because that makes it easier to poison the reindeer and paint stripes down their back and feed them to mink. Who made that happen? Which famous man will claim the credit for that? (*HWC* 97)

In her private life, Ferris is also abused by men like Greg, who is but a representative of the "they" men in reality life. As a young woman, Ferris is victimized by Greg's sexist attitudes, for instance. Greg often rows about animals with Ferris, thinking of her too soft, and even threatens to castrate her cat so as to render it less aggressive. Still, he often attributes his staying out and picking up girls at night to Ferris's nagging at him. As just mentioned, Greg believes that politics is men's business instead of women's, and often dismisses Ferris's fears and concerns about the world's political situation as mere symptoms of pre-menstrual tension. When Ferris endeavors to convince Greg that his remarks about pre-menstrual tension are truer than he thinks, for "women are more closely connected to all the cycles of nature and birth and rebirth on the planet than men, who are only impregnators after all," Greg just refutes, "[s]illy cow, that's just why politics are men's business" (*HWC* 89). Later, Ferris and Greg continue to argue about the "big accident," and Greg's remarks, as some feminist theorists would argue, reflect the very sort of phallocentric power domination in Western culture in that he thinks that Ferris's worry about "the end of the world" results from her "premenstrual tension," which signals the coming of her period, and that "other impregnators up in the north [Russia] would sort something out" (*HWC* 89). It is evident that Ferris's conflict with Greg "allegorizes the conflict between those who control the machinery of repressive power and those who are the victims of that power" (Sesto 72), Greg being the power controller and Ferris a victim of the sexist power domination.

Still, history in Ferris's view is full of cataclysmic disasters, and only "those who can see what's happening will survive" (*HWC* 97), which displays the skepticism about the hypothesis of "the survival of the fittest." Ferris has "always wondered about that phrase the survival of the fittest," and thinks of "The Survival of the Worries," believing that "[p]eople like Greg will die out like the dinosaurs. Only those who can see what's happening will survive, that must be the rule" (*HWC* 97). Ferris's ironic comments suggest her rebellion against Greg and the men alike and the phallocentric view of history behind— "the survival of the fittest;" it is a different view of the history of the world through the eyes of a woman anyhow. Barnes indeed describes Ferris's rebellion against the phallocentric power control embodied in Greg in this "chapter." Therefore, Ferris eventually leaves Greg without a note and "cast off" on a boat, of which Greg has a quarter share, on a day when Greg is out for work (*HWC* 90). On her travel on the sea, Ferris dreams that she is hospitalized. And all the doctors in her dreams are men, who try to control her mind and psychoanalyze her, in order to cure her "persistent victim syndrome." It is the male doctor who tells Ferris that she is fabulating her-stories (those mentioned above), but to the contrary Ferris vigilantly notes that it is the male doctor who tries to fabulate opposite stories for her, to brainwash her. Undoubtedly, Barnes fabulates all of these and leans to take Ferris's side, to which the ending of this "chapter" would attest: "The next day, on a small, scrubby island in the Torres Strait, Kath Ferris woke up to find that Linda [the cat] had given birth" (*HWC* 111). Seeing the kittens, Ferris not only feels "such love" but also visions "happiness" and "hope" (*HWC* 111).

This is then the end of the fabulated her-story of Kathleen Ferris. However, it is not delineated as what I have done here; instead, it is well emplotted and fabulated, composed of different pieces of writings, some long and some short, some plot narrative and some comment, some (fictional) reality and some (fictional) dreams, some facts and some fiction, some in the first person narration and some in the third; in a word, it consists of fragments with alternating first and third person narrative voices. As an independent (hi)story, "The Survivor" could be classified as one of the best short stories written by Barnes, just as any one of the (hi)stories in this "history of the world" would do. Moreover, we can situate it in the whole context of the "novel" to see its significance in an overall way, since Barnes insists on its status as a novel, contrary to some critics' repudiation of it not as a novel.

As one "chapter" of this "novel," "The Survivor" recalls several of the motifs suggested in the whole "novel." Firstly, we can see that history as (repetition of) disaster is implied in this "chapter," which could be also discerned in Chapter One "The Stowaway," Chapter Two "The Visitors" and Chapter Five "Shipwreck." Secondly, it is manifest that the journey on the sea is the main plot of this "chapter," in which Ferris recalls what happened in the past to unfold the (hi)story. The journey on the sea (accompanied by disasters) is also a vital image or motif represented in almost all the chapters of the "novel." As such, Barnes seems to indicate that the history of human beings issues from and continues to be a disaster, a journey on water, which to some extent confirms what Salman Rushdie has commented on this "novel" as a "footnote to history," or to be exact, to History of Christianity recorded in the Bible. In the third place, "The Survivor" reveals a sort of power relations between women and men and between the victim and the dominant, evidently embodied in the relationship between Ferris and Greg. In light of Foucault's theory of power discourse, it is reasonable to say that many (hi)stories in the "novel" deal with the conflict between those who control and those who are the victims of that power. In addition, Barnes also addresses such issues as the skepticism about "the survival of the fittest" and about the progressive view of history embodied in the technological development, and the interrogation of the written history dominated by "dates, achievements and famous men," which are recurrent and resonated throughout the narrative of the whole "novel" as well. As a result, we can say that "The Survivor" is thematically well-emplotted or fabulated, typical of the whole "novel."

In terms of formal structure, "The Survivor" could be also considered an exemplar of and in the "novel." As noted before, it is made up of a series of narrative fragments, with no specific location and chronology, alternating between the first person narrative voice and the third, intertwining reality and dreams, and blurring the boundary between fact and fiction, thus (re)presenting one "chapter" of (hi)stories of the world with fragmentation, discontinuity and the Other's voice. Such a "chapter" of the history of the world represented in such a way to a great extent mirrors the typical characteristic of the entire "novel," for it is evidently composed of a collection of different (hi)stories and essays, fragmentary in formal structure, discontinuous in time sequence, ontologically a blend of fact and fiction, and generically a mix of "[e]ssays, history, realistic fiction, beast fable, [and] dream" (Flower, "Story Problems" 317). Reading "The Survivor" in this way, we can also assert that it is formally well-emplotted or fabulated, a miniature of the whole "novel."

Still, it is enlightening to view the idea of "fabulation" by linking the introduction of it in this "chapter" with Barnes's writing of the entire "novel." As mentioned before in this part, the male doctor in Ferris's dreams assumes that Ferris is fabulating: "You make up a story to cover the facts you don't know or can't accept. You keep a few true facts and spin a new story around them" (*HWC* 109). If Barnes merely depicts the story of Ferris as the male doctor proposes, the (hi)story of the world in this "chapter" would turn out to be the cliché of a conventional narrative dominated by phallocentric thinking; nevertheless, Barnes postulates in it that it is the male doctor who is fabulating in order to brainwash Ferris, which is vigilantly observed by the latter. Therefore, through the introduction of the term of "fabulation," Barnes makes us deeply understand the complex and subtle power struggle between two sexes, which is no doubt one of the intentions implicated in his writing. In addition, seeing the introduction of this term in an alternative way, that is, drawing upon it to explore Barnes's postmodern historical writing in this "novel," it is not difficult to discern that it raises the her-story of Ferris to "a metafictional level" in that "fabulation" becomes a metaphor for exactly what Barnes himself is doing in the novel: "[W]e fabulate. We make up a story to cover the facts we don't know or can't accept; we keep a few true facts and spin a new story round them" (*HWC* 240). Simply speaking, all of the (hi)stories in this "history of the world in 10 ½ chapters" are based on historical facts, around which Barnes "spins" his own [hi]stories. Barnes articulated in an interview that "I quite like putting facts and real things and real stories into my fiction" (Koval 118), of which this "novel" is a very good instance. In short, the introduction of the term "fabulation" constitutes a footnote to Barnes's historical writing in the "novel," or it intertextually and self-reflexively represents what Barnes has written in this "novel."

More importantly, what is also suggested is that it is the very thing historians do in their historical writing, as referred to in "Parenthesis" by "Julian Barnes," pretending as a historian to think of historical writing or historiography (*HWC* 240). That is to say, what historians proper do in their historical writing is just like what Barnes the near-historian does do in his fiction, and the process of historical writing proper is similar to the process of writing the "history of the world" in this "novel," bearing the process of emplotment or "fabulation," with "a sense of form, control, discrimination, selection, omission, arrangement, [and] emphasis" (*LE* 14). Accordingly, we would maintain that "fabulation" is "a generic description of how Barnes perceives the writing of history and how his own [hi]stories are scripted" (Rubinson 168). In consequence, we can say that as a postmodern novelist, Barnes, in light of the form of fictional writing or from the angle of literary writing, " aligns history with fabulation and emphasises the crucial significance of narrativity in every representation of the past" (Kotte 125), thus highlighting the fictive character of history or historiography and eventually interrogating its objectivity and authenticity.

Although the statement that "[t]he Truth is rarely pure and never simple" (Wilde 368) is but a dramatic line, it could be used as an explanation or exegesis for Julian Barnes's writing in *Flaubert's Parrot* and *A History*. Barnes's unconventional (historical) writing in these two books also attests to the fact that "[t]here is not one true story about the past, but a multiplicity of complementary, competing, or clashing stories" and that "[s]uch stories do not come only in written texts purporting to tell us about the past, but in a variety of other ways too" (Lee, "Understanding History" 129). To realize this, Barnes's writing is thick with (inter)textual references and discursive heterogeneity, by way of parodic and metafictional devices of writing, so that his writing is replete with such postmodernist characteristics of fiction as parody (or pastiche), intertextuality, *bricolage* and metafiction, which nevertheless gives rise to the difficulty for the reading of his fiction and even results in the problematizing of whether some of his books could be defined as novels at all. That is to say, Barnes's writing is in fact a "subversion of the given" notion about the novel. This is a problem for some critics, so to speak. However, if we relate to Barnes what Jean-François Lyotard defines about "a postmodern artist or writer" — "the text he writes, the work he produces are not in principle governed by preestablished rules, and they cannot be judged according to a determining judgement, by applying familiar categories to the text or to the work," and "[t]he artist and the writer, then, are working without rules in order to formulate the rules of what *will have been done*" (81, italics original) —we would agree that Barnes is a very postmodern artist or writer in a Lyotardian sense. This also proves Barnes's continuous pursuit as an artist. With no doubt, the characteristics of Barnes as a postmodern writer would be necessarily examined in the next two chapters while analyzing his postmodern historical writing from the ontological and political perspectives respectively.

All in all, in his questioning and questing for historical truth, Barnes, in the texts discussed before, explores the issues of textuality and fictionality of history or historiography through his intertextual, self-reflexive writing (or narrative) strategy, epistemologically pointing to the fact that historical writing or historiography is a textual, fictional (and poetic) construction, foregrounding the relation of history to text and to fiction, and consciously or unconsciously calling into question the objectivity and authenticity of history or historiography espoused by conventional historians like Ranke. In spite of this, we should be aware that Barnes does not celebrate the impossibility of knowing historical truth,① although he often queries the authenticity of historical truth and his writing is fraught with elements of indeterminacy and ambiguity. This is but the very paradox embodied in Barnes as a postmodern writer and would be further referred to in the following chapters of this research.

---

① As "Julian Barnes" articulates in *A History*: "We all know objective truth is not obtainable, that when some event occurs we shall have a multiplicity of subjective truths which we assess and then fabulate into history, into some God-eyed version of what 'really' happened. This God-eyed version is a fake—a charming, impossible fake, like those medieval paintings which show all the stages of Christ's Passion happening simultaneously in different parts of the picture. But while we know this, we must still believe that objective truth is obtainable; or we must believe that it is 99 per cent obtainable; or if we can't believe this we must believe that 43 per cent objective truth is better than 41 per cent. We must do so, because if we don't we're lost, we fall into beguiling relativity, we value one liar's version as much as another liar's, we throw up our hands at the puzzle of it all, we admit that the victor has the right not just to the spoils but also to the truth" (*HWC* 243-244).

Chapter Three
Subverting and Revising Historical (Meta)Narratives

Simplifying to the extreme, I define *postmodern* as incredulity toward metanarratives.
—Jean-François Lyotard, *The Postmodern Condition: A Report on Knowledge*

Within the postmodernist view of history, the goal is no longer integration, synthesis, and totality, but it is those historical scraps which are the centre of attention.
—Frank Ankersmit, "Historiography and Postmodernism"

"You can't love someone without imaginative sympathy, without beginning to see the world from another point of view. You can't be a good lover, a good artist or a good politician without this capacity ... . " It is safe to add to the list that one cannot be a good historian and theologian without the capacity to see the world from another point of view.
—Gregory Salyer, "One Good Story Leads to Another: Julian Barnes' *A History of the World in 10 ½ Chapters*"

As a pioneering proponent for radical postmodernism or postmodern theory, Jean-François Lyotard in *The Postmodern Condition: A Report on Knowledge* launches his unflinching attack against "metanarratives," as the epigram heading the start of this chapter indicates. For his part, the grand systems of thought or metanarratives such as "the dialectics of Spirit, the hermeneutics of meaning, the emancipation of the rational or working subject, or the creation of wealth" (Lyotard **xxiii**) have dominated the Western world for centuries but are not sufficient to explain things. In effect, some of the grand narratives of history such as the (meta)narratives of Christian History or sacred history and Eurocentrism have influenced the Western mind for thousands of years; and they have affected not only the mind of the Western people but the process of Western civilization and the "history of the world" as well. Nevertheless, with the advancement of human society, their limitations and negative influences have turned out to be more and more manifest; and under postmodern circumstances, the "incredulity" toward and interrogation of them have turned out to be more and more intense. Such postmodern theorists as Jacques Derrida, Michel Foucault and Lyotard, among others, all display their critique on these (meta)narratives through and in their writings. Derrida's deconstruction and subversion of Western Logocentrism or Phallocentrism is a striking phenomenon in cultural and thinking areas of the Western world, and his deconstructive or subversive strategy appeals greatly to not a few of postmodern theorists, thinkers and novelists. Many contemporary British writers such as Peter Ackroyd, Antonia S. Byatt, Salman Rushdie, Graham Swift, all through their writings register their incredulity toward (the existence of) God, the linear concept of time and space, the truth value of knowledge (or history), and the progressiveness of the human world (or history), thus unfolding their interrogation of and subversion against the commonly acknowledged (meta)narratives or grand narratives.

Julian Barnes is such a postmodern novelist that he not only suggests his interrogation of (historical) metanarratives in his postmodern historical writing but also tries to deconstruct and subvert them, to revise and rewrite them, thus representing the alternative versions and different understanding of "the given" (meta)narratives. For instance, it is not difficult to discern that Barnes often discloses the disbelief in (the existence of) God, the skepticism about (the view of) progress, the subversion of the linear causality and the revision of the established power relation. This chapter will explore from the viewpoint of ontology Barnes's subversion and revision of historical (meta)narratives, which accordingly reveal a couple of postmodern views of history (discontinuity, fragmentation and plurality of history) implied in Barnes's unconventional writing about history, especially in his works such as *Flaubert's Parrot*, *A History of the World in 10½ Chapters* and *Arthur & George*. To realize this, I will draw upon some postmodern theories about historical discontinuity, fragmentation and plurality broached by Foucault, Frank Ankersmit, among others, aiming to point out that Barnes carries out these postmodern views of history into his fictional writing about history, exhibiting his insightful apprehension of the (conventional) historical (meta)narratives, the possible angles of viewing history, reality and truth indicated in his writing, and his deep concern for morality, humanity and the human condition. More specifically, this chapter is composed of two sections: the first section mainly explicates the discontinuous and fragmentary feature of history in light of Barnes's deconstructive and subversive writing about traditional historical continuity, causality and progressive view; the second section deals with the issue of historical plurality mainly through Barnes's revising of the established text and his digging out of some forgotten (hi)story about a racial victim.

I. Discontinuity and Fragmentation of History

As mentioned in Chapter One, there are two types of linear conception of history, viz., the view of sacred history or Christian History and that of secular history. The former view has dominated the Western world for centuries, whereas the latter one is but a product of the Modern Ages. For the believers of the former view, God with paternal authority stands over humanity, watches over the course of events, and regularly influences them through divine intervention. Thus, religion becomes the ultimate concern of humankind, and history moves teleologically according to design toward a foreordained conclusion directed by God. Without doubt, this view of history is based on the linear conception of history; that is, there is a beginning, a middle and an end in the progression of history, and certainly there is the cause for the happening of the event, God being the first and ultimate reason of motivation. Secondly, Christian History highlights objectivity and truthfulness as well. The truthfulness is certainly in accordance with God's divine will. Still, as a kind of grand narrative, Christian History puts a great emphasis on the writing of political and military affairs of the state, and therefore its historiography embraces a large measure of political utility, providing for politics and society a means of legitimating the *status quo* as consistent with the will of God. The views of Christian History still exist and take effects, which is to some extent the critique object of Julian Barnes's postmodern historical writing, especially in

A History. One of the secular views of history includes the progressive view of human society, figuring prominently in the progressive myth of the Enlightenment Age and later typically embodied in Marx's historical materialism. In a word, as grand narratives of history, they bear some common characteristics: they both hold that history is a linear process moving through time with a beginning, a middle and an end, with such features as linearity, continuity, causality and teleology; that history is a whole and a unity, with such features as totality, identification and unification.

Postmodern theorists (of history) such as Michel Foucault, Jacques Derrida and Claude Lévi-Strauss show no belief in such views of history; nevertheless, they uphold the non-linear, discontinuous instead of the linear or continuous, the fragmented, disordered instead of the total or universal, the pluralistic, multiple instead of the universal or monistic views of history. For instance, Foucault foregrounds the discontinuity of history in his writings such as *Madness and Civilization* (1961), *The Order of Things: An Archaeology of the Human Sciences* (1966) and *The Archaeology of Knowledge* (1969). In the last book, he views discontinuity as "one of the basic elements of historical analysis" (8) and "one of the most essential features of the new history" (9). For Foucault's part, discontinuity is no longer the "partita" but the "melody," not "the negative" but "the positive element" (9). In order to avoid and resist continuity, Foucault uses the views (or means) of Archaeology and Genealogy to take the place of the traditional concept of history. Both methodologies, as Best and Kellner contend, endeavour to "re-examine the social field from a micrological standpoint that enables one to identify discursive discontinuity and dispersion instead of continuity and identity, and to grasp historical events in their real complexity" ("Foucault and the Critique of Modernity"). Moreover, these two methodologies "attempt to undo great chains of historical continuity and their teleological destinations and to historicize what is thought to be immutable" (Best and Kellner, "Foucault and the Critique of Modernity"). In so doing, Foucault dismantles the traditional historiography typical of linearity, periodization and teleology. The concept of discontinuity in history can be also found in the writing of Lévi-Strauss. In *The Savage Mind* (1966), Lévi-Strauss explicates in detail the different meanings of history and/or historical fact from the traditional and points out with acumen that "[h]istory is a discontinuous set composed of domains of history, each of which is defined by a characteristic frequency and by a differential coding of *before* and *after*" (259–260, italics original). Then, he draws the conclusion that it is "not only fallacious but contradictory to conceive of the historical process as a continuous development" (260). Although he deconstructs the view of continuity from the perspective of structural methodology, Lévi-Strauss's contribution to postmodern theory (of history) cannot be underestimated, which, along with that of Foucault (and Derrida), ① accelerates the dismantlement of the view of historical continuity against the postmodern context. It is reasonable to contend that their efforts to deconstruct the feature of continuity in the traditional view of history has altered the ideas of historians and influenced the strategies of historical writing not only for historians proper but for postmodern novelists as well. In addition, the discontinuity of history also suggests the fragmentation of history. As noted in Chapter One, they are closely connected, or they are just like two sides of a coin and cannot be separated from each other. Therefore, to write about the one entails the writing about the other. This section will expound how Barnes breaks up the linear causality (of history) through and in his postmodern writing mode, to foreground historical discontinuity and fragmentation in *A History* and how Barnes displays his skepticism about progress or progressive narrative in *Flaubert's Parrot* and *A History*, so as to show Barnes's subversion and revision of such views as continuity, causality, totality and progressiveness embedded in historical (meta)narratives like those of the Enlightenment, Darwin's theory of evolution and Hegel's rational view of history.

i. "History Doesn't Relate"

The features of discontinuity and fragmentation of history are prominently represented in Julian Barnes's *A History*. First of all, these features are parodically and playfully implied in the title of the "novel." It could be a parody of the conventional historical writing about the "history of the world," such as Sir Walter Raleigh's *The History of the World*, as Brian Finney observes ("A Worm's Eye View of History" 49); it could be a "play with numeric orders, their inscription and simultaneous subversion" (Kotte 109). To be specific, instead of a definite article, Barnes uses an infinite

---

① Discontinuity is one of the basic concepts espoused by Jacques Derrida as well. For him, time is not continuous and linear any more, but netlike. The externalization of time constitutes space; metaphysically speaking, writing "weaves" the net of time, and as such the course of writing represents the "weaving" process of the time net and the process of meaning production. In the process of "weaving," the meaning of text or writing is deferred incessantly in time and space, thus transcendental signified can never be reached and the traditional ideas in history such as continuity, causality and totality are accordingly deconstructed. Such a view is in accordance with his idea displayed in *Positions*, that is, we must subvert the conventional concepts of history (67).

article to parody on the one hand the established writing of the "history of the world" and intimates on the other its potential possibility and indeterminacy of postmodern historical writing (Buxton 56; Rubinson 175). Moreover, the "½" in the title subverts "culturally encoded number systems" (Kotte 109) and the traditional (historical) writing modes, indicative of the discontinuity in the title reading. ① What does "a half chapter" mean? Is it possible to write "a half chapter" instead of "one chapter" in our writing? Customarily not. Obviously, a cursory glance at the title would tell us that it is a "subversion of the given." As to its contents, what Barnes has written in this "novel" all the more corroborates what Salman Rushdie comments on it, that is, it is a "fiction as critique," "footnote to history" and "subversion of the given" (241). Unlike the conventional historical writing which records the "history of the world" with linear continuity, causality and totality, Barnes's writing of the "history of the world" does the opposite, "ow[ing] little debt to traditional conceptions of history" (Monterrey 416). Or as Brian Finney rightly remarks:

> Where Raleigh's [*The History of the World*] was a monumental attempt to record the history of the world starting with the Creation, Barnes's modest book runs to some 300 pages and eschews any pretence of continuity or comprehensiveness. His is merely a history among many possible histories of the world. ... Barnes's entire book can be seen as a series of digressions from those events normally considered central to any historical account of the world. ("A Worm's Eye View of History" 49)

Then, a survey of the main contents in each "chapter" of the "history of the world" would exhibit how Barnes "digresses" from and subverts the

---

① Claudia Kotte has a very thorough analysis on the title of Barnes's novel: Barnes "divides his history into ten chapters and thus conforms to our system of counting, where ten denotes a certain totality, completeness and coherence. Yet Barnes simultaneously undermines this unifying order by inserting the fragmented half-chapter 'Parenthesis' after chapter eight. He thus subverts culturally encoded number systems and alludes to the incomplete nature of his supposedly universal history even in his title" (109); moreover, as this critic writes of it in the footnote: "Barnes's *History* might ironically allude to the historical work of the French historian de Condorcet (1743–1794), who divided his history of the world into ten epochs in order to show the perfection and progress of humanity" (Kotte 109). In this sense, we can see that Barnes's writing including the title is a parody of the orthodox writing of history done by historians proper.

conventional historical writing or historical (meta)narratives. ①

Chapter One "The Stowaway" in *A History* is a revision of the Biblical story of Noah, in which Barnes presents a different, negative image of Noah from that of Noah in the Bible, and a rewriting of the story of Noah's Ark and Flood, through the expression of a damagingly tiny insect, the woodworm, whose (hi)story is not recorded in the (hi)story of the Bible. Through his rewriting, Barnes displays his negation against the traditional, positive image of Noah, his disbelief in God, laying bare a suppressed or erased voice in the writing of "history of the world," presenting an alternative picture of the "history of the world," thus subverts and revises the grand narrative of sacred history implicated in the Bible. Chapter Two "The Visitors" shifts to the 1980s to another boat—a Mediterranean cruise ship where some Western passengers are held hostages by a group of Arab terrorists, which is loosely based on the 1981 Achille-Lauro highjacking incident. In this "chapter" of the "history of the world," Barnes explores such issues as the relationship between altruism and self-interest, the individual's participation and role in the (living) history of the world, and the cultural conflict and power relations between the Eastern countries and the Western ones. Barnes's conventional narrative and vivid description of the psychology of the main character from the perspective of third person narration endows this (hi)story of the world with the aura of psychological realism. Chapter Three "The Wars of Religion" transcribes sixteenth-century courts record of a case in the diocese of Besançon, France, in which the woodworms are accused of infesting the Saint-Michel church and causing so much damage to the diocesan bishop's throne that when the bishop sits on it, it collapses and sends him crashing to the floor, giving rise to serious injury to his head. Through the "transcription" of an unusual case about some trivial issues which have engulfed the church in conflict down through the ages, Barnes addresses such subjects as the religious extremism and the

---

① The historical (meta)narratives, intricately and subtly deconstructed by Barnes in this novel, include those of eschatology of (universal) history, the Enlightenment progressive view of history, Hegel's rational view of history, Darwin's evolutionary vision of history, and even Marx's pattern of history as a sequence of tragedy and farce. Here we can briefly mention the eschatology implied in Christianity (universal) history and the others would be more or less referred to in later discussion. On the one hand, Barnes foregrounds the role of God in several of (hi)stories, confirming the Christian providential view of history, but on the other Barnes's other stories "strongly disturbs the notion of historical patterns or regularities and a direction [of universal history], let alone benevolent divine guidance [of God], in history" (Kotte 115). In other words, when Barnes's writing advances beliefs in God's providential guidance and order in history, it undermines these religious assumptions and discloses them as human projections, to which the brief explanation of the novel's contents would testify.

exclusionism visited upon the Other (including the animals), thus "revealing the kind of fanatical excesses which promote intolerance and pave the way for such events as inquisitions and religious wars," and in the meantime examines the ways in which "truth, evidence, and testimony can be twisted to support opposing viewpoints" (Sesto 66). In this "chapter" Barnes evidently provides for the reader the historical information about the case (including the specific dates and the name of the defense attorney, Monsieur Chausenee a historical figure, the information of the archival or editorial history of the documents in which the case is recorded), so as to authenticate the actual occurrence of the trial. ① Therefore, through creating the illusion of historical actuality and authenticity, the execution of freighting this (hi)story of the world with documentary material enables Barnes to explore the relationship between historical reality and fictionality, one of the most important motifs of this "novel."

As discussed in the second chapter of this research, "The Survivor," the fourth "chapter" of this "novel," elucidates the issue of fictionality of history, among others, from the eye view of a female victim of the male domination. The random shifting of the first and third person narrative voices, the fragmented presentation of reality and fiction, and the well-fabulated scheme of the "chapter" *per se* and its self-reflexive reference to the whole book constitute the main characteristics of Barnes's writing in this "chapter" as well as the whole book. In Chapter Five "Shipwreck" Barnes's writing shifts to a historical disaster in the early nineteenth century in the history of France, in which, as noted before, Barnes first of all recounts very briefly the (hi)story of the *Medusa* shipwreck, and then examines one of the first and influential oil paintings of Romanticism—*The Raft of the Medusa* by Théodore Géricault. What merits attention is that Barnes in this "chapter," via juxtaposing three different types of texts, "focuses on the textual and artistic inscription of [historical] factuality" (Monterrey 415) and as such explores the relation of history to text(uality) and of history to art. Chapter Six "The Mountain," set in the 1830s, tells a story of a female character's pious belief in religion, her conflict with her father's faith in the progress of technology, and her (suicidal) journey with a friend to the mountain where Noah anchored his Ark, as written in the Biblical (hi)stories, to show her devout homage to Noah and God. Although it is a

---

① More specifically, its inconclusive ending not only informs us of the incomplete state of the transcript but depicts its physical condition: "*Here the manuscript in the Archives Municipales de Besançon breaks off* .... *It appears from the condition of the parchment that in the course of the last four and a half centuries it has been attacked, perhaps on more than one occasion, by some species of termite, which has devoured the closing words of the* juge d'Eglise" (*HWC* 79–80, italics original).

fictional story, Barnes in this "chapter" also refers to some historical events such as the exhibitions in the 1830s of the paintings related to the *Medusa* Shipwreck, which, as observed before, implies that through the association with the chapter "Shipwreck," different types of texts mediate, exchange and negotiate with each other, thus revealing the feature of the textuality of history in some sense.

The first story of Chapter Seven "Three Simple Stories" addresses a (hi)story about the two disembarkation from the *Titanic* of Lawrence Beesley (1877–1967),[1] a survival of the *Titanic* shipwreck and the writer of *The Loss of the SS Titanic* (1912). Beesley's first camouflage as a woman to disembark the *Titanic* demonstrates that the "fittest" in "the survival of the fittest" are "merely the most cunning" (*HWC* 174), and his second disembarkation from the facsimile *Titanic* in the making of a film named *A Night to Remember* then, as the narrator concludes, best exemplifies Marx's elaboration of Hegel on history: "history repeats itself, the first time as tragedy, the second time as farce" (*HWC* 175). However, the repeated (hi)stories are not always farces. The second story of Chapter Seven deals with a Biblical myth of Jonah being swallowed by a whale, schemed and manipulated by God. After a brief interpretation of the possible meanings of this myth about Jonah and the whale, Barnes retells an actual, tragic occurrence of a sailor named James Bartley, who was swallowed by a sperm whale on August 25th, 1891 off the Falkland Island but found "still alive," when the whale was slaughtered about one day later (*HWC* 180). Although modern science denies the possibility of the (hi)story of this modern Jonah, Barnes exposits the usage of the myth of Jonah: that is, "not that myth refers us back to some original event which has been fancifully transcribed as it passed through the collective memory; but that it refers us forward to something that will happen, that must happen. Myth will become reality, however sceptical we might be" (*HWC* 181). The third story in this "chapter" involves a true historical event happening before the eve of the Second World War. A liner named *St. Louis* left the port of Hamburg at 8 p.m. on May 13th, 1939 for Cuba with 937 passengers, all but 7 Jews, but the Cuba government later refused to honor the visas for these special passengers. After Cuba, other countries in South and Central America including the United States, all refused to admit the Jews and "declined to bear the world's shame single-handed" (*HWC* 186), so that the liner had to

---

[1] This is a true (hi)story occurring to Barnes himself. The young narrator is the incarnation of himself, for Barnes has actually met Lawrence Beesley and thus writes of his experience in the story: Barnes told an interviewer that "[t]hat simple story is completely true, that's about me" (Guignery, "History" 66).

float on the sea and eventually decided to turn back to Europe till suddenly Belgium announced that it would accept some of the Jews, which was followed by Holland, Britain and France. Ironically, when the Britain contingent from the *St. Louis* docked at Southampton on Wednesday June 21st, these Jews "were able to reflect that their wanderings at sea had lasted precisely forty days and forty nights" (*HWC* 188). Once again, Biblical history or myth had become modern reality. Thus, by retelling one of human history's most catastrophic events in a flat, documentary style, Barnes suggests his critique on human venality, hypocrisy and injustice.

Barnes's eighth chapter "Upstream!" comprises a series of fictional letters written by Charlie the protagonist to his estranged girlfriend in London about what he has experienced in film making. What Charlie has written takes place in a remote area in the jungles of South America, where the film about two Catholic missionaries who explored that region some two hundred years ago is being shot, in which Charlie is playing the role of Father Firmin, a stern and authoritarian Jesuit priest who is against baptizing the Indians while his co-star Matt, abrasive and egocentric, is playing Firmin's more moderate and open-minded colleague, Father Antonia, who favors converting the Indians. The remainder of the cast consists of the Indians who are hired as extras to perform the same tasks as their ancestors did before. When the civilized Western men aim to shoot a film about two missionaries' story, the primitive Indians hold that the two white men who dress in missionary robes and recite lines in front of a large glass eye are not actors but the real missionaries themselves; in consequence, the historical scene is duplicated except that an accident happening to Matt the actor results in his death. Herein Barnes investigates the relation of fiction to reality through his well-fabulated Chinese box structure via writing a series of fictional letters which recount the movie-making of a fictitious film in which fictitious actors impersonate two figures whose historicity, though supposedly real, is just as fictitious as that of the actors who perform them in the film.

Between the eighth "chapter" and the ninth "chapter," there is the "½" "chapter" — "Parenthesis." In this half "chapter," Barnes the writer's voice is brought to the fore to such a degree that the narrator identifies himself as "Julian Barnes," speaking to us directly as an author to his readers and that the narrator refers to the themes and motifs which have been discussed before and will be addressed in later "chapters."[1] Briefly

---

[1] Barnes insists that this half-chapter is the one occasion in the book where he dispenses with the mask of the fiction writer and offers his personal truth, just as he says: "I did this. You've got any complaints, look at me. ... I'm responsible" (Stuart 15).

speaking, "Parenthesis" is a meditation on love and its significance in human history and on its relation to truth and history, or in simpler words, it is "about the tension between love and history" (Salyer 226). It is here that love is offered as a substitute solution to history, for instance: "Love won't change the history of the world ..., but it will do something much more important: teach us to stand up to history, to ignore its chin-out-strut" (*HWC* 238). In addition, through his meditation on love and truth, Barnes also discusses the issue of history in an intensive way; that is, Barnes presents his postmodern view of history in his (re)thinking about the relationships between love, truth and history. More importantly, in this self-conscious or metafictional writing, Barnes expresses his questioning of historical objectivity or the objective historical truth, and intimates his endorsement of such postmodern views of history as the textuality of history and the fictionality of history.

Chapter Nine "Project Ararat," based on the career of American astronaut James Irwin (1930–1991), recounts the early life and career of Spike Tiggler (Irwin's fictional counterpart in this story), his exploration of the moon as a lunar astronaut in the Apollo space program, and his expedition to the mountain of Ararat to find Noah's Ark, through which Barnes depicts Tiggler's transformation from the man of science into the man of God and explores the subject of the tug-of-war, interplay or conflict between dogged faith and nudging doubt or between religion and science in general. Unlike this "chapter" which is loosely based on some historical facts, the final "chapter" of the book "The Dream" fictionalizes a "brave new" Heaven as the ending of the "history of the world." To be brief, this final "chapter" is "aptly a re-vision of heaven couched in the framework of a dream within a dream" (Salyer 229), or an illusionary or dreamy delineation of a New Heaven, in which Barnes speculates upon its blessings and paradoxes, and "reveals the tiny spark of 'Odyssean' restlessness in human nature which renders man unsuited for a life of eternal pleasure" (Sesto 108). What cannot be omitted is that as a final "chapter" of the "history of the world," it also briefly refers to some images or scenes turning up in the earlier "chapters" of the book, which nevertheless could be maintained as Barnes's writing strategy of rendering the collection of more than ten short (hi)stories as a whole, otherwise it could by no means be classified as a novel.

The brief reading of the "history of the world in 10 ½ chapters" evinces that Barnes "does not aim at replacing one sort of master narrative or all-englobing historical plot with yet another totalizing global order" (Kotte 123), that "it is difficult to derive one theme from this book as readers are often accustomed to doing with novels," that "history does not have one theme" (Salyer 221) but many and various ones, and that history delineated in this book is discontinuous and fragmented. It is just in this way of writing about history, i. e., in the strategy of what Lévi-Strauss has called *bricolage*, that Barnes exhibits his postmodern view of history, that is, history is discontinuous and fragmented. Hereinbelow, we can make a brief interpretation about Barnes's writing of discontinuity and fragmentation of history in this "novel." First of all, histories written as such are in a nonlinear causality. It seems that there are near-beginning and end in this "history of the world," but subsequent (hi)stories are not in a chronological order and with no causality as well, for "between chapter 1's origins and chapter 10's ends the remaining eight and a half chapters do not progress chronologically" (Finney, "A Worm's Eye View of History" 51). For instance, in terms of time or period, Chapter Two is set in the 1980s, Chapter Three in the sixteenth century, Chapter Four in the late 1980s, Chapter Five in the 1810s, Chapter Six in the 1830s, Chapter Seven in the 1950s, 1891, and 1939, Chapter Eight in the 1980s, Chapter Nine in 1977 and Chapter Ten in the very far future. This reveals that the (hi)stories in the "novel" are not linear at all, "thus undermining notions of a direction in [universal] history" (Kotte 107), that there is no cause-effect relationship between any two subsequently adjacent chapters, and that "[t]he relation between [Barnes's] narrative images or chapters is one of disjunction, ironic juxtaposition, disparity" (Finney, "A Worm's Eye View of History" 69). Or as a critic perceptively points out, "Barnes's *History* as a whole appears random and chaotic, since the sequence of chapters and stories resists any chronological order, let alone a plausible sequence of cause and effect" (Kotte 108). As the critic continues to contend:

> Apart from this constant moving back and forth in time, neither time nor place are continuous, for we are introduced to events in the Mediterranean, France, Australia, England, Germany, South America and the United States in consecutive chapters.
>
> Most conspicuously, *A History of the World* lacks causality and logical links, for none of the events can be explained in terms of a preceding chapter nor does it in any way account for subsequent stories. Events do not evolve or develop in time, but are simply accumulated and juxtaposed. The simple logic of cause-and-effect, before-and-after appears to be out of order. Given that the various episodes seem to have been selected and ordered at random, one might well wonder how these dispersed, fragmented pieces of narrative can add up to an integrated whole, *A History of the World*. (Kotte 108–109)

In short, we can say that the (hi)stories in this "novel" are in a discontinuous or disordered order, and that they are fragmented, denying "symmetry, teleology, totality, and hierarchy—all the expected conventions of realist [conventional] historiography" (Rubinson 174-175), which could be corroborated in and through its form and structure. ①

Still, the "novel" incorporates heterogeneous materials covering a number of genres, such as a playful parody of the Old Testament tale of Noah and the Ark, archival material of an animal trial in sixteenth-century France, letters and telegrams from an actor in the rain forest to his wife in England and a learned art-historical disquisition of Géricault's canvas *The Raft of the Medusa*. Or as other critics insightfully note, it is a mix of "fact and fiction, allegory, parable, art history and mythology" (Cape 38), "a multiplicity of … a fable, a political thriller, a courtroom drama, science fiction (or a psychiatric case history), a historical narrative, art criticism, epistolary fiction, an essay on love, and a dream-vision" (Finney, "A Worm's Eye View of History" 58); and in a more general sense, it is "a compendium and critical commentary of theological, legal, scholarly, literary, speculative, and traditional 'historical' genres of writing" (Rubinson 165). *Ergo* (therefore) the application of heterogeneous genres, the constant characteristic of Barnes's postmodern historical writing, foregrounds the presence of narrativity and its unavoidable role in postmodern historiographical writing, suggesting that "history is the sum of our attempts to make sense of our past through numerous narrative genres, whether they are traditionally considered historical or not" (Rubinson 165). In addition, the narrative voices behind this writing of the "history of the world" are also worth attention. There are the voices of the human beings including a female victim and of the lower insects; there are omnipresent perspectives, and the limited ones; there are first person narratives voices and those of the third. More specifically, Barnes's novel starts with the morally superior voice of the woodworm in Chapter One; there is the absurdly self-important voice employed in the French medieval law courts in Chapter Three; the art historian takes over in the second part of Chapter Five; there is the egotistical epistolary voice of the actor in Chapter Eight; there are several first-person narratives, including that of the possibly delusional character of Chapter Four, the eighteen-year-old prep-school master of the first simple story in

---

① What could not be denied is the fact that there are some recurrent images resonating in some of the "chapters" such as those of woodworm and a journey on the sea (water), which, however, does not cancel out the features of discontinuity and fragmentation of history in Barnes's "novel," and which is but made good use of by Barnes to illustrate the characteristic of historical repetitiveness.

Chapter Seven, and the dreamer of Chapter Ten who wakes up in a distinctly twentieth-century heaven; still there is the highly personal, mildly didactic voice of a narrator who takes the place of the position of the author in the half-chapter. In a nutshell, different perspectives and multiple voices (including a remarkably wide range of speech modes), intertwining with each other, endow the book with the attribute of discursive heterogeneity instead of a single, unifying (pseudo-third-person) narrative voice which is nevertheless the typical feature of conventional historical (meta)narratives such as *The City of God*, The Bible and other established historical writings. Accordingly, we can maintain that in so doing "Barnes was straining to differentiate his 'historical' work from that of [conventional] historians who aspire to a stance of objectivity" (Finney, "A Worm's Eye View of History" 52).

Under such circumstances, it is reasonable to contend that even if some of the chapters are thematically linked with each other, these "chapters" are nevertheless independent of each other, bearing the construction and significance of their own and as such each is "a discontinuous set composed of domains of history" (Lévi-Strauss 259); that even if Barnes himself defends its entirety, it is discontinuous and fragmented not just in the form but in contents as well. Or in other words, histories in this "novel" are but "historical scraps" (Frank Ankersmit's term); and their independence just manifests that they have turned out to be the focus of postmodern historical writing. That is to say, postmodern historical discourse focuses its attention on the discontinuity and fragmentation of history instead of the total, universal History or historical metanarratives. It is in this sense that Barnes refers to the "history of the world" in the "Parenthesis" like this: "The history of the world? Just voices echoing in the dark; images that burn for a few centuries and then fade; stories, old stories that sometimes seem to overlap; strange links, impertinent connections" (*HWC* 240). The emphasis on the "strange links, impertinent connections" is later echoed in Barnes's another postmodern fiction *England, England*: "History doesn't relate" (70). Therefore, what Jackie Buxton observes about Barnes's "theses on history" can be quoted to conclude this part:

> Taken together, these fragments [in *A History*] constitute anything but a grand narrative in the ordinary sense of the word. ... Barnes's theses specifically resist narrative coherence and specifically refuse the meliorative trajectory propounded by classical historicism. Barnes's history offers nothing like a traditional historicist approach, one that is dictated by cause and effect and wedded to a concept of progress. (65)

As indicated in the quotation, when Barnes's postmodern historical writing deconstructs the continuity and causality in conventional historiography by means of foregrounding historical discontinuity and fragmentation, it also undermines the "concept of progress" in traditional discourse of history or historiography.

ii. "Is This Progress?"

Besides showing his interrogation and subversion of historical continuity and totality implied in historical (meta)narratives, Julian Barnes through his writing displays his incredulity toward the progressive view or progressiveness of history, which is undoubtedly one of the prominent attributes in such historical (meta)narratives as that of The Enlightenment. In general, Enlightenment spirit highlights the emancipation of humankind from the dominance of the Providence, the significance of rationality, and the progressiveness of human society and history. The myth of history as rational progression is embedded in all of the major Western philosophies of history but is no longer justifiable. Or to put it another way, the belief in Enlightenment rationality[①] and progress(iveness) has dominated the Western world for centuries, but is pointedly questioned by postmodernists. Barnes, like most of the postmodernists, always queries the view of Enlightenment rationality and progress(iveness), just as he told an interviewer: "the idea that we've been making constant, inevitable, grand progress seems to me not really likely, not really plausible" (Guignery, "History" 67). This could also be testified in his writing in relation to the issues of history, be it in short stories or in novels.

In "Junction," one of the short stories in *Cross Channel* (21–42), Barnes through the expression of his several characters articulates one typical attitude toward the construction of railways between Rouen and Paris, France, in the 1840s. In the story, an artist, who is considered as "too young to be so old-fashioned," "cannot see the immense beauty of the railways" and maintains that "scientific advances make us blind to moral defects. They give us the illusion that we are making progress, which [tends] to be dangerous" (*Cross Channel* 39). Such a view about progress is

---

① According to James Martin Lang, Enlightenment rationality is the rationality "which ties the instruments and procedures of reason, aesthetics, history, etc. to a teleological or theological understanding of the world" (208) and "which had traditionally underpinned our understanding of history and the practice of historiography" (255). So is true of Enlightenment progress. *Ergo*, it is not unsafe to maintain that the incredulity toward Enlightenment rationality and progress signifies the one toward traditional history and historiography.

very similar to Flaubert's. In "Louise Colet's Version," the eleventh section of *Flaubert's Parrot*, we can find that Flaubert is such an artist who held such a view about the railways and "had already decided to be old before his time," when "he wasn't yet thirty" (*FP* 148). As Barnes notices, Flaubert "hated the invention" of railways, believing that "it was an odious means of transport" and pronounced it a boring subject (*FP* 108); and more significantly, Flaubert "didn't just hate the railway as such; he hated the way it flattered people with the illusion of progress. *What was the point of scientific advance without moral advance?* The railway would merely permit more people to move about, meet and be stupid together," thus for Flaubert it became one of "the misdeeds of modern civilization" (*FP* 108, italics added). Barnes refers to Flaubert's attitude toward "progress" in other places as well. In "Cross Channel" one of his most complex or heterogeneous chapters of the same book, Barnes in his pursuit of an authentic Flaubert makes some comments on Flaubert directly: "Flaubert didn't believe in progress: especially not in moral progress, which is all that matters. The age he lived in was stupid; the new age, brought in by the Franco-Prussian war, would be even stupider" (*FP* 85). Then Barnes poses his question about and voices his suspicion toward progress in modern society, in light of the narrator's observation on "a modern ship of fools" in a cross-channel ferry who are "working out the profit on their duty-free; having more drinks at the bar than they want; playing the fruit machines; aimlessly circling the deck; making up their minds how honest to be at customs; waiting for the next order from the ship's crew as if the crossing of the Red Sea depended on it" (*FP* 85). Later Barnes incessantly asks the questions about "progress:" "Is This Progress?" (*FP* 85), "Does the world progress? Or does it merely shuttle back and forth like a ferry?" (*FP* 105); "Does life improve?" (*FP* 167). Through his interpretation of Flaubert's view about progress and his incessant enquiry about progress through the voices of his narrator and other characters, we can sense that Barnes is more or less on the side with Flaubert, showing his incredulity toward the progress of human history with no moral advance.

Moreover, a close reading would convince us that Barnes's disbelief in progress(iveness) of history is also implied in *A History*, which will be examined in detail in the discussion below. First of all, in his writing about the "history of the world," Barnes continues his query on the development of technology. For instance, in "The Survivor," Barnes, through the consciousness of his character Kathleen Ferris, "reveals the underside of technological developments and thus questions notions of advance and progress in history" (Kotte 117–118). As the narrative goes:

Nowadays the ships had got bigger and bigger, while the crew had got smaller and smaller, and everything was done by technology. They just programmed a computer in the Gulf or wherever, and the ship practically sailed itself all the way to London or Sydney. It was much nicer for the owners, who saved lots of money, and much nicer for the crew, who only had to worry about the boredom. Most of the time they sat around below deck drinking beer ... . Drinking beer and watching videos.

... It said that in the old days there was always someone up in the crow's nest or the bridge, watching for trouble. But nowadays the big ships didn't have a lookout any more, or at least the lookout was just a man staring from time to time at a screen with a lot of blips on it. In the old days if you were lost at sea in a raft or a dinghy or something, and a boat came along, there was a pretty good chance of being rescued. You waved and shouted and fired off any rockets you had; you ran your shirt up to the top of the mast; and there were always people keeping an eye out for you. *Nowadays you can drift in the ocean for weeks, and a supertanker finally comes along, and it goes right past. The radar won't pick you up because you're too small, and it's pure luck if anybody happens to be hanging over the rail being sick.* There had been lots of cases where castaways who would have been rescued in the old days simply weren't picked up; and even incidents of people being run down by the ships they thought were coming to rescue them. ... That's what's wrong with the world, she thought. *We've given up having lookouts. We don't think about saving other people, we just sail on by relying on our machines.* Everyone's below deck, having a beer ... . (*HWC* 95-96, italics added)

For Barnes's part, the excessive reliance on machines or technological advancement makes humankind become inhumane, irrational and illogical and lose its essential humanity, and the progress in technology does not necessarily mean the advance of humanity, without which the progress of human society and history would turn out to be meaningless; without which the emancipation of humankind would turn out to be a vain dream. In this sense, Barnes calls into question the progressive spirit of The Enlightenment, like most of postmodernists do.

Still, we can perceive that in *A History* Barnes refers to Charles

Darwin's theory of evolution① and deconstructs what Darwin proposes about "the survival of the fittest." It is commonly acknowledged that Darwin discovers the law of development of the organic nature, or a specific theory of evolutionary mechanisms which could be used to explain the organic changes in the realm of nature. Later, Darwin's theory is transferred to the field of society so that social Darwinists uphold the survival of the fittest human race or the superior social group. In general, Darwin's theory, different from the Biblical (meta)narrative which foregrounds the role of God, from Hegel's theology which underlines the role of spirit of rationality, from Marx's historical materialism which emphasizes the roles of economic conditions and class struggles, highlights the role of nature in the mechanisms of its evolution; and like these (historical) (meta)narratives, it stresses continuity and progress in nature and human history. In some sense, Barnes's underscoring of historical discontinuity and fragmentation, as discussed before, suggests his skepticism about Darwin's theory of evolution as well. More directly, Barnes renders Darwin's theory, especially that of "the survival of the fittest," in a deconstructive way, so as to challenge its justice, thus undermining the progressive view or narrative of human history.

The Darwinian concept of the "survival of the fittest" includes the concepts of selection, the separation of "the clean and the unclean" —a phrase which reverberates throughout Barnes's *A History*. In light of Darwin's theory of natural evolution, the animals in "The Stowaway," the first "chapter" of the novel, know that they have "the way of things:" they are "brutal, cannibalistic and deceitful" in nature; they eat each other, and the weaker species know all too well what to expect if they cross the path of something that is both bigger and hungry, and one animal is capable of killing another (*HWC* 10). Therefore, only the robust, strong and healthy species can survive on Noah's Ark while the weak, small and sick animals and crossbreeds die out. Moreover, in "Shipwreck," the fifth "chapter" of the book, the brutalities, cruelties, and cannibalism on the raft of the *Medusa* also attest to the view of natural survival, not of the righteous but of

---

① Although Darwin merely discussed evolution of man in a few sentences at the end of *On the Origin of Species*, these sentences, as James Martin Lang perceptively points out, "are really suggestions that researchers in the sciences of humanity should consider the further applicability of his paradigm" (67). More specifically, Darwin's "a few sentences" go like this: "In the distant future I see open fields for far more important researches. Psychology will be based on a new foundation, that of the necessary acquirement of each mental power and capacity by gradation. Light will be thrown on the origin of man and his history" (359). What is implied in these sentences is more fully developed later in Darwin's *Descent of Man* (1871), as observed by Lang (68). Therefore, to discuss what is written in Julian Barnes's *A History* in light of Darwin's theory of evolution in a general sense would not be inappropriate.

those who are physically the strongest and brawniest: "On the raft, it was not virtue that triumphed, but strength; and there was little mercy to be had" (*HWC* 128). Similarly, in "Upstream!," as the narrator finds in the rain forest that the average life expectancy of the Indians is about thirty five years, he comments that "it's only the fantastically healthy ones who can get by at all" (*HWC* 205). A few instances as such could exemplify that Barnes endorses to some extent what Darwin's theory upholds— "the survival of the fittest."

However, what is implied in this "novel" is that Barnes undermines the concept of the natural survival of the fittest when he ostensibly substantiates it. In the first "chapter," the woodworm on Noah's Ark challenges Darwin's theory of natural selection through disclosing how "unnatural" the survival of some animals during the Flood is and how little it is linked with adaptation or fitness but rather with Noah's moody temper (*HWC* 12–16). Such animals as behemoth, salamander, carbuncle, basilisk, griffon, sphinx, hippogriff and unicorn are all killed and eaten by Noah and his family out of his arbitrary and brutal personality. Still, the woodworm intimates that "a mysterious outbreak of food poisoning" (*HWC* 8) and the death of both Simians, who are killed by a falling spar (*HWC* 24), are most likely not coincidences but the outcome of Noah's wily intrigue. More importantly, the woodworm undercuts Darwin's theory by stating that "man is a very unevolved species compared to the animals" (*HWC* 28). As the woodworm narrator continues to defend itself:

> We don't deny, of course, your cleverness, your considerable potential. But you are, as yet, at an early stage of your development. We, for instance, are always ourselves: that is what it means to be evolved. We are what we are, and we know what that is. You don't expect a cat suddenly to start barking, do you, or a pig to start lowing? But this is what, in a manner of speaking, those of us who made the Voyage on the Ark learned to expect from your species. One moment you bark, one moment you mew; one moment you wish to be wild, one moment you wish to be tame. We knew where we were with Noah only in this one respect: that we never knew where we were with him. (*HWC* 28-29)

In "Shipwreck," Barnes mentions the fact that "the strength" on the raft of *Medusa* triumphed, which to some degree confirms what Darwin postulates, "the survival of the fittest." However, when the frigate shipwrecked and the raft was built, there was a selection of those who embarked on the backup lifeboat and those who stayed on the raft. This "selection" certainly does not fit in with Darwin's theory: the aristocrats, the governmental officers and other upper class members got on the backup lifeboats and safely arrived at the destination; the lower officers, the sailors and the crews embarked on the improvised raft and only about one-tenth of them survived after fifteen days' ordeal on the sea. Still, as noted in the second chapter of this research, Kathleen Ferris "the survivor" also speculates about the survival of the fittest, poses her question about it, and defends "The Survival of the Worries" (*HWC* 97).

In addition, the "farce" about Lawrence Beesley in this "novel" also challenges Darwin's theory of evolution. The eighteen-year-old first person narrator knows of Beesley's (hi)story from the latter's family members that Beesley "escaped from the *Titanic* in women's clothing" (*HWC* 173). The knowledge of Beesley's (hi)story verifies the narrator's "view of the world": "Life's a cheat and all things shew it/I thought so once and now I know it" (*HWC* 173-174). Then the narrator thinks of it "on a wider scale" and refers to what theorists maintain, that is, "life amounted to the survival of the fittest" but reverses the notion of Darwin by way of questioning it:

> [D]id not the Beesley hypothesis prove that the "fittest" were merely the most cunning? The heroes, the solid men of yeoman virtue, the good breeding stock, even the captain (especially the captain!) — they all went down nobly with the ship; whereas the cowards, the panickers, the deceivers found reasons for skulking in a lifeboat. Was this not deft proof of how the human gene-pool was constantly deteriorating, how bad blood drove out good? (*HWC* 174)

It is evident that the narrator's wondering, especially the last questions in the above quotation, undermines the view of progress of humankind and history. The issue of natural or human selection appears again in the (hi)story about the Jews in Chapter Seven of this "novel." After negotiation with the Cuba authorities, 250 Jewish refugees on the liner *St. Louis* seemed to have the possibility of disembarkation at the Havana harbor, and at this moment, the narrator queries, "how would you choose the 250 who were to be allowed off the Ark? Who would separate the clean from the unclean? Was it to be done by casting lots?" (*HWC* 184). The enquiry patently contradicts what Noah (or God) has done on the Ark, i.e., separating the clean and the unclean animals in an arbitrary way; but more significantly, what is suggested in Barnes's writing is that it evokes the horrible Holocaust to our mind, "the Nazi project of purifying the German race, eliminating its 'imperfect' (Jewish) elements" (Kotte 118). "Is this progress?" Barnes would interrogate. It is a historical fact that the survival of the Aryan and the extinction of the Jewish people is anything but a natural selection; it is nevertheless savagely organized by the Nazis. All in all, Barnes's deconstructive writing of Darwin's theory of evolution just testifies that the theory of "the survival of the fittest" cannot represent a cogent pattern for the course of human history and that the progressive concept of the human world and of history implicated behind it cannot hold water either.

While deconstructing Darwin's evolutionary view of progress (in and of history), Barnes also subverts Hegel's rational view of progress embodied in his philosophical thinking of history. Hegel established his theory of world history via supplanting God with the objective and absolute spirit and the faith with Reason. History, for Hegel's part, is the rational development of the spirit in time, a linear, orderly, consistent, systematic and logical process. Nevertheless, what should be pointed out is that the absolute spirit or the principle of Reason must make use of the personal interests and passions of the "world-historical" figures such as Julius Caesar or Bonaparte Napoleon, who, in Hegel's view, can bring about new epochs that embody a higher stage of the absolute spirit (qtd. in Kotte 116). In a general sense, Hegel developed a dialectical model that underlines the progress of ideas, the transformation from thesis and antithesis to the culmination in a higher, transcending synthesis. Undoubtedly, Barnes's writing in *A History* also undermines Hegel's historical view. As mentioned before, Barnes's "history of the world" in this book bears no linear, orderly, consistent and systematic process; it is in general discontinuous and fragmented; the development of the "history of the world" as such is irrational, illogical, and inhumane, without rationality and with no process of the synthesis resulting from thesis and antithesis. Therefore we would agree with the view that:

> Contrary to Hegel's assumption, history does not unfold rationally, as the numerous arbitrary accidents portrayed in *A History of the World in 10½ Chapters* reveal. No principle of causality, no coherent agency can account for the terror of history [of the world], for events as contingent as killings, suffering, pain and death. The aleatory element inherent in catastrophes works against their rational interpretation. (Kotte 120)

For instance, the killing of some of the rare animals on Noah's Ark, as noted before, lacks rationality and logic; similarly, the course of events happening in "The Visitors" turns out to be arbitrary, and the killing of the Western tourists by Arab terrorists lacks any rationality as well. What's more, Barnes's writing in this book seems to stress the coincidences and accidents or aleatory elements, which would be otherwise rationalized in conventional historical writings and thus dismissed or eliminated from traditional historiography. In a word, Barnes's gainsay of Hegel's spirit of rationality and the process of synthesis signals his interrogation about the rational view of progress implied in Hegel's hypothesis of history.

It is safe to conclude here that Barnes in and through his postmodern historical writing, be it in *Flaubert's Parrot* or in *A History*, questions and subverts the traditional narrative or view of progress, which could be identified in such historical (meta)narratives as those of The Enlightenment and Hegel's rational view of (world) history. Unlike them, which emphasize progress, rationality and emancipation of human subject and society, Barnes's postmodern historical writing substantiates that such features as irrationality, illogicality, coincidence and arbitrariness have turned out to be the constant of the "history of the world," in which humanity is distorted and progress is under suspicion. Thus we can say that what Barnes delineates (in *A History*) is but a reflection of postmodern view of history, a postmodern presentation of the "history of the world" and a "subversion of the given" historical (meta)narratives.

II. Plurality of History

In terms of postmodern discourse of history, the plurality of history signifies that there is not only one kind of history or one pattern for the course of human history. This one pattern or model of historical discourse is often labeled as Eurocentrism, which to a great extent results in the domination of the Western countries over non-Western countries, excluding the diversity and variety of other races' cultures and histories. Similarly, this centrism also suppresses the female and non-human beings' voices in the design of the blueprint of the "history of the world." Human beings, as the master of the (natural) world, naturally, would not give voice to non-human beings or animals, for they are considered as a-rational, without thinking and subjective motility; and human beings turn out to be the protagonists of human history. The female voices are always suppressed in the patriarchy society of male domination, but not liberated from that domination till the 1960s. Accordingly, for a very long period of time, what dominates in the conventional writing of history is always the male voice of humankind, while racial minority voices, female voices (and non-human beings' voices) are all excluded, eliminated, erased or effaced. Different from the traditional discourse of history, postmodern discourse of history focuses its attention on micro-histories, such as local history, women's history, and histories of other cultures and races, and defends different patterns or models for the courses of different histories. In short, postmodern historical discourse rejects the monistic view of history, or to be exact, the Eurocentric view of history, and upholds historical heterogeneity, otherness, variety and plurality. With the diffusion and dissemination of postmodern theory and discourse of history, the pluralistic view of history turns out to be in the air as well. No wonder, it also affects the (historical) writing of postmodern novelists, which could be corroborated in the writings of such British writers as Antonia S. Byatt, Julian Barnes, Salman Rushdie and Jeanette Winterson.

As referred to in the Introduction, Barnes is considered as "the chameleon of British letters," never writes the same book twice, and known for his flexibility and variety embodied in formal experimentation and thematic profundity. It is also the typical feature of Barnes's postmodern historical writing. As a writer, Barnes never confines his vision to some single and sole perspective of Anthropocentrism or anthropolatric centrism, therefore there are voices, no matter how weak and peripheral they are, of some very tiny insects in *A History*. As a Western writer, Barnes never limits himself to some exclusive viewpoint of Eurocentrism or Westerncentrism so that it is no wonder that he devotes a half of his book to a racial victim to dig out and revise a forgotten history of racial prejudice in *Arthur & George*. As a Western male writer, Barnes never restrains himself from the female eye view of writing fiction to the extent that he writes *Staring at the Sun* from the perspective of Jean Sergeant a female protagonist, one section in *Flaubert's Parrot* about Flaubert from the angle of Louise Colet Flaubert's mistress, one "chapter" of "history of the world" in *A History* from the standpoint of Kathleen Ferris an abused woman and *England, England* with Martha Cochrane as the protagonist and centre of consciousness. Still, Barnes endows with virtue and sympathy some of female characters in his other novels and short stories, such as Annick in *Metroland*, Ann Mears in *Before She Met Me*, the heroine in "East Wind" (*Pulse* 3–18), Maria Solinsky in *The Porcupine* and Veronica Ford in *The Sense of an Ending*. Therefore, as a critic points out, "[a]s is usually the case in Barnes's novels, it is the woman who represents honesty and common sense" (Puddington 63). And as discussed in the second chapter of this research, Barnes draws upon the female perspective to (re)present alternative pictures of history or historical figure, thus proffering possibilities to rethink historical truth and verity and to recognize the fictionality of history or historiography, epistemologically. In a word, the female perspective plays a vital role in the postmodern historical writing of Barnes's work, though with different focalizations. Herein this section will examine Barnes's exploration on the historical plurality from alternative viewpoints; that is, it will deal with how Barnes in *A History* questions and revises sacred history recorded in the Bible about Noah and the Flood through the voice of a woodworm, to present an alternative version of part of Christian History, and how Barnes in *Arthur &*

George digs out and rewrites of a forgotten history about the racial discrimination impinged on a racial Other and of a famous historical figure's life (hi)story, so as to expose the implied anthropological bias in such historical (meta)narrative as Christian History and the (unconscious) racial prejudice in British official writing of history.

i. History in an Animal Version

As one of the grand narratives of history, Christian History focuses on the genesis, the process (or progress) and the transcendental emancipation of human subject. It is, as it were, written from the perspective of and for the humankind and as such the voices of other species are either marginalized or erased. Do other species have rationality and wisdom? Do they have a written history? Possibly not. However, we cannot deny that there are two kinds of worlds, the natural world and the human world; as a result, they would have their own respective (hi)story. It might not be possible for the non-human beings to write their own history, but it would be likely to write some human history from the non-human being's perspective. In fact, many a writer such as Jonathan Swift (1667–1745), Lev Tolstoy (1828–1910), Virginia Woolf (1882–1941), George Orwell (1903–1950) and Orhan Pamuk (1952–),[①] among others, all have written (hi)stories of human beings from the animals' focalization; and such execution of writing fiction is often labeled as the technique of "defamilarization." More or less, such stratagem of writing aims to subvert the exclusive perspective of anthropological centrism, in order to take in the possible viewpoints of perceiving the world and (re)present its diversity and plurality, which is a subversion of the grand narrative written by human beings. Julian Barnes, in "The Stowaway," the first "chapter" of *A History*, also makes good use of the animal angle to demonstrate a different version of the sacred genesis of human beings from that recorded (especially) in the Bible, to subvert scared history and revise the dominating (but perhaps not absolutely authentic) (meta)narrative of sacred history.

As many critics have observed, "The Stowaway" is a revisionist account of Noah's Ark and the Flood (Buxton 61; Kotte 108, 110; Monterrey 418; Rubin 13; Rubinson 165; Salyer 220), but not many reviewers have

---

① For instance, Swift's *Gulliver's Travels*, Tolstoy's novella about a horse, Woolf's *Flush: A Biography*, Orwell's *Animal Farm*, and Pamuk's *My Name Is Red* proffer different visions of the world from the perspective of animals, deconstructing to some extent the anthropological centrism dominating the writing of (hi)story for thousands of years.

examined it in detail. ① A critic points out that this "novel" "problematizes more than history—it problematizes the sacred" (Salyer 221), which could be considered as a footnote to Barnes's unconventional writing of history in "The Stowaway." How does Barnes problematize the sacred (history) in it? At first, the first person, animal narrator tells us that the Ark is "more than just a single ship" (*HWC* 4), and that the very name is given to "the whole flotilla," not for a single ship, for it is not possible "to cram the entire animal kingdom into something a mere three hundred cubits long" (*HWC* 4). According to the narrator's account, we know that Noah's Ark consists of eight vessels, but on the "journey" only Noah's Ark survives, the other lost in the Flood (*HWC* 5-6). Then, Barnes's narrator briefly mentions the duration of the Flood, questions and retools the Biblical record of it: "It rained for forty days and forty nights? Well, naturally it didn't .... No, it rained for about a year and a half .... And the waters were upon the earth for a hundred and fifty days? Bump that up to about four years" (*HWC* 4). However, if we are familiar with Genesis, we would know that "the rain was upon the earth forty days and forty nights" (Genesis 7: 12) and "the waters prevailed upon the earth an hundred and fifty days" (Genesis 7: 24). Barnes's revision of the authoritative, sacred text includes more than such simple queries, which is illustrated in his rewriting of the embarkation on the Ark, the image of Noah, the mission of the Ark, and other "truths" about the Flood (hi)story.

As a witness of the Flood, the animal narrator recounts in detail how Noah picks out the animals for the Ark, which is nevertheless not explained in the Bible. In light of the Bible, the description of the embarkation on the Ark is very succinct: "Noah went in, and his sons, and his wife, and his sons' wives with him, into the ark, because of the waters of the flood. /Of clean beasts, and of beasts that are not clean, and of fowls, and of every thing that creepeth upon the earth, /There went in two and two unto Noah into the ark, the male and the female" (Genesis 7: 7-9). Evidently, there is no delineation of how Noah selects other species for the Ark. Barnes rewrites it as such: Noah and his staff made an advertisement to "select the best pair that presented itself," and "[s]ince they didn't want to cause a universal panic, they announced a competition for twosomes ... and told contestants to present themselves at Noah's gate by a certain month" (*HWC* 6-7) ; such

---

① The (hi)story of Noah and the Deluge in the Bible covers about three pages, ranging from Chapter Six to Chapter Eight in Genesis. Barnes's rewriting of this (hi)story covers about 28 pages, extending it to a postmodern version of genesis of human beings, with profound readability and novel visionariness. The writing of this chapter originated from Barnes's idea of "rewriting the Bible," as he told James A. Schiff in "A Conversation with Julian Barnes."

a strategy did not arouse many an animal's interest and rendered many of them not embark on the Ark. What's more, as the animal narrator claims, "the arrangements" "were a shambles," for Noah "got behind with the building of the arks," thus giving insufficient attention to the selection of the animals (*HWC* 7). Therefore, the "normally presentable pair that came along was given the nod—this appeared to be the system; there was certainly no more than the scantiest examination of pedigree" (*HWC* 7). As to the selection of two of each species, the narrator corrects that, some creatures "were simply Not Wanted On Voyage,"① of whom the species of the narrator is one, so that they had to stow away, and that "any number of beasts, with a perfectly good legal argument for being a separate species, had their claims dismissed" (*HWC* 7). And then, the animal narrator provides more details it witnessed during the selection of the species for the arks: some splendid animals, arriving without a mate, "had to be left behind;" some families, refusing to be separated from their offspring, "choose to die together;" medical inspections were "often of a brutally intrusive nature," for all night long the air outside Noah's stockade was heavy with the wailings of the rejected (*HWC* 7). Still, the brutal medical inspections result in "much jealousy and bad behavior:" some of the nobler species simply paddled away into the forest, declining to survive on the insulting terms offered them by God and Noah; and harsh and envious words were spoken about fish; the amphibians began to look distinctly smug; birds practiced staying in the air as long as possible; certain types of monkey were occasionally seen trying to construct crude rafts of their own (*HWC* 8). Such a survey shows that Barnes's revision of the embarkation scene is not a mere expansion of what is recorded in the Bible; it is also a subversive rewriting of sacred history. This subversion of the "truth" of sacred history is all the more exemplified in Barnes's revision of the image of Noah, which will be illuminated in the discussion to follow.

First of all, the animal narrator mentions the physical features of Noah, which seems to be not recorded in the Bible: Noah "was a large man," "about the size of a gorilla, although there the resemblance ends;" Noah was "an ugly old thing, both graceless in movement and indifferent to personal

---

① As Jackie Buxton points out, the capitalized prohibition is Barnes's self-conscious citation of the fictional narrative on which the chapter under discussion is modeled: Timothy Findley's *Not Wanted on the Voyage* (1984), which presents Noah as an originary fascist, who persecutes both his family and the animals in his care, in order to maintain his power and his particular version of history (62). Thus, Findley's revision of the biblical account of Noah and his ark is an allegorical critique of the "apocalyptic" consequences of patriarchal and imperial oppression, and in this sense, Barnes's rewriting bears the intertextual reference to Findley's writing.

hygiene," and "didn't even have the skill to grow his own hair except around his face; for the rest of his covering he relied on the skins of other species" (*HWC* 17) ; and what's worse, Noah smelt. Such an image, in the animal narrator's view, cannot be compared with that of a gorilla, which is the superior creation with graceful movement, superior strength and an instinct for delousing (*HWC* 18). Then, why did God choose Noah as His protégé? It is a riddle for the animals, but it is recorded in the Bible. The Holy Bible reveals that "Noah was a just man and perfect in his generations" (Genesis 6: 9, 7), or it's believed that "Noah was sage, righteous and God-fearing" (*HWC* 8). Is it really the fact? The animal narrator who witnessed the deed of Noah has a different view about it. For the animal narrator, Noah was "an old rogue with a drink problem" (*HWC* 6), "a hysterical rogue with a drink problem," "a man who had his little theories" and "didn't want anyone else's" (*HWC* 8), "not a nice man" but "a monster, a puffed-up patriarch who spent half his day groveling to his God and the other half taking it out on us" (*HWC* 12). This is in line with Noah's brutal and cruel attitude towards the selection of other species for the arks, and the reason for other species' "Noah-angst," for their being poisoned, beaten, slaughtered, cooked and eaten by Noah and his family. Still, the animal narrator questions Noah's capacity as a captain of the Ark, not thinking of him as a good sailor, for when the seas were high Noah would retire to his cabin, throw himself down on his gopher-wood bed and leave it only to vomit out his stomach into his gopher-wood wash-basin (*HWC* 16). The narrator later scoffs at Noah's ability as the Admiral of the Ark, thinking that Noah was picked for his piety rather than his navigational skills, not any good in a storm, and not much better when the seas were calm (*HWC* 19). Besides, according to the animal narrator, Noah "was too proud" to make good use of the expertise of the birds, and just "gave them a few simple reconnaissance tasks—looking out for whirlpools and tornadoes—while disdaining their proper skills" but "sent a number of species to their deaths by asking them to go aloft in terrible weather when they weren't properly equipped to do so" (*HWC* 20). In a word, the character of Noah could be summarized as such: Noah "was bad-tempered, smelly, unreliable, envious and cowardly" (*HWC* 16).

When rewriting the image of Noah, Barnes also refers to Noah's creator God via the expression of the animal narrator. As to Noah's misconduct, the animal narrator reminds us that "it wasn't altogether Noah's fault," for "that God of his was a really oppressive role-model" (*HWC* 21). Noah's fear of God is obvious to such a degree that he "couldn't do anything without first wondering what *He* would think" (*HWC* 21, italics original). The narrator continues to scorn Noah's inflexibility of mind and takes Noah's construction of the Ark with the gopher-wood for instance to show his obeisance and submission to God. In the Bible, Noah was told to "[m]ake ... an ark of gopher wood" (Genesis 6: 14), but the animal witness tells us the fact that not much gopher-wood grew nearby but Noah ignored it and merely followed instructions from his role-model (*HWC* 21). Then the animal narrator queries and ridicules Noah's inflexibility of mind like this:

> Anyone who knows anything about wood ... could have told him that a couple of dozen other tree-types would have done as well, if not better; and what's more, the idea of building all parts of a boat from a single wood is ridiculous. You should choose your material according to the purpose for which it is intended; everyone knows that. Still, this was old Noah for you—*no flexibility of mind at all. Only saw one side of the question.* Gopher-wood bathroom fittings—have you ever heard of anything more ridiculous? (*HWC* 21, italics added)

After that, the narrator stresses that Noah "got it" from his role model and that the question always on Noah's lips is "What would God think?" (*HWC* 21). Therefore, in his ridiculing of Noah as the submissive subject, Barnes, through the voice of the animal narrator, also questions the authority and justice of God,① and even interrogates the nature of God, which is in keeping with his own disbelief in God in his work such as *Staring at the Sun*, *Nothing to Be Frightened of* and in his real life. The disbelief in God in this "novel" is, for instance, the continuation of Barnes's metaphysical and philosophical thinking about God in *Staring at the Sun*, in which Gregory the heroine's son reflects on the existence of God and proposes more than ten possible answers to it, but still gets no certain reply (*SS* 164-166). Accordingly, through the interrogation of his characters, Barnes poses questions for the truth of religion and knowledge. In an interview, Barnes spoke of his non-religious life in this vein: "I've never had a religious period in my life, I wasn't brought up in a religious family" (Freiburg 41). Later, Barnes confessed at the inception of *Nothing to Be Frightened of* that "I don't believe in God, but I miss him" (3), which could be rendered as a footnote to his writing of God in *A History*. That is, the rewriting of Biblical (hi)stories or the insinuation of the image of God is the very evidence of Barnes's missing God, but the subversive and deconstructive writing of the

---

① The animal narrator questions why God chooses Noah and human beings to stay on earth, for instance: for the narrator it is a riddle why "God came to choose man as His protégé ahead of the more obvious candidates," for most other species were a lot more loyal and "[i]f He'd plumped for the gorilla, ... there'd have been half so much disobedience—probably no need to have had the Flood in the first place" (*HWC* 18). The animal narrator suggests, "given the nature of God, that was probably the safest line to take" (*HWC* 11).

existence and the image of God exposits his disbelief in God.

In addition, the animal narrator discloses or digs out more "truths" about the (hi)story of the Flood so as to present the alternative possibilities of sacred history. As the narrator recounts, it is believed that "Noah, for all his faults, was basically some kind of early conservationist, that he collected the animals together because he didn't want them to die out, that he couldn't endure not seeing a giraffe ever again, that he was doing it for [the animals]," but the narrator refutes that this "wasn't the case at all," for Noah got the animals together "because his role-model told him to, but also out of self-interest," and "*He wanted to have something to eat after the Flood had subsided*" (*HWC* 22, italics original). Then the animal narrator relates more "facts" that "[f]ive and a half years under water and most of the kitchen gardens were washed away ... ; only rice prospered. And so most of us ... were just future dinners [for Noah]. If not now, then later; if not us, then our offspring," therefore, "[a]n atmosphere of paranoia and terror held sway on that Ark of Noah's" (*HWC* 22). Still, when "the Voyage was over, God made Noah's dining rights official" and Noah could choose whichever of the animals to eat for the rest of his life, which was the pay-off for Noah's obedience during the Flood (*HWC* 22). Thus, the animal narrator assumes that it "was all part of some pact or covenant botched together between the pair of [God and Noah]," for "having eliminated everyone else from the earth, God had to make do with the one family of worshippers he'd got left" (*HWC* 22). With no doubt, the narrator's recountal or Barnes's rewriting of this detail is justifiable and plausible.

Next, the animal narrator refers to the raven in this "early history." The Bible tells us that when the Ark landed on the mountaintop, Noah sent out a raven and a dove to see if the waters retreated from the face of the earth: the raven had a very small part, for it merely fluttered hither and thither, to little avail; whereas the dove made three heroic journeys, and returned to the Ark with an olive leaf. But the animal narrator rejects such a version and unearths that human beings have elevated the dove into something of symbolic value, and points out that "the raven always maintained that *he* found the olive tree; that *he* brought a leaf from it back to the Ark; but that Noah decided it was 'more appropriate' to say that the dove had discovered it" (*HWC* 25, italics original). The animal narrator argues for the raven like this:

> I always believed the raven, who apart from anything else was much stronger in the air than the dove; and it would have been just like Noah (modeling himself on that God of his again) to stir up a dispute among the animals. Noah had it put about that the raven, instead of returning

as soon as possible with evidence of dry land, had been malingering, and had been spotted (by whose eye? ...) gourmandizing on carrion. The raven, I need hardly add, felt hurt and betrayed at this *instant rewriting of history*, and it is said ... that you can hear the sad croak of dissatisfaction in his voice to this day. The dove, by contrast, began sounding unbearably smug from the moment we disembarked. She could already envisage herself on postage stamps and letterheads. (*HWC* 25–26, italics added)

Seen in this light, then, the (hi)story of the Flood has been rewritten or altered by Noah; and consequently the authority of Christian History or historical (meta)narrative is vulnerable to suspicion and interrogation, which is in accordance to the intent of Barnes's subversion and revision of sacred history.

At last, the animal narrator concludes that the Voyage teaches its species a lot of things and that the main thing is that "man is a very unevolved species compared to the animals," still " at an early stage of ... development " (*HWC* 28). More specifically, as the narrator reveals, men "aren't too good with the truth," "keep forgetting things" or "pretend to;" and "won't even admit the true nature of Noah;" and blaming someone else is always men's "first instinct:" "if you can't blame someone else, then start claiming the problem isn't a problem anyway. Rewrite the rules, shift the goalposts" (*HWC* 29). These are then the very nature of Noah, the "first father," "the pious patriarch" and "the committed conservationist" of humankind (*HWC* 29).

All in all, I would maintain that through the expression of the animal narrator, or by way of "bring[ing] to speech the voices of history that have been silenced by the one voice that passes itself off as the voice of God" (Salyer 224), Barnes's writing in "The Stowaway" subverts the conventional image of Noah and God and naturally "shame[s] the reader into rethinking sacred history" (Salyer 223). More importantly, Barnes "writes from the woodworm's point of view not to be merely 'daring' but to dramatize the beastliness and arrogance of man" (Flower, "Story Problems" 318) and thence undermines the anthropocentric viewpoint of seeing and perceiving the "history of the world," presents a novel possibility of knowing sacred history, thus taking cognizant of the plurality of history in an ontological way. Therefore, the writing in this "chapter" of "history of the world" fits in with the remark of Salman Rushdie on Barnes's work— "subversion of the given."

ii. History of a Racial Victim

In *A History*, Julian Barnes brings to the fore the voices of history that have been silenced by the dominating voices such as the voice of God, of Eurocentrism and of male domination. The silenced or marginalized voices in the book include those of non-human beings such as the woodworm and the termite, that of the female and those of non-Western ones and the minorities like the Arabs and the Jewish refugees. Their presence in Barnes's writing of the "history of the world" functions as "a reminder of those submerged voices of history" (Salyer 224). In such a fashion, Barnes's *A History* subverts the conventional paradigm of historical writing, which is characterized by one voice from start to finish, be it that of providential God, or that of the (pseudo-objective) male, and juxtaposes heterogeneous voices to represent the diversity and variety of histories, thus foregrounding the plurality of history. This part will examine how Barnes writes of and critiques the racial prejudice imposed on a racial Other in *Arthur & George*, his longest and deeply English novel.

Barnes in *Arthur & George* makes great efforts to adumbrate racial prejudice or racism at the post-Victoria period by means of digging out an (almost) forgotten history about George Edalji, a half Indian, whose father, from Bombay, born a Parsee[①] and married to a Scottish woman, was a vicar in a small church in the Midlands. After reading the novel we cannot deny the fact that the miscarriage of justice done to George relies heavily on racial bias, of which critics have taken note but not in detailed analysis (Berger 1613; Bernstein 146; Schwartz 42; Smee 34; Wilhelmus 348; Winder 50). Hence in the discussion below, I will illustrate specifically how Barnes depicts the racial prejudice in the novel through and in his characterization and story plot.

George Edalji was a shy, earnest child, raised according to a Victorian version of tough love, along with truth, righteousness and Anglicanism, due

---

[①] As Barnes told an interviewer, the Parsees were a favored race of the British, so that the injustice done to George Edalji, a half Parsee, is in fact one of the ironies of the novel: he was persecuted for his color (Lewis). More specifically, as Barnes recounted, "The Parsees were regarded as a pretty top quality sect in the British Empire. They were the merchant class. Highly educated. And indeed in the late 19th century there were two Parsee members of the British Parliament. The first Indian cricket team that came to Britain was a Parsee team, and they were looked upon, partly because they were pale-skinned and partly because they were a mercantile and lawyerly class, as sort of bridging the gap between the 'dusky races' and the white man. And so, in fact, George's father, Shapurji, would have been welcomed into the Church of England as sort of new blood. And yet it redounded on his son" (Lewis).

to his father's well-meaning but dauntingly austere discipline. Without doubt, George's life was cornered by his racial background from the very beginning and his world was thus limited to "the Vicarage, the church, the building where [his] Mother t[aught] Sunday school, the garden, the cat, the hens, the stretch of grass they cross[ed] between the Vicarage and the church, the churchyard" (*AG* 7). In fact, the situation of unsocialness surrounding George and his family was closely connected to the uncivilized, farm villagers: they were unwilling to contact this "odd" family. This invisible but influential prejudice, with the touch of Orientalism, eventually gave rise to the miscarriage of justice done to George when he was twenty seven years old. Certainly, more specific depiction of racial discrimination, laid bare in the act and speech of the local people, the police, the judge, the high officers in government and even Arthur Conan Doyle, will be necessarily enumerated in the following discussion, so as to point out the omnipresence and influence of racial bias or racism in the post-Victorian or Edwardian England.

When George was at the age of sixteen or so, his family was harassed by some evil hoax and inspected by Sergeant Upton, "a red-faced man with the build of a blacksmith" (*AG* 31), when they reported it to the police. With little knowledge of the personality of George, during the "inspection," Upton named George "uppish little fellow" (*AG* 32) and later without sound reason, troubled and pestered George on his way home. When George told the Sergeant he was going to be a solicitor, the latter laughed in George's face and spit down towards his boot, uttering that "Is that what you think? A so-li-ci-tor? What a big word for *a little mongrel* like you. You think you'll become a so-li-ci-tor if Sergeant Upton says you won't?" (*AG* 37, italics added). Later, George's father wrote to the Chief Constable of Staffordshire about what had occurred to his son but received, with no "expected apology and promise of action" (*AG* 38), an insinuative warning that the theft and hoax was done by George himself. Along with some vile hoaxes, anonymous, malevolent letters arrived day by day, and when the anonymous letters began to show violent intent, the Vicar feared for the family and decided again to approach the Chief Constable but his request was ignored for the second time. The persecution lasted for more than two years, in spite of the Vicar family's "counter-attack" (such as writing advertisements in the local newspapers to clarify the hoaxes and letters). And then it stopped, as suddenly as it began. This is, nevertheless, not the end of George's (hi)story.

Several years later in the Solicitors' Final Examinations, George received Second Class Honours, and was awarded a Bronze Medal by Birmingham Law Society, and accordingly opened an office: he was twenty-three and the world was changing for him (*AG* 80). In 1901, George published a pamphlet titled *Railway Law for The "Man in the Train*," which inspired his family and himself much, and supposed that he was on his way: "that journey in life [was] now truly beginning" (*AG* 85). The real journey in life started not as George imagined. The anonymous, iniquitous letters turned up again, but this time the real perpetration was done to some farm animals. The case of animals mutilated (to death) in an odd way puzzled the police, and in order to swiftly end the outrages, they focused their attention on George, whose name was deliberately mentioned in these spiteful letters. In fact, when George turned out to be an adult, racial prejudice accompanied his life but did not affect it severely until the occurrence of the animal mutilation. The typical racial discrimination could be identified in the police officers' dialogue:

> "Well, sir, *he's Indian*, isn't he? *Half Indian*, that is. *Little fellow. A bit odd-looking.* Lawyer, *lives at home*, goes up to Birmingham every day. *Doesn't exactly involve himself in village life*, if you understand me."
> " ... There was a campaign against the family a few years back."
> "I saw it in the day-book. Any reason for that?"
> "Who can tell? There was some ... ill feeling when *the Vicar* was first given the living. People saying they didn't want *a black man* in the pulpit telling them what sinners they were, that sort of thing. But this was donkey's years ago. I'm chapel myself. We're more welcoming, in my opinion." (*AG* 101, italics added)

Here in this conversation George was considered as not an Englishman but an Indian, "odd-looking," not involving himself in village life and, like his father, despised as "black," which represents the dominant view of the mainstream society and was later referred to in the novel for several times (*AG* 116, 120, 122). There is no wonder that when Inspector Campbell investigated the Vicar household, he could not help uttering that there was "something slightly queer about the family" (*AG* 120) and that it was a strange family (*AG* 122).

Then, with no solid evidence, "George Ernest Thompson Edalji was charged with unlawfully and maliciously wounding a horse, the property of the Great Wyrley Colliery Company, on August 17th [1903]" (*AG* 135). In the suit, racial prejudice turned out to be an invisible hand, controlling the process and the end; and the public and the media also played a complicitous role with the police and the jury.① Eventually, George was sentenced to seven years' penal servitude, despite a glaring lack of evidence and despite his attorney's great efforts to prove his innocence, on which Barnes comments as such: "From the start they presumed him [George] guilty, and the jury's decision had merely confirmed that presumption" (*AG* 182). Here what is perceivable is that behind this seemingly impartial commentary is Barnes's unspoken critique on those concerned in George's case.

Unexpectedly, the cursory sentence made by the court and the miscarriage of justice imposed upon George aroused not a few complaints and protest. As Barnes's writing shows, George in the prison learned from his father's letters that there had been a public outcry at his verdict (*AG* 189): The outcry is perhaps not out of the protest against racial prejudice but against the miscarriage of justice (short of evidence), although the former plays a vital role in the latter. In spite of this and of the fact that the case of George Edalji had become a sensation at that time, the essence of George's case could not be altered (*AG* 198), for the then Home Office would not change the verdict and the then convention of law system. However, unexpectedly again, after three years' penal servitude, George was released with no explanation or exoneration from the officialdom (*AG* 199–200). With no official explanation for his release, no apology and compensation for his incarceration, and his conviction not cancelled, George was locked in an "anomalous position" and could not "be readmitted to the Rolls" (*AG* 258), which was his basic request for and of life. In order to clarify his case, clear up his "moral despair and practical limbo" and return to work as he wished, George, like most of the victims of crime cases and of miscarriage of justice at that time, wrote to Arthur Conan Doyle, the world famous detective writer of the period for help (*AG* 257–258). George's case took a

---

① As Barnes described in the novel, when George was taken to the court, the crowd on the way "seemed more turbulent. Men ran alongside the cab, jumping up and peering in; some thumped on the doors and waved sticks in the air. ... [B]ut the escorting constables acted as if it were all quite normal" (*AG* 138). Still, the newspapers' reports were full of negative delineation of George: for instance, the Birmingham *Daily Gazette* delineated George biasedly to such a degree that "there was little of the typical solicitor in his swarthy face, with its full, dark eyes, prominent mouth, and small round chin" and that "[h]is appearance is essentially Oriental in its stolidity, no sign of emotion escaping him beyond a faint smile as the extraordinary story of the prosecution unfolded" (*AG* 140), while depicting William Greatorex a witness as "a healthy young English boy, with a frank, sunburnt face, and a pleasing manner" (*AG* 143).

turn when the creator of Sherlock Holmes intervened accidentally. ①

When Arthur Conan Doyle came across George Edalji and decided to "stir things up," to "knock some heads together" and let them "rue the day" (*AG* 258), the novel turns out to be not only a detective one, but also a historical, juridical and even political drama. Conan Doyle investigated George's case, via dialoguing with the defendant, the witnesses and the police officers, and tried to find out solid and sufficient evidence, based on his logical reasoning of the case from ending to beginning. On the other hand, Conan Doyle, in light of his enormous influence as a celebrity, planned to "make a tremendous noise" (*AG* 281), to make the Edalji case into as big a stir as the Dreyfus Case in France (*AG* 299), so that he published, with no copyright, his investigation results in newspapers. As a result, the noise Conan Doyle had made "had echoed far beyond Staffordshire, far beyond London, far beyond England itself" (*AG* 367). Eventually, the Home Office appointed a committee to deal with the verdict on George but due to its "corrupt inertia" (*AG* 261), it issued a report, refusing to recognize its embarrassment and shame, merely offering George a free pardon, without any grant of compensation (*AG* 381). The celebrated detective writer thought of the report as "a hypocrisy" (*AG* 382) and "continued his campaign" unflinchingly, but brought no alteration to the Home Office verdict. Conan Doyle's campaign, as Barnes relates, elicited the "constant questions in Parliament" for two months, and the Home Secretary answered all of the questions except the last one, that is, "Is Edalji thus being treated because he is not an Englishman?" (*AG* 387). That "no answer was returned" (*AG* 387) to the question evidently evinces that the Home Office recognized its shame on it.

In effect, during Conan Doyle's investigation, racial prejudice was an unavoidable issue; that is, Conan Doyle's investigation makes us see more

---

① As Barnes claimed, "[a]ll sorts of people wrote to Conan Doyle at the time. He'd invented Sherlock Holmes, and people logically thought that if he could invent and solve dreadful crimes, then he could help them in real life. Lots of people wrote to Sherlock Holmes, and, of course, he threw those letters away. Some wrote to Conan Doyle, and sometimes he would reply politely. But this was the very first case which he took up, and it's interesting why he did. It's a long story, but essentially, his first wife had died and he was in a pit of both depression and guilt over a secret relationship he'd had with another woman—honorable but secret, and he married her eventually. In my view, he believed that if he could prove George Edalji, who was thought by many to be guilty, was in fact innocent, it would be a sort of analogue for what was happening in his own life, that he was thought by some to have had a guilty relationship with another woman. He would prove that he was indeed innocent—if by innocence you mean sexually uninvolved—and I think that was true" (Schiff). Therefore, we could say that the original motivation for Arthur Conan Doyle to expunge George's conviction was accidental and not in a decent sense as imaged.

clearly the role racial bias played in George's case. Thus, an important plot occurring between Conan Doyle and Anson the Chief Constable cannot be omitted here. Before visiting Anson to know more details about the case, Conan Doyle had inferred that the Constable disliked people who were colored (*AG* 281), which was later substantiated by the latter's own words. Conan Doyle had a long conversation or dispute with Anson in the latter's house, in which the representative of the police spoke out his own ideas about George and his family without reservation:

> "A deplorable business, it has to be said. A series of mistakes. It could all have been nipped in the bud so much earlier."
> Anson's candour surprised Doyle. "I'm glad to hear you say that. Which mistakes did you have in mind?"
> "The family's. That's where it all went wrong. The wife's family. What took it into their heads? Whatever took it into their heads? Doyle, really: your niece insists upon marrying a Parsee—can't be persuaded out of it—and what do you do? You give the fellow a living ... *here*. In Great Wyrley. You might as well appoint a Fenian to be Chief Constable of Staffordshire and have done with it." (*AG* 327–328, italics original)

Still, Anson displayed his attitude toward the half-caste as such: "when the blood is mixed, that is where the trouble starts," for "[a]n irreconcilable division is set up" and "his soul is torn between the impulse to civilization and the pull of barbarism" (*AG* 339). It is clear that Anson's words and act (as mentioned before) to George and his family were thick with racial bias, which is the original root of George's tragic life.

Ironically, George himself had never thought that the jaundiced racial view or racism determined other people's attitude toward and judgement of him, although he was indoctrinated at an early age by his father that "[y]ou are an Englishman. But others may not always entirely agree" (*AG* 52). As to George's ignorance of the acts and words of racial prejudice from the "primitive people" (*AG* 52) in the local area and his request for solid evidence, Conan Doyle acutely pointed out to him that "[p]erhaps you should try occasionally not to think like a lawyer. The fact that no evidence of a phenomenon can be adduced does not mean that it does not exist" (*AG* 266). In actuality, one of the very powers of racial prejudice lies in its invisibility. Paradoxically, as a fighter for justice, Sir Arthur Conan Doyle was also locked in his sexist, imperial and Oriental biases. For his part, "in the interests of civil harmony," "the fair sex should be banned" from "the pooling booth" (*AG* 296), which is "resolutely against the notion of votes for women" (*AG* 201); and when the South Africa War broke out, Conan

Doyle volunteered as medical officer to make a good example for the young, thinking that Britain was getting into a fight which was a rightful one (*AG* 227). As to racism, although Conan Doyle fought against the injustice imposed upon George, he was biased in his opinion. In his autobiography *Memories and Adventures*, the creator of Sherlock Holmes wrote that "[h]ow the Vicar came to be a Parsee, or how a Parsee came to be the Vicar, I have no idea," making some ostensibly fair but partial explanation in this vein: "Perhaps some Catholic-minded patron wished to demonstrate the universality of the Anglican Church;" "The experiment will not, I hope, be repeated, for though the Vicar was an amiable and devoted man, the appearance of a coloured clergyman with a half-caste son in a rude, unrefined parish was bound to cause some regrettable situation" (qtd. in *AG* 414). These sentences are quoted by Barnes in this novel and later altered and drawn upon in Conan Doyle's conversation with Anson the Chief Constable of Staffordshire. These biased views dug out in Conan Doyle confirm that racial prejudice is so ingrained in the society that even an unflinching fighter for justice like Arthur Conan Doyle could not be uninfluenced by it and that our view of this great detective writer should be accordingly revised.

In short, it is not difficult to perceive that the racial identity of George was the key element affecting his conviction, and through Barnes's realistic, documentary depiction, we can sense that the "primitive people" in the Great Wyrley, the police and the jury in the Birmingham area, the higher officers of Home Office and even Conan Doyle who espoused fairness and justice, were all entrapped in the network weaved by racism (and Eurocentrism), which demonstrates to the full that racial discrimination as a collective unconscious was deeply embedded in the soil of the Victorian culture of England and generally, if I can say so, in the civilization of the Western world (the contemporaneous Dreyfus Case in France being another typical instance in point).

Then, why did Barnes write such a novel about racial prejudice or what promoted him to do so? There is a story about it. Barnes being Barnes, the original seed for *Arthur & George* was French. As Barnes told, he read a book *France and the Dreyfus Affair*, about the Dreyfus case by Douglas Johnson, an English historian of France, in which Johnson addresses the similarities between the infamous conviction for espionage of a Jewish officer in the French army and the contemporaneous victimization of the young Anglo-Indian, for both cases put a nation's attitude to its own minorities on trial (Rees). And as Barnes observed, "in both cases there is a shocking crime, a miscarriage of justice, key handwriting evidence, a sentence of hard labour, and a famous writer rides to the rescue [Emile Zola in France, Conan Doyle in Britain]" (Rees). Barnes thought this was extraordinary, for he had never heard of the case (Schiff), wondering, as Johnson did, "[w]hy has one case been forgotten and why is the Dreyfus case resonating throughout France even to this day?" Johnson's answer, according to Barnes, is that "because the Dreyfus case was about high treason and the British case was about animal mutilation," against which Barnes counter-argued that "in fact the British are much more shocked by animal mutilation than high treason" (Rees). Anyway, as Barnes recalled, "this was the story presented to me, and I thought that it was fascinating. I didn't know about the story, so I asked other people—no one had heard of this case," and as he continued to put it:

> I thought that I ought to read up about it, so I looked around. Conan Doyle himself wrote a series of articles for a newspaper, which he then collected into a pamphlet, when he was involved in trying to clear George's name. But *no one had written anything about this case for a hundred years*. In a way, I wrote this book in order to have something to read about the case. (Schiff, italics added)

However, at the very beginning, Barnes didn't have "any particular interest in Conan Doyle" and "deliberately didn't re-read the canon in order to write this book," because he "didn't want it to be that sort of book," but later Barnes's interest was pricked by Conan Doyle's modish espousal of spiritualism and by his long courtship of Jean Leckie while his invalid first wife was still alive (Rees). As Barnes said, " *[i]n his* [Arthur's] *autobiography he completely lies about Jean, and early biographers completely cover it up.* The spiritualist stuff is also about evidence, proof, knowledge, belief. And ... this is the point at which it starts to become potentially a novel" (Rees, italics added). This is then the reason for Barnes's writing of *Arthur & George* and his revision of the image of Sir Arthur Conan Doyle in the novel: to deal with Conan Doyle's sexist, imperial, Oriental, and idealist views historically and objectively, for in effect the creator of Sherlock Holmes was also a man who supported such views as sexism, imperialism, Orientalism and Spiritualism, which, as Barnes mentioned, was hidden away, distorted, or erased in Conan Doyle's autobiography and early biographies. In this sense, we would argue that *Arthur & George* turns out to be a revision of the orthodox (historical) narratives about Sir Arthur Conan Doyle.

What is equally significant is that Barnes foregrounds the description of George's (hi)story in this novel. Its title tells that it is composed of (hi)stories about "Arthur" and "George." What is manifest is that it is a piece of biographical writing about two historical figures with different racial backgrounds, personalities and social fames. The juxtaposition of them as done by Barnes proffers a novel possibility for the writing of biography; that is, Barnes's writing mode in it undermines the traditional mode or pattern of biographical writing: Barnes writes their biographical (hi)stories in turn in the early two parts of the novel and then intertwines or interconnects their (hi)stories in the later two parts; and as one of the twin protagonists, George Edalji, is endowed with an equally vital, if not more important, role in the novel. There is little evidence of biography in which the protagonist consists of two (or more) characters,① and, as it were, no evidence of biographical writing in which a (Western) celebrity is equally treated with an obscure, racial minority. In so doing, Barnes's biographical writing of these two historical figures subverts and revises the conventional (historical) (meta)narrative of biography. Certainly, the novel's genre, like that of most of Barnes's work, "refuses to be categorized" (Lewis) or "evades clear categorization" (Groes and Childs 3), for it blurs the boundaries among literary biography, historical novel, detective story, and psychological novel; or we can say that it is a mix of these (literary) genres or "a genre-defying hybrid" (Berberich 123). As a result, *Arthur & George* could be regarded as a postmodern(ist) novel, in which the conventional mode of (historical) writing is undermined: just as a critic contends, "[i]n this book, as in everything he does, Barnes was playing with and quietly expanding on the conventions of storytelling" (Lycett 133); for another, it could be also labeled as "historiographic metafiction" in that it "authentically represents history, while being aware of its own artificiality and questioning the dichotomy of fact and fiction as well as the claim to one objective truth" (Frey 1). All of these considered, one might argue that the writing in *Arthur & George* is no doubt a "subversion of the given."

Furthermore, from his critique of Arthur Conan Doyle's (unconscious) racial prejudice and view of Imperialism (or Orientalism) and his digging out and realistic, documentary delineation of George's case, we can sense that Barnes maintains a view of racial equality and racial plurality or diversity in

---

① There are certainly some contrastive and parallel biographies, which address two or more historical figures in one book. For instance, *Einstein, Picasso: Space, Time, and the Beauty That Causes Havoc* (2001) is such a kind of "biography," in which the author writes of Einstein's and Picasso's outstanding achievements in their respective fields and explores how they—the former by way of relativity theory while the latter cubism in painting—try to represent time and space much more deeply and satisfyingly than before. Ostensibly a biographical writing, it is in fact a critical study about the issue of aesthetics in science and science in aesthetics. It is certainly a sort of experimentation in biographical writing, but what Barnes does in *Arthur & George* is more innovative.

his mind, which can be also corroborated from his critical writing about the forgetting character of British people. More specifically, when asked about the similarity between George's Case and the Dreyfus Affair, Barnes displayed his critical view about France and Britain, the French and the English, thinking that

> [T]he British are quite good—and you can charge them with many things, hypocrisy included—but they are rather good at forgetting. Something was bad in the country and it sort of got fixed, and so we forget about it. Whereas in France they like to keep old wounds open, so to speak, and they like to remember the past in a way that the English certainly don't. The Scots, the Irish and the Welsh will have longer memories because on the whole they were not treated terribly well by the English. (Lewis)

In fact, Barnes also mentions the Dreyfus Affair in this novel and compares it with George's case, showing the similar view that the British people are good at forgetting. ① Certainly, Barnes's critique of the character of the English is impressive, but what is implied is the role racism and historical monism playing in the forgetting of the George's case. That is, historical monism and racism would repress and even erase the shameful pages but preserve and glorify the positively glaring pages of history, so that, as Barnes confirmed, "no one had heard of this case" and "no one had written anything about this case for a hundred years," for it has been repressed, though not entirely erased, from official history, due to the embarrassment and shame for British law system and officialdom. Therefore, it is reasonable to argue that Barnes's writing in *Arthur & George* mirrors his subversion and revision of orthodox and official history and thus substantiates to some extent his defense for racial and historical plurality.

The analysis in this chapter displays that Julian Barnes is a postmodern(ist)

---

① Compared with France, as Barnes put it in the novel, "England was a quieter place, just as principled, but less keen on making a fuss about its principles; a place where the common law was trusted more than government statute; where people got on with their own business and did not seek to interfere with that of others; where great public eruptions took place from time to time, eruptions of feeling which might even tip over into violence and injustice, but which soon faded in the memory, and were rarely built into the history of the country. This has happened, now let us forget about it and carry on as before: such was the English way. Something was wrong, something was broken, but now it has been repaired, so let us pretend that nothing much was wrong in the first place. The Edalji Case would not have arisen if there had been a Court of Appeal? Very well, then: pardon Edalji, establish a Court of Appeal before the year is out—and what more remains to be said about the matter? This was England" (*AG* 412).

writer with a strong spirit of deconstruction, which lies in the fact that Barnes in his *A History* deconstructs the conventional mode of historical writing overwhelmingly, endorsing the postmodern view or philosophical thinking of history such as discontinuity and fragmentation of history or historiography and the incredulity toward progressiveness of history in and through the form of fictional writing, and in *A History* and *Arthur & George* suggests his support for the plurality of history, by way of giving expression to the voices suppressed or erased in the orthodox writing of history, providing novel perspectives for the reading and understanding of history. That is, Barnes's postmodern historical writing evinces that postmodern discourse or philosophy of history underscores the discontinuity, fragmentation and plurality of history, via the emphasis of the "historical scraps" as "the centre of attention" (Ankersmit, "Historiography and Postmodernism" 149) and of "the capacity to see the world from another point of view" (Salyer 228). Or to put it another way, Barnes's postmodern historical writing in *A History* "highlights ruptures, subtle contradictions and inconsistencies, differences and conflicts" and "thus vehemently rejects the metaphysical concept of history as the history of a meaning or pattern which unfolds and fulfills itself" (Kotte 123), therefore undermining the speculative view of history or historiography; still, in *Arthur & George* Barnes's writing subverts the traditional pattern of biographical writing through the juxtaposition of (hi)stories of quite two different historical figures Sir Arthur Conan Doyle and George Edalji, digs out a piece of history about George Edalji repressed and forgotten by English society and people so as to disclose the evilness of historical monism and racism, and revises the officially positive image of a celebrated historical figure Arthur Conan Doyle to a historically truer one so as to expose the (possible) subjectivity in the conventional (meta)narrative of biographical (historical) writing, exploring in the meantime the national characteristic of English people. To achieve his aims, Barnes makes use of various kinds of postmodernist writing devices such as parody, intertextuality, irony, collage and self-reflexiveness, endowing with his writing a strong sense of deconstruction and spirit of subversion, so that "subversion of the given," a comment made by Salman Rushdie on Barnes's *A History*, could be used as a footnote to Barnes's postmodern (historical) writing on the whole, not merely to the specific one. All in all, we could restate that Barnes in these texts calls into question the conventional, speculative view of history and/or historiography through his postmodern historical writing modes and exhibits his postmodern view of history in the form of literary fictional writing, ontologically. Next chapter will move on to Barnes's political fiction to investigate how he deals with the issues related to history when politics and/or political ideology are involved.

Chapter Four
Fabricating and Representing Politics-History

All history was a palimpsest, scraped clean and re-inscribed exactly as often as was necessary.
—George Orwell, *Nineteen Eighty-Four*

Whether they wish it or know it or not, all men and women, all over the earth, are today to a certain extent the heirs of Marx and Marxism. ... [W]e cannot not be its heirs.
—Jacques Derrida, *Specters of Marx: The State of the Debt, the Work of Mourning, and the New International*

[T]here *is* no authentic moment of beginning, of purity ... . We may choose to freeze a moment and say that it all "began" then, but as an historian I have to tell you that such labelling is intellectually indefensible. What we are looking at is almost always a replica, if that is the locally fashionable term, of something earlier. There is no prime moment.
—Julian Barnes, *England, England*

As referred to at the end of the first chapter of this research, to explore Julian Barnes's postmodern historical writing from the epistemological, ontological and political perspective is merely an expedient strategy, which does not necessarily suggest that the work of Barnes and its study could be thus divided, for they are closely correlated with each other and a clear boundary line among them could never be drawn. As planned, this chapter will mainly address Barnes's historical writing from the political (and ideological) angle, another important focus of this research.

Postmodern theorists of history and New Historicists also deal with the relationship between history and politics when interrogating the conventional view or discourse of history or historiography. Michel Foucault and Keith Jenkins, for instance, emphasize the decisive role of power in or the power relation behind history and historical writing proper through their theoretical writings. This postmodern theoretical aura has affected the postmodern writing of history proper as well as the postmodern writing of history in literary works. Many a postmodern(ist) writers in Britain such as Martin Amis, Anthony Burgess, Kazuo Ishiguro, among others, all exposit the relation of history to (political) ideology and power in their writings, so as to rethink history, to "use the past to cast light on the present" (Furbank 112).

Julian Barnes is also such a postmodern writer, with a special concern for the political, ideological attribute of history, which is the reason why he is often called "a political writer" (Harris 26). Barnes, as "a novelist-philosopher" or a near-historian, often through the form of fictional writing illustrates his unconventional view or philosophy of history, which has been corroborated in the previous chapters of this research. Similarly, we can see that as "a political writer," Barnes demonstrates his politically critical instance in his postmodern historical writing, as manifested in his fiction such as *A History of the World in 10½ Chapters*, *The Porcupine* and *England, England*, which are related to the issue of politics, though to varying degrees. Therefore, in this chapter, I shall examine how Barnes through his unconventional historical (political) writing deals with the issues of history in connection with politics or those of politics pertinent to history, especially that of political power and ideology concerning history. The first section of this chapter would explore the issue of history and ideology, so as to indicate Barnes's insightful writing on the relation of history to political power and ideology, and his perceptive understanding of the issue of "The End of History," the one closely correlated with the political, ideological conflict, represented in his first political novel *The Porcupine*. And the second section would probe into Barnes's satirizing of the postmodern culture of simulacra, critique of the loss of national identity consciousness and concern for and rethinking of the political future (history) of England (and even the whole world), delineated in his another political fiction *England, England*.

I. History and Ideology

As noted in the first chapter of this research, postmodern theorists and/ or New Historicists have their own unique understanding of the issue of ideological attribute of history or the political power relation behind history. When they put forward their queries about the conventional historical discourse, they also take note of the (political) ideological attribute of history or historiography. According to Michel Foucault, for instance, the influence of power is everywhere, for power itself is everywhere and the production of knowledge is definitely restrained by power relations, or in other words, the exercise of power is the dominating factor for the production of knowledge, and there is no exception to history. Without doubt, such a view stands on the opposite side of the conventional discourse of history or historiography. Similarly, but more specifically and in a more empirical sense, Keith Jenkins defines history as follows:

> History is a shifting, problematic discourse, ostensibly about an aspect of the world, the past, that is produced by a group of present-minded workers (overwhelmingly in our culture salaried historians) who go about their work in mutually recognisable ways that are epistemologically, methodologically, ideologically and practically positioned and whose products, once in circulation, are subject to a series of uses and abuses that are logically infinite but which in actuality generally correspond to a range of power bases that exist at any given moment and which structure and distribute the meaning of histories along a dominant-marginal spectrum. (*Re-thinking History* 31–32)

Simply speaking, this definition suggests that history or historiography is in essence a discourse, is man-made, bearing a certain kind of political or ideological position, and corresponding to the exercise of power. Jenkins furthers his view of history to such an extent that "history is theory and theory is ideological and ideology just is material interests" and that "ideology seeps into every nook and cranny of history, including the everyday practices of making histories in those institutions predominantly set aside in our social formation for that purpose" (*Re-thinking History* 24). Therefore, for postmodern theorists of history and New Historicists, historical knowledge is but the (political) ideology constructed for some "material interests" and a great many ideological myths that are imposed on a certain community; in this sense, we can maintain that history is not a science, but the way utilized by every ideology on behalf of science to infuse their ideological doctrines to the common people. In a nutshell, postmodernist or new historicist notion of knowledge-power demolishes the objectivity and impartiality of history, no longer regarding it as a pure knowledge but discerning the power relation or political ideology behind its production. In this way, history turns out to be the tool of (political) power and ideology; and the purely or scientifically objective history and Ranke's "noble dream" of writing history "as it actually happened" would never be realized.

Julian Barnes's historical writing also touches on the ideological attribute of history, of which his brief reference to a historical figure Francis Drake in *England, England* is a good case in point. At university Martha Cochrane, the heroine of this novel, makes friends with Cristina, a Spanish girl. When Cristina speaks to Martha in a friendly teasing way that Francis Drake is a pirate, Martha disagrees with her and utters that he is an English hero and a Sir and an Admiral and therefore a Gentleman. And when Cristina says again more seriously that Drake is a pirate, Martha thinks of this as "the comforting if necessary fiction of the defeated" (*EE* 7). Later, Martha looks up Drake in a British encyclopaedia: while the word "pirate" never appears, the words "privateer" and "plunder" frequently do. Then she realizes that one person's plundering privateer might be another person's pirate, but "even so Sir Francis Drake remain[s] for her an English hero, untainted by this knowledge" (*EE* 7). It is evident here that the ideological implications behind the same historical figure are quite different for different people who are ideologically educated by official historical classes or historians, so that Barnes in his another novel asserts that "we need to know the history of the historian in order to understand the version that is being put in front of us" (*SE* 13).[1] Accordingly, we can say that Barnes is much concerned with the ideological attribute of history or historiography in his writing. This section will expound how Barnes's writing intimates power relations and/or political ideology behind history, and how his political writing responds to and explores the issue of "The End of History," principally demonstrated in his political novel *The Porcupine*.

---

[1] Here what Barnes articulates through his narrative comment is quite similar to what Edward H. Carr conveys in *What Is History?*, that is, "The historian, before he begins to write history, is the product of history" (40). This in fact emphasizes the subjective or ideological position of the author or historian situated in history rather than in some Rankean "objective" realm outside of it. In simple terms, Barnes here has implicitly rejected Ranke's objective history but pointed to the subjectivity and/or ideology-ness of historical writing.

i. History and Power Relation

Before the publication of *The Porcupine*, politics, be it domestic or international, plays no vital role in Julian Barnes's work, although it is more or less referred to in them. ① Naturally, *The Porcupine* turns out to be Barnes's first political novel, which was published in 1992, firstly under the title of *Bodlivo Svinche* and in the language of Bulgarian, six weeks before its publication in English in the United Kingdom, and caused an immediate sensation in Bulgaria, selling ten thousand copies in hardback and being recommended on the television news (Levy A10). As a political novel, *The Porcupine* appears to be conventional, so that it is often, but mistakenly, considered as "the simplest of all Julian Barnes's novels" (Moseley 150), "a bit monotonous" (Marien 13), falling "solidly into the conventional plot category" (Andreadis 228), with "the plainness of its prose" and "plot of devices reminiscent of 19th century novels" (Gosswiller 3). But in fact Barnes addresses the contemporary historical reality in this novel in a postmodern vein. In the following discussion, this part would first of all analyse how the political power relation is implied in *The Porcupine* and then refer to the historicity of the novel (text) or the reasons for Barnes to write it, Barnes's possible political positions, and finally the typically postmodernist feature of this novel.

The novel begins after the former Communist dictator of an unnamed country in Eastern Europe has been overthrown and imprisoned, his government replaced by a struggling new democracy. Now Stoyo Petkanov the deposed former President, probably the "Porcupine" of the title, is to be tried, relayed on television. His prosecutor is Peter Solinsky, a law professor, a former Party member but now a proponent of democracy and capitalism, who has many reasons for wanting to convict Petkanov, such as national feeling, his own ambition and the fact that his father, a former high government official, was purged by Petkanov. The narrative in the novel represents this (fictional) trial, in which Petkanov and Solinsky stand out and fight against each other for various reasons, personal and political, and

---

① There is a discussion of democracy in *Flaubert's Parrot*, but it is largely theoretical and justifies Flaubert's disdain for democracy; there are the events of Paris in 1968 in *Metroland*, but the point is that Christopher the protagonist is too busy with a girl to be aware that he is living through them; one of the characters in *Before She Met Me* also mentions some political views but in a throwaway line; political themes emerge at times in *A History*, but not in an important way. And as Merritt Moseley observes, Barnes's short story "One of a Kind" assumes some knowledge of the political situation in Romania, but it is hardly a political fiction (145).

with various strategies, rhetorically and practically. Petkanov is eventually convicted but retains his arrogance and honor, while Solinsky is portrayed as inept, and mocked for his shameless ambition and spitefulness.

As the former President of a totalitarian regime, Petkanov is an old-school communist hardened by prison in the 1930s and a crafty, ruthless politician with an enormous ego, considered by his opponent as "a tryant, a murderer, a thief, a liar, and embezzler, a moral pervert, the worst criminal in nation's history" (*P* 112). Undoubtedly, with the collapse of his regime, Petkanov is deposed and waiting to be tried, as the accused in the Criminal Law Case Number 1 in the new democratic court (*P* 9). Petkanov is found guilty of, as the new appointed Prosecutor General Solinsky wishes as most people of the nation do, "Theft. Embezzlement of state funds. Corruption. Speculation. Currency offences. Profiteering. Complicity in the murder of [a comrade] " (*P* 15) and "Complicity in torture. Complicity in attempted genocide. Innumerable conspiracies to pervert the course of justice" (*P* 16), but is actually "charged before the Supreme Court of this nation with the following offences: " "deception involving documents," "abuse of authority" and "mismanagement" (*P* 32). However, the trial goes on not in a smooth way, for the "straightforward proof of malpractice" is "hard to obtain" (*P* 38), due to the fact that "[l]ittle was written down; what had been written down was mostly destroyed; and those who had destroyed it suffered reliable attacks of memory loss" (*P* 38). Here Barnes's writing touches on one essential element in history or historiography, that is, record and memory as evidence of history, without which history or the past could not be approached, and which is later subtly dealt with in Barnes's *England, England* and *The Sense of an Ending*; and it also reminds us of the outstanding political novels *Nineteen Eight-Four* and *Animal Farm* by George Orwell (1903–1950). Unlike Barnes, Orwell articulates his political idea explicitly in *Nineteen Eighty-Four*, having an insightful understanding about history and the relations of history (truth) to political power and ideology. For instance, Orwell writes of history to the extent that past events "have no objective existence, but survive only in written records and in human memories" and that "[t]he past is whatever the records and the memories agree upon" (222). It is safe to say that Orwell in his writing interrogates the objectivity of history or historiography and manifests the complicated relation of history to text, which fits in well with Barnes's (re)thinking of history or historical truth, as noted in the former chapters of this research. Like Orwell, Barnes in his writing of the trial on Petkanov the former Head of State also highlights the vital role of records and memories, evidence of history. Without these records and memories as evidence, Petkanov could not be convicted. What is implicitly expressed in Barnes's writing is that Petkanov as the former President of a totalitarian state, like the "Big Brother" in *Nineteen Eighty-Four* and "the Pigs" in *Animal Farm*, has the authority or power to destroy "what had been written down" and to affect "those who had destroyed it." Or in other words, it is the power relation behind him that determines what would be written as and for history. Not surprisingly and contrastively, Petkanov's (personal) writings are well preserved and published as *Collected Speeches, Writings and Documents* with 32 volumes in 1982 by the then official publishing house (*P* 66). It is clear that what is destroyed or erased is what is not beneficial for Petkanov and perhaps the guilty evidence for his conviction; and what is recorded and preserved is for political propaganda and/or to glorify what he represents. What Petkanov represents is not merely Petkanov himself; besides, he is a representative of a party, a political ideology, and thus the act of recording or erasing is in fact a political, ideological activity, the exercise of power, the production of knowledge and the writing of history. As such, Barnes's contrastive depiction of the evidence of Petkanov's conviction and his writings exemplifies that the production of knowledge or truth is ultimately determined by the exercise of power, which is very similar to what Foucault argues about the production of knowledge: "the development of all ... branches of knowledge can in no way be dissociated from the exercise of power" ("On Power" 106). As a consequence, what Petkanov did just confirms what Lévi-Strauss has proposed— "[h]istory is ... never history, but history-for" (257).

Due to the lack of evidence, the trial on the former President goes on very slowly. The narrator tells us, "[p]erfectly well-attested examples of the former President's colossal greed, his brazen acquisitiveness, his kleptomania and furious embezzling, just seemed to vanish in open court before the eyes of several million witnesses" (*P* 66). Solinsky the Prosecutor General deliberately humiliates the former President by way of exposing him to the public in a not well-safeguarded car, but Petkanov later fights back against Solinsky through the disclosure of the fact that Solinsky, when a member of the former party and as part of a trade delegation in Turin, spent "the hard currency provided for him by the sweat of the workers and peasants at home" on a nice Italian suit, whisky and a prostitute (*P* 86). The "embarrassing disclosures" of Solinsky's past life renders the trial out of steam and into a quandary. How could Solinsky get out of it? Some evidence unbeneficial for Petkanov starts to appear with the help of Georgi Ganin, Head of the Patriotic Security Forces, who, after the "embarrassing disclosures," urges Solinsky that "[i]t is important to hold this trial, for the good of the nation. It is equally important that the accused be found guilty" (*P* 93), for, as Ganin continues to explain to Solinsky, "the nation expects from this trial something more than a technical verdict of guilty on a charge of minor embezzlement" and "expects to be shown that the defendant is the worst criminal in our entire history (*P* 94). What is suggested in Barnes's writing is that Solinsky represents the new state, a liberal democracy, while Petkanov the old regime, a totalitarian state and that the state experiences "a great moment," "a farewell to grim childhood and grey, fretful adolescence," and a moment to "delayed maturity," Petkanov's trial being the "last part of this process—the end of the beginning" (*P* 19–22). Being aware of this, Solinsky thinks of the evidence "discovered" by Ganin, a memorandum in which Petkanov's name initials instead of signature turns up, authorizing "the use of all necessary means against slanderers, saboteurs and anti-state criminals" (*P* 108), and eventually makes use of it to charge not merely against Petkanov in a personal capacity but against the entire criminal and morally poisoned system at whose head Petkanov stood (*P* 110–111). Publically, Petkanov is defeated by Solinsky, which nevertheless does not indicate the end of the struggle of different political ideologies embodied in them.

Does Solinsky, a representative of a new democracy, deal with Petkanov's case legally and justifiably? The answer is no. After the monumental show trial, when Solinsky goes back home, his wife Maria points straightforwardly out his vanity and hypocrisy in the "modern version" of "show trial" (*P* 113), and tells him that she can't love him any more and doubts that she could even respect him (*P* 112). More importantly, she despises Solinsky's act of "inventing fake evidence" (*P* 112), saying that, "Peter, you don't really think the worst criminal in our nation's history would sign such a useful document which Ganin just happened to discover when the prosecution wasn't having the success he'd hoped?" (*P* 113). Naturally, as the narrator recounts, Solinsky has considered this and is ready with his defence, in a Machiavellian way:

> If Petkanov hadn't signed that memorandum, he must have signed something like it. We are only putting into concrete form an order he must have given over the telephone. Or with a handshake, a nod, a pertinent failure to disapprove. *The document is true, even if it is a forgery. Even if it isn't true, it is necessary.* (*P* 113, italics added)

This is then the logic of Solinsky to convict Petkanov, the logic of "ends justify means," which is also the logic used by Petkanov himself to manage his former state, as implicated in the novel. Certainly, it is the power relation that Solinsky represents renders him act as such, that is, to use forgery evidence, so as to alter and/or rewrite history, which is also what "Big Brother" does in *Nineteen Eight-Four* and "the Pigs" do in *Animal*

Farm. Solinsky seems to realize this so that he has "a sudden, nauseating vision of the ... future rehabilitation," in which he is cast as a villain (*P* 78). Because history, as Orwell writes, "not only changed, but changed continuously" (83). If Petkanov is the dictator or "Big Brother" in the old regime, then we can say that after this trial Solinsky, like "the Pigs" in *Animal Farm* after the expulsion of their human master, has turned out to be the "Big Brother" in the new democracy. In other words, Peter Solinsky has become another Stoyo Petkanov, or they "are, in fact, alter egos of one another" (Kakutani C19), just as they share the same initials in their name (SP and PS) though in reversal (Duplain 34) ; because of this, in their last meeting, the convicted President warns Solinsky that "[y]ou cannot get rid of me" (*P* 136). This is with certainty one of the ironies or satires in the novel: the conviction of the former dictator of the "old" regime is built on the faked evidence concocted by the "new" democracy, which constitutes Solinsky's first charge against Petkanov: "deception involving documents" (*P* 32) and is no doubt the very strategy or means ("all necessary means") for the former dictator to suppress and purge "slanderers, saboteurs and anti-state criminals" (*P* 108), which include Anna Petkanov, the former Minister of Culture, Petkanov's own daughter (*P* 111).① This political power or politics not only changes the life of the individuals, but also alters the profile of history and certainly the writing of history or historiography. As Keith Jenkins theorizes, it is "those with the most power distribute and legitimate 'knowledge' *vis-à-vis* interests as best they can" (*Re-thinking History* 31), of which Petkanov in *The Porcupine* and the "Big Brother" in *Nineteen Eighty-Four* are both typical examples. The discussion so far proves that Petkanov is such a person with political power; as to the "Big Brother," we know that in his regime "[e]very record has been destroyed or falsified, every book has been re-written, every picture has been re-painted, every statue and street and building has been re-named, every date has been altered" (Orwell 162). It is in this sense that Barnes's political writing is in line with the inheritance of Orwell or is "Orwellian" (Freiburg 44) : they both, through the form of fictional writing, display the relation of political power and ideology to the writing of history or historiography; that is,

---

① What is implicitly critiqued by Julian Barnes is perhaps not ideological matter, but the "means" for the service of "ends," just as a critic acutely asserts, in the novel "Julian Barnes offers a portrait of political changes in Eastern Europe to criticize corruption, deception, craftiness and ambition, both in the old Communist system and in the emerging democratic order of the post-Communist transition period. It is not a question of bad and good ideologies, or Soviet Communism versus Western capitalism, but of a struggle between the unacceptable corruption that often entraps politicians and the implicit honesty that should reign over the political sphere" (Lázaro 123).

history or historiography is an ideological construction and the corollary of the exercise of (political) power. Considering what Barnes writes in *A History* and what he discloses in *The Porcupine*, it is not unsafe to say that Barnes's historical writing and postmodern textual practice corroborate the politically ideological attribute of history, which subverts the given view of history or historiography upheld by Ranke and the like.

The conflict between Petkanov and Solinsky ultimately represents the one between two different kinds of political ideologies, which is dramatically delineated in the novel and would be addressed in the next part about the issue of "The End of History." And the following discussion would refer to the historicity of this novel (text) or the reason for Barnes to write it, so as to make a more clear understanding about the critical positions implied in Barnes's writing, in light of his interpretation of the relation of art (literature) to politics. Critics have noticed that the novel or, to be exact, the trial of Stoyo Petkanov is based on the trial (from 1990 to 1991) of Todor Zhivkov the former President of Bulgaria. Why does Barnes base his novel on Todor Zhivkov's show trial? Because he knows well of the political and social contexts of the trial. Although the country is not revealed in the novel, Barnes later made it clear in an article published in 1992: "The novel deals with the trial of a former communist leader somewhere in the Balkans: the only such country where an ex-leader has actually been brought to trial is Bulgaria" ("How Much Is That in Porcupines?" 5); moreover, as mentioned before, the novel was firstly published in Bulgarian. Why Barnes has such an interest in Bulgaria? There is a story about it. Barnes's interest in Bulgaria started with the publication of *Flaubert's Parrot* in Bulgarian: in order to promote the novel about parrot, Barnes spent nine days there in November 1990 and for months before that he had cut out and collected every reference to Bulgaria in newspapers; and there Barnes noticed the disastrous political and economic situation of the country in the wake of the fall of old Communism and at the dawn of the introduction of a free market economy, such as the food shortages, the lack of petrol, the ration coupons, the electricity cuts, the queues, the upsurge of pornography and erotica, and the pollution, which were all noted down by Barnes in his notebook (and written in his novel); six months later, drawing inspiration from these notes, Barnes started composing *The Porcupine* (Guignery, *The Fiction of Julian Barnes* 86). This is no doubt the immediate reason for Barnes to write the novel. However, since most of Barnes's novels are non-political, why does he alter his subject matter at this juncture? Certainly, we can say that, as noted in the Introduction of this research, as "the chameleon of British letters," Barnes never writes the same book twice, and "his development has never been predictable" (Parrinder 18). In spite of this, we cannot deny the fact that the then political and social context has affected the Western intellectuals' mind so that, besides Barnes, other writers such as Malcolm Bradbury (1932-2000), Ian McEwan, Günter Grass (1927-), Philip Roth (1933-), Saul Bellow (1915-2005) and John Updike (1932-2009), among others, all show their interest in the then political event and ideological clash in Europe in their writings. Barnes, born in 1946 and spending his childhood and part of his adult life in the shadow of the Cold War, is captured by the *zeitgeist* of his times.

However, another reason that could not be dismissed is the "impatience with England" (Moseley 147). The England in the later 1980s and early 1990s "appears less ... *interesting*. Less ... *mythic*. Less like a place where important things are happening. And [...] if England seems a more diluted, washed-out kind of country these days, maybe that's because it *is*" (Leith 13, qtd. in Moseley 147, italics original). Therefore, when asked about his choice of an Eastern European political situation for *The Porcupine*, Barnes answered that "[t]here is no point in doing a little-England version of the American novel—the Empire is long dead. What is London the centre of in the world? Symphony orchestras, maybe. Symphony orchestras and royalty. But that doesn't make me want to write a novel about the Royal Family" (Leith 13, qtd. in Moseley 147-148). The then political conservatism and economic decline, as it were, renders British intellectuals despair; though perhaps not despaired, Barnes in his *Letters from London 1990-1995* criticizes Mrs. Thatcher, John Major and the Conservatives, and feels frustrated at the futile situation of British politics. Simply speaking, while at that time the political situation in Britain appeared to be a stagnant pool of water, the whole societies in Eastern Europe were in rough water, "moving from entrenched Marxism to something like western-style liberal democracy, the market economy, and civil freedoms" (Moseley 148). In addition, as Barnes observes, "Bulgaria [for the West] is the forgotten item in the Eastern European unshackling, a country that is doggedly down-page" ("Candles for the Living" 6-7). Then, under these circumstances, the writing of this political novel becomes not difficult for Barnes.

Many reviewers note that Stoyo Petkanov, a man of ideals, is depicted as much more impressive and compelling than his dull opponent Peter Solinsky. For instance, as Michael Scammell rightly remarks, Petkanov is presented as "a rugged, hearty, indomitable Communist scrapper, still fit in his 70s, capable of dominating not only his inquisitor but an entire courtroom and, through television, an entire country with the power of his will," whereas Solinsky as "not just a Hamlet," "also a turncoat, a former Communist who left the Party for the 'Greens' at the most propitious moment and made a career for himself in the opposition" and "a vacillating wimp, an intellectual tortured by self-doubt" (37). Therefore, the critic concludes that Barnes "weighs the scales in his favor, privileging Petkanov's utopian ideals, however twisted, and power politics, however unscrupulous, over Solinsky's democratic doubts and tortured moralism" (Scammell 37). Such a view seems to be verified by the very ending of the novel: an old woman stands silently in the rain, holding a small picture of Lenin tightly. Is Barnes on the side of the old woman and Leninism? Barnes is often considered as "a man of the Left" (Moseley 146) and one of the writers on the left (Hutchinson 243) ; but most of his work are not politically aware novels. Barnes's defence for Gustave Flaubert's uninterestedness in politics could give some hint about his attitude toward political writing: "*Literature includes politics, and not vice versa*" (*FP* 129, italics original).① This view is later echoed by Barnes in an interview that "art is greater than politics and that art includes politics, rather than vice versa," that "art isn't at the service of politics; politics is instead a potential subject for art" (Lewis). Accordingly, as Barnes contends, his job is "to describe life as it is and put that description into a particularly pleasing form of a story," but "in the describing of life, there is inevitably, if it's accurate, an implicit description of what's wrong with some of it. And to that extent writers can end up being political, depending again on the circumstance of society in which they live" (Lewis). The "description of what's wrong with some of it" in *The Porcupine* is that truth, justice and freedom are all ideologically distorted, be it in the old totalitarian regime or the new liberal democracy. In this way, the ostensibly simple ending of the novel does not show what Barnes's political, ideological proclivity is. However, it is reasonable to contend that Barnes displays his suspicion toward the master narratives of Communism and Capitalism, since both Petkanov (or old Communism) and Solinsky (or Capitalism) are treated with skepticism in his writing. This is, however, a sort of ambiguity or paradox in Barnes and in the Western intellectuals in general, which is decided by the power relation of the society in which they live politically and historically.

What should be pointed out at last is that *The Porcupine* also blurs the demarcation between fiction and reality, as Barnes does in many of his novels, which endows the novel with a typical postmodern aura.

---

① Barnes has a more detailed explanation about this view: "Novelists who think their writing an instrument of politics seem to me to degrade writing and foolishly exalt politics. No, I'm not saying they should be forbidden from having political opinions or from making political statements. It's just that they should call that part of their work journalism. The writer who imagines that the novel is the most effective way of taking part in politics is usually a bad novelist, a bad journalist, and a bad politician. " (*FP* 129-130)

Undoubtedly, it is "fabricated" by Barnes, and as such we can find that there are some differences between Stoyo Petkanov and Todor Zhivkov, as observed by critics (Duplain 35; Scammell 37). However, Barnes tends to write it as a serious comment on the contemporary Eastern Europe, so that not a few real historical figures (such as Frank Sinatra, Mikhail Gorbachev, Erich Honecker, Janos Kadar, Gustave Husak, Wojciech Jaruzelski and Nicolae Ceausescu) and historical events or facts are alluded to in the novel, thus authenticating the historical and geographical context and establishing the continuity between fiction and reality. Just as Linda Hutcheon remarks, "[i]n many historical novels, the real figures of the past are deployed to validate or authenticate the fictional world by their presence, as if to hide the joins between fiction and history in a formal and ontological sleight of hand" (*A Poetics of Postmodernism* 114). Thus considered, Barnes's writing represents the historical reality of that time so that many Bulgarian readers applaud the book, regarding it as a truth-told novel (Barnes, "How Much Is That in Porcupines?" 5). On the other hand, the introduction of real-world figures into a fictional world also "foregrounds the ontological boundaries between fiction and reality" (Sesto 125), which is nevertheless not conventional at all and is a postmodern(ist) execution of historical writing, not identified by some critics such as Merritt Moseley, who argues that "[t]here is nothing postmodern about it; it is not tricky, or experimental or dazzling" (148). Brian McHale explains that "[t]here is an ontological scandal when a real world figure is inserted in a fictional situation, where he interacts with purely fictional characters" (85). The encounter between Stoyo Petkanov and Mikhail Gorbachev is a good case in point. As written in the novel, in one conference Petkanov puts forward a union between his country and Russia. But Gorbachev, suspicious that Petkanov is employing this as a ploy to evade payment of his country's debts, rejects the proposal. From then on, the relationship between them deteriorates. Then we can see that in his consciousness Petkanov curses Gorbachev as "that weak cunt with birdshit on his head" (*P* 87) and "that cunt in the Kremlin" (*P* 88) and denounces Gorbachev for betraying Communism and selling out to the West. Perhaps because of this, Vanessa Guignery asserts that the insertion of real-world figures in a fictional situation would "deprive the historical figures of their authenticity, turning them into puppets which have been manipulated by a fictional protagonist" (*The Fiction of Julian Barnes* 91). In short, we could say that on one hand Barnes endeavors to achieve a sense of documentary verisimilitude by way of introducing some historical figures, the device used in some conventional historical writing, but on the other he also attempts to explore the effects of blurring the conventional boundaries between fiction and reality, as many postmodern novelists do; in consequence, as "a new form of political fiction" (Byrne 253), *The Porcupine* both involves contemporary historical reality and insists on maintaining its status as a work of fiction, a juxtaposition vital to the postmodern(ist) literary experience, and a recurrent ambiguity in Barnes's postmodern historical writing.

ii. Not "The End of History"

With the collapse of the Berlin Wall in 1989 and the disintegration of communist regimes in Eastern Europe in the early 1990s, a sanguine mindset turns up in the Western world, which claims that the clash between Socialism and Capitalism has ended and that the world would be dominated by Capitalism and liberal democracy. In such a political and historical context, American political theorist Francis Fukuyama (1952-) puts forward his hypothesis, firstly in "The End of History?" (1989) and then in *The End of History and the Last Man* (1992), that history has ended because Western liberal democracy has triumphed over Communism and by implication Marxism too. Fukuyama's bold contention has many adherents in the ensuing period immediately following the collapse of old Communism in Europe in the 1990s. But soon a growing body of dissenting voices turns up and queries Fukuyama's assertion, among which Jacques Derrida's is an intriguing one, mainly demonstrated in *Specters of Marx: The State of the Debt, the Work of Mourning, and the New International* (1994, later in this research abridged as *Specters of Marx*). Eventually, "The End of History" becomes a catchy word, and the issue of "The End of History" turns to be a heated topic not only for political theorists, philosophers, but also for literary theorists and even novelists. This part will firstly refer to Fukuyama's hypothesis of "The End of History" and Derrida's refutation against it[①], its imprint on postmodern historical writing, and then substantiate how Barnes's writing in *The Porcupine* addresses the politically ideological conflict, pointing out that, as a politically aware writer, Barnes is in effect responding to the issue of "The End of History" through the form of fictional writing.

According to Fukuyama, "a remarkable consensus concerning the legitimacy of liberal democracy as a system of government had emerged throughout the world over the past few years, as it conquered rival ideologies like hereditary monarchy, fascism, and most recently communism" (*The*

[①] The issue of "The End of History" and Derrida's writing are complicated; thus, what is dealt with here is but a brief introduction to them, so as to provide a social, cultural and theoretical context for the discussion of the political, ideological implication in *The Porcupine*.

End of History **xi**), for it represents "the most rational form of government, that is, the state that realizes most fully either rational desire or rational recognition" (*The End of History* 211-212) ; thus Fukuyama contends that liberal democracy may constitute the "end point of mankind's ideological evolution" and the "final form of human government" and therefore represents the "end of history" (*The End of History* **xi**). Based on empirical facts, Fukuyama concludes that "the *ideal* of liberal democracy could not be improved upon" (*The End of History* **xi**, italics original), which implies that the ideological conflict would become a thing of the past and that a new world order beckons. This is then the "good news" he announces in his writing: "liberal democracy and free markets constitute the best regime, or more precisely the best of the available alternative ways of organizing human societies" and "[i]t most fully (though not completely) satisfies the most human longings, and therefore can be expected to be more universal and more durable than other regimes or other principles of political organization" ("Reflection on the End of History, Five Years Later" 29). With no doubt, Fukuyama's declaration of "The End of History" elicits a flurry of discussion and debate. Postmodernist thinkers, as Stuart Sim suggests, "have been particularly attracted to notions like the end of history" (22). For instance, Derrida, Jean-François Lyotard and Jean Baudrillard all contribute their writing to this issue, among which Derrida's *Specters of Marx* seems to be more compelling to be referred to here but briefly.

When Marx's reputation is perhaps at the lowest point of his intellectual history, Derrida tends to resurrect it in the timely book *Specters of Marx*. At the beginning of his work, Derrida firstly points out the necessity and significance of (re)reading Marx or Marxism, by claiming that there is "no future without Marx, without the memory and the inheritance of Marx: in any case of a certain Marx, of his genius, of at least one of his spirits" and that "*there is more than one of them, there must be more than one of them*" (*Specters of Marx* 13, italics original). Thus, Marx or Marx's spirit, for Derrida, is plural (*Specters of Marx* 75, 86). Then Derrida insightfully indicates that Fukuyama's hypothesis is "a dogmatics" built on "paradoxical and suspect conditions" (*Specters of Marx* 51) and "is essentially a Christian eschatology" (*Specters of Marx* 60), so as to predominantly in his second and third chapters demolish Fukuyama through the analysis of the ideological nature of the latter's hypothesis, his philosophical and political naivety and pseudo-evangelism, among others. For instance, unlike Fukuyama who spares no effort to celebrate liberal democracy, Derrida criticizes and satirizes it instead.① It is certain that, with the intervention of Derrida, the issue of "The End of History" will not end, so that the specter or spirit of Marx would be haunting us for all time.

In fact, the issue of "The End of History" also results in various responses from the then writers or novelists.② As Del Ivan Janik comments, "[o]ne product of the 'end of history' is literary postmodernism" (160), which does not necessarily intimate that history and the notion of history could not become the subject and theme of fiction. Instead, as the critic observes, "[i]ndeed, a significant number of the more ambitious English novels of the 1980s and 1990s have in common an acute consciousness of history and a sharp focus on its meanings or potential for meaning" (Janik 160-161). The hybridization or combination of "literary postmodernism" and the "consciousness of history," naturally, engenders one kind of particular historical fiction, that is, "new historical fiction" or historiographic metafiction. The novels of British writers such as Peter Ackroyd, Julian Barnes and Graham Swift represent this category of historical writing. As to Barnes, his *Flaubert's Parrot* and *A History* are often considered as historiographic metafiction, as noted before. With no doubt, the much more concern for history in literary works, in whatever ways or modes, registers that the writing of history does not end in literary

---

① More specifically, Fukuyama in his book glosses over the discrepancy between reality and ideal with regard to liberal democracy, while Derrida discerningly discloses that "the gap between fact and ideal essence does not show up only in these so-called primitive forms of government, theocracy, and military dictatorship" but "also characterize, *a priori* and by definition, *all* democracies, including the oldest and most stable of so-called Western democracies" (*Specters of Marx* 64, italics original); while Fukuyama applauds the acceptance of liberal democracy, Derrida queries with a hint of asperity that "is it still necessary to point out that liberal democracy of the parliamentary form has never been so much in the minority and so isolated in the world? That it has never been in such a state of dysfunction in what we call the Western democracies?" (*Specters of Marx* 78-79). Derrida then substantiates his idea with the enumeration of numerous failings of liberal democracy, including mass unemployment, the plight of the homeless, the ruthless economic war between European countries, thorny problems in free market and foreign debt, the spread of nuclear weapons, inter-ethnic wars, and the manipulation of the United Nations, etc., with a view of calling for the construction of a "New International" of left-wing interests, "to continue the fight against injustice that had spurred Marx on to the composition of his most work" (Sim 55-56). This theoretical blueprint is not merely out of Derrida's debate with Fukuyama, it also results from his inheritance from Marx's spirit or Marxism, just as the second quote heading this chapter tells, Derrida, like all of us, cannot not be the heir of Marx or Marxism.

② In the year of 1992, besides Barnes's *The Porcupine*, other two important European writers Ian McEwan and Günter Grass also published their politically, historically aware novels: the former's *Black Dogs* is about the ideological estrangement of a couple of Communists, the latter's *The Call of the Toad* about the overthrow of Communism.

imagination. Barnes's *The Porcupine*, we would argue, deals with the issue of "The End of History" in a subtle way, displaying the intense conflict of politics and ideology, prominently illustrated in the encounters between the protagonist and the antagonist, suggesting that "the end of history" does not beckon, with his ambiguous "positions" and an open ending.

The main focus of *The Porcupine* lies in the dramatic conflict between two political ideologies, that is, Communism and Capitalism, which is mainly delineated in the encounter between Stoyo Petkanov, an old school Communist, and Peter Solinsky, a new proponent for liberal democracy. The discussion to follow will exemplify how Barnes describes the ideological clash between these two characters as to their respective defense for their own ideological stance.

In the novel, Petkanov is depicted as an orthodox, staunch Communist, steadfast in his belief in Socialism and Communism, never giving in to his opponent. From the start in his encounter with Solinsky, Petkanov seems to be on the upper side, by not "play[ing] the part allotted him" and keeping his own "script in mind" (P 17). When firstly imprisoned, "quite illegally, without mentioning any charges," Petkanov, as the Second Leader of the country for thirty-three years, refuses to be treated as a criminal, asking protestingly for more food supply (P 9-12), and " refuse[s] legal representation" (P 14), which gives rise to his encounter with Solinsky the Prosecutor General in person (P 39). It is in these personal encounters that their personalities and past are unearthed, so is their ideological clash. In their first meeting, the issues of food shortage and the woman's rights are mentioned, for instance. For the old leader, women should be cornered in the kitchen, and should not come out to protest on the street for any reason; when Solinsky answers that it is "their right," the former President satirizes that " [a] government that cannot keep its women in the kitchen is fucked" (P 13), and tells to the point that "they were only protesting against the fact that there is now less food in the shops than at any time under Socialism" (P 16). Solinsky evades Petkanov's sharp interrogation by saying that he is not "to discuss the difficulties inherent in the changeover from a controlled economy to a market economy" (P 16). Fukuyama would agree with Solinsky that economic difficulties are temporary and would be solved at last, for he believes that "liberal democracy in reality constitutes the best possible solution to the human problem" (*The End of History* 338). On the contrary, Derrida would not hold such a view in that he discloses many thorny problems in liberal democracy, which are not solved but deteriorate. Barnes, though considered as a left-wing writer by some critics, does not show any hint of agreement with Petkanov or Solinsky. On the other hand, through Solinsky's ten-year old daughter's naïve questions and Solinsky's responses, Barnes exhibits his incredulity toward Petkanov's theory of "food in the shops" (*P* 12). One of the questions and answers goes like this: "Why were there so many apricot trees in the countryside but never apricots in the shops?" "Because we sell them abroad for hard currency that we need" (*P* 26). More significantly, in the recountal of the rise of the opposite Green Party, the more serious issue of environmental pollution is referred to, which turns out to be a crucial reason for the collapse of the old totalitarian regime: there was "a river from which no fish had been taken for years. The trees above the town grew twisted and low, rarely putting out leaves," and "[c]hildren developed chest ailments from infancy; women wrapped scarves round their faces before going out to shop; doctors' surgeries were full of burnt lungs and tortured eyes" (*P* 27). In this sense, Petkanov's accusation of Solinsky pertinent to economic situation is but a self-deception. Therefore, in this round of debate, there is no victor.

In the following encounters between these two ideological opponents, various economic, social and political issues are brought to the fore gradually, such as the issues of food shortage, inflation, pollution, black market, pornography, prostitution, freedom, truth, etc. As "a true believer in Socialism and Communism," who has "never wavered from the path" (*P* 130), Petkanov, via the "tactics" he used at the very beginning, fights against Solinsky at their every meeting. When Solinsky refers to the fact for the former President that newspapers under new liberal democracy have the freedom to express their views, Petkanov refutes that " [a]ll newspapers belong to some party, some interest. Either the capitalists or the people" (*P* 41). When Solinsky tells the former "helmsman of the nation" that Americans and Germans invest in the country, Petkanov rebuts that they come here "to rape and pillage," for "[t]hey put a small amount of money into our country in order to take a larger amount out. That is the way of capitalism and imperialism and those who allow it are not only traitors but economic cretins" (*P* 60). When Solinsky discloses that Petkanov despises people, never trusts them and spies on them all the time, the former Head of State argues that he is "a man of the people" (*P* 68), "a hard-working man of the people" and "knows what people want" (*P* 69). Here their ideological clash seems to reach to the highest point and the former President's speech appears to be more reasonable and impressive:

> And what do people want? They want stability and hope. We gave them that. Things might not have been perfect, but with Socialism people could dream that one day they might be. You—you have only give them instability and hopelessness. A crime wave. The black market. Pornography. Prostitution. Foolish women gibbering in front of priests

again. The so-called Crown Prince offering himself as saviour of the nation. You are proud of these swift achievements? (*P* 69)

To this, Solinsky admittedly responds, "[t]here are difficulties," for "[t]his is a period of transition. There have to be painful readjustments. We must understand the realities of economic life" (*P* 70). There are still more similar attacks and counter-attacks occurring between Petkanov and Solinsky in the novel, which will not be enumerated here. It is manifest that they are not (merely) personal, but political and historical, with the rich implications of ideological conflict. We can assume that Solinsky, just like Fukuyama, spares no effort to defend liberal democracy and capitalism, and eventually out of his character and moral conscience convicts Petkanov of being guilty, while Petkanov sticks to his own belief in Socialism and Communism, which has been tested out through such ordeals as imprisonment, the fighting against fascism and against Gorbachev's selling out to the West, as delineated in the novel. Nevertheless, Barnes's point is not merely to describe two graphic characters, but more meaningfully to substantiate the ideological conflict represented in them, thus mirroring a certain picture of contemporary historical reality.

From the adumbration of the characterization of Petkanov and Solinsky, Barnes appears to be in favor of the former leader, who has a staunch belief in his faith and fights to the last minute, and against the ambitious but self-doubted intellectual Solinsky, who is unfaithful not only to his wife but to his belief (Scammell 37). Does this mean that Barnes upholds the belief that is engrained in Petkanov's mind, or that he totally opposes what Solinsky now pursues? Barnes's own remarks is a possible answer to this: " It's a political novel about that old but still true problem: the weakness of liberalism confronted by the certainty of a system that believes it has all the answers" (Freiburg 46). In fact, Barnes does not give us a definite answer in his remarks, or perhaps there are no definite answers to it. Still, we can look at " the problem" that is represented in the novel and that has an affinity with the issue of " The End of History" again but in a different way.

As the President of the old regime, Petkanov is accused of many crimes, as discussed before. However, the crimes are not merely out of his personal vices such as greed and hypocrisy, but also out of the political power endued with him by the regime. Thus, the charge against him is not merely against him but against the regime that he represents. Then what is accused of about the old regime in the novel? Alberto Lázaro perceptively points out that " Petkanov's political regime was an absolute and oppressive single-party government that permitted no individual freedom and attempted to control all aspects of people's life through coercion and repression" (124), which is expressed or implied in the novel.① Still, an indirect reproach of the main flaws of this regime is subtly suggested when Solinsky's daughter, at the age of ten, asks her father four "naïve" questions: "Why were there so many soldiers when there wasn't a war? Why were there so many apricot trees in the countryside but never apricots in the shop? Why is there fog over the city in the summer? Why do all those people live on that waste ground beyond the eastern boulevard?" (P 124). These naïve questions and the possible answers, as Lázaro notes, underscore four basic maladies that Barnes indicates as characteristics of the old regime in Eastern Europe: police repression, deficient centrally planned economy, disregard for the environment, and social inequalities (124). Some of the features and the references to torture, genocide, and manipulation of history or historiography, remind us of the world depicted in *Nineteen Eighty-Four*. Therefore, we can discern that, in spite of the fact that Petkanov claims that there is no lack of food in shops and that there is stability under his old regime,② Barnes in effect displays his incredulity toward the "certainty" of this old Communist regime. Similarly, Barnes also substantiates the "weakness of liberalism" or liberal democracy, as mentioned in the attacks and counterattacks between Petkanov and Solinsky. Could Solinsky become justifiable by saying that "[t]his is a period of transition. There have to be painful adjustments"? Such an excuse would be echoed by Fukuyama, but rejected by Derrida. Derrida describes the weakness or vices of liberal democracy in contemporary capitalist world in his third chapter of *Specters of Marx* (77 – 94) to testify that the weakness of liberal democracy or the situation as Solinsky acknowledges in the novel is constant, not temporary, due to its nature, as Marx presaged. In this sense, it is not unsafe to say that Barnes's and Derrida's writings bear the similar spirit of critique of capitalism. All in all, both old Communism and Capitalism are undermined in the novel, which prefigures the novel's ambiguous conclusion, anyhow.

Unlike Derrida, who puts forward, though theoretically, a plan of

---

① For instance, demonstration would be "ringed by troops under the command of an officer" (P 2), and "any public gathering of more than eight people had to be officially registered, and the registration procedure might be very *ad hoc*, consisting of men in leather coats demanding to know names and addresses" (P 52); apartments were bugged by security police (P 7); there were "routine purges" of Party members (P 25); loyal citizens were executed for being traitors and then became martyrs whenever the political situation called for (P 101–103).

② In his final speech in the court, Petkanov glorifies his regime as such: "I have been helmsman of this nation for thirty-three years. Unemployment has been abolished. Inflation has been controlled by scientific methods. The fascists have been routed. Peace has been uninterrupted. Prosperity has increased. Under my guidance, this country has grown in international stature" (P 121).

constructing a "New International," Barnes does not propose any plan but wisely leaves an open ending. In the coda of the novel, Petkanov is sentenced to thirty years of internal exile, although his crimes are not actually proved; and Solinsky is not the victorious side in the political trial, for he is abandoned by his wife due to his dishonest behavior in the trial. On the whole, we can see that for one thing the demise of Petkanov's regime and the signs of approaching spring (symbolically) suggest the possibility that liberal democracy would take root and Solinsky will survive his personal crises, while for another the new democracy is itself deeply flawed, as is tested by Solinsky's expediential use of forged evidence to convict Petkanov and by the new government's failure to improve life quality for the common people. This ambiguity implied is enhanced by its very ending, which goes like this:

> In front of the vacant Mausoleum of the First Leader an old woman stood alone. She wore a woolen scarf wrapped round a woolen hat, and both were soaked. In outstretched fists she held a small framed print of V. I. Lenin. Rain bubbled the image, but his indelible face pursued each passer-by. Occasionally, a committed drunk or some chattering thrush of a student would shout across at the old woman, at the thin light veering off the wet glass. But whatever the words, she stood her ground, and she remained silent. (*P* 138)

Here before examining this ending, we first of all should get to know this old woman. The old woman is the grandmother of Stefan, one of the four young students, who has "gone along to those first anxious protests" and "watched and marched and shouted" (*P* 20), thinking that it is "a great moment in their country's history" (*P* 20), "the nation's sudden passage from enforced adolescence to delayed maturity" (*P* 22), and the time to "learn the truth" (*P* 23). They watch the proceedings of the trial on television, and their talks and curses about Petkanov are inserted intermittently in the narrative in italics and square brackets, as the instant responses to Petkanov's courtroom statements, functioning as a kind of chorus like that in the drama. When these students watch the trial on television, Stefan's grandmother refuses to do so, but sits "a few metres away in the kitchen, underneath a small framed colour print of V. I. Lenin" (*P* 53), speaking little nowadays, just like a specter, ignoring the existence of the young students. When Solinsky is exposed to a scandal by Petkanov, a dramatic scene turns up in the novel: "*the students were momentarily silent*, Stefan's grandmother cackled to herself quietly in the kitchen while the television played to an empty sitting-room" (*P* 87, italics original), which tells that the grandmother shows concern for the trial, not watching it but listening to it. Evidently, the young students are on the side of Solinsky, while the old woman is on the side of Petkanov; therefore, as Petkanov and Solinsky constitute a set of binary opposition, the old woman and the young students represent another one. Thus there are different classes of supporters for different ideologies, their opposite views and acts differently explored in the novel.

However, there is no clear resolution, as Alberto Lázaro puts it (125), although the very ending of the novel would make critics assume that Barnes is on the side of the old woman. It is perhaps not in accordance with Barnes's own intent, that is, "to describe life as it is and put that description into a particularly pleasing form of a story" (Lewis; Freiburg 48). But it is reasonable to say that the ending of the novel intimates that "clean breaks with the past simply don't exist" (Duplain 35) and that it is not "the end of (hi)story," either, which represents Barnes's postmodern, critical response in the form of fictional writing to the contemporary historical reality happening in Eastern Europe and witnessed by himself and to the contention of "The End of History" (particularly) upheld by Fukuyama. In light of this, we would maintain that, like Derrida, Barnes demonstrates his postmodern critical attitude toward the vice and weakness of both authoritarian regime and liberal democracy in a deconstructive way, implicitly demolishing Fukuyama's view of "The End of History" by way of his writing and especially an open ending in *The Porcupine*, which indicates that the disintegration of old Communism in Eastern Europe does not necessarily entail that liberal democracy and its attendant capitalist economic system have won.[①] Moreover, the whole situation around the world in this post-Marxist period all the more corroborates the absurdity of Fukuyama's, the rightfulness of Derrida's and the insight of Barnes's. In this sense, Barnes's writing also evinces that literary writing is a sort of practice: when literature represents the contemporary historical reality, it has already engaged in this history and become part of it.

Coincidently or not, we can find in Derrida's *Specters of Marx* the reference to "Porpentine" (93), an obsolete version of "porcupine," the very title of Barnes's novel. As noted before, Barnes is very familiar with French language and culture, and he once told that he had "read a few pages of Derrida" (Freiburg 37); no wonder, his critical attitude or critique spirit is similar to Derrida's, both bearing the strategy of deconstruction or

---

[①] In the novel, the grandmother and "a few hundred other loyalists" in the country, just like the specters of Marxism, still exist and protest (*P* 54), and the grandmother even envisions "the moment when men and women would rise and shake themselves, recovering their rightful dignity and starting again the whole glorious cycle of revolution," believing that "it would come to pass" (*P* 55).

"subversion of the given." Whether Derrida has ever read Barnes or not is a mystery, despite the fact that *The Porcupine* was published two years before *Specters of Marx* and made some sensation in (at least) Bulgaria. Nevertheless, this is not important here; what I would contend is that Barnes and Derrida are both heirs of Marx or Marxism and they, in their writings about politics and history and their relations, critique what Marx once critiqued, by way of Marx's spirit.

The next section will expatiate on how Barnes aims his critique spirit at England, showing his deep concern for its present and future conditions, not merely politically.

II. History and Hetero-topia[①]

"Utopia" is an imagined form of ideal or superior human society, or a written work of fiction or philosophical speculation describing such a society that does not exist in reality (Baldick 269). The word "utopia" was coined by Sir Thomas More in his Latin work *Utopia* (1516), as a pun on two Greek words *eutopos*, meaning "good place," and *outopos*, meaning "no place" (Abrams 328). More's account of an ideal commonwealth was followed by several others such as Francis Bacon's *New Atlantis* (1627), Samuel Butler's *Erewhon* (1872), Edward Bellamy's *Looking Backward: 2000-1887* (1888), William Morris's *News From Nowhere* (1890) and H. G. Well's *A Modern Utopia* (1900). Utopian fiction has been often used as the basis of satire on contemporary life or to "satirize humanity's dreams about and longings for utopia in general" (Murfin and Ray 493). The term "dystopia," the opposite of utopia, represents a "bad place," usually set at some point in the author's future, and describes a society in which we would not want to live. The writing of dystopia aims to "alert readers to the potential pitfalls and dangers of society's present course or of a course society might conceivably take one day," by way of "depicting unpleasant, disastrous, or otherwise terrifying consequences for the protagonists as well as humanity as a whole" (Murfin and Ray 122). The typical instances of such a genre include Aldous Huxley's *Brave New World* (1932), George Orwell's *Nineteen Eighty-Four* (1949) and Margaret Atwood's *The Handmaid's Tale* (1985). As a writer with humanistic thought and a strong awareness of

---

① Here in this section I will refer to the idea of hetero-topia in a literal sense. Michel Foucault made a thorough analysis on hétérotopies, consisting of six different types of spaces or places (see a brief introduction to this concept by Foucault in Shang Jie 82–91). What I would discuss here about hetero-topia could be included in the sphere of Foucaultian hétérotopies; but the reversal is not true.

history, Julian Barnes does not only rethink the past, but also show concern for the present and the future of human beings (history) ; in other words, he often critiques the present through his (re)writing of the past so as to make suggestions for the future or writes of the future to criticize or satirize the present so as to warn people of the present against the potential dangers or perils.① A close reading of Barnes's novels like *Staring at the Sun*, *The Porcupine* and *England, England* would evince that what Barnes depicts in his novels are neither utopias nor dystopias. For Barnes, a writer with postmodern thoughts (of deconstruction), to write about "a good place" or "a bad place" would be both involved in metaphysical traps, which is against Barnes's own will, for he, like Jacques Derrida, prefers the diversity or variety of "positions" to a certain one, as he does in *The Porcupine*. Therefore, it is appropriate to use the word "hetero-topia," a heterogeneous place, to describe the worlds adumbrated in Barnes's fiction since they are neither utopia nor dystopia. This section will explore how Barnes creates a world of historical simulacra in *England, England*, through his parodying the theory of (postmodern) simulacra and how he delineates a place "neither idyllic nor dystopia" to show how a region like England could deteriorate in the future, and to write a warning letter to its people before the dawn of the third millennium.

i. "We Must Demand the Replica"

Julian Barnes's *England, England* deals with such themes as authenticity, history, Englishness, the commodification of historical heritage and the invention of cultural tradition in an original, postmodern way. Or to quote Barnes himself, the novel is about "the idea of England, authenticity, the search for truth, the invention of tradition, and the way in which we forget our own history" (Marr 15). It is often considered as "a stinging caricature of contemporary England's spiritually void heritage industry" (Landon 174) and a satire " of corporate ambition gone wild in a culture that values

---

① In *Staring at the Sun* (1986), for instance, Barnes depicts a future world dominated by technology, in which the whole of human knowledge is stored in computers for people to get easy access. In spite of this, as Barnes's writing confirms, the future technology could not solve such speculative questions as the meaning of life, the status of death and the existence of God, intimating that it is human heart or humanity instead of technological evolution that plays the decisive role in human society. Barnes's concern for the human future is also demonstrated in his first political novel *The Porcupine* (1992), in which Barnes delineates the contemporary historical reality after the fall of old Communism in Eastern Europe and implicitly presages that the future of human society would not be overwhelmingly reigned by one political system like liberal democracy but consists of different forms of political systems.

convenience above all else" (Charles 19). It is composed of three sections: "England;" "England, England;" and "Anglia." Here in this part I will focus on the second section of the novel, in which Barnes creates a world of historical simulacra and hyperreality, satirizing the heritage tourism via his parodying the theory of simulacra put forward by Jean Baudrillard; and in the next part I will turn to its third section to examine Barnes's depiction of a world "neither idyllic nor dystopia" to exhibit Barnes's concern and rethinking of the future of England.

In the second section of *England, England*, Barnes makes great efforts to present a postmodern world of simulacra labeled as "England, England." To profile this world of simulacra, we have to start with its creator Sir Jack Pitman. As Barnes introduces, Sir Jack "is a big man in every sense of the word," "[b]ig in ambition, big in appetite, big in generosity," and "[f]rom small beginnings, he has risen like a meteor to great things" to become "[e]ntrepreneur, innovator, ideas man, arts patron, inner-city revitalizer" and "a man who walks with presidents" (*EE* 30). As the story begins, Sir Jack asks his employees: "What is there left for me?" (*EE* 32), to which he responds boastfully: "I have built business from the dust up. I have made money … . Honours have come my way. I am the trusted confidant of heads of state. I have been the lover … of beautiful women. I am a respected … member of society. I have a title. My wife sits at the right hand of presidents" (*EE* 32). Then the tycoon asks another question "What is real?," which is central to the understanding of the novel, and speaks arrogantly to his inferiors: "Are you real, for instance […] You are real to yourselves, of course, but […] My answer would be No. […] *I could have you replaced with substitutes, with … simulacra*" (*EE* 32, italics added). Next, the magnate continues to question his employees and answer himself, concluding that what he needs is "one last great idea. One for the road" (*EE* 35). Then Barnes writes out his character's thought as such: "Yes, one last great idea. The world had not been entirely respectful in recent years. Well then, the world needed to be astonished" (*EE* 35). Bearing this in mind, Sir Jack then solicits his consultant for advice about his new client "England." The latter articulates his view about England metaphorically: "So England comes to me, and what do I say to her? I say, 'Listen, baby, face facts. We're in the third millennium and your tits have dropped. The solution is not a push-up bra'" (*EE* 38). This consultant considers himself as a patriot, yet he does not believe in modern ancestor-ship; instead, for his part, patriotism should be pro-active: if one day the whole of Ireland, Scotland and Wales would declare independence as a sovereign state respectively, England should not stand in the way,① just as "the noble discipline of philosophy" had let go of other "sorts of skill-zones" such as medicine, astronomy, law, physics and aesthetics when they down the centuries "had spun off from the main body and set up on its own" (*EE* 39). Thence, in his mind, England, just like philosophy that still addresses life's central problems, would not lose her strong and unique individuality established over so many centuries. The consultant admits that England has lost its past glory but it has what others don't, that is, "an accumulation of time" (*EE* 40) and speaks out his suggestion for Sir Jack: "England—my client—is ... a nation of great age, great history, great accumulated wisdom. Social and cultural history [is] eminently marketable, never more so than in the current climate. ... We are the new pioneers. We must sell our past to other nations as their future!" (*EE* 41). Undoubtedly, such a view has won a great popularity right now and especially for heritage tourism in Britain. More importantly, what this consultant utters indicates "a combination of nostalgia and mourning for a lost Englishness with an anxiety for, or a coming to terms with, the present condition and future projections of England" (Bentley 483). That is, through this character, Barnes discloses the fact that there is a general sense of "perceived diminution of national identity" among the English (Corner and Harvey 45), and that the concern for and the stress on heritage have become their response to the loss of Empire (and the threat of assimilating English identity into the EEC).

Getting his "last great idea" from his consultant for his Project to build an essence-of-England theme park to show his patriotism and make a fortune as well, Sir Jack then invites an unnamed French intellectual to educate the Project's Co-ordinating committee. After the intertextual reference to some French thinkers or philosophers like Pascal, Rousseau, Lévi-Strauss and Baudrillard, the French intellectual points out that Sir Jack's Project is profoundly modern and underlines that "*nowadays we prefer the replica to the original. We prefer the reproduction of the work of art to the work of art itself*" (*EE* 55, italics added). Then the intellectual cites evidence to show that "the number of visitor minutes spent in front of the replica exceeds by any manner of calculation the number of visitor minutes spent in front of the original" (*EE* 55), emphasizing that it is "important to understand that in

---

① Here Barnes refers explicitly to the (historical) reality of the inclination of Scotland, Wales and Northern Ireland for independence from the United Kingdom, as referred to in Chapter One of this research. For instance, it is reported that in the year of 2014, Scotland will have another referendum as regards the separation from the Kingdom. And the council of the Isle of Wight also has the intent to separate itself from the United Kingdom, as reported. That is also one of the reasons why Barnes chooses the Isle of Wight as the site for Sir Jack's last *magnum opus*.

the modern world we prefer the replica to the original because it gives us the greater *frisson*" (*EE* 56), followed by his explanation that "[t]o understand this, we must understand and confront our insecurity, our existential indecision, the profound atavistic fear we experience when we are face to face with the original" and that "[w]e have nowhere to hide when we are presented with an alternative reality to our own, a reality which appears more powerful and therefore threatens us" (*EE* 56). To get his idea across, the French intellectual quotes more instances, especially the theory of an old French thinker, "one of those old *soixante-huitards* of the last century," to support his view (*EE* 56). More specifically, the old thinker has pointed out a profound truth in his remark that "[a]ll that was once directly lived" "has become mere representation,"① which is nevertheless not praise but criticism, according to the French intellectual. Then the unnamed French intellectual further interprets the old thinker's thought in such a fashion:

> Once there was only the world, directly lived. Now there is the representation—let me fracture that word, the re-presentation—of the world. It is not a substitute for that plain and primitive world, but an enhancement and enrichment, an ironization and summation of that world. This is where we live today. ... In conclusion ... the world of the third millennium is inevitably, is ineradicably modern, and that it is our intellectual duty to submit to that modernity, and to dismiss as sentimental and inherently fraudulent all yearnings for what is dubiously termed the "original." (*EE* 57)

What is implied in the speeches of this French intellectual is, as Barnes writes, that "[w]e must demand the replica, since the reality, the truth, the authenticity of the replica is the one we can possess, colonize, reorder, find *jouissance* in, and finally ... it is the reality which, since it is our destiny, we may meet, confront, and destroy" (*EE* 57). Here it is not difficult to see that the profile of the French intellectual is playful, "a clear parody of Jean Baudrillard" (Bentley 491), who nevertheless acutely critiques the culture of simulacra.

---

① The "old thinker" referred to here is Guy Debord (1931–1994), a French Marxist theorist, writer, filmmaker, member of the Letterist International and the founding member of the Situationist International (SI). His best known works are his theoretical books, *The Society of the Spectacle* and *Comments on the Society of the Spectacle*, the former of which had made a great influence on the movement of Paris in May 1968. The sentence that "All that was once directly lived has become mere representation" is quoted from thesis 1 in *The Society of the Spectacle*, which proves that Barnes is familiar with French culture and has read not a few theoretical books about contemporary cultural thoughts.

With such theoretical underpinnings, Sir Jack sets out to implement his Project. First of all, he instructs his Concept Developer to target "[t]op fifty characteristics associated with the word England among prospective purchasers of Quality Leisure" and his Official Historian "to find out how much people know" (*EE* 60) so as to build a perfect replica of people's conceptions of England and Englishness, and then asks his employees to suggest a place for his Project. Finally, he decides to select as the site for his Project the Isle of Wight, an island with little historical heritage but a "mixture of rolling chalk downland of considerable beauty and bungaloid dystopia" (*EE* 76), a "location dying for makeover and upgrade" (*EE* 79). When the Fifty Quintessences of Englishness[①] are searched out through the survey conducted by the Concept Developer, Sir Jack and his committee have not a few discussions about these quintessences connected with Englishness, trying to remake or reposition some myths for modern times, for most people in the third millennium don't want what historians think of as history but just want to "enjoy what they already know" (*EE* 73-74), and also plan on how to pursue the Island and persuade the Royal family to relocate to it. When everything is prepared, Sir Jack chooses his sixty-fifth birthday as the appropriate date for action (*EE* 173) : on the day, the Council of the Island

---

[①] The Fifty Quintessences of Englishness include: 1. Royal family; 2. Big Ben/Houses of Parliament; 3. Manchester United Football Club; 4. Class system; 5. Pubs; 6. A Robin in the snow; 7. Robin Hood and his Merrie Men; 8. Cricket; 9. White cliffs of Dover; 10. Imperialism; 11. Union Jack; 12. Snobbery; 13. God save the King/Queen; 14. BBC; 15. West End; 16. *Times* Newspaper; 17. Shakespeare; 18. Thatched cottages; 19. Cup of Tea/Devonshire Cream Tea; 20. Stonehenge; 21. Phlegm/Stiff Upper Lip; 22. Shopping; 23. Marmalade; 24. Beefeaters/Tower of London; 25. London Taxis; 26. Bowler Hat; 27. TV classic serials; 28. Oxford/Cambridge; 29. Harrods; 30. Double-decker buses/Red buses; 31. Hypocrisy; 32. Gardening; 33. Perfidy/Untrustworthiness; 34. Half-timbering; 35. Homosexuality; 36. Alice in wonderland; 37. Winston Churchill; 38. Marks & Spencer; 39. Battle of Britain; 40. Francis Drake; 41. Trooping the colour; 42. Whingeing; 43. Queen Victoria; 44. Breakfast; 45. Beer/Warm beer; 46. Emotional frigidity; 47. Wembley stadium; 48. Flagellation/Public schools; 49. Not washing/Bad underwear; 50. Magna Carta (*EE* 86-88). This "eccentric list," as Vera Nünning correctly contends, indicates that "the construction of Englishness and its concomitant deconstruction are intricately intertwined in the novel" (63). Accordingly we can find in the novel that, such features of Englishness as the Beatles, pragmatism and the mercantile spirit are not listed in the survey result but implicitly referred to in the novel, the latter two typically represented in Sir Jack Pitman himself. In short, I would agree with the view that "[w]hat the novel ultimately suggests is that Englishness is nothing but a heterogeneous mixture of invented traditions. This English tradition thereby presents itself as the result of a process of invention and comes dangerously near to being chauvinist, xenophobic and racist, for Sir Jack's island like other accounts of Englishness does not include any Scottish, Welsh, or Irish features, let alone immigrants, blacks or slaves." (Pakditawan 9)

declares its throwing off the yoke of Westminster and pronounces its independence, the title of Island Governor bestowed upon Sir Jack Pitman; after that a petition is delivered to the International Court at The Hague requesting annulment of the 1293 Island Purchase [the original purchase of the Island in 1293, by Edward I from Isabella de Fortuibus, for the sum of six thousand marks], and an application for instant emergency membership of the European Union is also prepared, which encapsulate "the long struggle for liberation on the part of the Islanders, a struggle marked by courage and sacrifice down the centuries" (*EE* 177), thus an invented tradition for the Islanders (Nünning 67) as well; and then the Islanders look towards Brussels, Strasbourg, and The Hague for the safeguarding of their rights and freedoms (*EE* 177). Here, Barnes has addressed the history of the Isle of Wight, its relationship with the main body England and its fictional independence in the future from it, rendering the novel much more touch of politics-history. It is in effect one of the crucial parts in the novel that is directly related to political matters, without which the novel could not be classified by Barnes himself into the same category with his political novel *The Porcupine* (Freiburg 46).

However, these actions are but Sir Jack's political, diplomatic maneuvers, not his real aims. Sir Jack has no intention of taking the Island into the European Union, and he just needs Europe to keep Westminster out of his face until everything has settled down; still, he plans to prorogue the Parliament of the Island within a week, for in his mind there is nothing for it to do and nothing he wants it to do (*EE* 178). Therefore, Sir Jack's real aim is to build an authoritarian kingdom in the Isle of Wight, manipulated by his Pitco Group and governed by himself. Sir Jack being Sir Jack, at the juncture of the success of his Project, he immediately decides to sack his two employees and also lovers, Martha Cochrane and Paul Harrison. But to his surprise, Martha the Special Consultant and Paul the Ideas Catcher have been already wary of him and found out the evidence of his patronizing in an abnormal brothel, thus blackmailing him to let them carry out the Project. The dramatic story occurs after Martha becomes the CEO of this Project on the Island of simulacra.

What would this Island of simulacra be like? As aforementioned, Sir Jack's project is to sell the past, social and cultural history of England to foreign visitors, and most typical features as regards Englishness have been figured out, so that on this Island, now named "England, England" by Sir Jack, there are Buckingham Palace, Big Ben, the King and Queen and their guardsmen, William Wordsworth's daffodils, Stonehenge, Anne Hathaway's cottage, the White Cliffs of Dover, the Harrods emporium inside the Tower of London, Wembley Stadium, Sherwood Forest, the grave of Princess Di-,

Robin Hood and his Band, Dr. Samuel Johnson and such historic scenes as the Battle of Britain, the Trial of Oscar Wilde and the Execution of Charles I, among others. Thus, in "England, England," which reproduces the original and Old England metonymically, tourists can meet icons like the King and Queen of England, chat with historical celebrities like Samuel Johnson or Nell Gwyn, share pastoral idylls with shepherds, and even encounter myths, Robin Hood's Band of Merrie Men being especially popular with the visitors. Because the Island experience is "more convenient, cleaner, friendlier and more efficient" (*EE* 188), a vast number of visitors come to the Island to visit these "replicas" instead of going to the Old England to see the "originals." As to the reasons, Martha tells a journalist that "[w]e're merely following the logic of the market:" "First, that tourists had hitherto flocked to 'original' sites because they simply had no choice in the matter;" and "Second, and more laterally, that if given the option between an inconvenient 'original' or a convenient replica, a high proportion of tourists would opt for the latter" (*EE* 185). As to its economical and political changes, "England, England" also holds lessons for the rest of the world:

> For a start, there is full employment, so there is no need for burdensome welfare programs. ... Pitco shipped the old, the longterm sick, and the socially dependent off to the mainland. But Islanders are not heard to complain, any more than they complain about the lack of crime, which eliminates the need for policemen, probation officers, and prisons. The system of socialized medicine, once popular in Old England, has been replaced by the American model. Everyone, Visitor or resident, is obliged to take out insurance. (*EE* 187)

Naturally, as a financial analyst in the novel observes, the Island "is a pure market state. There's no interference from government because there *is* no government. So there's no foreign or domestic policy, only economic policy" (*EE* 187, italics original) ; and as a result it becomes "a pure interface between buyers and sellers without the market being skewed by central government with its complex agendas and election promises" (*EE* 187-188). This is considered by the observer as the recognition of man as "a market-driven animal" and as "the future" of human society (*EE* 188). In short, it seems that the Island has become a sort of utopia or tends to become a utopia. However, it is but a world of simulacra and hyperreality, replete with historical replicas and bogus historical figures, who are actually played by "actors." What happens next on this Island substantiates that it is not a utopia and not the future for humankind, either.

In this world of simulacra, everything is predesigned, based on "history" or what happened in the past, and also monitored and surveilled by Martha the CEO, to cater to the visitors' interest in "history." As such, what the "historical figures" turning up in some "historic scenes" should do is merely to play the roles and recite their lines as accurately as designed and written in their contracts with Pitco Group, so as to entertain the visitors. This is theoretically feasible and workable. However, to make the thing complicated is the complication and sophistication of human nature or humanity, which is to some extent ignored by the Project's Coordinating Committee. Things do not go smoothly by the book. One important thing occurring on the Island is the "separation" or "adhesion" of personality taking place in the actors. Most of its manifestations are harmless, as Barnes writes of it: within a few months of Independence, certain members of Backdrop could no longer be addressed as Pitco employees, only as the characters they are paid to inhabit; they are initially thought to be showing signs of discontent, whereas in fact they are showing signs of content and happy to be who they have become and don't wish to be others (*EE* 202-203). But now it seems to be spreading beyond Backdrop: the "smugglers" who played the historical smugglers in the villages of the Island start to smuggle practically, for instance. How does Martha deal with such a problem? To deal with these smugglers, Martha commands a raid against them, captures the ringleaders and punishes them according to contract, the new smugglers, operating under more tightly-drafted contracts, thoroughly trained and introduced. So in this way everything on the Island works, because complications are not allowed to arise. Just as Barnes comments in more detail on the operation of the Island: "The structure was simple, and the underlying principle of action was that you did things by doing them" (*EE* 207) ; therefore,

> there was no crime ... and therefore no judicial system and no prisons—at least, not real one. There was no government—only a disenfranchised Governor [Sir Jack] —and therefore no elections and no politicians. There were no lawyers except Pitman lawyers. There were no economists except Pitco economists. There was no history except Pitco history. ... [W]ealth was created in a peaceful kingdom: what more could anyone want, be they philosophers or citizen? (*EE* 207)

However, complaints arise again, this time against "Dr. Johnson," who dines with visitors at "The Cheshire Cheese as the Dining Experience" of the Project. Whatever the complaints turn out to be, Martha realizes that the actor playing "Dr. Johnson" has gotten inside the skin of his role, or become *the thing itself*, i. e., this talented actor behaves exactly like Dr. Johnson:

Chapter Four Fabricating and Representing Politics-History   173

this "Dr. Johnson" displays his authentic attitudes especially his moodiness or melancholy of the original toward modern visitors, which is unacceptable for those who *de facto* don't know the real Dr. Johnson but simply want to have a good time with "Dr. Johnson." It is certain that tourists are less than delighted when they are actually confronted with "the real." As a critic notes, "[t]he 'English malady' of melancholy may be English, but it is not accepted as such by visitors, who prefer and demand an idealized version of Englishness that is adjusted to the tastes of the present" (Nünning 65), with which we cannot agree more.

The same thing occurs to Mr. Hood and his Band; that is, they also get inside the skin of their roles. To be specific, they complain about what they eat, and start to hunt for their own food, insist on more privacy and are going to curtain off the viewing windows to stop everybody looking in, claim that "staged fights are hopeless and wouldn't it be more realistic if the Sheriff's men were given an extra financial inducement to capture the Band, and if they, the Band, were allowed to ambush the Sheriff's men anywhere" (*EE* 230), and this "Robin" even complains that "it's unfair and unjust and a crime against his manhood that he hasn't ... had a shag in months" (*EE* 231). In a word, they really behave like unscrupulous outlaws who become a threat to the community. For Martha, this is "a major crisis, and a challenge to the very philosophy of the Project" (*EE* 234); so she decides that a raid on Robin's cave must be carried out and done as "a one-off cross-epoch extravaganza" (*EE* 234). As a consequence, this time the "Island SAS," whose routine work is the restaging of the Iranian Embassy Siege of 1980, is summoned to complete this new task. Without rehearsals, the leader of the "Island SAS" worries that "the show might not have a true enough look to it" (*EE* 235); however, out of everyone's anticipation, the fight between the "Island SAS" members and Robin Hood and his Merrie Men goes very realistically. Through Martha's consciousness, we can discern that "[t]he special effects had been terrific; ... utterly convincing; any mishaps merely confirmed the action's authenticity" (*EE* 238). Nevertheless, this is unacceptable for Sir Jack, who, with the "help" of Paul, Martha's partner, has erased the evidence of his patronizing in a kinky brothel and regained his executive control, demands Martha's immediate resignation. Eventually, Martha is expulsed from "England, England" the Island of simulacra and declared by Sir Jack as *persona non grata* in perpetuity.

After Martha's departure, Sir Jack deals swiftly with the subversive tendency of certain employees to over-identify with the characters they are engaged to represent, and "England, England" turns out be "a peaceful kingdom" again. Sir Jack himself has even taken up the reins once more after Paul's leaving, and is later voted by both Houses of Parliament of the Island as the first Baron Pitman. The Official Historian then elaborates a plausible family tree for the new baron, whose mansion begins to rival Buckingham Palace in both splendor and visitor throughput. Ironically, as the ideas man, Sir Jack's "last great idea" also comes true as regards himself. In the first months after his death, the visitors come to pay their homage at the Pitman mausoleum, to read Sir Jack's "wall-wisdom" (his big words inscribed on a wall) and depart thoughtfully. Yet they also continue to tour the Pitman mansion at the end of the Mall, and such loyal enthusiasm points up the emptiness and melancholy of the building after its proprietor's death, which renders the then executives realize that "Sir Jack must live again," following the logic of marketing once again (*EE* 258). The replacement Sir Jack swiftly becomes a popular figure and "The Pitman Dining Experience at The Cheshire Cheese" proves to be a jolly option for visitors, which nevertheless renders throughput at the Pitman mausoleum drop rapidly and greatly. As such the real Sir Jack has been forgotten and Time or more exactly the dynamics of Sir Jack's own Project has its revenge ironically (*EE* 258).

All in all, this is then the world of simulacra established by Sir Jack the mogul and "fabricated" by Barnes the writer. When Barnes started to write this novel, there was something in the air of the British Isles that suggests a broader dissatisfaction with heritage tourism, on which another British writer Penelope Lively's novel *Heat Wave* (1996) makes not a few attacks, for instance. As a satire, this novel skewers the tourist industry at large and heritage tourism specifically. It is perhaps a known truth that visits to historic sites or history museums are educationally valueless unless preceded by assiduous preparation and followed up by post-visit testing, of which the depiction in the novel is a very good instance. Without doubt, the French intellectual in the novel is also satirized by Barnes (Freiburg 50). To be more specific, a few pages of the novel in which the French intellectual appears detail how this great philosopher is flown in, gives his speech to Sir Jack's Project committee members, stops off in London to buy fishing waders, flies and a quantity of aged Caerphilly (a sort of cheese) with his conference fee and then flies off to his next international conference. The caricatural adumbration of this French intellectual registers that when Barnes critiques the fact that "history" or historical heritage has turned out to be a sort of commodity, he also insinuatively criticizes the intellectuals and the role they play in the commodification of history as cultural capital. As a critic underscores, "[w]hat is being satirized is not the ideas or theories themselves, but the way in which they have been incorporated into a commodity culture—where intellectualism is itself a commodity in the pay of corporate projects" (Bentley 492). Certainly, when referring to the French intellectual, we cannot ignore the theory he put forward for Sir Jack's

Project, without which "England, England" a world of simulacra would become a castle in the air.

The whole project of rebuilding a replica of Old England is built on the hypotheses that the authentic has lost its value, and that people under postmodern circumstances prefer the (well-made) simulacra to the real. Thus in the novel a French intellectual is invited to propaganda the views about simulacra, as noted before, which could be easily identified with those criticized by Baudrillard. It is not difficult to sense that the theory of Baudrillard is being evoked for the support of Sir Jack's corporate project; that is, Baudrillard's critique of postmodern culture is in effect recycled as a celebration of the market economy. The success of the "brave new venture" testifies what the French intellectual predicates, in that the Island prospers because it proffers the convenient replicas, which proves to be far more attractive to tourists than viewing the authentic historic(al) sites in real England. It is not unsafe to contend that the replicas on the Island is not (merely) a representation of the real, or what Baudrillard calls a "first-order" simulation, but more a blurring of the boundaries between reality and representation, a "second-order" simulation, which gives rise to much of the novel's humor and irony when the Project's employee-actors start to behave as if they are really the characters they play. The real King and his wife Queen Denise, lured to the Island, are exceptions, but "interchangeability of the authentic and the imitation" demonstrated and managed by his Majesty himself at the same time complicates *the thing itself* (Nünning 69). What's more, we can see that, in the planning and developing of the Project, Barnes highlights postmodern notions of the construction of history and reality, suggesting that the Project really belongs to what Baudrillard calls the "third order" of simulation, a "hyperreal" in which the model precedes (or at least overtakes) the real (Baudrillard 2; Lane 86). Therefore, while Baudrillard uses his theory of "the hyperreal order" to critique postmodern (American) culture, by means of stressing that it functions not as "a false representation of reality" but as a concealment of "the fact that the real is no longer real" (25), and when Baudrillard fears that "hyperreality will be the dominant way of experiencing and understanding the world" and cautions against the day when we can no longer "negotiate the differences between a true and false state of affairs" (Lane 87), Barnes on the contrary fabricates and represents such a world of hyperreality, but then satirizes it and that of critical theory as well. Accordingly, we would agree with the view that the "novel is not a critique of postmodernity, but a lament that the theories underpinning postmodernism are likely to be the most accurate in understanding how the contemporary nation can be articulated" (Bentley 493). Then in light of the definitions about utopia and dystopia, we would maintain that the world of simulacra and hyperreality on the Island is neither a utopia nor a dystopia, but a world of "hetero-topia," in which simulacra and hyperreality are the dominant, the so-called history and reality but constructed.

Certainly, what should not be dismissed is that Barnes's writing seems to intimate that economic factors play a vital role in the whole process of the implementation of Sir Jack's Project as well as in the matters of politics. More specifically, Sir Jack's enormous wealth renders him the possibility and feasibility of persuading the council of the Isle of Wight to seek for independence from the Westminster and the real King and Queen of England to relocate to "England, England," both bribed by Sir Jack, making it a real independent kingdom; the operation of the Island according to market rules renders all the Islanders participate in Sir Jack's Project and leads to its success with people's preferring the replica to the original in the third millennium's postmodern society. The economic recession in Old England also determines its political fall and seclusion, which will be examined in the next part.

ii. "Neither Idyllic nor Dystopic"

Julian Barnes's postmodern (historical) writing in *England, England* exposits the historical ignorance of common people, critiques heritage tourism which exploits "history" as a cultural capital in an irrational vein, addresses the decline of the Empire and the potential inclination of political independence of some components of the United Kingdom, and more significantly explores such issues as Englishness and the relation of authenticity to simulacra by way of drawing upon the theory of simulacra and hyperreality put forward by Jean Baudrillard. Some of the important issues discussed before will be still mentioned in this part. Barnes in the novel has fabricated and represented two quite different worlds, one of which is a world of simulacra and hyperreality and has been illuminated, and the other of which is up to now not clear to us. Instead of a world of simulacra with political independence and economic prosperity, operated according to market rules, what would be the other world in Old England be like? The following passages will endeavor to clarify this question.

Critics have noted that *England, England* bears some resemblances to the fiction of dystopia. In consequence, the novel is regarded as a "dystopian fable" (Tate 63) and as "the first classic dystopia of the 21st century" (Charles 19). Notwithstanding, a close reading would show that these comments are not accurate enough; and Barnes himself would not agree with them much, for he depicts the world in its third section as "neither idyllic nor dystopic" (*EE* 265). Or in other words, what he has fabricated and represented in the novel could not be easily classified, just like his writing itself. Therefore, it is appropriate to term what Barnes has fabricated as "retrotopia" (qtd. in Hutchinson 236) and more apposite to name it as, for my part, a "hetero-topia," a place consisting of heterogeneous elements and components. In this world of hetero-topia, described in the third section of the novel, Martha Cochrane is still the protagonist, through whose consciousness Barnes presents a fictitious future of England.

In fact, in the second section of the novel, Barnes also mentions the situation of Old England, as a contrast to what has occurred in "England, England." As Barnes's writing exhibits, while the Island turns probably to be "a peaceful kingdom, a new kind of state, a blueprint for the future," there is "unremittingly negative news about Old England" (*EE* 207). To be specific, "the place [Old England] had been in a state of free-fall, had become an economic and moral waste-pit," and "[p]erversely rejecting the established truths of the third millennium, its diminishing population knew only inefficiency, poverty, and sin; depression and envy were apparently their primary emotions" (*EE* 207). Decades later, what would Old England be like?

Simply speaking, we know through Martha's consciousness that in Old England "the whole thing had unravelled" quickly (*EE* 259): Old England has "progressively shed power, territory, wealth, influence, and population," is "to be compared disadvantageously to some backward province of Portugal or Turkey," has "cut its own throat," "lying in the gutter beneath a spectral gas-light, its only function as a dissuasive example to others," and has "lost its history, and therefore—since memory is identity—[has] lost all sense of itself" (*EE* 259). As to the decline of Old England, Barnes remarks that there are two distinct periods. The first period begins with the establishment of the Island Project and has lasted for as long as Old England has attempted to compete with "England, England." It is a time of "vertiginous decline" for the mainland: the tourist-based economy collapses, speculators destroy the currency; the departure of the Royal Family makes expatriation fashionable among the gentry; and the country's best housing stock is bought as second homes by continental Europeans; a resurgent Scotland purchases large tracts of land down to the old northern industrial cities and even Wales expands into Shropshire and Herefordshire. Internationally, Europe declines to throw good money after bad, and various attempts at rescue. It is rumored that, as Barnes fabricates, there is "a conspiracy in Europe's attitude to a nation which had once contested the primacy of the Continent," that during a secret dinner at the Elysée "the presidents of France, Germany, and Italy have raised their glasses to the words 'It is not only necessary to succeed, it is necessary that others fail' "

(*EE* 260). Documents leaking from Brussels and Strasbourg, as Barnes puts it, verify that many high officials regard Old England less as a suitable case for emergency funding than as an economic and moral lesson: "It should be portrayed as a wastrel nation and allowed to continue in free-fall as a disciplinary example to the overgreedy within other countries" (*EE* 260). Symbolic punishments are also introduced: the Greenwich Meridian is replaced by Paris Mean Time and on maps the English Channel becomes the French Sleeve (*EE* 260). To respond to such crises, a Government of Renewal on the Old England is elected, which pledges itself to economic recovery, parliamentary sovereignty and territorial reacquisition. Its first step is to reintroduce the old pound as the central unit of currency; and its second step is to send the army north to reconquer territories officially designated as occupied but which in truth had been sold. However, Old England has to make a humiliating treaty with the Scottish, who are backed up by the United States; and what is worse, when Old England fights with Scotland, the French Foreign Legion invades the Channel Islands, with the endorsement from the International Court at The Hague (*EE* 261).

Then after the war with Scotland, Old England, burdened with reparations, discards the politics of Renewal, which marks the start of its second period: economic growth, political influence, military capacity and moral superiority are now all abandoned (*EE* 261).[1] And the world begins to forget that "England" has ever meant anything except "England, England," a false memory which the Island works to reinforce; in the meantime, those who remain in Old England or Anglia start to forget about the world beyond. However, poverty ensues. The Anglians discard much of the communications technology that was once indispensable; and a new chic applies to fountain-pens and letter-writing, to family evenings round the wireless and dialing "O" for Operator; then cities dwindle, and mass transit systems are abandoned and horses boss the streets; coal is dug again and the kingdoms assert their differences; new dialects emerge, based on the new separations (*EE* 262). It is probably because of this that some critics think of Barnes's writing as "dystopic." It is not a "dystopia," however, which could be corroborated by more details

---

[1] For instance, the new political leaders proclaim a new self-sufficiency, extracting the country from the European Union, declaring a trade barrier against the rest of the world, forbidding foreign ownership of either land or chattels within the territory, and disbanding the military; emigration is permitted, immigration only in rare circumstances; the country bans all tourism except for groups numbering two or less; the old administrative division into counties is terminated and new provinces are created, based upon the kingdoms of the Anglo-Saxon heptarchy; and finally Old England declares its separateness from the rest of the world and from the Third Millennium by changing its name to Anglia (*EE* 262).

about Old England as follows: over the years the seasons have returned to Anglia, and become pristine; crops are once again the product of local land, not of airfreight; weather, long since diminished to a mere determinant of personal mood, becomes central again; and accordingly fogs have character and motion, thunder regains its divinity, rivers flood, sea-walls burst, and sheep are found in treetops when the water subsides (*EE* 263–264). Besides the great transformation occurring to Anglia as regards seasons and weather, the wild and wildlife also prosper in Old England. This is nevertheless a global view about Old England. According merely to this description, it appears to have become a pastoral or idyllic land, or some sort of genuine Old England. Ostensibly, it is not untrue, but following Martha and living with her vicariously, we can find that the village where she lives is "neither idyllic nor dystopic" (*EE* 265).

This village, as noticed by Martha, displays a picture of rural idyll: Hens and geese wander proprietorially across cracked tarmac onto which children have chalked skipping games; ducks colonize the triangular village green and defend its small pond; washing, hung on rope lines by wooden pegs, flaps dry in the clean wind; as roof-tiles become unavailable, each cottage returns to reed or thatch; without traffic, the village feels safer and closer and without television the villagers talk more; nobody's business goes unobserved; peddlers are greeted warily and children are sent to bed with tales of highwaymen and gypsies rustling their imagination, though few of their parents have seen a gypsy and none a highwayman (*EE* 265). This is no doubt a portrait of an authentic rural life with peace and serenity. There are, however, under the ostensibly authentic rural idyll, some bogus figures, which reduces the authenticity of the rural pastoral life into question. For instance, Jez Harris the farrier of the village is "formerly Jack Oshinsky, junior legal expert with an American electronics firm obliged to leave the country during the emergency," and prefers to stay in this village and "backdate both his name and his technology," therefore nowadays he shoes horses, makes barrel hoops, sharpens knives and sickles, cuts keys, tends the verges and brews a noxious form of scrumpy into which he would plunge a red-hot poker just before serving; and after marriage with a local woman he localizes his accent; his inextinguishable pleasure is to play the yokel whenever some anthropologist, travel writer, or linguistic theoretician would turn up inadequately disguised as a tourist (*EE* 251). Thus, it is not difficult to perceive that instead of featuring people who are themselves and live simple and authentic lives, the characters in the last section of the novel provide another curious mix of the real and the bogus, which "underscores the idea that the boundaries between the real and the imitation have become blurred" (Nünning 70), hence adding weight to the complexity of Barnes's exploration of the relation between the fake and the authentic, which is one of the main concerns of (the second section of) the novel. What is more crucial is that Jez Harris this fake figure is delighted to tell self-made copies of legends and myths for "monetary exchange or barter" to those who want to pry into the (hi)stories of Old England, which seems to serve the purpose even better than the real ones. In spite of his short knowledge of true legends or (hi)stories, Jez Harris continues to fabulate or fabricate, for the very good reason that visitors prefer them to the "original" (*EE* 252). As a result, we can infer that life in this Anglia village is by no means "authentic," although the life of the villagers to some extent attests to the idealized notion of ruralism. In other words, the regression to a pre-industrial society or the "adjustment to economic circumstances does not entail genuine friendliness and communal values" (Nünning 71). Instead, the negative sides of the village life could be also witnessed: prying and xenophobia has become part of the life style of the villagers.

Moreover, as Martha realizes, the villagers of Anglia could not re-experience or relive the old times. Although the external forms and economic conditions bear a great resemblance to those of the far past, or a pre-industrial society, the villagers do not return to the "authentic" pre-industrial attitudes and lifestyles; instead, they look for models in the past to establish manners and rituals that would be in accordance with the economic situations and with the modern values internalized in their mind. For instance, in order to "revive—or perhaps, since records were inexact, to institute—the village Fête," an official delegation of schoolmaster and vicar on one afternoon call on Martha to exchange memories and study old books so as to make sure how to conduct such a celebration, for Martha "had actually grown up in the countryside" (*EE* 254-255) many years before. The result is a blend of the old and the new, sporting a Queen of the May, a dressing-up competition, a three-legged race, a demonstration of Cornish wrestling, refereed by Coach Mr. Mullin "with an open encyclopaedia in hand," while the band plays traditional tunes and Beatles' songs (*EE* 269-273). However, in spite of the lack of orientation at the beginning and their conscious efforts to revive the Fête tradition, the villagers soon realize that the Fête has become a *fait accompli* (accomplished fact) and part of their lives: "It had been a day to remember. The Fête was established; already it seemed to have its history. Twelve months from now a new May Queen would be proclaimed and new fortunes read from tea-leaves" (*EE* 275). That is, another tradition has been invented, although the authentic past plays little role in the process. Therefore, we can say that the villagers on Anglia, just like Sir Jack, in their search of tradition and authenticity, invent new traditions rather than celebrate the original traditions. Here again the notion of Englishness is satirically critiqued by Barnes; and it is in this sense that a critic realizes that "Englishness is nothing but a heterogeneous mixture of invented traditions" (Pakditawan 9). Still, one of the results of the dressing-up competition in the Fête is that the villagers have a dispute about "what is real?". Martha's consciousness reveals that there are "Queen Victoria," "Lord Nelson," "Snow White," "Robin Hood," "Boadicea" and "Edna Halley" in this competition (*EE* 273). When Martha gives her vote to "Edna Halley," the question of whether or not Edna Halley is a real person is broached. The question of "what is real?" once put forward by Sir Jack in the second section of the novel is again referred to. Barnes's satire is suggested in his description of the dispute: "Some said you were real only if someone had seen you; some that you were real only if you were in a book; some that you were real if enough people believed in you. Opinions were offered at length, fuelled by scrumpy and ignorant certainty" (*EE* 273). What is ironic is that some of the villagers themselves bear no real but fake identities and that what they really celebrate is not the old traditions but those invented by themselves.

Thus considered, we would maintain that Anglia is not an idyllic land, in which the boundaries between the real and the fake and between authenticity and simulacra have been blurred, thence similar to "England, England." For another, it would be reasonable to contend that Anglia is not a world of dys-topia either. Hints of "spiritual renewal and moral self-sufficiency" emerge, in spite of its economic ruins and political seclusion. As Martha observes, PC Brown hasn't "caught a single criminal since his arrival in the village" (*EE* 274). Moreover, the villagers are trying to create a sort of life which is in keeping with their economic circumstances, the invention of the Fête tradition being an instance. There are truly real things in Anglia, i. e., the innocent children. For Martha, these children have not yet reached the age of incredulity, only of wonder, and they show the willing yet complex trust in reality, so that even when they disbelieve, they also believe (*EE* 273-274). Therefore, this innocence is no doubt real, just as Martha's incredulity toward the bogus "England, England" is real.

In the end, what should be emphasized is the form or narrative mode of the novel, which is the one with, as a critic acutely argues, "a sufficiently amorphous form to accommodate apparently conflicting elements" (Head 20). The first section "England," about one-tenth of the novel, is an evocation of the childhood of Martha and her memory of later encounter with her long-forgotten father. In this section, Martha, as the third person narrator, is also the central consciousness of the narration; and the social setting seems to be located in the post-war English past, recognizable and even familiar to those growing up during the given period. It is not difficult to note that this section is written in a mode of (psychological) realism, through which Barnes explores the relation of memory to identity, be it individual or national. Or as a critic stresses, this section "is presented as realist because it is concerned with an evocation of a traditional English past. The form of the writing, therefore, evokes the sense of that past as much as the details it supplies us with" (Bentley 493). The second section "England, England" is postmodern in style, which fits in well with its purpose of building a postmodern world of simulacra and hyperreality. Simply speaking, it is fragmentary in structure, and the situations and characters in it turn out to be unbelievable in some sense. Textual hybridization is also one of its typical stylistic features. More specifically, there is the French intellectual's speech, which is a parody of the theory of Baudrillard, and there is a newspaper's report about the theme park, which ostensibly renders the novel the aura of authenticity but on the other hand highlights its fictionality and artificiality. There are also intertextual references in this section to Guy Debord's works since some words are directly taken from *The Society of the Spectacle*, and to Michel Foucault's *The History of Sexuality* as Barnes refers to Martha's and Paul's "history of sexuality." Still, the retelling or repositioning of some myths in the past of Old England gives Barnes's writing a touch of Magic Realism. In short, the elements of parody, pastiche and intertextuality, among others, foreground the postmodern(ist) features of this novel, which is in line with Barnes's exploration of the phenomenon of postmodern culture of simulacra. Then in the third section "Anglia" Barnes seems to adopt a writing form of "pastoral elegy," which could be confirmed by Barnes's delineation of the natural scenes, as mentioned before. However, when depicting the images of the villagers and their celebration of the Fête, Barnes's writing seems to become ironic and parodic rather than in the sense of pastoral elegy. Just as the artificiality that fuels the second section of the novel "contaminates" the third section, Barnes's writing mode in the second section also "contaminates" those in his third one of the novel, if I can say so. The different writing modes in the three different sections of the novel make it distinct in Barnes's work, which, in the words of Salman Rushdie, is also a "subversion of the given." Therefore, it is correct to contend that "Barnes is sometimes considered as a postmodernist writer because his fiction rarely either conforms to the model of the realist novel or concerns itself with a scrutiny of consciousness in the manner of modernist writing" (Childs, *Contemporary Novelists* 86), but plays with the possibilities of novel writing.

  In a word, I would assert that Barnes fabricates and represents two worlds of hetero-topia (of history) in *England, England* via the writing modes with postmodern heterogeneity, and explores such issues as national identity consciousness, construction of history, and their relations to national political future, suggesting his concern for and thinking of the political future and historical orientation of England (and even the whole world).[1]

This chapter examines Julian Barnes's two political novels *The Porcupine* and *England, England*, with a view of exploring Barnes's concern for and rethinking of the relations of history to (political) power relation and ideology, and of simulacra culture to construction of history and future (history), predominantly embodied in Barnes's deconstructive writing of contemporary historical reality in *The Porcupine*, which foregrounds his deep insight into the influence of power relation on history or historiography and his timely response to the then heated issue of "The End of History," and also embodied in Barnes's satiric or parodic writing of postmodern simulacra culture in *England, England*, which represents his acute observation about the impact of simulacra culture on the construction of history, (national) identity and even the future advancement of economy and politics of a region like England.

To be more specific, the unconventional, postmodern historical writing in *The Porcupine* indicates Barnes's emphasis on the significance of power relation or (political) ideology in history or historiography, his thinking of history (like other kinds of knowledge production) subtly affected by power relation or the execution of political power, and his perceptive understanding of the conflict of political ideology and incredulity toward the master narrative of history (or political system), accordingly critiquing like Jacques Derrida and by way of Marx's critique spirit the hypothesis of "The End of History" put forward by Francis Fukuyama. Then, Barnes's postmodern historical writing in *England, England* constitutes his thinking about the future (history) of England. Through the parody of the postmodern simulacra culture, the satire of the historical tourism's rendering of history as cultural commodity, and the fabrication and representation of two heterotopia worlds, Barnes's writing in this novel attests to the possibility and practicability of theories which are criticized by Jean Baudrillard but articulate the very underpinning of postmodern society, and displays his lament that the real is no longer the real, that there is "no prime moment"

---

[1] The issues of heritage tourism and simulacra culture are not merely encountered by England but by other countries as well. The problems related to them such as construction of history, national identity consciousness and economic development have aroused great interest and been widely discussed all around the world. Barnes's writing in this novel provides a good text for us to rethink these issues; therefore what he writes of is not merely about England but of the whole world as well.

but "always a replica" "of something earlier" (*EE* 135), that the replica rather than the original is preferred, and that economic and political situations of England in the future would be greatly affected by postmodern culture of hyperreality and reduced to be near-primitive but unpromising. Again, we can see that Barnes's (historical) writing is unconventional and postmodern, due to the fact that the postmodern fabrication and representation of contemporary political-cum-historical reality and futuristic history in his novels rely heavily on his deconstructive, satiric or parodic strategy of writing, which is in fact in accordance to his writing strategy identified in his most postmodernist fiction such as *Flaubert's Parrot* and *A History*, although ostensibly not the same.

In summary, Barnes in *The Porcupine* and *England, England* explores the issues related to history at the political level, foregrounding the importance of politics in history or historiography or the vital relation of (political) power relation or ideology to history, and presenting different pictures of future history (of England) from the conventional delineation of utopia or dystopia, thus broadening our vision about politics-history and the future history of human beings. Therefore, labeling Barnes's historical writing in these two texts as "subversion of the given" would not be inappropriate, which constitutes the typical feature of Barnes's postmodern historical writing and the kernel of argumentation of this research.

Conclusion

The distinctive feature of [Julian] Barnes's work taken as a whole is its diversity of topics and techniques, which confounds some readers and critics, but enchants others. While some underlying themes can be identified, such as obsession, love, the relationship between fact and fiction, or the irretrievability of the past, it is clear that in each novel Barnes aims to explore a new area of experience and experiments with different narrative modes.
—Vanessa Guignery, *The Fiction of Julian Barnes*

Julian Barnes is often considered as a writer whose fictional writing always brings new faces to the formal experimentation of British fiction, and as such labeled as "the chameleon of British letters" and "the inscrutable Mr. Barnes," as noted in the Introduction of this research. The reason mainly lies in his "willingness to experiment in every one of his novels" (Massie 48), but essentially results from his ambition as a writer, just as he explains, "[i]n order to write, you have to convince yourself that it's a new departure for you and not only a new departure for you but for the entire history of the novel" (Billen 27). As a result, Barnes is regarded as "perhaps the hardest of all his generation to assess" (Massie 48), and the specificity of his work taken as a whole is "the sense of heterogeneity," which certainly brings about the difficulty for Barnes scholarship: various kinds of articles could be searched out but a comprehensive research on Barnes could not be easily completed. However, after reading Barnes's works including his interviews, we can sense that Barnes is in actuality much concerned with one vital issue, that is, the issue of truth. He articulates in public more than once his view about the relation of fictional writing to truth. For instance, in an interview, he commented, "prose fiction is the best way to describe the world and to tell the truth about the world, which is what we're here for" (Schiff) ; and on another occasion, he told an interviewer that "fiction is untrue but it's untrue in a way that ends up telling greater truth than any other information system ... that exists. That always seems to me very straightforward, that you write fiction in order to tell the truth. People find this paradoxical, but it isn't" (Freiburg 39). Not coincidentally, the characters in almost all of Barnes's fiction such as *Before She Met Me*, *Flaubert's Parrot*, *A History of the World in 10½ Chapters*, *The Porcupine*, *England, England*, *Arthur & George* and *The Sense of an Ending* all endeavor to figure out some sort of truth about themselves, about the society and about the world. It is safe to say that Barnes is telling the (hi)story of truth through his characters and in the form of fictional writing, which is also the main concern in Barnes's postmodern historical writing. Considering this, we can also (re)view Barnes's postmodern historical writing in light of his exploration of the issue of truth.

In *Flaubert's Parrot*, Barnes calls into question the truth of the past or history through the constant querying of "How do we seize the past?". The writer's main concern is "how do we know the true Flaubert?", resulting from his encounter with two parrots in his visiting in 1981 to two museums of Flaubert, which were both assuredly considered as the authentic parrot used by Flaubert when he was writing his short story *Un Coeur Simple*. The second "authentic" parrot gives rise to Barnes's questioning and questing for truth about Flaubert and the past. How does Barnes seize the true Flaubert?

His writing evinces that to know the true Flaubert the only way is through the texts written by and related to Flaubert, and in consequence various kinds of texts are presented in the novel, accompanied by various interpretations about Flaubert, but there is still evidence absent. Could we trust these surviving texts? Barnes's interpretation of Flaubert appears to be built upon these "texts," nevertheless he occasionally and self-consciously intimates his skepticism about their authenticity. More importantly, through the reading of various types of (historical) texts, Barnes explores the relationships between life and text and between history and text(uality), indicating that historical truth is under suspicion. In his another postmodern fiction *A History*, Barnes also exposits the relation of history to text(uality). In "Shipwreck," one section of this "novel," Barnes presents us three heterogeneous texts about a historical disaster: an overview of a historical text *Narrative of a Voyage to Senegal in 1816*; a color replica of an oil painting named "The Raft of the *Medusa*" and an artistic review of this painting based on *Narrative of a Voyage to Senegal in 1816* and *Géricault: His Life and Works*. Barnes's writing in Chapter Five and Chapter Six of this "novel" suggests that the understanding of the specific historical disaster and the interpretation of Géricault's painting both rely heavily on other (prior) texts, which as the "surviving textual traces" are "consequent upon complex and subtle social processes of preservation and effacement" and "subject to subsequent textual mediations." Thus we would hold that the mingling and intertextuality of heterogeneous texts foregrounds Barnes's concern for the relation of history to text. This then constitutes the main points of "Textuality of History," the first section of Chapter Two of this research.

Its second section "Fictionality of History" expounds the fictive character of history epistemologically. Barnes's view of history as "merely another literary genre" in *Flaubert's Parrot* is often quoted to corroborate his agreement with the suggestion that history is a fictive narration or fiction, just like literature, as expressed in Hayden White's writing. Such a reading does not distort its literal meaning, but Barnes has his own explanation about it, that is, when there is lack of evidence, "if you try to write a more complete history, then you have to fictionalize or image." What Barnes argues is a constant situation encountered by historians. Unconsciously Barnes refers deconstructively to one of the original meanings of "history," i. e., "any kind of narrative" or "story," as noted in Chapter One of this research. Accordingly, this research discusses three texts in light of Barnes's own understanding of history as fiction: a (hi)story of Flaubert from the viewpoint of his mistress Louise Colet in *Flaubert's Parrot*; one short (hi)story about the love affair between Old Turgenev and a young actress in

"The Revival"; and a (hi)story of the life of Sir Arthur Conan Doyle in *Arthur & George*. Then, Barnes's another comment about history is also regarded as his understanding of history or postmodern view of history. Barnes (through his character) articulates that "the technical term is fabulation. You make up a story to cover the facts you don't know or can't accept. You keep a few true facts and spin a new story round them," which is later echoed in his authorial "Parenthesis" self-reflexively. Considering this and Barnes's reference to the writing of history as "art" in his another postmodern novel *Love, Etc.*, we would contend that Barnes's view of historiography fits in with what Hayden White indicates in his writing such as historiography as a "poetic process." This part subsequently demonstrates how Barnes "fabulates" a (hi)story of the "The Survivor" and how this (hi)story represents the whole "novel" structurally and thematically and how the introduction of the term "fabulation" intertextually and self-reflexively refers to what Barnes has written in the whole "novel," suggesting what historians do in historical writing. This chapter, in short, illustrates Barnes's understanding of the relation of history to text(uality), embodied in his heterogeneous, intertextual writing which aims to search for historical truth, and his view of history or historiography as fiction, exemplified in his self-conscious, fictional writing which stresses the very execution of fabulation. Epistemologically, whether stressing the relation of history to text(uality) or highlighting the fictive character of historiography, they both call into question the historical truth or true history.

The conventional view of history or the speculative philosophy of history often views history as a whole, emphasizing its continuity, causality, totality and progressiveness, and regarding the West as the subject of human history and civilization, thus suppressing history of the Others. Barnes's postmodern historical writing also displays his incredulity toward such a view of History, especially exposed in his subversion and revision of some historical (meta)narratives such as those of The Enlightenment, Christian History, and Darwin's theory of evolution and Hegel's rational history. Postmodern theory of history underscores discontinuity instead of continuity, fragmentation instead of totality of history, which is best substantiated in Barnes's *A History*. The title of this "novel" tells that it is about the writing of history of the world but in an unconventional way, for "10 ½" undermines the "culturally coded number systems," and a close reading would confirm that it is in fact parodying and deconstructing the traditional history and historiography through and in its content and form. More specifically, the "novel" breaks down the continuity and totality of conventional history but presents "a history of the world in 10 ½ chapters" with discontinuity and fragmentation, with not one voice but various (and suppressed) voices, with different person narrations, speech modes and language styles. In other words, the "chapters" are not held together by a single narrative progression but by a series of themes, events, objects and personae which recur in different historical contexts with "radical use of genre" (Rubinson 164-165). Thus, Barnes uses the postmodern writing modes to represent postmodern view of history, which might not be accepted and done by conventional historians. Moreover, when Barnes employs postmodern modes of writing to undercut the continuity, causality and totality of historical (meta)narratives, he also manifests his incredulity toward the progressive view in these (meta)narratives. That is, Barnes expresses his suspicion about progress, especially that of technology without moral advance in *Flaubert's Parrot*, *A History* and a short story "Junction" in *Cross Channel*; he also undermines Darwin's evolutionary view of progress in a deconstructive way in *A History*: some of the (hi)stories in it attest to what Darwin hypothesizes, while more of (hi)stories refute Darwin's theory; still, Barnes in this "novel" also queries Hegel's rational view of history, due to the fact that the terror of history disclosed in this "history of the world in 10 ½ chapters" testifies that history does not unfold rationally and logically. This constitutes the main ideas in "Discontinuity and Fragmentation of History," the first section of Chapter Three of this research, which is followed by the exploration of the issue of the "Plurality of History" in its second section.

Although Barnes does not explicitly express his view about the plurality of history, we can infer from his heterogeneous writings that he endorses diversity and variety instead of unification and singleness, complexity instead of simplicity, ambiguity instead of explicitness; as to the narrative voice, it is not difficult to find that there are various voices in his work such as those of the female, the animal and the racial Other, besides the (white) male. His presentation of other voices in his (historical) writing indicates on the one hand his constant questing for artistic innovation and on the other hand his agreement with the view of the plurality of human history, which is mainly exemplified in his rewriting of sacred history in the Bible from the viewpoint of a very tiny insect in *A History* so as to subvert the conventional Anthropocentrism embedded in such a kind of historical (meta)narrative as Christian History, and in *Arthur & George* his digging out and rewriting of a forgotten history about a racial Other so as to critique the racial prejudice in British official history and collective unconscious and of the indecent page of a historical figure (like Sir Arthur Conan Doyle) so as to revise the orthodox narratives about this historical figure, which, by way of blending the biographical writings of two totally different historical figures, undercuts the conventional (historical) (meta)narratives of biography. In a word, this chapter evinces Barnes's incredulity toward and revision of the truth in historical (meta)narratives from the angle of ontology.

Chapter Four of this research deals with Barnes's two political novels *The Porcupine* and *England, England*. Its first section firstly examines *The Porcupine* from the viewpoint of the relation of history to (political) power and ideology, implicating that the power relation, especially the exercise of political power often plays a vital role in history, and then in light of the dispute about the issue of "The End of History" discusses the ideological conflict in the novel and its political response to the then heated issue. Certainly, the genesis of Barnes's writing and/or the historicity of this text are also referred to in order to make Barnes's writing intent and the novel's practical significance understood. This section thus exhibits Barnes's concern for and thought of the contemporary historical reality and truth, mirroring his intense perception of the (political) ideology-ness of history yet paradoxical attitude toward political reality. The second section of this chapter analyzes the two heterogeneous worlds in Barnes's *England, England*, pointing out that Barnes delineates differently from the conventional writing of utopia and dystopia two worlds of hetero-topia: the one, built on the Isle of Wight, is composed of historical simulacra with typical features of Englishness, now a political independent nation from its homeland England, with economic prosperity and under the control of a corporation; the other, Old England has declined into a pre-industry country, "neither idyllic nor dystopic," with economic ruin and political seclusion. One vital common feature of these two hetero-topia worlds lies in their similar heterogeneity, i. e., the boundary between authenticity and simulacrum is blurred in both places. Thus, via his satiric, parodic and futuristic depiction of the future (history) of a nation like England, Barnes explores such important issues as the construction of history or historical tradition and its relation to future, the phenomenon of simulacra culture, and national identity consciousness and its relation to political independence. In short, this chapter deals with Barnes's political historical writing, revealing Barnes's deep critique and perceptive rethinking of contemporary historical reality and truth and of the future of England.

All in all, this is a brief review of Barnes's postmodern historical writing from epistemological, ontological and political angles, which to a great extent demonstrates that Barnes is a unique writer who has "an overt interest in [philosophically historical] ideas and a flair for formal innovation" (Locke 40). Undoubtedly, the three aspects are pertinent to each other and cannot be completely separated. For instance, when asking "How do we seize the past?" we have already pre-hypothesized the questions such as "what is the past?" and "who writes the past?" and when discussing the issue of "The End of History" politically, we also touch on the issue of the master narrative of history. In fact, their relationships are much complicated so that, we would emphasize, the writing of Barnes's postmodern historical writing from these angles respectively is but an expedient strategy. Certainly, Barnes's historical writing is closely connected with the issue of truth; in simple terms, his postmodern historical writing could be viewed as a "subversion of the given" truth about history. This mirrors that Barnes's postmodern historical writing bears an intense spirit of deconstruction, which does not necessarily suggests that Barnes as a postmodern writer denies and repudiates everything including truth, of which it is his intent to tell as a writer, as noted at the beginning of this Conclusion. It is no wonder that Barnes articulates such an idea about truth: "What we should do eventually is believe that truth is obtainable. History may not be 56 per cent true or 100 per cent true, but the only way to proceed from 55 to 56 is to believe that you can get to a hundred" (Guignery, "History" 65). This view about historical truth could be also identified in "Parenthesis" the authorial half-chapter in *A History*, as mentioned at the coda of the second chapter of this research. Similarly, Barnes does not deny the progress of human society and history absolutely, believing that there are "small pieces of progress" (Saunders, "From Flaubert's Parrot to Noah's Woodworm" 9), though his historical writing to a high degree attests that "things are chaotic, free-wheeling, permanently as well as temporarily crazy" and that "human ignorance, brutality and folly" is a "certainty" in history (*FP* 66). Therefore, Barnes's historical writing, being "part of a project of reassessing the past, our own ancestry, without the old framing certainties" (Byatt, "A New Body of Writing" 444–445), does not necessarily entail an absolute denial of historical truth, the progressiveness of human history and the significance of historical (meta)narratives. As a consequence, we can maintain that Barnes's postmodern historical writing does not fall into historical pessimism and nihilism and "beguiling relativity" (*HWC* 244), but challenges and deconstructs the given knowledge about history, presenting a postmodern view or philosophical thinking of history in the form of literary fictional writing, and proffering novel perspectives for the reading and understanding of history or historiography and very good texts for the study of literature (and even history) from the angle of postmodern discourse or philosophy of history.

Calling into question and questing for the (historical) truth is a recurrent motif in "new historical fiction" of contemporary British literature, which is, for instance, also embodied in the historical writing of Graham Swift and Salman Rushdie, the peer writers of Barnes's generation. A brief comparison of their historical writing with Barnes's would be helpful for the understanding of the *sui generis* feature of heterogeneity in Barnes's historical writing. Considered as one of "the golden generation of British novelists," Barnes, along with Swift, Rushdie, among others, lives under the shadow of contemporary historical reality such as the decline of the British Empire and the political conflict of the Cold War, which enhances their historical consciousness as an individual and a writer; in the meantime, these writers also live in a society of postmodern culture and thoughts, in which various isms "in the air" affect their mind as well. When postmodern view or philosophy of history comes across literature, a new sort of fiction comes into being, generally named as "new historical fiction," which is "an outgrowth of the wider postmodern questioning of Enlightenment and positivist philosophies and traditional disciplinary authority" (Rubinson 161) and as such "emphasizes postmodern uncertainties in experimental styles, tells stories about the past that point to multiple truths or the overturning of an old received Truth, mixes genres, and adopts a parodic or irreverently playful attitude to history over an ostensibly normative mimesis" (Keen 171). These are the commonly acknowledged features of "new historical fiction" and can be perceived in these British writers whose writings are concerned with postmodern historical writing.

Here we can briefly examine the similarity and difference between such writers as Swift, Rushdie and Barnes. The similarity between these three writers is in general thematic in that histories are rewritten in their works so as to approach contemporary issues, or to use the past to cast light on the present, or to stress the importance of history to the understanding of the contemporary. The difference in their writing is mainly technical, although they could be all considered as postmodern(ist) writers. Swift, for instance, in his most outstanding fiction *Waterland*, predominantly utilizes such modernist narrative strategies as multiple points-of-view and time shift, foregrounding the inner consciousness of the protagonist; Rushdie in his prominent works such as *Midnight's Children*, *Shame* and *The Satanic Verses*, usually employs the writing strategies of Magic Realism, "mingling realism with the supernatural and history with spiritual and philosophical re-interpretation" (Brooke-Rose 137), presenting a fantastic, magic world. Barnes, as discussed before, prefers the writing strategem of (inter)textuality and deconstruction, through putting together heterogeneous texts with different genres to (re)present a heterogeneous postmodern world, to such an extent that his books such as *Flaubert's Parrot* and *A History* are often questioned whether they should be labeled as novels at all. However, if we bear in mind what a postmodern writer would be in Lyotardian sense, we would not deny that Barnes is a typical postmodern artist or writer, who defies to be categorized not only in formal experimentation but also in his writing about the "subversion of the given" truth about history or historiography. Certainly, for the conventional or orthodox readers, Barnes's most postmodernist texts such as *Flaubert's Parrot* and *A History* could not be read as novels, for in their mind these texts cross the boundary of the novel genre too far, which would constitute the shortcomings of Barnes's writing in some sense. In a word, a comparative study of these writers is an interesting topic, rendering us know more about contemporary British literature in a global way, which does nevertheless not occupy a vital place in Barnes's scholarship yet.

It is evident that focusing on the interpretation of Barnes's "subversion of the given" truth about history or historiography, this research does not commit itself to the specific analysis of the features of formal experimentation in Barnes's works, although in the end of some sections it also refers to them but briefly, which is one of the salient characteristics of Barnes postmodern writing and could become another significant topic for Barnes scholarship, which is not thoroughly explored up to now. As "one of the great innovators of English literary form" (O'Regan 117), Barnes in his writing, while exploring different areas of human experience, makes his peculiar contributions to the innovation of the novel form for British literature in his trans-generic texts such as *Flaubert's Parrot* and *A History* through such narrative or textual strategies as parody, intertextuality, collage and metafiction and writing every one of his books with a new face, which, along with Barnes's incessant exploration of postmodern historical and philosophical notions—such as the concept of history as fiction, the (im)possibility of absolute knowledge, the (un)attainability of truth—renders him the name of a postmodernist novelist. Barnes also underscores the ontological status and the role of the reader in his novels such as *Flaubert's Parrot*, *Talking It Over* and *Love, Etc.* and often blurs the boundary between fact and fiction to examine the relation of reality to fiction in his fiction such as *The Porcupine*, *England, England* and some short stories, and adopts multiple points-of-view to write about the same event to investigate the nature of truth in his writing such as *Talking It Over* and *Love, Etc.* All of these, as it were, add many a weight to the studies of Barnes from the perspective of narratology. Moreover, the issue of intertextuality and of generic heterogeneity in Barnes's writing, which is "profoundly dialogic," "mixing several traditions and voices while aiming for originality" (Guignery, "A Preference for Things Gallic" 45), and related to Mikhail Bakhtin's novel theory, constitutes another new area for Barnes studies.

Still, a specific and detailed reading of the female characters in Barnes's works has not turned up yet, another perspective for Barnes study, with no doubt. Why does Barnes, a male writer, offer prominent positions for female characters in his fictional world? Why are virtues often detected in his female characters rather than in the male? Why does Barnes constantly put his views about love and marriage into his narratives? Such questions are waiting to be answered. In addition, Barnes's writing is permeated by existentialist thoughts, or in other words his writing is replete with existential questions, especially in his works such as *Staring at the Sun*, *A History* and *Nothing to Be Frightened of*; and a critical study of Barnes from the perspective of existentialism has not turned up yet and would be a rewarding though challenging area for Barnes scholarship. Certainly, there are not a few other issues about Barnes to be explored, the investigation of which would be worthwhile for anyone who wants to focus his or her study attention on Barnes. Therefore, the writing of Barnes from the epistemological, ontological and political perspectives and in light of postmodern historical view or philosophy in this research is just a beginning, which would elicit more interest in Barnes studies, not only in his historical writing but in his writing on the whole.

All in all, it is not unsafe to say that Julian Barnes is "by now one of the most intelligent, cosmopolitan and precise of British writers" (Bradbury 488) and a prominent and prosperous writer with a profound awareness of rethinking and strong spirit of critique, who has pursued his goal unflinchingly and unfailingly on the way to paying his homage to the Muses. The year of 2011 is the lucky year for Barnes, but would not be the final year of his literary creation. We hope that "Mr. Barnes, who previously proved himself with a subsequent work" (Krist) would not disappoint his readers by the next one, which would create, in his own words, "a new departure" "for the entire history of the novel."

References

Abrams, Meyer H. *A Glossary of Literary Terms*. 7th ed. Boston: Heinle & Heinle, 1999.
Allen, Brooke. "Lives in Miniature." *The New Leader* 87. 3(2004): 32–34.
Andreadis, Athena. Rev. of *The Porcupine* by Julian Barnes. *Harvard Review* 5(1993): 228–229.
Ankersmit, Frank R. "Historiography and Postmodernism." *History and Theory* 28. 2(1989): 137–153.
—. "Historical Representation." *History and Theory* 27. 3(1988): 205–228.
Antakyalioğlu, Zekiye. "Mourning and Melancholy in Julian Barnes's *Levels of Life* and *The Only Story*." *Cankaya University Journal of Humanities and Social Sciences* 14. 2(2020): 158–169.
Aristotle. *Poetics*. Trans. Joe Sachs. Newburyport, MA: Focus Publishing/R. Pullins Company, 2006.
Atkinson, Ronald F. *Knowledge and Explanation in History: An Introduction to the Philosophy of History*. London and Basingstoke: The Macmillan Press Ltd., 1978.
Baldick, Chris. *The Concise Oxford Dictionary of Literary Terms*. 2nd ed. New York: Oxford University Press Inc., 2001.
Balée, Susan. "Swimming Lessons." *The Hudson Review* 57. 4 (2005): 663–674.
Barnes, Julian. *Arthur & George*. New York: Vintage Books, 2007.
—. *Before She Met Me*. London: Picador, 1986.
—. "Candles for the living—Julian Barnes in Bulgaria." *London Review of Books* 12. 22(1990): 6–7.
—. "Carcassonne." *Pulse*. London: Jonathan Cape, 2011. 185–195.
—. *Cross Channel*. London: Vintage Books, 1997.
—. "East Wind." *Pulse*. London: Jonathan Cape, 2011. 3–18.
—. *England, England*. New York: Vintage Books, 2000.
—. "Evermore." *Cross Channel*. London: Vintage Books, 1997. 89–111.
—. *Flaubert's Parrot*. New York: Vintage Books, 1990.
—. "The Follies of Writer Worship." *The Best American Essays 1986*. Ed. Elizabeth Hardwick. New York: Ticknor & Fields, 1986. 1–8.
—. "Hamlet in the Wild West." *Index on Censorship* 23(1994): 100–103.
—. "Harmony." *Pulse*. London: Jonathan Cape, 2011. 158–184.
—. *A History of the World in 10 ½ Chapters*. New York: Vintage Books, 1990.
—. "How Much Is That in Porcupines?" *The Times* Oct. 24, 1992: 4–6.
—. "Julian Barnes in Conversation." *Cercles* 4(2002): 255–269.
—. "Junction." *Cross Channel*. London: Vintage Books, 1997. 23–42.
—. *The Lemon Table*. London: Vintage Books, 2011.
—. *Letters from London 1990–1995*. London: Picador, 1995.

—. *Love, Etc.* New York: Alfred A. Knopf, 2001.
—. "Melon." *Cross Channel.* London: Vintage Books, 1997. 63–87.
—. *Metroland.* London: Picador, 1990.
—. *Nothing to Be Frightened of.* New York: Vintage Books, 2009.
—. *The Porcupine.* London: Pan Books Ltd., 1993.
—. *Pulse.* London: Jonathan Cape, 2011.
—. *The Sense of an Ending.* New York: Vintage Books, 2011.
—. *Something to Declare.* London: Picador, 2002.
—. *Staring at the Sun.* New York: Vintage Books, 1993.
—. "The Story of Mats Israelson." *The Lemon Table.* London: Vintage Books, 2011. 23–48.
—. *Talking It Over.* London: Pan Books Ltd., 1992.
—. "When Flaubert Took Wing." *The Guardian* (Mar. 5, 2005): 30.
Barthes, Roland. "The Discourse of History." Trans. Stephen Bann. *Comparative Criticism: A Year Book* 3(1981): 7–20.
Baudrillard, Jean. *Simulations.* Trans. Paul Foss, Paul Patton, and Philip Beitchman. New York: Semiotext(e), 1983.
Beard, Charles A. "That Noble Dream." *The Varieties of History*: *From Voltaire to the Present.* Ed. Fritz Stern. New York: Vintage Books, 1973. 315–328.
Bentley, Nick. "Re-writing Englishness: Imagining the Nation in Julian Barnes's *England, England* and Zadie Smith's *White Teeth.*" *Textual Practice* 21. 3(2007): 483–504.
Berberich, Christine. " 'All Letters Quoted Are Authentic: ' The Past after Postmodern Fabulation in Julian Barnes's *Arthur & George.*" *Julian Barnes: Contemporary Critical Perspectives.* Eds. Sebastian Groes and Peter Childs. London and New York: Continuum, 2011. 117–128.
Berger, Joseph. Rev. of *Arthur & George* by Julian Barnes. *Psychiatric Service* 58. 12(2007): 1613–1614.
Berlatsky, Eric. "'Madame Bovary, C'est Moi!:' Julian Barnes's *Flaubert's Parrot* and Sexual 'Perversion'." *Twentieth-Century Literature* 55. 2(2009): 175–208.
Bernard, André. "The Casual Reader." Rev. of *Arthur & George* by Julian Barnes; *I Feel Bad about My Neck: And Other Thoughts on Being a Woman* by Nora Ephron; *The Man in the Gray Flannel Suit* by Sloan Wilson. *The Kenyon Review* New Series 29. 2(2007): 2–10.
Bernstein, Stephen. Rev. of *Arthur & George* by Julian Barnes. *Review of Contemporary Fiction* 26. 1(2006): 146.
Best, Steven, and Douglas Kellner. "Foucault and the Critique of Modernity." Sept. 4, 2012. <http://pages.gseis.ucla.edu/faculty/kellner/pomo/ch2.html>.

—. *The Postmodern Turn*. New York: The Guilford Press, 1997.
Billen, Andrew. "Two Aspects of a Writer. " *The Observer Magazine* July 7, 1991: 25-27.
Birnbaum, Robert. "Julian Barnes, Etc. " *Identity Theory* Mar. 8, 2000. <http://www.identitytheory.com/people/birnbaum8.html>. Rpt. in *Conversations with Julian Barnes*. Eds. Vanessa Guignery and Ryan Roberts. Mississippi: The University Press of Mississippi, 2009. 83-95.
Boyd, William. "Late Sex. " *London Magazine* 20. 7(Oct. 1980): 94-96.
Bradbury, Malcolm. *The Modern British Novel: 1878 - 2001*. Beijing: Foreign Language Teaching and Research Press, 2005.
Brooke-Rose, Christine. " Palimpsest History. " *Interpretation and Overinterpretation*. Ed. Stefan Collini. Cambridge, UK: Cambridge University Press, 1992. 125-138.
Brooks, Neil. "Interred Textuality: *The Good Soldier* and *Flaubert's Parrot*. " *Critique* 41. 1(1999): 45-51.
Brooks, Peter. "Obsessed With the Hermit of Croisset. " *New York Times Book Review* Mar. 10, 1985: 7, 9.
Buxton, Jackie. "Julian Barnes's Theses on History (In 10 ½ Chapters)." *Contemporary Literature* 41. 1(2000): 56-86.
Byatt, Antonia S. *On Histories and Stories: Selected Essays*. Cambridge, Massachusetts: Harvard University Press, 2000.
—. "A New Body of Writing: Darwin and Recent British Fiction. " *New Writing 4: An Anthology.* Eds. Antonia S. Byatt and Alan Hollinghurst. London: Vintage, 1995. 439-448.
Byrne, Jack. Rev. of *The Porcupine* by Julian Barnes. *Review of Contemporary Fiction* 13. 2(1993): 252-253.
Candel, Daniel. "Nature Feminised in Julian Barnes's *A History of the World in 10 ½ Chapters*. " *Atlantis* 21(1999): 27-41.
Cape, Jonathan. "The Ship of State. " *New Statesman* June 23, 1989: 38.
Carr, Edward H. *What Is History?* New York: Vintage Books, 1961.
Catană, Elisabeta Simona. "History as Story and Parody in Julian Barnes's *The Noise of Time*. " *Romanian Journal of English Studies* 16. 1(2019): 25-31.
Charles, Ron. " O, Brave New Venture That Has Such People In't! " *The Christian Science Monitor* May 13, 1999: 19.
Childs, Peter. *Contemporary Novelists: British Fiction Since 1970*. Basingstoke and New York: Palgrave Macmillan, 2005.
—. *Julian Barnes*. Manchester: Manchester University Press, 2011.
Coe, Jonathan. "A Reader-Friendly Kind of God. " *The Guardian* June 23, 1989: 27.
Collingwood, Robin G. *The Idea of History.* Beijing: China Social Sciences

Publishing House, 1999.
Cook, Bruce. "The World's History and Then Some in 10 ½ Chapters." *Los Angeles Daily News* Nov. 7, 1989: 12.
Corner, John, and Sylvia Harvey. "Mediating Tradition and Modernity: The Heritage/Enterprise Couplet." *Enterprise and Heritage*. Eds. John Corner and Sylvia Harvey. New York: Routledge, 1991. 45–75.
Craig, Amanda. "Do not Go Gentle." *New Statesman* 17.798 (Mar. 15, 2004): 55.
Croce, Benedetto. *History: Its Theory and Practice*. Beijing: China Social Sciences Publishing House, 1999.
Darwin, Charles. *On the Origin of Species*. Ed. Gillian Beer. New York: Oxford University Press, 2008.
Derrida, Jacques. *Of Grammatology*. Trans. Gayatri Chakravorty Spivak. Baltimore and London: The John Hopkins University Press, 1976.
—. *Positions*. Trans. Se Biping. Beijing: SDX Joint Publishing Company, 2004.
—. *Specters of Marx: The State of the Debt, the Work of Mourning, and the New International*. Trans. Peggy Kamuf. New York and London: Routledge, 1994.
Descombes, Vincent. *Modern French Philosophy*. Trans. L. Scott-Fox and J. M. Harding. London: Cambridge University Press, 1980.
Domańska, Ewa. "Hayden White." Interview. *Encounters: Philosophy of History after Postmodernism*. Charlottesville and London: The Press of Virginia University, 1998. 13–38.
Duguid, Lindsay. "Before It Becomes Literature: How Fiction Reviewers Have Dealt with the English Novel." *On Modern British Fiction*. Ed. Zachary Leader. Oxford: Oxford University Press, 2002. 284–303.
Duplain, Julian. "The Big Match." *New Statesman and Society* Nov. 13, 1992: 34–35.
Eder, Richard. Rev. of *Cross Channel* by Julian Barnes. *Los Angeles Times* Mar. 17, 1996: 2.
Elias, Amy J. "Meta-mimesis? The Problem of British Postmodern Realism." *British Postmodern Fiction*. Eds. Theo D'haen and Hans Bertens. Amsterdam: Rodopi, 1993. 9–31.
Finney, Brian. "Peter Ackroyd, Postmodernist Play, and *Chatterton*." *Twentieth Century Literature* 38.2 (1992): 240–261.
—. "A Worm's Eye View of History: Julian Barnes's *A History of the World in 10 ½ Chapters*." *Papers on Language and Literature* 39.1 (2003): 49–70.
Fleishman, Avrom. *The English Historical Novel: Walter Scott to Virginia Woolf*. Baltimore and London: The Johns Hopkins Press, 1971.

Flower, Dean. "Cynicism and Its Discontents." *The Hudson Review* 52. 4 (2000): 657–674.
—. "Politics and the Novel: Julian Barnes, Isaac Bashevis Singer, José Donoso, Etc." *The Hudson Review* 46. 2(1993): 395–402.
—. "Story Problems." *The Hudson Review* 43. 2(1990): 311–318.
Foucault, Michel. *The Archaeology of Knowledge*. Trans. A. M. Sheridan Smith. New York: Pantheon Books, 1972.
—. *The History of Sexuality, Volume I: An Introduction*. Trans. Robert Hurley. New York: Pantheon Books, 1978.
—. "On Power." *Politics, Philosophy, Culture: Interviews and Other Writings, 1977–1984*. New York: Routledge, 1990. 96–109.
Freiburg, Rudolf. " 'Novels Come out of Life, Not out of Theories:' An Interview with Julian Barnes." *"Do You Consider Yourself a Postmodern Author?" Interviews with Contemporary English Writers*. Eds. Rudolf Freiburg and Jan Schnitker. Münster: LIT, 1999. 39–66. Rpt. in *Conversations with Julian Barnes*. Eds. Vanessa Guignery and Ryan Roberts. Mississippi: The University Press of Mississippi, 2009. 31–52.
Frey, Olivia. *Narrative Technique in Julian Barnes' Arthur & George: Negotiating Truth and Fiction*. GRIN Verlag, 2009.
Fukuyama, Francis. *The End of History and the Last Man*. New York: The Free Press, 1992.
—. "Reflections on the End of History, Five Years Later." *History and Theory* 34. 2(1995): 27–43.
Furbank, Philip N. "On the Historical Novel." *Raritan* 23. 3(2004): 94–114.
Gilderhus, Mark T. *History and Historians: A Historiographical Introduction*. 6th ed. New Jersey: Pearson Education Inc., 2007.
Gosswiller, Richard. "After the Fall." *Chicago Tribune* Jan. 3, 1993: 3.
Groes, Sebastian, and Peter Childs, eds. *Julian Barnes: Contemporary Critical Perspectives*. London and New York: Continuum, 2011.
—. Introduction. "Julian Barnes and the Wisdom of Uncertainty." Eds. Sebastian Groes and Peter Childs. *Julian Barnes: Contemporary Critical Perspectives*. London and New York: Continuum, 2011. 1–10.
Guignery, Vanessa. *The Fiction of Julian Barnes*. New York: Palgrave Macmillan, 2006.
—. "'History in Question(s):' An Interview with Julian Barnes." *Sources* 8(2000): 59–72.
—. "'A Preference for Things Gallic:' Julian Barnes and the French Connection." *Julian Barnes: Contemporary Critical Perspectives*. Eds. Sebastian Groes and Peter Childs. London and New York: Continuum, 2011. 37–50.

Guignery, Vanessa, and Ryan Roberts, eds. *Conversations with Julian Barnes*. Mississippi: The University Press of Mississippi, 2009.
—. "Julian Barnes: The Final Interview." *Conversations with Julian Barnes*. Eds. Vanessa Guignery and Ryan Roberts. Mississippi: The University Press of Mississippi, 2009. 161–188.
Guppy, Shusha. Interview. "Julian Barnes, The Art of Fiction, No. 165." *The Paris Review* 157(2000). Aug. 18, 2012. <http://www.theparisreview.org/interviews/562/the-art-of-fiction-no-165-julian-barnes>.
Harris, Robert. "Full of Prickles." *Literary Review* 172(1992): 26.
He, Zhaohui, and Gan Ximei. "On the Introduction, Translation and Studies of Julian Barnes in China." *Journal of Hubei University of Economics (Humanities and Social Sciences)* 19.6(2022): 123–128.
Head, Dominic. "Julian Barnes and a Case of English Identity." *British Fiction Today*. Eds. Philip Tew and Rod Mengham. London: Continuum, 2006. 15–27.
Heptonstall, Geoffrey. "A Francophile on France." *Contemporary Review* 281.1639(2002): 116–117.
Higdon, David Leon. *Shadows of the Past in Contemporary British Fiction*. Athens: University of Georgia Press, 1985.
—. "'Unconfessed Confessions:' The Narrators of Julian Barnes and Graham Swift." *The British and Irish Novel Since 1960*. Ed. James Acheson. Basingstoke, Hampshire, London: Macmillan Academic and Professional Ltd., 1991. 174–191.
"History." *Oxford Advanced Learner's Dictionary*. 8th ed. Electronic. Oxford, UK: Oxford University Press, 2010.
Holmes, Frederick M. *Julian Barnes*. London: Palgrave Macmillan, 2009.
The Holy Bible. King James Version. New York: Ivy Books, 1991.
Hou, Weirui, and Li Weiping. *A History of English Fiction*. Nanjing: Yilin Press, 2005.
Huang, Jinxing. *Postmodernism and Historiography: A Critical Study*. Beijing: SDX Joint Publishing Company, 2008.
Huntchinson, Colin. "The Abandoned Church and the Contemporary British Novel." *The Yearbook of English Studies* 37.1(2007): 227–244.
Hutcheon, Linda. *A Poetics of Postmodernism: History, Theory, Fiction*. New York and London: Routledge, 1988.
—. *Narcissistic Narrative: The Metafictional Paradox*. New York and London: Methuen, 1984.
Hutchings, William. Rev. of *Cross Channel* by Julian Barnes. *World Literature Today* 71.1(1997): 149–150.
Jameson, Fredric. *The Political Unconscious: Narrative as a Socially Symbolic Act*. Ithaca, New York: Cornell University Press, 1981.

—. "Marxism and Historicism." *New Literary History* 11.1 Anniversary Issue II (1979): 41–73.

Janik, Del Ivan. "No End of History: Evidence from the Contemporary English Novel." *Twentieth Century Literature* 41.2(1995): 160–189.

Jenkins, Keith. *Re-thinking History.* London and New York: Routledge, 2003.

—. *Why History? Ethics and Postmodernity.* London and New York: Routledge, 1999.

Johnson, Douglas. *France and the Dreyfus Affair.* London: Blandford Press Ltd., 1966.

Joseph-Vilain, Mélanie. "The Writer's Voice(s) in *Flaubert's Parrot.*" *Q/W/E/R/T/Y: Arts, Litteratures et Civilisations du Monde Anglophone* (2001): 183–188.

Kakutani, Michiko. "Confrontation Between Post-Soviet Bureaucrats." *New York Times* Nov. 10, 1992: C19.

Karl, Frederick R. *A Reader's Guide to the Contemporary English Novel.* Beijing: Foreign Language Teaching and Research Press, 2005.

Keen, Suzanne. "The Historical Turn in British Fiction." *A Concise Companion to Contemporary British Fiction.* Ed. James F. English. Oxford, UK: Blackwell Publishing Ltd., 2006.

Kennedy, John. Rev. of *Cross Channel* by Julian Barnes. *The Antioch Review* 55.1(1997): 110.

Kotte, Claudia. "Random Patterns? Orderly Disorder in Julian Barnes's *A History of the World in 10½ Chapters.*" *Arbeiten aus Anglistik und Amerikanistik* 22.1(1997): 107–128.

Koval, Ramona. "*Big Ideas*—Program 5— 'Julian Barnes.'" ABC Radio National Oct. 31, 2004. <http://www.abc.net.au/rn/bigideas/stories/2004/1228319.html>. Rpt. in *Conversations with Julian Barnes.* Eds. Vanessa Guignery and Ryan Roberts. Mississippi: The University Press of Mississippi, 2009. 118–128.

Krist, Gary. "She Oughtn't to Have Been in Pictures." *New York Times Book Review* Dec. 28, 1986: 12. Aug. 18, 2012. <http://www.nytimes.com/books/01/02/25/specials/barnes-before.html>.

Landon, Philip. Rev. of *England, England* by Julian Barnes. *Review of Contemporary Fiction*(1999): 174.

Lane, Richard J. *Jean Baudrillard.* London: Routledge, 2000.

Lang, James M. *Dialogue with History in Post-War British Fiction.* Dissertation. UMI Company, 1998.

Lázaro, Alberto. "The Techniques of Committed Fiction: In Defence of Julian Barnes's *The Porcupine.*" *Atlantics* 22.1(2000): 121–131.

Lee, Alison. *Realism and Power: Postmodern British Fiction.* London and

New York: Routledge, 1990.
Lee, Peter. "Understanding History." *Theorizing Historical Consciousness*. Ed. Peter Seixas. Toronto, Buffalo, London: University of Toronto Press, 2004. 129–164.
Leith, William. "Where Nothing Really Happens." *Independent on Sunday* May 2, 1993: 13–14.
Levenson, Michael. "Flaubert's Parrot." *The New Republic* Dec. 16, 1991: 42–45.
Lévi-Strauss, Claude. *The Savage Mind*. London: George Weidenfeld and Nicolson Ltd., 1966.
Levy, Paul. "British Author, French Flair." *Wall Street Journal* Dec. 11, 1992: A10.
Lewis, Georgie. "Julian and Arthur and George." *Powells.com*. Feb. 13, 2006. Aug. 18, 2012. <http://www.powells.com/blog/interviews/julian-and-arthur-and-geo-orge-by-georgie/>.
Liu, Wenrong. *A Historical Survey of Contemporary British Fiction*. Shanghai: Wenhui Press, 2010.
Locke, Richard. "Flood of Forms." Rev. of *A History of the World in 10½ Chapters* by Julian Barnes. *New Republic* Dec. 4, 1989: 40–43.
Lukacs, John. *The Future of History*. New Haven & London: Yale University Press, 2011.
Luo, Xiaoyun. "Aftereffects of Shock: Power Discourse in Barnes's *A History of the World in 10½ Chapters*." *Foreign Languages Research* 3(2007): 98–102.
Luo, Yuan. "Searching for the Truth: On the Reading of Julian Barnes's *Flaubert's Parrot*." *Contemporary Foreign Literature* 3(2006): 115–121.
—. "A Thematic Study of *England, England*." *Contemporary Foreign Literature* 1(2010): 105–114.
Lycett, Andrew. Afterword. "Seeing and Knowing with the Eyes of Faith." *Julian Barnes: Contemporary Critical Perspectives*. Eds. Sebastian Groes and Peter Childs. London and New York: Continuum, 2011. 129–133.
Lyotard, Jean-François. *The Postmodern Condition: A Report on Knowledge*. Trans. Geoff Bennington and Brian Massumi. Minneapolis: University of Minnesota Press, 1984.
Mallon, Thomas. "As Young as You Feel." *New York Times Book Review* June 27, 2004: 7.
March, Michael. "Into the Lion's Mouth: A Conversation with Julian Barnes." *The New Presence* Dec. 1997. <http://www.new-presence.cz>. Rpt. in *Conversations with Julian Barnes*. Eds. Vanessa Guignery and Ryan Roberts. Mississippi: The University Press of Mississippi,

2009. 23-26.
Marien, Mary W. "Twilight in the Balkans." *The Christian Science Monitor* Jan. 20, 1993: 13.
Marr, Andrew. "He's Turned Towards Python." *The Observer* Aug. 30, 1998: 15.
Martin, Tim. "Julian Barnes Is Back to His Old Tricks in *The Only Story*." *The Telegraph* Jan. 31, 2018. May 14, 2023. <https://www.telegraph.co.uk/books/what-to-read/julian-barnes-back-old-tricks-story-review/>.
Martino, Andrew. Rev. of *The Sense of an Ending* by Julian Barnes. *World Literature Today* 86.1(2012): 56-57.
Massie, Allan. *The Novel Today: A Critical Guide to the British Novel 1970-1989*. New York: Longman Inc., 1990.
McGrath, Patrick. "Julian Barnes." *Bomb* 21 (Fall 1987). Aug. 18, 2012. <http://bombsite.com/issues/21/articles/980>. Rpt. in *Conversations with Julian Barnes*. Eds. Vanessa Guignery and Ryan Roberts. Mississippi: The University Press of Mississippi, 2009. 11-19.
McHale, Brian. *Postmodernist Fiction*. New York and London: Methuen, 1987.
Mengham, Rod. "General Introduction: Contemporary British Fiction." *Contemporary British Fiction*. Eds. Richard J. Lane, Rod Mengham and Philip Tew. Cambridge, UK: Polity Press, 2003.
Messud, Claire. "Tour de France: Julian Barnes Loves the Country and, Especially, Its Writers." *New York Times Book Review* Oct. 6, 2002: 25.
Miller, Arthur I. *Einstein, Picasso: Space, Time, and the Beauty That Causes Havoc*. Trans. Fang Zaiqing and Wu Meihong. Shanghai: Shanghai Technology and Education Press, 2006.
Miracky, James J. "Replicating a Dinosaur: Authenticity Run Amok in the 'Theme Parking' of Michael Crichton's *Jurassic Park* and Julian Barnes's *England, England*." *Critique* 45.2(2004): 163-171.
Monterrey, Tomás. "Julian Barnes's 'Shipwreck' or Recycling Chaos into Art." *Clio* 33.4(2004): 415-426.
Montrose, Louis A. "Professing the Renaissance: The Poetics and Politics of Culture." *The New Historicism*. Ed. H. Aram Veeser. New York: Routledge, 1989. 15-36.
Moseley, Merritt. *Understanding Julian Barnes*. Columbia, South Carolina: The University of South Carolina Press, 1997.
Murfin, Ross, and Supryia M. Ray. *The Bedford Glossary of Critical and Literary Terms*. 2nd ed. Boston and New York: Bedford/St. Martin's, 2003.
Nünning, Vera. "The Invention of Cultural Traditions: The Construction and Deconstruction of Englishness and Authenticity in Julian Barnes's *England, England*." *Anglia* 119(2001): 58-76.

Oates, Joyce C. "But Noah Was Not a Nice Man." *New York Times Book Review* Oct. 1, 1989: 12–13.
O'Regan, Nadine. "Cool, Clean Man of Letters." *Sunday Business Post* June 29, 2003. Rpt. in *Conversations with Julian Barnes*. Eds. Vanessa Guignery and Ryan Roberts. Mississippi: The University Press of Mississippi, 2009. 115–117.
Orwell, George. *Nineteen Eighty-Four*. London: Penguin Books, 1989.
Pakditawan, Sirinya. *An Interpretation of Julian Barnes Novel "England, England."* GRIN Verlag, 2004.
Parrinder, Patrick. "Sausages and Higher Things." *London Review of Books* Feb. 11, 1993: 18–19.
Pateman, Matthew. *Julian Barnes*. Tavistock, Devon, UK: Northcote House Publishers Ltd., 2002.
—. "Julian Barnes and the Popularity of Ethics." *Postmodern Surroundings*. Postmodern Studies 9. Ed. Steven Earnshaw. Amsterdam: Editions Rodopi B. V., 1994. 179–191.
Puddington, Arch. "The Porcupine." *Commentary* 95. 5(1993): 62–64.
Rafferty, Terrence. "Watching the Detectives." *The Nation* 241. 1(1985): 21–22.
Ranke, Leopold von. "Preface: *Histories of the Latin and Germanic Nations from 1494–1514.*" *The Varieties of History: From Voltaire to the Present*. Ed. Fritz Stern. New York: Vintage Books, 1973. 55–58.
Rees, Jasper. "The Inscrutable Mr. Barnes." *The Telegraph* Sept. 23, 2006. Aug. 18, 2012. <http://www.telegraph.co.uk/culture/books/3655483/The-inscrutable-Mr-Barnes.html>.
Roberts, Ryan. "Inventing a Way to the Truth: Life and Fiction in Julian Barnes's *Flaubert's Parrot*." *Julian Barnes: Contemporary Critical Perspectives*. Eds. Sebastian Groes and Peter Childs. London and New York: Continuum, 2011. 24–36.
Rosenau, Pauline M. *Post-Modernism and the Social Sciences: Insights, Inroads, and Intrusions*. Princeton, New Jersey: Princeton University Press, 1992.
Ruan, Wei. "Barnes, Flaubert and 'Flaubert's Parrot': On *Flaubert's Parrot*." *After Modernism: Realism and Experimentation*. Ed. Lu Jiande. Beijing: China Social Sciences Press, 1997. 390–404.
—. "Barnes and His *Flaubert's Parrot*." *Foreign Literature Review* 2(1997): 51–58.
—. *Texts Against Social Contexts: The Study of British Fiction After the Second World War*. Beijing: Social Science and Literature Press, 1998.
Ruan, Wei, Xu Wenbo and Cao Yajun. *A History of the 20th Century British Literature*. Qingdao: Qingdao Press, 1998.

Rubin, Merle. "From Nebulae to Noah's Ark." *The Christian Science Monitor* Jan. 10, 1990: 13.

Rubinson, Gregory J. "History's Genres: Julian Barnes's *A History of the World in 10½ Chapters.*" *Modern Language Studies* 30. 2(2000): 159-179.

Rushdie, Salman. "Julian Barnes." *Imaginary Homelands: Essays and Criticism 1981-1991.* New York: Penguin Books, 1992. 241-243.

Salyer, Gregory. "One Good Story Leads to Another: Julian Barnes' *A History of the World in 10½ Chapters.*" *Journal of Literature & Theology* 5. 2 (1991): 220-233.

Saunders, Kate. "What Death Has Taught Him." Rev. of *Pulse* by Julian Barnes. *New Statesman* Jan. 3, 2011: 50-51.

—. "From Flaubert's Parrot to Noah's Woodworm." *Sunday Times* (London) June 18, 1989: G8-9.

Savigny, Jean B. H., and Alexander Corréard. *Narrative of a Voyage to Senegal in 1816.* London: Schulze and Dean, 1818.

Scammell, Michael. "Trial and Error." *The New Republic* Jan. 4, 1993: 35-38.

Schiff, James A. "A Conversation with Julian Barnes." *Missouri Review* 30. 3(2007): 60-80.

Schwartz, Lynne S. "An Unlikely Convergence." *The New Leader* 88. 6 (2005): 42-44.

Scott, James B. "Parrot as Paradigms: Infinite Deferral of Meaning in *Flaubert's Parrot.*" *ARIEL: A Review of International English Literature* 21. 3(1990): 57-68.

Sesto, Bruce. *Language, History, and Metanarrative in the Fiction of Julian Barnes.* New York: Peter Lang Publishing Inc., 2001.

Shaffer, Brian W. *Reading the Novel in English 1950-2000.* Oxford, UK: Blackwell Publishing Ltd., 2006.

Shang, Jie. *A Survey of Contemporary French Philosophy.* Shanghai: Tongji University Press, 2008.

Sim, Stuart. *Derrida and the End of History.* New York: Totem Books, 1999.

Smee, Sebastian. "The Curious Case of the Slashed Horse." *The Spectator* 298. 9231(2005): 34.

Smith, Amanda. "Julian Barnes." *Publishers Weekly* Nov. 3, 1989: 73-74.

Stern, Fritz, ed. *The Varieties of History: From Voltaire to the Present.* New York: Vintage Books, 1973.

—. Introduction. *The Varieties of History: From Voltaire to the Present.* Ed. Fritz Stern. New York: Vintage Books, 1973. 11-32.

Stevenson, Randall. *A Reader's Guide to The Twentieth-Century Novel in Britain.* Lexington: University Press of Kentucky, 1993.

Stout, Mira. "Chameleon Novelist." *New York Times* Nov. 22, 1992. Aug. 18,

2012. <http://www.nytimes.com/1992/11/22/books/barnes-interview92.html>.
Strout, Cushing. "The Case of the Novelist, the Solicitor, and a Miscarriage of Justice." *Sewanee Review* 115. 1(2007) : **xi-xiii**.
Stuart, Alexander. "A Talk with Julian Barnes." *Los Angeles Times Book Review* Oct. 15, 1989: 15.
Swift, Graham. *Waterland*. London: Picador, 2010.
Tate, Andrew. "'An Ordinary Piece of Magic:' Religion in the Work of Julian Barnes." *Julian Barnes: Contemporary Critical Perspectives*. Eds. Sebastian Groes and Peter Childs. London and New York: Continuum, 2011. 51-68.
Taunton, Matthew. "The Flâneur and the Freeholder: Paris and London in Julian Barnes's *Metroland*." *Julian Barnes: Contemporary Critical Perspectives*. Eds. Sebastian Groes and Peter Childs. London and New York: Continuum, 2011. 11-23.
Taylor, D. J. "A Newfangled and Funny Romp." *The Spectator* June 24, 1989: 40-41.
Turner, Frederick J. "The Significance of History." *The Varieties of History: From Voltaire to the Present*. Ed. Fritz Stern. New York: Vintage Books, 1973. 198-208.
Updike, John. "A Pair of Parrots." *New Yorker* July 22, 1985: 86-90.
Vonnegut, Kurt. *Slaughterhouse-Five or The Children's Crusade: A Duty-Dance with Death*. New York: Dell Publishing, 1988.
Versteegh, Adrian. "Meta-Analysis Goes Mainstream." *Poets & Writers* May 1, 2012: 16-18, 20.
Walsh, William H. *Philosophy of History: An Introduction*. New York and Evanston: Harper & Row, Publishers, 1960.
Wang, Shouren, and He Ning. *A History of British Literature in the 20th Century*. Beijing: Peking University Press, 2006.
White, Hayden. "The Fictions of Factual Representation." *Tropics of Discourse: Essays in Cultural Criticism*. Baltimore and London: The Johns Hopkins University Press, 1978. 121-134.
—. "The Historical Text as Literary Artifact." *Clio* 3. 3(1974) : 277-303.
—. *Metahistory: The Historical Imagination in Nineteenth-Century Europe*. Baltimore & London: The John Hopkins University Press, 1973.
—. "New Historicism: A Comment." *The New Historicism*. Ed. H. Aram Veeser. New York: Routledge, 1989. 293-302.
Wilde, Oscar. "The Importance of Being Earnest." *The Plays of Oscar Wilde*. Ware, Hertfordshire: Wordsworth Editions Limited, 2000.
Wilhelmus, Tom. "Ah, England." Rev. of *The Inheritance of Loss* by Kiran Desai; *Shalimar the Clown* by Salman Rushdie; *Arthur & George* by Julian Barnes; *on Beauty* by Zadie Smith; *The March* by

E. L. Doctorow. *The Hudson Review* 59. 2(2006): 345–351.

Williams, Raymond. *Keywords: A Vocabulary of Culture and Society.* Revised ed. New York: Oxford University Press, 1985.

Wilson, Keith. "'Why Aren't the Books Enough?' Authorial Pursuit in Julian Barnes's *Flaubert's Parrot* and *A History of the World in 10½ Chapters.*" *Critique* 47. 4(2006): 362–374.

Winder, Robert. "Bumps in the Night." *New Statesman* July 11, 2005: 49–50.

Wood, James. "The Fact-Checker." *The New Republic* June 24, 1996: 40–43.

Yang, Jincai, and Wang Yuping. "Dissolution of the Real in Julian Barnes's *A History of the World in 10½ Chapters.*" *Journal of Shenzhen University (Humanities & Social Sciences)* 1(2006): 91–96.

Yin, Qiping. "Querying the Narrative of 'Progress:' A Brief Analysis of Three English Novels." *Journal of Zhejiang Normal University (Social Sciences)* 2(2006): 12–19.

Zhai, Shijing. "The Young- and Middle-Aged Novelists in Contemporary Britain." *After Modernism: Realism and Experimentation.* Ed. Lu Jiande. Beijing: China Social Sciences Press, 1997. 405–429.

—, and Ren Yiming. *A History of Contemporary British Fiction.* Shanghai: Shanghai Translation Press, 2008.

Zhang, Helong. "The Inter-genre and Inter-art Aspects in the Fiction of Julian Barnes." *Foreign Literature* 4(2009): 3–10.

Zhang, Li, and Guo Yingjian. "An Existential Approach to the Thanatopsis in *Nothing to Be Frightened of.*" *Contemporary Foreign Literature* 3(2010): 81–88.